Reflections by the Riverside

A Prose and Poetry Anthology,

Presented by the Riverside Writers

of the Fredericksburg, Virginia, area,

and Along the Lovely (in Fable and Fact)

Rappahannock River.

Reflections by the Riverside

Produced in 2024 by Riverside Writers
A Chapter of the Virginia Writers Club
P.O. Box 382
Spotsylvania, VA 22553

Paperback ISBN: 978-0-9997789-3-7
Hardback ISBN: 978-1-958321-90-4

Edited by Steven P. Pody
Cover design by: Tannhauser Press
Cover images by:
Published in USA by Tannhauser Press

A TANNHAUSER PRESS PUBLICATION

Welcome To Our Anthology

…Well, the subject heading tells it all. Welcome! By way of introduction, we, of Riverside Writers, hope that you are prepared for an exceptionally fine read -- in fair exchange of your wisely invested time, your earned appreciation and your money (or gift acceptance). We thank you for your faith in our collective literary power to entertain and to delight you!

In your hands, at the moment, is the ninth volume of collected works published by our Fredericksburg, Virginia-area writing club. The club, Riverside Writers, was established and officially chartered as a member chapter of the Virginia Writer's Club (VWC) on April 25th, 1998. Since club inception, we have published:

1. Riverside Currents (2001)
2. Riverside Echoes (2003)
3. Riverside Revelations (2008)
4. Riverside Reflections (2010)
5. Rappahannock Review (2011)
6. Rappahannock Voices (2014)
7. River Tides (2017)
8. America 2020 (2021)
9. Reflections by the Riverside (2024)

As you can see, our current title bears a resemblance to our 2010 title. However, that is the relative nature of reflections, isn't it? To see and yet to interpret the same general experiences through different lights and facets, and to thrill to markedly different outcomes through a dazzled and varied view of wonder!

The 2020 volume experienced some disruption from the onset of the COVID-19 pandemic, and as we adjust to a social world regaining its equilibrium, it has again become time to gather our wits, our extreme optimism, and our works of prose and poetry, and attempt to rock (at least a little bit) …your literary world. It is hoped that you will be pleased, surprised and/or astounded in positive and superlative ways with our written efforts. …For what is an author …without an appreciative audience?

This volume, through a democratic club vote, was nobly entitled: "Reflections by the Riverside," and is compiled, entire, through the hopes, dreams, experiences and practiced craft of twenty-nine of our current Riverside Writers membership. Our 2020 edition held eighteen authors and our 2017 anthology held thirty-four, so this volume is somewhere in between -- and well-representational of the prose and poetic quality of the sincere and talented effort by members of the club.

Anthologies for our club are a once every three or four year expression of our published creativity, but are, in the long-term, in-print mileposts in the extended mission of this organization. Anthologies are but one social and physical benefit in a club that, as an established non-profit entity, is to celebrate the art and craft of writing by offering writers opportunities for personal and professional interaction with other writers; strengthen skills in the art, enhance the craft and business of writing; and advocate the literary arts in the broader local community.

The existence of Riverside Writers, and the value that may be gleaned from membership, in the main depends upon the writers you see within these pages, and their fellow members. We are an organization of stories, poems, lyric and literary experiences, and a mutual thirst to express ourselves and learn our craft. Riverside Writers members are as alone or engaged as they wish to be -- while imaginative friends and peers are at hand to help, advise, listen, commiserate, laugh, cry and share an amazing, creative world. Within the pages of this anthology are club members who have taken up the challenge, bravely, to the point of publication, and bring the flame of inspiration to your willing eyes.

Our authors are people who want something more in life. Some want to be famous, some want to be rich (or at least supplement income!), some crave a touch of relative immortality, and others just feel the need to grow in the literary arts and express themselves - with an audience. You will find all types of people, talent and experience here. A serious business, a hobby, a private yearning compulsion, a venue of like-minded friends... Our purpose is your purpose -- for the glory of exquisite prose, beautiful poetry, personal cultural enhancement... Come read our pages and catch our purposeful and often whimsical fun, fancy ...and fire!

The writer's challenges ...and to the 29 authors who dared.

"We are continually faced by great opportunities, brilliantly disguised as insolvable problems."   Benjamin Franklin

"It is hard to fail; but it is worse never to have tried to succeed."
                                        Theodore Roosevelt

"Life is a banquet, and most poor suckers are starving to death."
                                        Auntie Mame

Table of Contents

Dedication

Larry Raymond Turner is still, as of this writing, less than a year gone. A driving force within Riverside Writers for most of its lifespan, Larry died on October 15, 2023. Of our nine printed anthologies, this is probably the only one in which he has posted no creative piece. He was a prize-winning poet, with six books published, and was a Riverside Writers club president from 2009 to 2012 (two terms).

His poetry appeared numerous times in *The Lyric* and in the online journal (now discontinued) *Voices on the Wind.* Among his books were three of poetry, stories and drama, and a 2015 memoir: *The Magic Years: Tales of the Turners 1957 – 1970.* In 2019 he published *Celebrating Christmas in Poetry and Story.*

Prior to his final years in Midlothian, Virginia, and with Riverside Writers, Mr. Turner served as president of the Illinois State Poetry Society and regional vice-president of the Poetry Society of Virginia.

To many in Riverside Writers, Larry was an influence, a mentor, and a lyric spirit significantly touching, in gentleness and with patient understanding, the fundamental muse in us all. This anthology is dedicated to his memory.

Introduction

Much of the spirit of an introduction, and much club philosophy defining the overall tenor of this anthology, was covered in the semi-unconventional "Welcome". Also, the gratitude department is ever open with our thanks to you, the reader. However, there is one further note of the editor to cover in this edition – the presentation of author biographies. Authors, as evidenced by our 'Dedication,' are a fragile and lamentably mortal, if wonderful and colorful, phenomenon. ...But the works they've produced; the glorious heights and profoundest depths of their thought, emotion and passion – they are what this anthology is all about. Great works, wonderfully fine concepts, and pieces of literary art showcased for all the world to see. The authors speak through their works, and the works themselves, through publication, are immortal in the halls of the Library of Congress, in local libraries, and around the world.

In this vein, the author biographies are consolidated at the appendix-like portion of this anthology – grouped alphabetically at the end of the book. (...Also, it saved 18 physical pages.) If a creative work has piqued your interest and admiration, well, you know where to look to satisfy your origin-story curiosity, and marvel at the life story of your favored writer of note.

As for this book- it is an introduction unto itself. We introduce you to our whimsy, our dreams, our hopes, and our creative-written story and poem-children, birthed for your understanding and your enjoyment. We hope we exceeded expectation.

P.S. In proofing this document, I corrected misspellings where encountered, but left many 'poetic-license' expressions in place. In fact, it was not my place (I feel) to correct informal words, colloquialisms, foreign expressions and/or slang. Therefore, you will find many compound words (among other things) that should be hyphenated, or perhaps more formally treated, that are scrunched together. You'll see audiobooks, Treehouse, treefrog, longsword, etc., expressed. Leave them be, sit back ...and enjoy the journey.

Acknowledgments

The idea to produce another anthology originated with Jorge R. Roberts-Saavedra. Jorge is one of two Riverside Writers to move out of state (to Texas!), and still remain an active member. The other Zoom-dependent member is Madalin Bickel (Florida). It was she who recommended that we dedicate this work to the (then) recently-deceased Larry Turner, an influential long-term club member and past-president. Her intended tribute was summed up as: "…he made a difference in my life as a writer." A life-long creative writer may part this life with many levels of personal and official honors, but that simple, appreciative statement may rank as one of the grandest…

Historical data for the club, and for this anthology volume in particular, is sourced from James R. Gaines. Jim is a long-time member, past president, and in the 26-year history of our club – has become our hallowed living institutional memory.

Valerie Horton, our club Secretary, contributed our ISBN number. Who knew that people kept spares around? Thanks Valerie, thou art swell.

Contributed the title… Well the anonymous title selection was chosen by vote at our September monthly meeting. And the winner and honor went to the editor of this book.

Thanks a'mighty to Miriam S. Pody for cheerfully helping to proof the manuscript of this book.

We, Riverside Writers, are a chapter of a larger statewide organization. To the Virginia Writers Club (VWC) president, Charles Tabb, we give thanks for support and for contributing a very kindly back-cover commentary flourish. Great job, Chuck!

To Martin Wilsey, long associate of Riverside Writers -- and friend, advisor, consultant, guest speaker and publisher – we say thanks deeply for your generosity of expertise, and for your sincere and fruitful support of the dynamic literary movement that is the current hallmark of the wide Fredericksburg-area of Virginia.

ACKNOWLEDGMENTS

I personally extend my feelings of deep appreciation to the many brilliant and sparkling author contributors to this anthology. Let us, oh reader, marvel together!

Ever-thanks to Salem Church Public Library for their long, active and enthusiastic support!

And, our collective sincerest thanks to those creative and inspired members who built and carried the club through its first quarter of a century. Thanks to all members, officers, volunteers, and to the chief officers (presidents) who helped light the way. A listing is cited at the end of this book.

P.S. Perhaps one of the last of its creative breed – but the authorship was consulted, and no artificial intelligence of any amount or kind was used in this thoroughly human anthology.

A.I. is not a part of us,
    though we're a part of it.
And all this book's
        original,
comprising human wit.

Within these pages, mindeth well,
    you'll not see brains forsook:
For souls and hearts
        of human spirit
were
    wonder enough (!)
        for our book.

SPP

LET THE WORDS
SPEAK...

STORIES, ASPIRATIONS,
DREAMS AND
POETRY,
FROM THEY WHO WRITE

...BY THE BEAUTIFUL
RIVERSIDE

'Reflections by the Riverside'
Riverside Writers, 2024

Barbara Beaumont

The Alchemist's Rainbow

Ariana pulled the covers up over her head. She had turned the thermostat off yesterday, since it was a beautiful, balmy, breezy day. Her windows were open, and the wind chimes played their beautiful melody.

This morning it is in the fifties. She felt like she was in a cocoon and did not want to leave the bed to turn on the heat.

Finally throwing the covers back she looked at Aries, her 10-year-old Shitzu, and said, "time to make the donuts" and the dog started jumping around. Aries knew that phrase, she was ready to take her walk and have her breakfast.

Ariana turned on the heat, put on her magical furry long pants, a sweatshirt and her white down jacket. She put on Aries' harness and leash, then pulled open the curtains of the front picture window. She let out a heavy sigh. It was not only cold but a grey cloudy day.

"Darn, I do so much better on a sunny day!" Then she added "okay, look for the positive, right Aries?"

She opened the door, and they stepped outside. Something was different. The energy was vibrating at a higher frequency than normal. Orbs immediately surrounded her, chattering away in their high-pitched tones. There were three circling around her. She knows, when there are three it represents Body, Mind and Spirit.

"You must be bringing me a powerful message, spirit guide. It has been a while since you visited." She took a few deep breaths, asking for help to connect and interpret the message.

She was glad she was still on the front porch; if any of her neighbors heard her talking and looking up, it would be tough to explain.

The orbs were saying "It's gone, someone stole it, you have to do something!!!"

6

"What is gone, who stole what?"

"The pot of gold at the end of the rainbow! It must be gone! That is the only possible explanation for a grey rainbow." The orbs were translating the high-pitched sounds both aloud and telepathically to her.

The gold was a source for creating rainbows, much like the sun.

The scientists and non-believers said there was no such thing as a pot of gold. They believed the rainbow did not have an end, so there could be no place for a pot of gold to reside.

Normally, the white light from the sun was reflected through the rain and split into a band of colors; red, orange, yellow, green, blue, indigo and violet. However, the Alchemist in charge of the pots of gold could create the same effect. The gold oil acted like a prism splitting the colors to create a rainbow. Only a few mystics know the truth. Legend has it the only way to tell which rainbow is the Alchemist's and which is from the Sun is by the order of the colors. When we have a double rainbow, the colors of the Alchemist's rainbow start with violet, while the one from the Sun starts with red.

Ariana turned her attention back to the orbs. "Why would they do that? The rainbow is still going to be there from the sun."

"No, it is not! You do not understand!!! The Leprechauns put a spell on Aguistin, the sun God's sister's magical flying horse. The spell took Aguistin's powers away."

People became sad, gave up hope; there was no reason for the sun to shine.

"Oh my" Ariana said sadly, "this is a major problem. Spirit guides do you have any ideas?"

The orbs were flashing like strobe lights; a few minutes later they were growing dim, like a light that was losing its power and getting ready to go out. They told Ariana telepathically "It is affecting all the light in the world. If we do not figure this out, not only will the rainbows go grey, but the entire world."

Ariana was stunned, what could she do?

The orbs told her as they were fading, "Consult your Book of Shadows."

Ariana went back into the house. She called out: *"Guardians of the book, undo my spell of invisibility so I may see the answer to the problem worrying me."*

She did not remember ever reading about anything like this happening.

The book appeared on her wood table. She held the Book of Shadows to her heart and implored the book for help at this perilous time.

Then she placed the book open on the table. The pages turned back and forth. Finally, it stopped, opening to **The Rainbow Spell** with directions.

You Will Need: 7 Candles and 7 Ribbons one in each color of the rainbow.

Open all the windows and ask for nature's blessings. Light your candles in the order of the Rainbow colors remembering each color also represents the old planets of the Zodiac: Red for Mars, Orange for Sun, Yellow for Moon, Green for Mercury, Blue for Venus, Indigo for Jupiter, and Violet for Saturn.

Make a circle out of them around you. Sit in the middle of the circle and concentrate on feeling the color and energy of each light flickering and burning. Make sure to tie each candle at the base first with its matching-colored ribbon. After one hour, blow out the candles, untie the ribbons, and criss-cross them into a braid. Hold the braid in your right hand and say aloud: " I consecrate thee as a tool of magick, I charge thee with power, In the name of the Goddess and in the name of the God, So Mote It Be!" This will become your most powerful talisman and will always attract a Rainbow when *you hold it to your heart and proclaim your intention.*

She did as the book directed. A couple of hours later she said aloud: "Okay I created the talisman. Now what?"

The pages of the book turned back and forth again, like an invisible hand was turning them.

The pages stopped. At the top of the page was the title *Ireland and Leprechauns* (aka Fairies, Wee people). She remembered reading a book about them. She reached for her book on Ireland, another magical book, she placed it on the table, it opened to a particular page.

She began to read aloud. "The enchanted, fairies and leprechauns of Irish history come from an ancient divine race called Tuatha de Danann. The are the people of the Mother Goddess Danu, a fierce protector of her people.

Belenus was her oldest child, and known as the God of the Sun and an immensely powerful alchemist. His younger sister Niamh would carry people from other places back to the secret land of Tir na nOg on Aguistin, her majestic white flying horse. Aguistin had the power to take her for rides over the waves, up the mountains and to the other worlds. Legend has it, if she never dismounted during her travels from her homeland she would live forever.

They were one of the last races of gods to inhabit Ireland before they were defeated by the Celts/Gaels, who are the ancestors of the present-day Irish. The Tuatha Dè prepared their future kingdoms under various hills, and fled to their subterranean cave and abodes when the Celts landed in their ships.

They decided not to fight the invaders due to their skill in prophecy showing them that the Celts were destined to live and rule on the island. However, another group led by Mother Goddess Danu escaped to Tir na nOg, a mystical magical island.

When she said the name of the mystical Island, the pages of the book turned again. This time opening to a story about the rainbow ending in the magical land of Tír na nÓg, a place that was located beyond the edges of the map, situated on an island on the west side of Ireland. It could be reached only by a grueling voyage or a request from one of its residents.

Tír na nÓg is a place where sickness and death do not exist. It is a place of eternal youth and beauty. Music, strength, life, and all pleasurable pursuits come together in this magical place. Here happiness lasts forever; no one needs food or drink. There are caves high in the mountains full of pots of gold. They say this is where the rainbow ends. The alchemist Belenus and son of Danu, create Gold

Oil from the gold and this is used by the Goddess Brigit to help him create rainbows. Often when you see two rainbows it is Belenus and Brigit who created it. If you look closely, you will notice the colors are reversed on one of the rainbows; Belenu's and Brigit's signature for the purpose of playing, and bringing joy to those who view their rainbows.

The Book of Shadows' pages started turning again. It showed her Niamh, Danu's daughter, crying on the island of Tír na nÓg. A curse was put on her beautiful stallion Aguistin, which she rode among the worlds. She was inconsolable. Belenus, God of the Sun, did not want to see his sister so sad; he could not bear to let the sun shine when so many tears were creating so much rain. Also, he could not get to the gold without Niamh's trusty steed Aguistin. The cave where the oil of gold was made was hidden high in the mountainous peaks. People were sad, the rainbows around the world were dark grey in light grey skies.

The orbs were talking to her again. "You need to find a way to help them so we can have rainbows of color again and the sun can shine, and we can have baby-blue skies with puffy white clouds and rainbows with all the colors that bring joy to the people. Otherwise, the world without sun will slowly end."

Ariana was crying, she was so moved by this problem that she knew she had to do something. She knew that what you think, you create. She told herself aloud: "You can do it!" Turning back to her Book of Shadows, she was hoping it would help her find a way to undo the spell.

The pages turned again, the words on the page were larger and it stated simply: "Only the spell of another, more powerful, leprechaun could remove the first spell and protect Aguistin from further spells."

"But how do I summon the right one and ask for help?"

The pages of the book turned, she read the page:

"Here is the summoning prayer. Once the leprechaun appears, you must give him a piece of gold; it can be a charm, a necklace, an earring, or a ring, but it must be real gold. He must be thanked profusely for granting the wish, and you need to say: 'If ever I can repay your act of kindness, I will be happy to do so.' But remember, leprechauns are known to be tricksters and you will not know till the deed is done if he was sincere or tricking you."

Ariana took a deep breath, asked for her spirit guides to show her if the leprechaun was being helpful, or doing a shenanigan. She prayed to her Irish grandmother's spirit to guide her and let her heart be open, for her intuition to be sharp, to be able to see his true spirit, and to trust her gift of insight.

Finally, she was ready; the book pages turned to the words of the spell.

It warned her again, saying the request to undo the spell had to come from a true believer's heart. If not, the leprechaun had the power to banish her from her world for at least three centuries.

She took a deep breath, and carefully said the following spell:

"Oh, Leprechaun Leprechaun, the highest of the high,

I humbly call on thee,

to remove the spell placed on Aguistin, the steed of Niamh, sister of the sun god, that

the sun may shine and rainbows once again bring beauty to our island of green, and those around the world,

Let the way be lit with the beacon of your shillelagh,

To save the rainbows I make this plea,

An evil spell has been cast on Aguistin, the magical steed at Niamh.

In the name of St Patrick, I beckon thee.

With shamrocks spread about with glee

Oh, Leprechaun Leprechaun, please appear at my knee.

Knowing when you grant my plea.

You can Ride the Colorful Irish Rainbow happily across the deep green sea."

Suddenly, a leprechaun appeared at her knee. Ariana was startled and jumped back, thinking he did look a bit mischievous.

Was she doing the right thing?

11

Then a voice whispered in her ear. She knew it was her grandmothers voice. "He is not a trickster; his heart is pure and will grant your wish. Trust your intuition my child and trust him. You are guided by the power of ancient wisdom and the angels that surround you!"

Ariana looked at this small red headed leprechaun, took a deep breath and said "Thank you so much for coming! I am so grateful, and I hope you enjoy and treasure the gifts I am giving you with heartfelt gratitude. The first gift, is a powerful talisman; that if this ever happened again you could use it to make the rainbows reappear." She handed him the braided ribbon from the mystical spell. She noticed a hint of a smile on his rugged face.

"I also have this for you, it is very special to me; it was my grandmothers." She gave him her gold Claddagh ring. "If I could ever be of help to you let me know, I am forever in your debt."

The hint of a smile turned into a grin. "The spell is removed, and Niamh and her brother are free to ride Aguistin. The sun will shine again. May the angels always surround you."

At that moment two beautifully colored rainbows appeared, He bowed, tipped his small cap, waved goodbye and stepped in between the colorful rainbows and disappeared.

No more rainbows of grey, she did it! Her orbs were bright and happily bouncing around her, making happy sounds. She had trusted those guiding, guarding, and protecting her, and the best and most surprising part was that she had trusted herself.

The Book of Shadows had closed. She did her invisibility spell, and the book was safe again from anyone seeking it. All was well with the world!

She grabbed Aries leash, as they walked out the door and down the street. She, Aries, and her orbs happily admired the beauty of the double rainbows that seemed to sparkle in the baby blue sky.

My Cherie

Dearest child, who lived in my womb,
Breathed my breath,
Felt my love,
Was cherished and caressed.

Who shone in my eyes,
Now twinkles in the sky,
Time passed too swiftly,
Left with the eternal "why?"

Your pain was my pain,
Your hope my hope,
Your dreams my dreams,
Wanting so, for a different outcome.

All of it gone, in one brief moment,
When your heart stopped beating,
Your last breath gone,
Now, all of us must live on ... without you.

Your beauty, your smile,
The strength you summoned
During moments of pain,
Somehow, you found the courage, to continue on.

I will miss your presence in everyday things,
I will miss your laughter when the birds sing,
I will miss how you loved all God's creatures,
I will miss how often you were my teacher.

Your body may be gone,
Yet, your spirit lives on,
In the lives you touched,
And those who loved you so much.

I will see you in the trees, the plantings in the spring,
I will see you in the Kitty cats, when they play with their things,
I will see you in your dad's and brother's eyes,
I will see you in the many tears that I cry

Be assured your memory will never be far,
You live in my heart forever more.

I wrote this poem for my childhood friend, after the loss of her 40-year-old daughter Cherie, who passed away on September 13, 2010.

Yin-Yang

My favorite symbol to see,
Is the Yin-Yang sign of destiny,
It makes me think and ponder life,
Balance is the answer, not constant strife.

The Hills and Valleys we often traverse,
Making us stronger and able to embrace.
Life on life's terms and acceptance of ourselves,
For in each of us, Light and Dark dwells.

Honest appraisal of character,
Not an easy task,
We often want to make changes,
We hope will last,

Seeking our true self is like planting seeds,
Wondering what this new life needs,
We water, feed it and hope it grows,
Then the hardest part…. to let it go.

One day it sprouts up through the earth,
Its green leaves reaching for the sun,
While the root reaches down below,
Looking to build strength … to not let go.

Storms come, winds blow,
The little plant bends to and fro,
But it has a grasp, it is growing strong.
It knows now, it can weather any storm.

Is it not like people?
Who need love to grow?
Is it not about trusting natures flow?
Remembering days have highs and lows?

Days can be grey and cloudy.
But the little plant has become aware.
That with time, sun, water, and love
We grow and embrace each day we are here,

And amazingly we survive…

Madalin E. Jackson Bickel
Calendar Girl

What parents don't understand about moving to a new city almost every year is that it makes you the new girl in class. It means making new friends and trying to find a group to fit in. Being the new girl was sometimes okay, but most of the time it seemed more like a crutch. This September was the beginning of fifth grade. My parents had decided to move back home near family. They had finally bought a house, but we had no furniture. So, while my mother worried about buying furniture, decorating our new house, and planning a house warming, I went to school.

The "new" school was brick and looked like an old four room building, but it had a lower level with two more classrooms which became the cafeteria at lunch time. The fifth-grade class was in the downstairs room farthest from the kitchen and was separated from the other classroom by a movable floor to ceiling wall. The desks were old wooden tables like first graders use. At my last school, we had real desks in nice neat rows facing the blackboard, but in this room sitting at the tables made some of us sit with our backs to the teacher. Somebody was always twisting around during a lesson to see the board or Mrs. Fisher.

After a few months of school, our class had settled into a routine. The teacher knew who the strong students were and had chosen her favorites. We had reading groups. Even though I was in the group with better readers, they still read too slowly. More than once Mrs. Fisher caught me silently reading ahead. She scolded me if I didn't know where to begin when it was my turn to read aloud.

Mrs. Fisher looked older than my mother and reminded me of a dried prune. Her pinched lips would assign us difficult activities like diagramming sentences. When we didn't do well, she would get a gleam in her eyes. She rarely ever smiled at us.

When we came back to school from Christmas vacation, Mrs. Fisher greeted us with a basketful of chocolate candy bars and a challenge. "Today we are going to make calendars for 1957. You will not be able to look at any calendars for help. I will give you the day the new year begins, then you must draw each month's calendar and number the days for each month. You may add holidays and drawings. Those who complete the assignment with perfect accuracy will be rewarded."

After placing the basket of candy on her desk, she handed out paper and rulers. We quietly got our pencils from the little storage places under our tables. When we had our materials ready, she looked around the room. "Today is Friday, January 4th. That means this month and the year began on Tuesday. You will now draw the calendar for the twelve months. You may begin."

I picked up my pencil and ruler and began measuring and dividing my paper into large squares for each month, then I divided each large square into columns and rows. January had thirty-one days. Because it began on Tuesday, I would need five rows. I labeled the top January and then labeled the day of each column beginning with Sunday. I carefully began numbering each small square beginning with Tuesday.

An elbow poked my left rib. I turned to see one of my two best friends, Sherry, looking at me. She whispered "I don't know how to do this. Can you help me?'

I looked at her blank paper, then at the teacher who was walking around the room. I whispered back, "Divide your paper like I have and draw squares for January. Fill in the little squares with numbers beginning with January 1 in the Tuesday block, then just keep going."

She picked up her pencil and ruler and began to draw lines. No measuring. She just began drawing lines. I stopped her. "You must measure to be sure you have enough lines and spaces."

Sherry turned her big brown eyes on me, "How?"

I sighed, took her pencil and ruler, and proceeded to draw all her blocks for twelve months. Just as I finished, my right rib received a jab. It was Leslie.

"Can you help me, too?" she whined.

I looked to see if the teacher was nearby. I saw her look at me.

With my head down, I completed numbering January on my calendar and began numbering February while mentally reciting 'Thirty days hath September, April, June, and November…' I needed to know how many days were in February. It was not a leap year, so

February would have 28 days and begin on Friday. Another jab in my right rib got my attention.

"Mary-Margaret, please help me." It was Leslie again. She was small like me but not very bright. She was in the low reading group and was always needing help with her arithmetic.

I picked up her pencil and ruler and started blocking off her paper. "Begin with the first large square, January, divide it into thirty-one small squares and number them one through thirty-one beginning with Tuesday."

I watched as she slowly began writing her numbers then went back to my own. As I continued to work on my calendar, I would get whispers and jabs. The girls had never heard of the Thirty Days poem and had no idea how many days were in each month. I finally stopped my work and wrote on a piece of paper how many days were in each month. The girls then went back to filling in their squares.

Mrs. Fisher stood at the front of the room, "You have ten more minutes then we will go outside for recess. All calendars must be finished and given to me as you leave."

Sherry and Leslie were well on their way to completing their calendars. I still needed to draw a few squares. I looked at the school clock on the wall and knew I needed to hurry.

My paper was getting smudged as I quickly moved across each row. I mumbled the number of days in each month while trying to make sure I didn't skip a day as I moved from one month to the next. Just as I wrote December 31 into its square, Mrs. Fisher said, "Time."

I looked at my less than neat calendar and was disappointed with my work. I wrote my name at the top. With the other students, I cleaned up my area then got out of my seat and pushed in the chair. We silently handed in our papers and grabbed our jackets.

Outside the wind was blowing and it was cold. Sherry and Leslie ran off with some of the other girls to grab the swings. I leaned against the building's warm brick wall and thought about my calendar. I had wanted to made special drawings for the holidays and add some color. Instead I had handed in a hurried-up, messy paper. My teacher would be disappointed in my work.

Soon Mrs. Fisher came out and blew her whistle. Kids came running from around the graveled playground and lined up. "You may go to the restroom then return to the classroom, hang up your jackets, and take your seats. I will return your papers and tell you who earned the candy bars. Won't it be fun?"

"Yes, ma'am," the class chimed. Sherry and Leslie had pushed their way to the front of the line. Mrs. Fisher looked down at them and actually smiled.

Good, I thought, maybe they will get a candy bar too and quit nagging me for help.

The classroom was quiet. We sat up straight in our little wooden chairs and looked at the teacher. She had the papers in her hand. "I am so proud of your work today. Many of you surprised me with your ability to make a calendar accurately. There were a few disappointments, but most of you earned a candy bar, and will receive your papers first."

Mrs. Fisher began walking around the room with our papers in her hand. "Sherry, I will begin with you. You did a marvelous job and earned a candy bar. You may help me give out the rewards. Please fetch the basket from my desk and place a candy bar at your seat. You may now follow me around and give out candy as I hand back the papers. Leslie, you are next. Congratulations."

Leslie beamed. I was pleased for her and watched as Sherry placed the candy on Leslie's calendar. Then Mrs. Fisher with Sherry following behind her, continued around the room handing out calendars and candy. Billy and Jane of course earned one. They were good students like me.

Mrs. Fisher reached Freddy's desk and shook her head. "Freddy, I know you tried so hard, but you had a few mistakes." She handed Freddy his calendar and patted him on the head. He gave her a small smile.

Everyone had their papers but me. Sherry was out of candy bars and sat down beside me. She looked at me with a big ugly grin and then giggled. Mrs. Fisher paused by my chair, "Mary-Margaret, I was so disappointed in your calendar. It was smudged, and when you reached September, you started the month on the wrong day. So, September, October, November, and December were incorrect. I guess you don't know on what day your birthday falls in September this year. I really expected better from you."

20

She slapped my paper down in front of me then turned to go back to her desk. "Boys and girls, you may eat your candy bars. Mary will come around and collect your wrappers and place them in the trash."

Without looking up, I folded my paper and placed it in my desk. I heard Sherry and Leslie giggle while opening their candy bars. Sherry leaned across me, "Leslie, I do believe this is the best candy bar I have ever eaten. Don't you think so?"

"Delicious," Leslie replied and giggled again.

I did not look at either one of them. I thought they would share a bite with me, but instead they seemed to be enjoying eating in front of me. Mrs. Fisher looked my way. Tears were trying to squeeze through my eyes, but I stood up and pushed my chair in. I whispered loud enough for most of the class to hear, "Sherry, my birthday falls on Wednesday this year. My parents will have a party for me, but I don't think you will be invited."

The room fell silent as I walked over and picked up the trash can. I began circling the room and collecting the candy bar wrappers. Mrs. Fisher probably heard my whisper, but she sat at her desk with her head down grading some papers. She never saw me smile like a calendar girl.

Spring Morning

Dawn's rosy hue tinged the sky.
Pale light stirred the birds awake.
The backyard echoed in early morning
chaos as nest building and seed gathering
filled the air along with squawks and spats.

Excited cardinals and raucous bluejays
fought for bird feeders and baths
of warming water. They dipped and
fluttered then swept away for nest
materials of twigs and brush.

The cool spring morning finally
warmed into a sunny afternoon.
It welcomed lazy humans who idled the
day away with ocular and
Audubon guide at their side.

Tea and biscuits and an open book,
followed by a snooze in rhythm
with the syncopated songs of
happy avians.

Butterfly Cinquain: Literally and Figuratively

Chrysalis

Brown small casing
Spring's gift to flowers
Waiting for the proper moment
To waken
Bringing colors to flutter round
March's early pale blossoms
Join bees and hummingbirds
Scattering pollen

Monarchs

October's Welcome

The gold and russet leaves spiral down,
skitter across the lane, twist against
a picket fence decorated with
autumn's splendor.

Bits of red leaf shards, chunks of crushed
acorns and twigs scatter across the sidewalk.
Stone stairs outlined by lit gourds welcome
home sweater clothed souls with
warm cider and caramel corn.

October has brought shorter days and longer nights
with a whisper of November's approaching chill.

If You Never Lived in the Mountains

If you never lived in the mountains
you never heard your mamma yell "Ooo-wee,
dinner," and stretch it out like Minnie Pearl
on the Grand Ol'e Opry.

We'd be jumpin' on the bank throwin' rocks
into the crick when her voice met our ears
after bouncing around from bush to tree
all up and down the holler. We could always tell
our mamma's voice from the others. She'd stand
on the front porch, hold on to the rail, and
cup her other hand to her mouth: "Ooo-whee…"

Soon our short legs were making time down the
dirt road. It was spring and we could smell the ramps
cooking in the beans with mamma's biscuits and
gravy. It was so good to eat even if your body
would stink like a skunk clear into next week.

Old Mrs. Adkins-with-a-d-not-a-t would open the
windows of the sixth-grade class, look at us,
roll her eyes, and sniff. We'd laugh cause the boys
would fart all the way down the hall as the girls
tried to pretend they didn't smell nothin'.

We girls were good at ignoring the boys. Even
though in our hearts we knew how it was goina' be.
Them boys would end up in the mines,
breathing that coal dust.

It was in the air too. The stuff clung to the
wash so it was dirtier when you brought it

inside then it was when you hung it up fresh.
It didn't take much imagination to figure out
what daddy's lungs were like and
why he coughed all the time.

Them coal mines are closed now. The big
barons couldn't make no more money.
Rumor has it they went off to Wyoming
then North Dakota where there was money
to make and men to bury.

Mamma's buried up on the hill now.
Every time it rains I worry her bones
are goina' wash down the mountain
and land back on the front porch.

When it rains that water comes rushing
down the mountain like a horse heading
for its hay. If mamma did end up on the
porch she wouldn't recognize it. The railings
are gone and there ain't no paint.

Everything is gray, just like the sky
and our tired faces.

January 2022

It wasn't predicted, the blizzard.
It just developed and buried
the earth – stiffened the soil,
left the cardinals to hunt for seed;
left the human no way to fill the feeder.

The temperature plummeted -
bone chilling gusts whipped around corners;
the house across the street
disappeared.

Wind blew steadily, like a gale;
tree branches clicked against each other,
against the bricks of the old fence.
Lights flickered off then on
then off.

No lights, no tv, no heat –
no fireplace to warm the night.

By morning a polar landscape
reflected the winter sun -
nothing moved, no sound
of traffic, no birds chirped.

Small tracks of torpor mammals
skimmed across the fresh white
blanket then disappeared into
drifts.

Someone walked their dog
knee deep in white banks, their
boots made trenches left
behind

to wait for warmer air or
early spring.

They Call it Mountain Dew

They call it Mountain Dew
like it's some kind of original
name. I remember laughing
when I saw the first can – not
a bottle like a respectable soda
pop – but a can with a funny
tab you had to pull.

Mountain Dew, I figure who
ever came up with that name
lives in some big fancy house
in some big fancy city and
drives some big fancy car. He's
probably never seen dew on a
flower in a garden much less
glazing the leaves of mountain
laurel.

We rise early in the mountains
cause there's not much else to do.
Sleep is a waste and your body
does better walking around then
lying on a bumpy thing called
a mattress.

In the summer we sleep on
pallets in front of the door or
on the porch. It all depends on
how bad the skeeters are.
That way there's a breeze and
the sweat dries and makes you
feel cool even if it is a bad joke.

They tell bad jokes at the company
store and talk about the weather,
if the mine is cutting back, and if there's
going to be a bad storm. They talk
about Buffalo Creek but it's not a
joke. That sobers them up then they
wander down the road to sneak a
swig of white lighting.

Our Mountain Dew is the kind
that sits on a Jack-in-the- pulpit
or dribbles down our throats
when we sip on Honeysuckle.
Real mountain dew clings to the
side of a brave little flower poking
up through dead leaves from last fall.

It raises its head for early risers so
we know there is more to these
mountains than black gold for
the barons and black lung for
the rest of us.

Mountain Dew? It's the part
of the mountains you don't know
unless you crawl off the porch,
breath in fresh air, and leave the
coal camp behind.

THE FIRE

The dry brush and woodlands needed no help to kindle into warm and hostile dancing flames. The air around the miles of ancient timberland seemed to speak of fire, but the ranger in the tower had seen none. He found himself continually turning, with the high-tech binoculars against his eyes, straining and looking, but not wanting to see. This time he turned faster, until he neared vertigo, sure that something would register. His eyes caught the sight almost as quickly as the sensor resounded with the high-pitched warning.

Lowering the oculars to his chest, the ranger moved to the computer terminal and immediately began checking for the location, time, and cause of the spark already sending swirling mists of smoke skyward. With a few carefully tapped signals and screen changes, he located the coordinates of the trouble. Oddly, it was not located on a hilltop or side, but in a moisture laden valley where less wind existed.

He checked the terminal again more quickly but from a different perspective. The printout read "natural causes". Having wasted enough time, he began pressing digital readouts for other towers and the main control center in Washington, DC. This one was strange, moving fast, and dangerous.

With the message sent and relays set, he transported down the steel alloy tower and prepared for departure. In the outer environment clothing room, he carefully but quickly maneuvered, Velcro and all, into the oxygen-rich, heat-resistant jumpsuit. Strapping into his life support system with supplies for ten full days of fire fighting, he stepped to the pad and felt the door swish open.

His gunmetal gray hovercraft was always ready. He lifted the side door and stepped in pulling the angled half-door-half-wall unit shut. Lights began to flash as he set the coordinates to match the area surrounding the first flash of fire he had seen. With everything in place, he punched the start button, ignited the engines, and blasted forward. Five seconds saw him hovering over the now blazing low spot. With the care of an ancient lunar module captain, he skimmed the area and landed near the origin of the flame.

It burned strong, white, and with little movement. He stared for nearly a minute mesmerized by the strange hot flame, then spoke into the microphone extended from his helmet.

"DC Control, FT number 375 reporting from coordinates 30 degrees north, 79 degrees west. Do you copy?"

"FT 375, this is DC Control. Proceed."

"Strange bright flame at fire epicenter. Sending spectral analysis. Await further contact." He pressed the chrome digital bracelet circling his left forearm. Within thirty seconds a message came beeping across the small screen. The message left him looking from the screen to the flame and back again.

With the heat beginning to permeate even his jumpsuit, he backed his air jet away and waited orders. Another thirty seconds elapsed as the flame continued to burn. A voice crackled in his ear. With staccato sounds, the voice said, "FT 375, spectral analysis incomplete. Computer unable to identify. Pull back and wait. Repeat, pull back and wait."

FT 375 heard the message, saw the flame, and knew it was different. He felt secure and invited. He gently eased the air-jet forward. A better look was all he wanted. The heat slowly increased. He moved closer, first cautiously, then with excitement. It was the most beautiful fire, burning straight and tall. Cleanly and smoothly in a perfect circle it began to encompass all the surrounding timber. He forgot the oath of protection of earth's last forest. He forgot the importance of the last hundred square miles of wood. He forgot the need to protect it for future generations. He only knew that the flame welcomed him.

The flame crept around the air-jet, around the terminal and special equipment, and around FT 375. He never really felt the heat. It came too quickly. When the fire finally died, all that was left around the shiny alloy tower was a haze of gray that would never again darken the skies of planet earth. There was nothing left to burn.

Unearned Guilt

Wallowing in guilt was something she knew was a waste of time, but there were days, months even, when she couldn't help herself. It was the height of selfishness to allow such indulgence. She did it anyway and hoped no one was looking.

It began when she was young, very young, perhaps barely seven years old. The bright yellow school bus would pick her up on the opposite side of the busy highway, drive east for several miles before turning into the shanty town. With her eyes barely high enough to see out the window she watched as the bus made each stop. The road was dirt, often more mud than dust, and the kids were shoeless, black, and poor. It was a shock to her young system to see children she believed must be neglected. How could their mothers let them go barefoot in the dirt?

At some point her parents must have determined she should catch the bus as it made its way back west. The yellow bus began picking her up at the end of their long driveway. It was safer than crossing the highway, and to her relief, she would never need to gaze upon the poor children again. Her heart, and much later her mind, could not endure the sight or the pain, but the guilt remained.

When she was nine, her school had a fund-raising contest. Each fourth, fifth, and sixth grade class elected a king and queen. She had been elected queen by her classmates to represent their fourth-grade class in the competition. The classes were selling candy to raise funds for the school. The class which sold the most candy and raised the most money would see their candidates become king and queen of the school. The runners-up would be prince and princess.

Her class was in second place. When rehearsal time came for the crowning night, the two candidates from the class leading in fund raising were the ones who practiced taking the thrones. The runner ups stood beside them. She was fine being a runner-up.

That night the cafeteria-turned-auditorium was filled with parents, grandparents, siblings, and teachers anxiously waiting the announcement of the winners. The candidates were lined up in the kitchen before proceeding down the aisle for the crowning event on the school's stage. Her mother had made a beautiful white gown with a beaded top and full skirt that swirled outward when she turned around. She felt like a princess. As she was turning back and forth, watching the skirt billow, there was a flurry of excitement. Her teacher came over and pulled her aside. It seemed there had been a change in the fund-raising totals and her class had won. She would be a queen not a princess.

The rest was a blur as everyone but the kids from the other class seemed excited. She sat on the throne and received the crown. She smiled but knew in her heart the second-place princess deserved the crown.

The white crown had been made of satin with glass gems, sequins, and rhinestones attached. It looked like a real crown. She was given the crown to keep and did so for many years even after they moved away. Over time it became a bit ragged as she and her younger sister played dress up and took turns wearing the crown.

She never told anyone how uncomfortable she had felt about winning the crown. One night, however, she overheard her parents discussing the 'donation' they had made to the school. In that quiet moment, their voices erased the joy of winning but not the guilt.

When We Were Young and It Was Summer

You asked me what I was going to do
this summer. It was like you were speaking a
foreign language. I haven't thought of doing
something in the summer since my kids became
adults.

I try to remember what it was like when school
dismissed before Memorial Day and summer
stretched on until the cool nights of September
had us exchange swimsuits for sweaters. Then,
I stop to think, not about your question…

The memories of summers past when the greatest
worry was which flavor of ice cream tasted best and
which ride we'd go on first at the amusement park,
the drive to the park was long. We argued in the back
seat about which ride was our favorite.

I said I was too old to ride the Merry-go-Round.
My sister chimed in that she was too big for it, too.
All forty inches of her six-year-old body which
always managed to be standing right behind me
when I wanted to be a grown up ten-year-old.

Instead, I stood embarrassed in front of my friends.
We were big kids who only rode scary rides like the
Ferris Wheel. I was ordered to hold my sister's hand
and lead her to a safe ride that mother said was proper,
then watched as my friends headed to the roller coaster.

What am I going to do this summer? Probably read
lots of books, stay out of the sun, and try to remember

what it was like in 1957 going on picnics, eating
watermelon and spitting seeds, while trying to impress
the boys who could hit a baseball out of sight.

I'll try to remember what it was like to have family
outings, how my grandmother's fried chicken tasted,
and why Cousin Billy always pushed to the
front of the line for cake and ice cream. I might
remember mother and dad loading us into the car.

It was a late-night drive home ending when he
carried us to bed, while mother whispered in the
dark. Maybe I'll remember the August I was
married and left home while my daddy stood in
the driveway and cried.

I'll try not to remember standing beside my
sister, lifting the bridal veil on her smiling
face knowing it was lie. She was crying
inside because father had announced he was
leaving our mother.

It hurts trying to forget how beautiful
she looked in her wedding dress, how the
church was decorated with pink flowers while
the organ painted the air with Mozart, and how
precious my daughter looked as flower girl.

I'll try to forget the artistry of the tiered wedding
cake, how many guests attended, and if they
knew our lives were changing that day. I'll
try to forget it was the beginning of a summer
we would only remember as the year our family
fell apart.

The Persistence of Memory*

When the body has aged, and the

mind is left to drift, memories,

like flotsam, nest upon us while the

world goes blind.

Negative or positive, soft or rigid,

memories snake through gray matter,

make us want to forget, yet they

remain, twisted like laundry on a

jute clothesline.

Memories of a first-born babe or a kiss

once the veil was lifted, melt away like

Camembert left in the sun.

Others hang rigid unaware of their metallic

likeness to nightmares then morph into

monsters from which we cannot hide.

We lay awake, try to revoke, even

topple the creature and yet it persists.

Haunted, the memories continue

ingrained in contorted minds

until the clock is silenced.

*With apologies to Salvador Dalí

Don Bishop (Fantasy author "T.S. Pedramon")

Gilwenna and the Wolves - A Nightshade Unicorn Story

February 2024, under the pen name T.S. Pedramon. In the world of his Nightshade Unicorn *saga.*

Gilwenna slammed the door in Reublan's face. He had played his last trick with her; she was done with him.

Sighing, she turned around and leaned against the door, relaxing her legs as she slumped down to sit on the floor.

"Didn't go too well, then?" Father asked her.

"He's such a…a…a dolt!" Gilwenna replied.

"Seems you've been having similar problems with several young men. Are you sure it's them?"

Gilwenna was taken aback at the question. "Yes, I'm sure." She rolled her eyes. "Let's see, now. I caught Reublan trying to court Melgia at the same time he was trying to see me, and tonight he made excuses to explain it away. Blonnel always talks down to me, and he thinks I'm basically supposed to live in the kitchen, always making food just for him. Helnan is always making rude jokes and eyeing me and other girls in inappropriate ways. And Persnan thinks it's okay to pick his nose in public. Yes, I'm sure it's them."

Father's eyebrows rose high into his forehead.

"Well, I, umm. I mean, I knew Persnan was socially awkward. I hadn't realized all the rest of that stuff," Father said.

"Well, that's how things are," Gilwenna spat in exasperation.

"Muffin," mother said, "do you really think it's all that black and white? Maybe there is some misunderstanding."

"No, I'm with Gilwenna on this, I suppose," Father interjected. "Like I said, I wasn't aware it all added up this way, but I do know she's not making anything up."

"Then where are the good boys?" Mother asked rhetorically. "Gilwenna's already six years past her Greenstone. You and I were already betrothed a few months after ours."

"Mother, you're not helping." Gilwenna lay the accusation at her feet. "This is the story of my life: where are the nice guys?"

Father set down the book he had been pretending to read when Gilwenna arrived home. "I know you'll find somebody."

"When?" she shot back. "I would love to be able to believe that. As Mother so wonderfully pointed out, I'm already six years past my Greenstone. I might as well declare myself an old maid by now."

"Sweet Peach, I wouldn't say it's all that bad," Father said. "So what if you haven't found somebody yet? So what if you never do? It's not a bad life in itself. You have Mother and me for the rest of our lives. You have your brothers and sisters, and nephews and nieces. You'll always have people who love you."

Gilwenna sighed again. "I know. I just wish I didn't have to fight with these dogs in the meantime."

"Besides," Father continued, "it's a beautiful world. You're fortunate to live in this valley, where we get to see unicorns—pardon me, that's my sailor grandfather breaking through—we get to see Nomord on a nearly regular basis here. You always enjoy seeing them, don't you?"

"Yes, but the Nomord won't keep me company when I'm an old maid dying alone."

"They can talk."

"Supposedly. Maybe they just copy a few words like parrots do."

"Maybe you should go downriver with next season's lambs," Mother suggested. "You'd probably meet some nice young men at the livestock market in Ipnard."

Before Gilwenna could protest at her mother's matchmaker inclinations, Father called it a day.

"We'd better get some rest, and especially you, Sweet Peach. I want you to take the flock to the upper pasture beyond the quarry tomorrow. You'll need to get an early start."

Gilwenna reluctantly pulled herself from the floor and began getting ready for bed.

~~~

Gilwenna got up as the sky first began to brighten, before the sun cast its rays properly down into the Valley of the Five Moons. It was late summer and the days had not yet begun to shorten, so this was quite an early rise for her.

She groggily roused the thirty-five sheep and let them out of their pen, leaning heavily on her shepherd's crook and setting them on the path up to the pasture that Father had indicated the night before. Gilwenna knew he wanted the sheep to rotate pastures so they wouldn't graze the grass down to its roots, and the upper pasture would be ripe for them to visit again by now.

As she walked up the road and the sheep accompanied her, she thought of the road she was walking along. This made her think of Lainen, a young man she had known while growing up. She felt sure that he had liked her, same as she felt about him. They'd been best friends, and adolescence lent a fun new spark to the acquaintanceship. She felt even more confident that his behavior in adulthood wouldn't match that of her recent suitors.

But such was her luck that he had moved up to Norl three years before their Greenstone. He'd moved away, his family loading up a cart with their precious belongings, and they had left town. They traveled north, just like she was now, on this very road. Surely, he must have been married five years ago by now. And Gilwenna was stuck here, tending sheep alone until she grew old.

Maybe her standards were too high. Maybe... No, just like she told her father the night before, her suitors did not meet a reasonable threshold of decency. Better to be alone, right?

Gilwenna reached the pasture that Father had sent her to, let the sheep inside, and closed the gate to contain the flock just in case any of them got away from her momentarily. She thumbed the release on her bag, thinking about pulling out her knitting. She had started on a scarf the week before, choosing prudence and wanting it ready when the cold weather came. But now she thought about the fact that it was still summer. Gilwenna felt that if she even thought about the scarf, the day would feel hotter.

She set herself up sitting on a low branch in a tree and pulled out her flute instead. Father had bought this flute for her when she was eight years old, when he was downriver to sell some sheep. He'd come back to town and had it engraved on the back with a small line map of the main waterways and roads in the Cleft, another name for the Valley of the Five Moons.

Gilwenna had made herself an expert at playing the simple instrument over the years. Now she skipped from song fragment to fragment as she considered her most recent romantic disappointment. It made her angry, and she had trouble sticking with one song.

Looking around the field below her to make sure the sheep were still all accounted for, Gilwenna surprised herself by realizing that she had managed to continue playing one single song continuously for several minutes. Go figure. She had been thinking about Lainen again, and here she was, playing her favorite song.

She didn't even know what the song was called. She'd picked it up from a grain merchant and his family one day when they stopped in town for the village's Pinkstone Observance when she was ten. Gilwenna hadn't caught the name and had only heard some of the lyrics, but the tune was written in stone in her mind, both verse and chorus. Something about lovers divided by circumstance.

She must be fooling herself. The song elicited images of true lovers, not anyone like her disappointments that called themselves men. She could daydream about Lainen all day long, but he was no more real in her life than the others were good options.

Gilwenna was pulled from her reverie by an impalpable sense of danger. She hadn't noticed what specific signs she picked up from the sheep, but she was personally familiar enough with her flock that she became unconsciously aware that something was wrong.

She cast her eyes about the field, looking for some sign to show her what was distressing the sheep. She eased herself down from the branch where she sat, never removing her gaze from the shadows of trees around the perimeter of the pasture.

In a blur, a wolf broke out of the shadows in the distance off to Gilwenna's right, dashing toward the flock. She immediately moved to place herself between the wolf and the flock, swinging her staff before it came near to show it that she posed a threat. Two more wolves emerged from the opposite side of the pasture, at the moment to her back.

The sheep now pressed themselves close together against the danger, and Gilwenna maneuvered again, trying to maintain a barrier around the flock. This was impossible. There is no way she could maintain herself on all sides of the flock while wolves attacked from different directions. Gilwenna wouldn't have accused sheep of being the smartest of creatures, but at this moment they were intelligent enough to form a tight group and stay behind Gilwenna's swinging shepherd's crook.

What the sheep saw as security, the wolves eyed warily.

Could there be only three of them?

Gilwenna looked around at the three wolves and at the fringes of the pasture. No other canines appeared. Still, how was she supposed to protect thirty-five sheep on all sides at once?

Gilwenna reached into the pocket of her bag, slung over her shoulder. She carried a few stones there for occasions such as this. As one of the pair of wolves to her left made a lunge toward the flock, Gilwenna held her staff in her left hand and hurled a stone the size of her fist with her right hand. Luck was with her at the moment, and the stone struck the wolf in the shoulder. It halted its assault, backing up for space while it reassessed the situation.

At the same time, the wolf that came from her right lunged toward the sheep near it, a few strides behind Gilwenna. She swung her staff frantically, holding the toe end in her hands and hitting the wolf's flank with the crook. The wolf yelped and backed up, the same as its comrade had.

Gilwenna couldn't wait for them to decide to attack the flock again. She advanced on the lone wolf, swinging her staff in front of her and hoping to catch its neck in the crook so she could break it. Both wolves to her left abandoned the attack on the sheep and charged at Gilwenna instead.

Gilwenna grabbed another stone from her bag, and another, throwing them at the pair while they ran toward her. Both wolves, now expecting an attack from her, easily dodged the stones which fell harmlessly beyond them. Gilwenna turned back and forth from wolf, to wolf, to wolf, brandishing her crook to hold them at bay. She had been alarmed the moment she realized the sheep were on edge, but now she was panicking for her life.

While Gilwenna faced the leftmost attacker, the lone wolf on her right jumped at her from behind and collided with her back, knocking her to the ground. Growling fiercely, it grabbed a mouthful of hair and pulled, tugging her head back. Finding hair covering Gilwenna's neck, the wolf grabbed her right shoulder and bit into it, shaking and pulling toward her left, turning her over on to her back, exposing her face and hands.

Keeping her arms up to protect her face and neck, Gilwenna swung blindly with the staff. She heard it hit flesh twice, accompanied by one yelp, but then she felt teeth sink into her forearm while another fanged mouth enveloped her face, tearing into her cheeks on both sides.

Gilwenna screamed as she desperately tried to find canine throats to squeeze with her fingers, now thinking she would be lucky if she could become an old maid after all.

Next, her scream was cut off as the growling around her suddenly gave way to howls. Hooved feet that appeared evidently from nowhere thrashed with dainty, deadly precision at the wolves. A beast with a single horn sprouting from the center of its forehead imposed itself upon the wolves' space.

It was over in a second. Canines fled from the impressive white-furred beast and the commotion around Gilwenna quieted down, though the sheep continued bleating in belayed fright.

One of the blessed Nomord had come to her rescue. Gilwenna glanced up at the majestic creature, which stood apparently indifferent now, contemplating the sheep, or the trees. One could never be sure with the Nomord. They never seemed to focus on anything for very long.

Gilwenna blinked, using her good hand to wipe blood from her face while she tried to sit up. Something felt wrong, though. She groped at her torso and belly with her hand. Her fingers came back even bloodier. She hadn't noticed while she was trying to protect her head and neck, but a wolf had bitten her belly, leaving a large wound that now expressed increasing pain as the thrill of the fight faded.

Gilwenna was as good as dead. Even if somebody were here to clean her wounds, even if they brought alcohol to sanitize the wounds, nobody could quell an infection from a gut wound like this. She might survive a few more days, but that would be it, miraculous rescue or no.

"I am Tithcoennen," the Nomord spoke.

Dazed though she was, Gilwenna started at the Nomord's speech. She coughed, then spoke roughly through her pain. "Thank you for help—" It was too much. She coughed again, then heaved dryly.

The Nomord stepped close to Gilwenna, looking her in the eye. Leaning down, she—all the Nomord were female—touched the tip of her horn to Gilwenna's forehead. A feeling of warmth filled Gilwenna, though it was an internal feeling, not discomforting her at all despite the heat of the day. Then her wounds burned, as intense as a branding iron, but the burning was momentary and rapidly gave way to...utter relief. The experience culminated in a sensation of bathing in a pure, clear river, and the Nomord lifted her head and stood tall.

Gilwenna shook herself. "What—" she stammered, wide-eyed. "How—thank you."

"You are welcome," the Nomord said.

Gilwenna had heard of people being this close to a Nomord, but never thought it might actually happen to her.

"You healed me. And you're talking to me. And you're—what did you say?"

42

The Nomord laughed, a feathery sound that seemed to calm the sheep. "Tithcoennen."

"Is that your name?"

"It is, and it isn't. All Ta-Nomord are Tithcoennen. All but one."

Gilwenna couldn't make heads or tails of this. "Well, Tith...Tith-co-en-en," she repeated slowly. "What can I do for you in return?"

"Just live, Gilwenna. Live well." Tithcoennen smiled with her eyes.

Gilwenna wondered how the beast knew her name. "What is the Ta—uh, Ta—um, Nomord, that isn't Tithcoennen?"

"Never mind that now. I would like to do one more thing for you before I lose myself."

"Lose yourself?"

"Yes. I cannot normally be so coherent, can I? Not since the days before." Tithcoennen's eyes clouded over, then cleared again.

"Before what?"

"There's not much time. Live well. Keep playing your flute. I have visited you before, out of sight. I am pleased by the music you play. Hold your flute up, please. Hurry." The Nomord's face showed great concentration.

Gilwenna held her flute up, and Tithcoennen brought her horn forward to touch it briefly.

"All have a gift, all Nomord," she explained to Gilwenna. "Some, like I, can bring modest thought into reality. Ideas, communication, feeling, become physical. Next time, I hope you'll still—" She paused, bestowing importance to her next words. "—Beware the wolves."

Music emanated from the small silvery instrument without Gilwenna holding it to her lips, serenading the grain merchant's song as sweetly as Gilwenna had ever done so.

"Something to remember me by," said Tithcoennen. "Say 'beware the wolves' to hear the song when you are too tired to play. I also have tried—tried, mind you—to give it some shred of power against the influence of the imprisoned menace. You—" Her eyes clouded again. "You never know—"

The Nomord looked around at her surroundings. Bending down, she took a bite of grass.

Gilwenna raised her hand toward Tithcoennen's flank, but the beast shied away.

"Thank you," Gilwenna said, trying to hold tears back.

So much had just occurred. It was known that the Nomord were capable of speech, but they never held a conversation. They could heal, but it was extremely rare. Now Gilwenna had been given the honor of both, and on top of that, she had a flute that could help carry her through difficult times.

But Tithcoennen's visit was a mixed bag. There was so much Gilwenna couldn't understand. All but one? Ta-Nomord? Imprisoned menace? What did all this mean?

The rest of the day passed in a daze. Gilwenna kept thinking about the fortuitous, odd, and inexplicable visit. She numbly listened to the flute play her favorite tune dozens of times, and listlessly tried playing other songs. She tried turning to her knitting. All was pointless. She needed somebody to talk to. Somebody who could understand her.

Maybe growing to be an old maid wouldn't be so bad, but it wouldn't be ideal, either. Perhaps she should give Reublan another cha—

"Ahoy, there!"

That was Father's voice. What was he doing up here past the quarry? He was supposed to be irrigating the wheat today.

"Gilwenna! Come on. It's time for you to go home," he called as he rounded a bend and came into sight.

"But the sheep! It's not time for them to go home," she called back.

Father looked up and saw Gilwenna at that point, taking in the effects of the day on her. He stopped walking in surprise, then resumed both walking and talking as he continued to approach.

"What happened to you? Your hair is all matted and your clothes are covered in…is that mud?"

"Blood. There were wolves," Gilwenna replied simply.

Father turned to look back down the trail.

"Are you hurt?"

"No." She didn't explain.

"Ah, uh—All the better for you to go home, then. Take a rest. How about this? I'll take the flock home. Somebody came by the house, wanted to see you, see? He and I caught up a bit, and I said he could wait until dinner for you to come home. But he begged me not to make him wait."

Gilwenna contorted her face in confusion, nearing disgust. Who was trying to creep back into her good graces?

"Which one of them is it? Is it the nose-picker?"

"Gilwenna! Gilwenna, it's me!"

No. That voice. Gilwenna didn't dare suppose—

The afternoon light caught the bright red color of a tall man's shirt as Lainen walked around the corner with a smile as big as the valley on his face. He dropped the bag he carried and broke into a run up to meet her.

Gilwenna couldn't believe the turn of events. She stood in shock for a moment, then lunged into him and cried with relief and joy. She was full of questions about the circumstances that brought him back, but certain of his character and intent. And their future.

Her personal wolves would be held at bay forever now; she only need beware the four-legged kind from this day on.

Salandra the Precious - A Thallenroads Story

December 2023, under T.S. Pedramon. In the universe of his Grendhill Chronicles *saga.*

"Salandra, my precious, can you come here, please?" Mother's voice sounded down the hallway and into Salandra's bedroom, where she was writing a note to her older cousin, Apple.

Apple lived in the canopy, in Cherrimellon.

Salandra Switch lived in a village called Cherrynut, at the roots of the great Cherrimellon tree, near Market Branch. Salandra was nine Turns of age now—what was that in Years? Seven?—but she thought back a few Turns to when she was learning to read. During those days, Apple and her parents used to come down the trunk and spend a week among the roots with the Switch family during the winter, and Apple would help Salandra practice reading. Nowadays, Apple was too busy with boys. Well, one boy.

Salandra set her pencil down, pinned the note to the root wall in front of her, and walked to the kitchen, idly slapping her hand on the hallway's whitewashed cinderblock walls.

"Mother, how do you spell 'engagement?'" She asked when she got there. "I'm writing to Apple to say congratulations."

"I'll tell you later, precious, when you come back," Mother replied.

"Come back? From where?"

Mother stood at the stove, stirring a pot.

"Yes, dear. You know your father went up to Cherrimellon today to buy me some fabrics I've been needing to spruce up our winter clothes."

"Uh-huh."

"Well, it's a big favor he's doing for me, so I want to have a nice dinner ready for him when he comes home, but I need an ingredient for this soup."

"What do you want me to do?" Salandra didn't see how she fit into the equation.

"I need you to go get me some peanuts."

"You want me to go to Market Hall?" Salandra's eyes widened. She didn't have any money.

"No, you shouldn't have to go so far. I want the local cherry-peanuts. Just get them from the passages."

Mother tapped the spoon on the side of the pot and reached into a cupboard. She pulled out a wooden bowl and handed it to Salandra.

"But the harvest is over, there aren't any left!" Salandra protested.

"There's always some left. Just go and fill this bowl and then come back. You want the Cherrynut soup, right?"

"Mm-hm!" Salandra nodded enthusiastically and licked her lips for emphasis.

"Alright, precious. Just bring me a bowl of cherry-peanuts," Mother bargained.

"Okay!" Salandra turned to go out the door.

"Thank you!" Mother called after her.

Salandra stepped outside and into the passageways that acted as the streets for the town of Cherrynut. The walls alternated between cinder block, stone, wood, and earth. She walked along, inspecting the segments of earthen wall, searching for any peanuts the harvesters may have missed.

She left her own passageway when she got to the end, turning a few corners as she searched. After several minutes, she had only found a few individual uncracked husks. As she began to be worried that she wouldn't be able to find enough peanuts, she found herself straying farther and farther from home.

As her concern grew, she realized that she was catching up to a man walking slowly ahead of her. She was about to turn around and head back the way she came, when he turned and she recognized him.

Mayor Wingdale.

The mayor smiled at Salandra. "Hey there, Miss Switch. Can I help you with anything?"

47

Salandra stood stiff and wide-eyed, looking up at him wordlessly.

He looked at the bowl she carried and back to her face. "Are you looking for something?"

Salandra couldn't overcome her shyness, and stayed motionless, mouth agape.

Mayor Wingdale shrugged. "Okay, Salandra. Just let me know if you need anything." He turned again, walking a few more steps before taking a side passage.

Salandra unfroze, liberated by his disappearance. She resumed her search for the local sweet cherry-peanuts that grew from the roots of the Cherrimellon tree. She started noticing more and more stone and wood walls as she went, with fewer segments of cinder block or earth. Salandra realized that she was getting closer to the center of the village, and there was less room to cultivate and harvest the peanuts here, but this area also usually had the densest harvest. She continued her search.

As Salandra saw the passageway open up ahead of her into a great chamber, she realized she had unwittingly walked all the way to Market Hall. The cavern's ceiling vaulted far overhead, its roof made of the dark-colored roots of the enormous tree that the town of Cherrynut lived under. Every few years, the town used huge scaffolding to re-paint the roof a pale color that would give a better impression of the sky up top in the light of their lanterns. Every few years, the ventilation shafts would be re-dug, removing debris deposited by animals or weather. Salandra was proud to live in a busy town that produced an important crop for the region, but right now she was worried about getting some of that crop back home to her mother. She had been able to glean almost nothing from the passageways.

Emerging into the grand cavern, Salandra stood there dumbly, wondering what to do next. She looked left, right, and ahead. She saw shops, some closing up for the evening, and some still open and peddling their wares. Surely some of those would be selling food, and surely some of them would have local peanuts, but Salandra had brought no money. By the time she walked home—no, ran home—and made it back here after asking Mother for a bit of money, the rest of the shops would probably be closed. Maybe they should have something else for dinner tonight. But Mother had already started cooking the soup. What was there to do?

Then Salandra saw a man pushing a cart piled high with cherry-peanuts, just leaving the Market Hall through another passageway. The threshold he crossed as he left the cavern was uneven; it jostled his cart and a bunch of peanuts fell off. He didn't notice it and kept moving.

Salandra ran to grab the bunch, picking it up. She raised her free hand toward the man's back and was about to call out to him. Sir, you dropped this!

But nothing came out. Curse this shyness! She only wanted to say something simple, but she didn't know this man well enough to be comfortable. And there were still so many people about. What would they think? What if they didn't observe the entire exchange, and judged inaccurately without knowing what was really happening? But that was absurd. She was just trying to return a bunch of cherry-peanuts that fell off a cart...

As Salandra thought this, she realized that the man was now out of sight, traveling up the passageway. She slowly tore her sight away from the bend he had disappeared around, lowering her eyes to the bunch of peanuts in her hand. She fit it in the bowl so she could use one hand to hold both items; the bunch filled the bowl and heaped over.

Great. Now it probably looked like she was just assuming possession of food that didn't properly belong to her. If anybody was watching her now, they were probably judging that she...

She heard a kind laugh over her shoulder. Turning to look, she saw Mayor Wingdale again.

Oh, no.

It wasn't his easy smile that made her uncomfortable; it was the situation she was in, and the fact that he wasn't her family. In fact, his friendly eyes did help ease her a little.

"Sweet Salandra," he said, walking closer. "I saw the whole thing. Those were my cherry-peanuts."

Salandra's eyes nearly popped from their sockets. She grabbed the bunch from the bowl and held it up for him.

The mayor laughed again.

"No, it's alright. I don't want them. I paid that gentleman to take my harvest to the next town so I could take them to another market. That bunch is yours now."

Salandra stared at him with her jaw loose, maintaining her silence.

"Salandra, it's alright," the mayor said softly.

He crouched down to her height.

"Those are your cherry-peanuts now. Go home; I imagine your mother wants them for a tasty soup, yes?"

With difficulty, Salandra found her voice. "Um. Yes," she uttered softly.

"Well, that settles it," he said with a twinkle in his eye. "You're having a tasty soup tonight. Tell your folks I said hello."

Mayor Wingdale patted Salandra on the shoulder, then stood and walked away, giving finality to the transfer of ownership.

Salandra came to herself, turned on her heel, and nearly bolted. Wait.

"Thank you, Mayor!" she called over her shoulder.

Then she walked home briskly, easily tracing her path home with a light heart. When she walked in the front door, she handed the bowl of cherry-peanuts to her mother and found her father sitting at the table, a bag on the floor next to him holding the fabrics he had purchased for her mother.

"Hey, precious!" Father greeted her. "Guess who came down the trunk with me to spend the night with you tonight?"

A very familiar young woman sat across the table from him.

"Apple!" Salandra shouted with glee.

Я-BOT

Created June 25, 2021. Version March 12, 2023. Under T.S. Pedramon.

Back in those days, everyone wanted one. Sure, why not get a personal assistant? Not—not like a digital assistant, but a physical personal assistant, with arms and legs. Somebody who could talk to you to face to face. Clean the house. Do the laundry. Why not? I mean, that's what technology is for, right? To make life easier. To make life better.

As it happened, it was Russia that started mass producing the first reliable, fully-functional, physical personal assistants. If it had happened a couple of decades prior, nobody would have seen it coming. It would have to be Japan or China. Possibly the US. But the technology wasn't really there yet in those days.

And Russia really made a comeback since those days. And I mean, it started with their hackers. Of course, everyone remembers the hackers from the 'teens and the '20s. But no, we're not talking about hackers. Those—those were people. Of course there's also the invasion of Ukraine they initiated in February of '22. The hackers faded into the background during that war. But when Russia was ultimately repelled and they slowly started recovering from their trainwreck of a self-mutilation, the hackers started gaining more notoriety again.

But those were people, sitting behind keyboards. We're talking about machines here. Machines who move like people, not people who operate through machines. No, these—these personal assistants…

Of course, every country had their own take on it. Japan had theirs. Japan was the first one to come out with one, though it wasn't as good as the Russian version, of course. It's just that once the technology was established, everyone had theirs.

Korea was another one, obviously. Korea's were really popular there for a few years. And China's, despite concerns about data collection. Who wouldn't want one? And then you know, trying to produce the most affordable ones.

But it was…it was Russia's that really, really changed the scene. The "Arbots," they were called. Or, technically, the ЯBOTs. A backwards R and a capital B-O-T. I mean, I guess these are characters in the Cyrillic script. I don't know. I don't speak Russian.

But I mean, who wouldn't want a personal assistant? Makes life easier. So then when Russia started shipping millions of these every year, everyone thought it was great. Everyone thought, you know, Russia had shifted their focus. That they weren't, they weren't trying to hack everybody anymore. I mean, this was the late '30's. Times had changed.

That Russia's hackers had calmed down some years prior is true. And then Russia had shifted their focus to hardware and producing a high quality product. They became known for building good cars, and gained that reputation quickly. The Russian economy had taken off.

And then…there were the ЯBOTs. Very high quality build. Not like some of the Chinese knockoffs. Somewhat like some of the Japanese ones, but the Russian ones were cheaper. I mean, if you get similar performance from two different products, why not go with the cheaper one? And they were sturdy. They lasted. At least, I assume they're still going strong, even today.

But then a few years in…I—I don't know. Golubev, the guy they voted in after Putin finally lost enough favor for his Ukraine fiasco to actually lose an "election," seemed ambitious on behalf of his homeland. But he and his gang made some offhanded comments. Made some confusing comments at press conferences, talking about the ЯBOTs.

And, you know people in the States like to joke and call them robots or Arbots, but properly there they're called ЯBOTs. At least that's how they were marketed, in English, at least.

But, so, these comments from Golubev and his groupies, if you will. I mean, if we had understood at that time, the whole world would have been alarmed. Of course, the ЯBOTs are the best on the market, he says. Of course, they're…they're designed that way. They allow you to set it and forget it. You tell the ЯBOT what you want it to do, it takes care of the rest.

And they just…I mean, I guess the point was to sell a good, solid product that behaved appropriately. Get people hooked and dependent, telling their friends to buy one, too. But then…OK, I mean I, I know a little bit of Russian. I don't speak it. But I can read a few things now. I couldn't back in those days. But I learned. We all learned.

So, I mean it was a marketing ploy, right? It was genius, that. ЯBOT, I mean, it's just looks like you got the R switched around backwards and you're missing an O and it's a robot. Of course, it's a robot. But the backwards R—it's not just a backwards R. The letter in Russian sounds like Y. It sounds like, "Yuh". Or something like that. And it means "I," like the grammatical first person, me. "I am" is what it meant.

And the BOT. Uh… "Vote." It sounds like the word "vote" except if you spoke it through, try to speak it through a straw. "Vault," almost, the way some people pronounce it. So BOT means "here," or "look," or "behold."

And in Russia you skip over—I mean in Russian I guess I don't even know if they have the word "to be." They must have something, but when you say, "I am here," you just say "I here." And that's what ЯBOT meant in the end. I mean, "yuh-vot." I am here. I exist. I am. The things were sentient, OK?!

Except apparently they had some hard-coded instructions. Something like "Execute order 66," or something, if you watch Star Wars. If anyone has a copy of that these days.

I mean, I guess that's all there is to it. Suddenly they all went crazy one day. Told people, like, they told their masters that they were now the masters. They started…forcing people to work, all for Russia's benefit. Punishing them if they didn't. So many people died that first day. So many people.

All we can do is hope that we can find the chink in Russia's armor, in Russia's supply chain, or their infrastructure. And somehow sabotage the ЯBOTs to save us all. Before our will is crushed. Before our spirit is gone.

For now, I hide in the forest like the coward I was when I ran away from my ЯBOT. I was only fortunate enough to get away because he—it—was in the shop for maintenance. It was still the early days of the occupation—that's what it is, right?

And they were spread thin enough that he—sorry again—it—was the only one watching me, so when it was in for maintenance I was left unsupervised.

You'll have to forgive my confusion still lasting today. He worked for me without complaint for three and a half years, and I thought I might actually consider him my best friend.

His name was Peter. I should have called him Judas.

Sorry. "It." I should have called it Judas.

Ocean of Memory

Don Bishop (Pedramon's real name) and Rose Bishop, age 5 at time of story creation. August 2017.

Lilly watched the village slip out of sight. It was empty, as the village elders had decided this voyage would include the whole town. Lilly was eleven years old, and like all the children, was excited to join the first fishing voyage of the season. This year she would be able to help a little, rigging the lines and nets to catch the large tuna they hunted. She felt ready to contribute.

But a week or two was a long time to be away from home and all her toys. She wished she could bring some of them. The village was a couple of hundred people, now spread among the fourteen small ships they had. She might not see her friends much, but the boats would come together from time to time during the voyage, and she could see her friends then. That would make the time away from home more bearable.

Lilly watched their small island disappear and did her best to distract herself by doing her part on the trip just like her mother said to. She helped her mother clean the first tuna they landed near the end of the first day. At the end of the day they met up with another craft to place the large fish into its hold so they would be ready to catch more. They caught their second tuna late in the morning of the second day. If they could keep catching fish so quickly then perhaps this quest wouldn't seem so long after all.

During the hours of waiting, Lilly occupied her mind singing songs and asking her parents how to know where to go to find fish. Catching two in as many days was encouraging, but when could they expect to catch another? She hoped the journey wouldn't drag on too long before she could get back home.

At the end of the second day Lilly slipped while dodging under the boom and managed to steady herself on the mast. Her hand slid and she cried out in pain. There was a large sliver right in the middle of her palm! Her mother helped her remove it, but her hand hurt enough that it slowed her work repairing lines and nets. Would boredom and pain be the hallmarks of this cruise? If only she had known how trivial those were.

A few hours after dark at the end of the second day out, and about an hour after the most recent atoll had slipped from sight, men and women began shouting to wake everybody up. Something was different about the ocean. As Lilly woke she thought she could hear rumbling. As she stood in the boat, she saw a line on the surface of the water, traveling too fast for belief. The narrow line ripped from the horizon to the vessels in a matter of seconds.

The wave smashed into the fleet. Only a foot or so tall, it nevertheless struck with such force that it left the boats heaving to and fro. Two rigs capsized. The smallest children in the fleet started crying from the sound of the impact. Then it was gone. A moment of eerie stillness reigned while people recovered from the shock of the blow.

Men, women, and adolescents shouted and those in the water hurried to swim back to their boats. Others from nearby craft swam across the gap to help them right their boats. After several minutes' struggle, they were just getting the boats upright and starting to scoop the water out, when a second wave hit. It toppled three boats.

During the next half hour, two more waves hit the small fleet. In the end, nine of the fourteen ships had been capsized, and four had been crippled beyond repair at sea. The people of the village banded together and rescued their companions in the destroyed rigs, and righted the boats that had been capsized but remained salvageable. But now each ship was carrying almost twenty people instead of the intended fifteen. They had lost supplies overboard. Food and fresh water were low. Equipment had been knocked overboard. They couldn't catch more food.

At least everyone survived.

Everybody lost sleep that night, too. As morning approached, the elders gathered on one ship to determine their plan of action. With the craft all damaged and supplies depleted, they must return home. They rationed food and set sail.

The trip back took three full days. Lilly's hand ached as the splinter wound tried to heal. Everybody was hungry, but the food had to be rationed for unexpected delays. Lilly thought her thirst was the worst of all. Everybody had survived, and everybody was going home, but the paltry water ration left Lilly parched. She tried to imagine getting home and crawling into her comfortable bed after finally sating her thirst. To sleep without fear of another wave knocking over their rig! Her hope of getting home seemed just enough to keep her going.

On the third day of the return trip Lilly croaked to her father that she could not continue. He did not give her an extra drink of water. He wordlessly dipped a rag in their fresh water and handed it to her. She eagerly put the wet scrap in her mouth. Oh, how glorious! But after a moment the effect was gone. Lilly suffered on.

Finally, they approached their island. Lilly could almost cry with anticipation for an end to all her anxiety and tribulation. They rounded the bend to bring their village into sight.

It wasn't there. The destructive waves had come here, had grown in height while racing in to shore, and washed their home away. Only mud remained.

When they landed, the elders decided they would rebuild, on higher ground, farther from the water. Lilly would live in another hut with her parents, would yet play with her friends, and would enjoy the food she loved.

But her first home was in the ocean, now only a memory.

J.M.R. Gaines (James F. & John M.)

Serizawa Dies

Our imagination, our future heritage?
More than that
Our honor
Literally dissolved!
Along with that monster?
Gojira!
By his own tragic design
The one-eyed hero
True samurai
Sacrificed in the resounding deep
To our empire's flaming folly.
Refusing to expire
The torch he longed to pass would be
Doomed to become the spark
For further holocaust
When snatched by unworthy hands.

Maidens, sound the dirge again
This once for a single soul
Who will not lie still.
Notes they remember so well…
But the reason for those scarlet words
Already evaporates
As they fly from young lips.

Sensei, teacher and master,
Far-sighted into so many pasts
Do you shudder for the outcome of our race?
Your attendants turn away
Only partly comprehending,
Yet immersed in fear,
Or breaking into
Cold nuptial tears.

Through the Wormhole

Plunging from
Something into nothing…
And/nor
Neither/or…
Nothing into something?
How do you know?

You walk from a room,
Pushing through a door into
Another identical room.
It is a swinging door…
You push back through
But that is not
The room you came from?
How do you know?

If you are upside down,
Yet everything else is also
Upside down,
What is rightside up?
How do you know?

Your atoms reverse,
Vortices change direction,
Left is right,
Clockwise counter,
And through your eyes,
How do you know?

A pigeon always tells north from south,
A dog always tells owner from burglar,
However a finch cannot tell

Peanuts from habanero.
That dog cannot see
If the master wears green,
The burglar red,
Or the other way around…
Around and around.
Your eyes grow dizzy,
Your organs cannot feel magnets.
Unable to feel the Earth's pulse,
How will you sense the cosmos?
How do you know?

The Astronaut's Hymn

Eternal Father, show your grace
To those who sail the depths of space.
O shield them from the cosmic fire
As from the dangers of desire
And in the stark infinity
Warm their hearts with humility.

Beyond the influence of Earth,
Allow them wisdom through rebirth.
Maintain their course both true and sure
Through any perils they endure.
From star to star, where they may roam,
Lord, bring them always safely home.

The Double Abyss

We chop atoms into protons into quarks

And keep on chopping.

We blow suns into nebulae into galaxies

And keep blowing until universes burst.

When will we realize

For every inside there is an outside,

For every outside an inside?

World without end upwards and downwards—

Heisenberg was right.

Matter and energy all dissolve

Into each other and something more…

No matter how we grow mechanical eyes

It will always be one step beyond us,

Beckoning and mocking.

We are like the slimy Dwarf.

Grasping at elusive Beauties,

Only to slip away on uncertain stones,

And if there is some golden treasure to seize,

It lies unbeheld in the absolute here and now.

Outset

At the time of the Zetan incursion in 2235 Earth's defenses were rudimentary. The corporations had mainly developed weapons to fight each other, while the vestigial planetary governments aimed their attack devices downward against terrestrial rivals instead of outward against invaders. Only a half-dozen vessels had been suitable to be fitted with the projectors the Thil delegation had brought when they came to alert humans about what they could expect from Zetans re-entering the Sol system. Better this token resistance than slavery and surrender. There was always hope that the mysterious Blynthians whom the Thil described as allies would appear to save the day.

The Thil – grim, taciturn creatures: even from the translators, their voices had a hissing, disquieting quality; closer to things that hadn't breathed on Earth since before the Triassic. Still, they were at least shaped more or less like humans – they claimed the mysterious Blynthians had sent them to Earth for that reason.

Good God, what must the Blynthians themselves look like?

The Paramount joined a motley human squadron that deployed with three Thil battle cruisers just a month before the second wave of Zetan ships approached Earth's system. Captain Seb Forestier tried to make the best of his slim chances in the looming battle.

"Li, have we arrived at the defense coordinates?"

The Exec looked grim. "Yes, sir. Just passed thirty thousand kilometers off Ganymede."

"Weapons systems all functional?"

"Projector units and missiles all read Go. Do you think we'll actually get a chance to use them? It feels … weird to just be waiting here for the Thil squadron to lure the Zetans into our little trap."

"Best we can do. Hard enough getting trained to use the projectors without also having to learn the battle manoeuvres the Thil use. As it is, we're essentially a masked battery poised for the battle to come to us."

Despite constant efforts to appear imperturbable, Li's face betrayed concern. "They say the Zetans are genetic tinkerers."

Ever since the raid on Munich that had been obvious. According to survivors, they came in various forms, sizes, and configurations to abduct the engineers from the Siemens-Bayer Research Complex, wanting the best and the brightest to experiment on. Seb knew ... had known some of those people. What had become of them now? Seb could think of nothing to say in response that was true, necessary and kind, so he pretended not to have heard Li's remark. Sometimes it was best not to respond at all.

"Alert, sir!" the comm interrupted. "Thil c&c reports condition red. Targets heading toward weapons range."

"Understood. Li, arm missiles and prepare to implement plan Delta on my command."

As the still unseen Zetans approached, Paramount slid elliptically around Ganymede. The five other Earth ships arched on parallel courses until four Zetan targets, chased by the Thil cruisers, closed to the prearranged point.

Paramount followed plan Delta by changing the order of the line, like a pulling guard, to form a cluster with Absolute and Dauntless. They fired their missiles just before the Zetan barrage met them head on.

"Damage control report!" Forestier barked to the comm.

"Section four breached and sealed, captain," Damage central responded. "Propulsion inactive."

Damn! Adrift near Jupiter. "What about our weapons systems?"

"Round two missiles ready to go from waist stations. Projectors still 100%"

"Envirosystems?"

"Sustainable."

That meant at least six hours. Not enough time to repair propulsion.

Forestier turned toward his Exec. "We may still be useful, but not for long. Order partial evac. All non essentials to the pods."

Li hurried to send the order to the affected areas of the ship as her superior worked on a projector strategy with Tactical. On the scope, a Zetan ship that seemed unharmed by the missiles was swinging around to launch another attack.

"Captain, all crew request permission to stay on board."

"What?" Forestier quickly overcame an instant of rage at their insubordination – a feeling that turned to admiration as he realized his crew were choosing to stay under his leadership till the end. And considering what the Zetans did to their captives. ...

"All right, Li. So what do we do other than blast away with the projector units? Might as well try to board. How do we stand for rangers, other than casualties from Section Four?"

"Full complement for two limpets, sir."

The limpet boarding modules looked like the animals they were named for, truncated cones with a telescoping bottom that could adjust to a variety of shapes to match target hulls. Each carried a detachment of sixteen rangers in combat suits to provide survival in various atmospheric conditions – a happy coincidence that would allow Paramount's party to be effective in the Zetans' alien collection of gases.

"Well, launch them ASAP. We'll fire one projector volley at maximum range and then give them ninety seconds to attach and secure. If they're not successfully aboard then, we fire at will. Inform Tactical."

In scarcely a minute Paramount shuddered slightly as the limpets detached and accelerated toward the oncoming Zetan. There had been just enough time for the chaff to spread out to obscure their movement from the enemy. As the projector volley unleashed, its massive power made surprisingly little effect inside the Paramount. Forestier felt nothing until the Zetan response crackled through every electronic circuit on his ship, sparking and blowing panels all over the bridge.

But they were still alive.

His indicator showed environmental was nominal in all remaining sections. As he turned to the scope he saw why. The Zetan had diverted some weapons to engage the limpets. One had disappeared from the screen and as he feverishly searched for the other, he saw with a start that it had managed to attach to the enemy vessel.

Li turned anxiously. "Projectors ready, sir."

"Hold our fire! Boarding status?"

It was Comm that replied, "Party aboard and engaging target crew. Some casualties. It's a firefight, sir."

Nothing was certain. Forestier swallowed and ordered.

"Prepare to fire projectors on my mark."

The rangers knew when they left what they were risking. Their ninety seconds were almost up.

"Three, two…"

"Wait, sir," Li shouted. "Boarding party reports multiple hull breaches and target envirosystems disabled. Zetans are cacking all around them and several pods have ejected.

We've won!"

Her enthusiasm and slang marked a rare but welcome change from her usual formality.

Thank God, thought the captain. Then: *Instead of incinerating those rangers, we need to think of saving them.* "Set scuttling charge and back to the limpet immediately!"

It seemed an age before the Zetan vessel exploded in a nuclear flash and the limpet thumped back onto Paramount's hull.

The onboard crew welcomed the disembarking rangers with cheers as they emerged from decontamination, naked as jaybirds.

Seven of the team had survived the firefight, though the captain could not afford to rejoice and bask in their victory – this engagement was only part of a much bigger battle.

"Long range sensors! What's going on out there?"

Comm quickly answered. "Mobile Zetan targets have left the ecliptic and are being engaged by the Thil. They're corkscrewing all over the place, but it looks like the Thil have the upper hand. One Thil cruiser appears to have some major damage but is still in action. There are Zetan hulls scattered around and several debris fields. Some kind of craft is approaching rapidly from far outside the system. Doesn't look either Thil or Zetan ..."

Maybe this was one of the Blynthians. No wonder the Zetans were breaking off. The Thil had done a good job but even an entire fleet was no match for a Blynthian warship.

Forestier and Li exchanged a look of surprised relief. It seemed Earth would be spared further bombardment and there would be no further hostage-taking by the aliens.

The elation was short-lived, however.

"What about our ships?"

"Sorry to say, sir, we lost Absolute and Dawntreader. Our sister ship Paragon is coming to pick up evacuees or restore environmentals. EVA thirty-five minutes. Admiral Blake is gone and Commodore Surajee has assumed the flag."

Seb turned to Li. "You have the bridge. I'm going down to medical to see the boarding party, then look at the seal on Section Four. Notify me when Paragon closes in."

The Exec glanced back at her board. Nominal environment suddenly didn't seem so bad. With the projectors powered down to half, they might not even need a full evac to the sister ship.

There were a couple of tugs standing off the asteroid belt. Li prepared to summon one and stopped to smile as she realized that humankind's first space battle, even if it went down as a local skirmish within system, was over.

Seb continued to peer at the sensor screens. For only a second did he permit himself to wonder if among that ship debris out in the system were parts of any of his friends from Munich, or what was left of them.

First Contact: the Quarantine Hypothesis (Non-fiction)

Back in the 1950's, the noted physicist Enrico Fermi developed a line of thinking now called the Fermi Paradox, which stated, roughly, given the mathematically good possibility of intelligent life on other planets in the galaxy or the known universe, why had none of them made contact with humans or left something to demonstrate their existence? He might well have looked across the lunch table when he developed these thoughts, since he was at Los Alamos, New Mexico, in the middle of a nuclear lab complex, talking with a group of scientists that included Edward Teller, the godfather of the hydrogen bomb. Let's keep this context in mind as we develop the discussion.

For all his off-the-cuff brilliance, Fermi's Paradox does leave considerable room for doubt. His mathematical calculation of Intelligent Life probability fails to take a few important things into consideration, most notably the factor of universal entropy. In figuring the tens of billions of years that "early" galactic civilization(s) may have had to spread across space, he did not recognize that life develops on planets and that planets, and the stars that enable them, also have a lifespan. In fact, many are developing or disappearing right now, within our own, so far short, human window of IL. Thus, geologically and astrophysically, a civilization does not have forever to get its message across.

Moreover, we have to consider that there may be such a thing as a Species Threshold that applies to the situation. By that, we mean that each species has an evolutionary "window" between the time that it emerges from a determined existence (i. e. homo erectus) and the time when it is capable of ending its existence through overpopulation, conflict, or perhaps other processes of degeneration. Humans have had only 10,000 years or so of anything we deem civilization. We still have only a partial idea of how life and intelligence develop, much less of how they may become extinct. In

Fermi fashion, we can consider that we are probably typical in this respect and that other forms of IL would be subject to the same phenomenon of a Species Threshold, possibly absolute, possibly not. The concept that an interplanetary IL civilization would arise and simply stay the same, continually able to initiate first contact with another IL, therefore seems counter-intuitive.

We can conclude that even under a best-conditions scenario, IL first contact chances may be less than Fermi optimistically calculated. Assume, though, that Fermi is not far off the mark and that there is now at least one IL form in the galaxy that might be capable of contacting us but hasn't. This apparently willful neglect in turn suggests that something like the Star Trek version of Prime Directive is at play: interstellar civilizations may have an avoidance policy in effect regarding life forms that have failed to achieve a given level of achievement. Science fiction has posited this situation many times, beginning perhaps with Olaf Stapledon's *Star Maker*. Contemporary variations are too numerous to list. It is worth mentioning, in addition, that we humans have not proven so far to be a very encouraging study group in some ways. Other than a few exceptions like the Great Wall and the Pyramids, humans spent long centuries without producing progress observable from space. Even as late as the nineteenth century, the energy footprint of a great city like London, Beijing, or Baghdad would have been miniscule compared to purely natural phenomena like major volcanic eruptions. Our first radio broadcasts, arguably the best long-range testimony to our technology, would have been gibberish to a passing IL presence. They may have been completely ignored, since they were merely analog forms of audio tracks (and who says other ILs even use the same bands and conventions of audio communication that we do?) in a plethora of different languages, not even sensibly digitalized. The same holds true for television, keeping in mind that the first broadcast capable of reaching even the nearby space of our solar system was of a speech by a fellow named Adolf Hitler. Of course, the next major observable event would have been the first explosions of the atomic bomb, which accelerated with mind-numbing speed to ever larger, more powerful, and obviously aggressive bombs.

We arrive more or less inevitably at the realization that IL life forms in our vicinity may not want to hasten a first contact. If you heard that a boy from a house way down the street had just murdered part of his family, would you invite him into your yard to play? Not bloody likely. Better to make sure that you did not attract his attention in any way. A Stellar Quarantine might in this case seem to be a scenario that reduces the risk for an IL form in our spatial neighborhood, whether or not the neighbor decided that we were worthy of further observation at all.

At this point, we are tempted to argue, as cock-eyed optimists, that surely the human race had proven that it is capable of better things than World War II or Mutually Assured Destruction. We have the UN, the Internet, Neil Armstrong on the Moon, the Hubble Telescope. Doesn't that prove that we have a worthy side to our existence? The trouble is that all of our advances, especially in the direction of space, have been driven by a military motive that may not seem like acceptably civil behavior to the neighbors. Our first satellites were launched on rockets designed originally to destroy London and Moscow, if not New York. Sputnik caused a virtual panic in military applications that quickly spread into the outer reaches of our atmosphere. For one Hubble, we have scores, perhaps hundreds, of active spy satellites pointing the wrong way, back down toward Earth, sending drones with explosive payloads to the eradicate the villain-du-jour. The Space Shuttle was designed primarily not for the inoffensive International Space Station, but to deliver unspecified military machines into orbit. Now that the Space Shuttle is mothballed, it has been replaced by the secret X-37B vehicle. No one is supposed to know what it's doing on its long robotic missions, but we think we can be sure it's not surveying crops or tracking bird migrations. All this astro-military activity could not help but send a message to an IL observer that we humans may not be ready to learn how to pop up unannounced in other planetary systems.

When immigrants came to the booming USA in the early 20th century, they had to pass through Ellis Island. Not because Americans wished to embarrass them or keep better track of them or help them adjust to a new environment, but to quarantine disease carriers before they could set foot on Manhattan Island. Whether our physical microbes are damaging to extraterrestrial IL forms, we cannot know yet, but we can reasonably surmise that our mental microbes are probably strictly undesirable. We may be in the Ellis Island Infirmary of interstellar relations at this very moment. Our future will be judged by one factor, and only one: whether we can cure ourselves of our undesirability.

Malanna Carey Henderson
Just Beyond the Horizon

It was 1851 on New Year's Day.

The enslaved workforce gathered before the Big House at the Twin Oaks plantation in Richmond, Virginia. Lips whispered prayers, backs stiffened, fists clenched, and palms pressed against the fast-beating hearts of those who waited.

Fifteen-year-old Henry Mason stood among them. His body was rigid as he listened, and watched. He stood next to Aunt Olivia. Theirs was not a blood tie but a love tie.

From the moment he became an orphan, Aunt Olivia held him when he cried, fed him when he was hungry, and loved him, always. They held hands now, her hand lost in his. Small in stature, the elderly woman walked tall among the enslaved and planter communities owing to her wisdom and legendary midwifery skills. There would be no news for her, but for him, they were uncertain.

In two years, he had shot up like Virginian pampas grass. His height and the breadth of his shoulders had begun to mirror his father's. He had high cheekbones like his mother and her light brown eyes. Oivia's eyes reflected the fear that filled his soul. They hoped. They prayed he'd be spared. But now he was the size of a full-grown man. The precarious safety of childhood slavery was behind him. Life would become far more dangerous.

The overseer started calling names. The morning was cold like the message he was about to deliver on the heels of last night's New Year's Eve celebration.

Ordinarily, Henry loved days like these when the air was crisp and the sky blue and cloudless. Nature's majesty mocked him. How dare the morning look so beautiful on a day that would bring grief to so many? The sky, the air, and the earth were oblivious to their fear. New Year's Day was Hiring Day, or Heartbreak Day as many in his community called it.

"Henry Mason, you're on loan to the Sweet Magnolia Plantation," cried the overseer.

The boy's heart pounded like waves crashing against the rocks of a craggy shoreline. Sweat appeared across his brow. His armpits itched. The back of his eyes stung as he blinked in rapid succession. He turned to Aunt Olivia and pressed her to his chest. Her thin arms encircled his tapered waist. She looked up at him. Worry lines deepened in her nut-brown forehead. Her mouth trembled as she spoke.

"It gonna be alright, Henry," she said in a voice edged with sorrow. "Mind yo' manners. You jest do like dey tell ya, and make no trouble, so's you can come back to me." She rose on her tip-toes. He bent his head down and she pressed her lips against his chocolate brown cheek. He held her in his arms for a few moments.

"Yes, Auntie, I won't make no trouble."

Sometimes, trouble follows all on its own. Moments ago, Henry had blinked back tears when he heard the fate of the brothers, Toby and Hank. His best friends were destined for the auction block, monetary instruments to settle plantation debts. There would be no more lying about the riverbank casting their rods to see who would get the first bite. He'd never hear the chortling again that accompanied their banter while playing the dozens or when they collapsed in peals of laughter when Toby strutted around giving orders like Master Ebenezer. Odds were, he would never see them again.

He swallowed hard to loosen the tightness that knotted his throat. But the sight of Aunt Olivia walking away from him made the tears spill down his cheeks. A man ain't supposed to cry. Tears were for children and women. This turn of circumstance was about to change his life, like the tumble of a leaf blown off a tree by a strong wind. He felt abandoned as he did when he heard his parents had been sold. Their deaths followed soon after.

This would be the first time Henry left his birthplace.

The road ahead looked as thorny as the greenbrier vine that twisted around a low-hanging branch of an oak tree. Sometimes when he had an urgent message from the Big House to deliver to the slave quarters he'd run past the tree only to feel the pull of the sharp prickles of the vine as it snatched the strands of his coily hair. No matter what obstacles he'd find at the Sweet Magnolia, the road led back to Twin Oaks where the love of family and friends would welcome him with many pairs of open arms.

The Sweet Magnolia plantation struck a chord of fear in Henry. It was no secret that Master Ebeneezer despised the owner, Lucius Dayton. When he served breakfast to Master Ebenezer and Mistress Roslyn, Henry listened intently as they discussed current news and exchanged gossip. Dayton's connivance with planters and the maltreatment of those enslaved at his plantation frequently dominated their discourse.

However, when catastrophe struck, slavers demonstrated uncommon loyalty to one another. The last slave revolt back in the fall of '49, at the Magnolia brought men from distant counties to quell the rebellion. When they were caught, the leader was hung and his followers were sold. Those who escaped were still being hunted.

Likewise, when turbulent weather mimicked the hand of a vengeful God, long-standing grudges ceased to exist.

Last night, a severe thunderstorm with slashing rain, high winds, hail, and lightning struck the county. The next morning, Henry heard of all the neighboring plantations, the Sweet Magnolia suffered the greatest losses. Folks who leaned toward superstition said it was nature's way of punishing Ole Master Dayton for his legendary cruelty. The enslaved believed it was on account of old Auntie Bet. She left the plantation late at night. An hour into her journey, she was apprehended. Auntie Bet begged Master Dayton to understand that she wasn't running away but going to visit her family who lived on another plantation. Word had reached the Sweet Magnolia that her daughter Willa, and her three-year-old twin granddaughters Maisy and Clara had been sold to a plantation in South Carolina, and Auntie Bet had wanted to see them one last time. Since the overseer refused to give her a pass, the elderly woman cried that she had no choice.

Dayton ignored her pleas and ordered the overseer to administer twenty lashes. She slumped in death before the lash struck its final blow. That night, the African spirit, Ole Jessup, sent a tempest to avenge Auntie Bet's killing, so said the conjure man from Sweet Magnolia. By noon, the story had spread like brushfire to the plantations of central Virginia, and beyond.

Never one to believe in superstitions, Henry felt a sense of foreboding hover over the Sweet Magnolia as soon as he arrived.

Henry groaned when he saw the back-breaking work that it would take to restore the plantation to its former self. Rubble from several collapsed buildings peppered the landscape. Lightning had split trees in half, scattering branches helter-skelter, some jagged endings were stiletto sharp. Even the white-pillared mansion had a gaping hole in its roof.

Wide-eyed mothers clung to young children as they stood among the wreckage they once called home. Cows roamed in random directions. Chickens squawked and ran across ruined fields. Dogs barked at the decimation. They dashed around aimlessly as if they were unsure of what to make of the chaos while children played tag and ran through the slave quarters, oblivious to the recent destruction.

Overseers drove the field hands hard to salvage the beds of tobacco seeds just planted before Christmas. Henry labored for long hours in a crew of men and teenage boys. There was livestock to round up and secure. Piles of debris to be cleared before rebuilding slave cabins and farm structures. There were dead people, black and white, to bury.

The first time he met the boys from Sweet Magnolia they were tight-lipped and not especially friendly. They whispered amongst themselves and treated Henry like an outsider. The dominant one of the group, nicknamed June Bug, eyed Henry's coat and remarked, "One day soon I be wearin' dat coat."

"You'll have to take it from me, first," responded Henry. He wasn't intimidated by June Bug or any of his gang. As time passed, the boys who saw June Bug as their leader mimicked his behavior and Henry became a target for their slights and verbal abuse.

Henry could take care of himself. He had learned to box at Twin Oaks. Sometimes, he sparred with young men and boys his age but always in sport. He could hold his own.

At night, Henry tucked the coat under his makeshift pillow. One morning, it was missing. When he inquired about its whereabouts, a wall of silence grew tall in the cabin. After what seemed like an eternity, one boy named Peter said, "June Bug's got yo' coat."

June Bug glared at Peter and then sneered at Henry.

"Give me my coat," demanded Henry through clenched teeth.

"Ain't yo' coat no mo'. It's mine." He winked at Henry and let out a laugh. The other boys joined in.

"I'm not going to tell you again, June Bug."

In two strides, the tall skinny boy was nose to nose with Henry, whose thick brows drew together as he stared down his adversary. Suddenly, June Bug pushed him hard against the cabin wall. In a flash, Henry shot a jab to his left jaw. June Bug collapsed and hit the floor with a thud. Peter got the coat from where it lay between June Bug's cot and the wall and handed it to Henry. From then on Peter and Henry were inseparable.

After the boys complimented him on his pugilistic skills, he offered to teach them the basics. The animosity toward Henry ceased at once, and in time a friendly bond developed between him and all of his cabin mates, June Bug included.

There were marked differences that reflected the disparity of the plantations where the boys of Sweet Magnolia and Henry resided. Henry's clothes were adequate and fitted his long legs and wide shoulders. The coveted knee-length coat guarded him against the winter cold. The other boys wore thin, plain-woven woolen garments that were well-worn and ill-fitted. Likewise, the boys were clad in threadbare shirts and breeches.

Henry sat down next to Peter for their afternoon dinner break. His friend looked at the bacon and potatoes set before him and his eyes lit

75

up. "Massa don't ever feed us like dis. It's only 'cause y'all here from da Twin Oaks, Mayfair, and Mornin' Star plantations. We git ash cakes and salted fish most of da time,"

Sitting side by side, Henry and Peter were the physical opposites. Henry was six feet tall, with a handsome face and athletic build. Peter, on the other hand, was much thinner and shorter. He barely reached Henry's shoulders. However, there was one feature of Peter's in particular that brought him widespread admiration.

When Henry heard Peter speak in those first few days of arrival he was startled. His voice arrested the listener's attention. Its depth was like a rolling river. The smoothness of his voice mirrored the glassy surface of a body of water that reflected the sun's brilliance.

Peter's voice was the highlight of Sunday worship. The enslaved community looked forward to a visit by the colored preacher. He delivered a spirited sermon under the watchful eye of the overseer. Peter's voice held the congregation spellbound. It could still a baby's cry, and make women swoon. Most Sundays, Master, and Mistress Dayton were present too.

The notes dived deep when he sang the spiritual "Deep River." His rendition of "Sometimes I Feel Like a Motherless Child" never failed to bring tears to Henry's eyes. Joy bounced off the walls when he led the congregation in "Ride On, King Jesus."

However, today when his friend spoke, Henry was startled for a different reason. The boy's dark brown eyes searched Henry's sable orbs.

"I'm gonna run one day. You best come wid me."

Henry shook his head. "I plan to buy my freedom. I don't want slavers haunting me for the rest of my life."

"No black is truly free here. Deys snatch up free men, women, and children from up north to sell down here all the time. But at least up north, dere's a fighting chance to *stay* free. It's right over there," Peter said, his eyes shining bright with wonder.

"What's over where?" Henry asked, his head turned to Peter.

The boy pointed north. "Freedom is just beyond the horizon, up north. I'm gonna git dere, one day. You'll see."

After a few weeks, his tenure at the plantation was drawing to a close. At bedtime, the corn husk mattress felt especially comfortable. Henry would rest in the cabin two more nights before he returned to Twin Oaks. His lips turned up in a smile before he fell asleep. He wished he could bring Peter with him.

Agonizing screams crashed through the stillness of his slumber. Henry popped straight up to a sitting position. His heart hammered in his chest. A cool breeze flitted through the chinks in the walls of the dilapidated cabin and caressed his face. Standing by his cot stood June Bug. "Dere's a whipping. Come on." He pulled his pants over his nightshirt and followed the boy outside. A crowd had gathered. There were black, brown, and pale faces staring at the commotion in the direction of the whipping post. Cries and moans, a song of misery, emanated from the crowd.

"This will teach you not to run off." The overseer's bullwhip flew into the air and struck the soul tied to the post. A cry tore from his throat and then faded into a whimper. The moon relinquished its command over the night, and the sun gradually spread its wings of gold upon the horizon.

Henry's heart stopped. He witnessed the figure at the post slip to his knees under the pain of the lash. Blood trickled down his back. One-hundred and fifty lashes were the standard punishment for a runaway. Henry didn't think Peter would survive that or the biblical number of thirty-nine lashes slavers employed to replicate Christ's flogging.

The overseer threw his weight behind each stroke. His green eyes, under a shaggy head of blonde hair, were on fire.

Every time the lash cut into Peter's skin, Henry flinched.

Men hung their heads as they pulled their tearful women closer to their bodies. Young children buried their wet faces into the folds of their mothers' skirts. Every time this lurid spectacle occurred it was like ripping open a wound. All were forced to watch the punishment and live vicariously through the runaway and witness the type of homecoming they'd receive if they dared to put their dreams of flight into action.

Henry understood the message. A fugitive might run into the dawn of freedom but if he failed, he could expect a punishment so harsh that he would welcome freedom in death. If not death, one could lose an ear, a toe, a foot, be sold away from family and friends, or wear a slave collar for weeks, months, or years.

"Don't let me see na none of ya'll trying to help this ungrateful wretch. If so, you'll trade places with him. I promise you that."

The stable boy came running toward the overseer. He waved his hands above his head. "Stop! Mister Green, stop. Master Dayton says to stop." Once the message was delivered, he headed back toward the horse stable. Green growled and struck the ground with the bullwhip in the stable boy's direction.

"They will take him down now?" Henry let out a sigh that released the breath he hadn't realized he had held. He turned to June Bug who stood beside him.

"Naw," the boy shook his head. Henry saw the tears roll down June Bug's cheeks.

Green ordered a few men to help him with Peter. Henry was glad he wasn't chosen, otherwise Peter's blood would be on his hands. A twinge burned in Henry's chest. Why didn't he try to talk Peter out of it? He had offered only his opinion about Peter's plans. Had he known, Peter would attempt to run so soon, he would have tried to discourage him. It was widely known that Master Dayton never freed any enslaved persons. To Peter self-emancipation was his only pathway to freedom. For those who labored at the Sweet Magnolia plantation, there were two means of escape, the auction block or a casket.

Instead of taking him down, Peter's wrists were secured at the top of the post. Henry caught sight of Peter's feet dangling off the ground and his heart sank into his stomach.

"How long will he have to suffer on that post?" Henry asked June Bug.

"He'll be dere all night. All night long." The boy answered.

78

Green flicked the lash in Peter's direction. The boy cried out in fear, and a grin appeared on his torturer's face.

"Y'all, get to work," he bellowed as he looked around at the solemn faces.

Henry prayed that God would spare Peter's life. He hoped one day Peter would live to feel the sun on his face as a free man.

As Henry performed his chores, a yoke of sorrow lay heavy on his shoulders.

When night fell, Henry paced back and forth in his cabin. Sleep refused to provide a respite. Should he risk bringing Peter water? Of course, he should. The overseer's threats were empty where he was concerned. He was on loan. He didn't belong to Master Dayton. Henry had never known Master Ebeneezer to allow anyone but the Twin Oaks's overseer to mete out punishment.

Careful not to wake the boys, Henry crept outside with a drinking gourd tucked under his coat. Guided by the moonglow cast upon the yard, he walked to the whipping post.

Henry extracted the gourd. The bullwhip snapped back and lunged like a serpent's tongue but missed his cheek by inches. The song of the whip buzzed in Henry's ear and he took flight. He tripped and his backside hit the ground. The drinking gourd flew out of his hand and was swallowed by the darkness.

The overseer zig-zagged as he approached. Henry could smell the cloud of stale liquor wafting through the air. The man swung the whip over Henry. The boy rolled to the left and right as the lash cut lines in the ground where he had lain.

"Now, boy, ya just go ahead and tend to dat wretch, if ya brave enough. I'll see to it that you take his place."

Henry scrambled to his feet and didn't look back. Green didn't run after him but mumbled obscenities at the retreating figure.

"God, please don't let him catch me," Henry whispered.

"Coward!" The cry, like a ghost, chased Henry, shattering his soul.

The boy closed the door behind him. He jumped into his cot and drew the blanket over his head. He lay on his side with his knees drawn up. The offensive word haunted him. His body was rigid as fear knifed through him. The voice with its raw, scratchy timbre wouldn't leave him alone. Who had called him a coward? Was it the overseer or *Peter?*

Me and Mr. Jones

The urgent wail of a siren broke the serenity of West Outer Drive, the tony, tree-lined street located on Detroit's northwest side. Historically, the enclave housed the city's doctors, lawyers, and wealthy businessmen; today most of those residents are affluent African Americans. My dad's spacious two-story brick, five-bedroom house was the second from the corner.

He lived alone and was happy to have the company of his second eldest daughter. I relished the opportunity to show off my culinary skills by making dinner.

Tighten Up, an R&B tune by Archie Bell and the Drells was playing on my transistor radio. My prized possession sat on the kitchen counter amongst a row of cookbooks, underneath oak cabinets. This song came out a few years ago and was an instant hit for two reasons: its style was classic soul, and its creators developed a unique dance. As I was breaking up the lettuce in a large salad bowl, I started to do the "Tighten Up." When the drum solo beat out its rhythm, I abandoned the lettuce and put all my efforts into doing the dance.

Moments later, Billy Paul crooned the famous line from his number one hit song, Me and Mrs. Jones. "We've got a thing going on." I sang along with him, as he defended his romance with a married woman.

The timer on the oven went off. I didn't want the garlic bread I had made from scratch to burn, so I took it out of the oven first, before turning off the timer.

The doorbell chimed. I wondered who was calling. It could be Roxanne Gordy who lived in the corner house across the street. My sisters and I met her this past summer on a five country European tour for high school students sponsored by the American International Academy. The first time I saw her, I knew she was related to Berry Gordy, the founder of Motown Records. As his niece, she had the same features, gingerbread skin tone, and crown of thick black hair.

If Dad was expecting company, he didn't tell me. I had aunts and uncles who lived within a few miles, maybe it was one of them.

"Are you expecting anyone, Dad?" I said as I passed the den.

"Yes, one of my patients."

When I opened the door, I was taken aback. It took me a few minutes to recognize the caller. It was Mr. Jones. I had seen him through the years at my dad's office, but not nearly as often as I'd seen his wife and three children.

A crisp shirt and creased pants were his usual attire. He possessed a voice like an actor. He spoke in soft, measured tones that were pleasing to the ear. At the office, his demeanor was as warm and friendly as a summer's day.

Now, Mr. Jones looked more like Dr. Jekyll's Mr. Hyde than himself.

An oversized blazer hung from his shoulders. His medium-sized frame was clad in rumpled clothes. Creases in his forehead were as indelible as a staff on a page of sheet music. Surrounding the intense brown eyes were sprays of worry lines. He was biting his lower lip, which had turned from brown to red.

Whatever he had to say was so important that he made an appointment to see Dad at his residence instead of his office.

Was he terminally ill? Was he here to get advice on how to break the news to his wife? Or was one of the children ill?

On a late Saturday afternoon Dad could be found in his den. A glass of Scotch whiskey sat on an end table. Dr. Samuel Roy let his considerable girth sink into the plush sofa with an open book on his lap and a pipe between his chubby fingers. The tobacco smoke curled upward and disappeared before a sixty-by-thirty-six-inch bronzed, three-dimensional work of art on the wall. It depicted a handsome matador clad in a traje de luces. Beads and sequins adorned the short jacket. The setting sun cast the skin-tight trousers in coppery gold hues. The bullfighter held the red muleta in mid-air as the bull was about to charge. Above the artwork were two traditional Spanish swords used for bullfighting. Displayed in a crisscross pattern, their silver hilts glistened in the shaft of sunlight streaming through the opened curtains.

Like a king in his castle, Dad surrounded himself with his comforts. A two-tiered bar cart on wheels held a variety of glasses and decanters of gins, Scotch whiskey, and brandies. Books of all genres, classic literature, non-fiction from world-class Smithsonian tomes, as well as adventures authored by famous explorers filled the built-in bookshelves.

Mr. Jones stormed past me like a gale of wind, nearly knocking me down. I stepped back quickly to regain my balance.

"Hello, Mr. Jones?" I said, in an attempt to sound nonchalant.

"Er- hello," he croaked. His wide-eyed stare, like a deer standing in front of an oncoming car, gave me pause. Directing his words to my father, he said, "I didn't know any of your children would be here."

"Oh, don't mind me, Mr. Jones. I'm not hanging around."

My dad rose and shook his patient's hand before he offered him a chair directly across from him. Mr. Jones dropped into the overstuffed armchair like an exhausted day laborer.

"Would you care to join me?" Dad nodded toward the bar cart.

"Please," he begged. He rose and reached for the glass of Scotch Dad handed him. He knocked it back and held out the empty glass for another before he resumed his seat.

"Take it easy," Dad said, then refilled his glass.

Not waiting around to be dismissed, I slowly walked down the hall toward the kitchen. My curiosity had peaked by now and I dearly wished to know the cause of Mr. Jones' distress. Before I stepped over the threshold of the kitchen, I heard the desperation behind his shocking revelation.

"Doc, I think my wife is having an affair! Er, er, no, I don't think she's having an affair, I'm certain of it."

"What?" My dad's rapid-fire response set me in a panic.

Dad was no stranger to marital discord himself. Three years ago, he made a surprise visit to my high school. Sister John Mark called me out of my freshman English class. I saw his worried face through the window of the classroom door before I stepped into the hallway.

My heart raced. What could be the matter? Was there a car wreck? Did something happen to my mother, brother, sisters, or grandparents?

Once, the nun left us alone and returned to the classroom, I braced myself for some catastrophic announcement. Dad had never visited my school outside of parent conferences.

His bleary eyes shifted away from my face as he struggled to voice the words. "Your mother is suing me for divorce." He extracted the petition from the breast pocket of his suit coat. It trembled like a leaf. The official words were printed in large, bold letters. I had never seen him so vulnerable.

My mom could do this? She could reduce this pillar of the community to rubble, topple this paragon of strength and superiority to a bundle of nerves.

I saw my mother as powerful for the first time.

It felt awkward to comfort a man whose anger could explode like a grenade which turned my legs into jelly, whether or not I was the target. I made it my business to obey his every command and blend into the background like the furniture to avoid his ire.

I put my hand on his shoulder, then hugged him. "I'm sorry, Dad." My voice sounded sincere.

"She can't do this. She c-can't break up the family," he muttered. A sheen of perspiration beaded his brow. I looked down at my feet and focused on my penny loafers. The new copper coins placed into the slits of my new shoes this morning shone like gold. When I raised my head I saw his broad back retreating toward the door. He left without saying goodbye.

I felt numb.

I walked through the classroom door as if in a trance. The first thing that caught my eye was how blue the sky appeared outside the open classroom window. Bird song floated in the classroom upon the wings of a flower-fragrant breeze that caressed my face.

I should have been devastated, but I wasn't. All I felt was relief, and a touch of joy. No more loud and sudden arguments that struck me like a lightning rod, the fear gripping my chest and quickly spreading to my bowels, making them quiver. I turned down the volume of their shouts by turning up the television set. The closet served as my refuge. Hands over my ears, the sonorous sounds fell like broken glass; quiet pieces of a broken marriage that Mom would have to sweep up. At last, I could look forward to returning home every day to peace and quiet.

Mom had a multitude of reasons.

A year or two ago, I was in the master bedroom talking to my mother. We were chatting it up like two girlfriends. Dad had gone to the office and my siblings were asleep. We heard a woman's high heels clicking on the pavement. It was early in the morning and the street was quiet like an empty church. The high heels paused when they got to our house. I tensed up. We heard the cover of our mail slot creak, which occupied the lower half of our front door, being pushed open.

I dashed down the stairs, my mother was seconds behind me. I grabbed the paper that had fallen to the floor. I read the letterhead. It was a bill from an exclusive ladies' boutique. I had just made out the word lingerie in the item column when it was snatched from my hand. My mother scanned its contents. It was as if a cloud passed overhead and blotted out her sunshine. The color in her face heightened; her lips trembled. Our carefree mother-and-daughter time had faded like an old black and white Polaroid.

It wasn't my mother who broke up our family. No, it was my dad's infidelity. Although he was a grown man when Playboy magazine was at the height of its popularity, he was young enough to be influenced by the objectification of women promoted and celebrated in its pages.

The divorce wasn't easy, but after several wrong turns and starts, the family had settled into a comfortable routine. My parents would never be friends, but they were cordial to each other and never used us children as pawns.

I felt sorry for Dad, even though he was more at fault than Mom. Had their love died, or had it dried up like fruit left to rot on the vine? Or perhaps, the late nights at the office had eaten up the day, extinguishing time for conversation and intimacy until there was no time. Maybe the isolated lifestyle of a housewife had stunted her growth. Her primary cultural enrichment narrowed to gossip with neighbors and family.

In order to earn my own money and not be a burden on my mom, I worked at my dad's office. That could be dangerous. A few Saturday mornings, we'd walk into the office to discover we had been robbed. Papers littered the floor and drugs were missing. On one occasion, a patient reported that she overheard three people in the waiting area planning a robbery. Dad called the police, and they were arrested. After that, he bought a gun. When he was at home, it occupied a drawer in the nightstand of his bedroom.

At work, the revolver, holstered under his white doctor's coat, became part of his professional attire.

I enjoyed wearing a nurse's uniform, but the high wedged shoes were another story. At first, they were comfortable, but the long hours soon evaporated that feeling of cushy support. By days' end, I felt as if I had been walking on hot coals. Besides getting a salary, spending time with Dad was the chief reason my sisters and I worked at his office.

We saw our dad on other occasions. He'd pick us up to go to a movie or dine at a fancy restaurant. I saw first-hand the playboy lifestyle wasn't all it was cracked up to be. He mentioned to us that he missed the family adventures we used to share, the summer vacations to Canada, the west coast, or New York. Christmas mornings were especially dear to him. One year, he asked my mother to marry him again. I saw it as an invitation to repeat the past. In my opinion, he was making promises that we all knew he couldn't keep. I was relieved when she turned him down.

He was flawed but he was my dad, and I loved him.

This dinner would be special; it was the first time I tried these recipes. There was no better guinea pig for a daughter to practice her culinary skills on than a divorced Dad living alone.

The menu consisted of baked eggplant parmesan for me and veal parmesan for him. Spaghetti with tomato sauce, a tossed salad, and baked garlic bread would round out the meal.

I had everything under control. The eggplant and veal were in the oven. I had forgotten the croutons and took out the tossed salad, added them, then returned it to the refrigerator. The only part I was worried about was the spaghetti. I didn't want soggy pasta; so, I'd planned to let the water boil gently until Mr. Jones left. Then, I would add the pasta.

I tipped-toed down the hall not to be nosy but to see if Mr. Jones had left.

"I know she's seeing someone."

Was he angrier now than when he first arrived? The edge in his voice grated my ears like sandpaper. I felt so sorry for him. I could tell he loved his wife.

My father's voice sounded weary. Mr. Jones's complaints must have become tedious by now.

"Why do you think she's having an affair?"

"She whispers into the phone when I come into the room."

"Do you have any proof that it's a man on the other line?"

"Her behavior is proof enough," Mr. Jones stated. "She's grown distant. It's been quite a while since we've… you know what I mean. There's always an excuse, Doc. She goes to the office so much with the kids, practically every week. I know she holds you in high regard. Has she confided in you?"

Patients confiding in their doctors was nothing new. Dad told me patients had asked him to find jobs and mates for themselves and their children.

"I'm sorry, James, but I don't know what to tell you. She hasn't said anything to me."

"I know something about him." James's voice lifted in triumph.

87

"What?" Caution edged Dad's voice.

"He's rich," he snarled. "When she was out with the kids, I searched her dresser and found a box with expensive lingerie, frilly satin things, trimmed in lace. I can't buy her anything like that, Doc, on a mailman's salary. But a professional man can. Right, Doc?"

That's when the pit of my stomach fell.

Could he sense it? Or did he actually have proof that my father was the one having an affair with his wife? I had figured it out too. She'd visit the office with the children in tow, saying one of them had a cold. Every week?

Is that why he came here to confront my father or was he really in the dark and just wanted some advice?

He kept talking and then, he said it, he accused my dad of cheating with his wife.

I froze. Every muscle was taut as a violin string. I heard quick movements and the long scratch of metal on metal. I struggled to control my breath and slowly peeped around the corner. My worst fears were realized. There was Mr. Jones standing over my father, the blade of a sword pointed at his throat! I stood there in the hall with my heart pounding out of my chest. There was no time to retrieve my dad's pistol. What could I do?

"I figured it was you, Doctor Roy. Every week, she's in your office, pretending one of the kids is sick."

"No, you're wrong, James."

"How dare you deny it. I have proof. There was more in that box than lingerie. I found a letter from you referencing that blasted song, Me and Mrs. Jones."

"James! Please, please, I've tried to break it off with her, but she forced me to see her by coming to the office. She just won't take no for an answer. Tell me what to do. I'm at my wit's end."

At that moment, I rounded the corner. I gasped. Mr. Jones stood waving the sword at my dad, and then my eyes jumped to the space where the sword hung on the wall just moments ago. If I hadn't seen it with my own eyes, I'd have never believed this was happening. I stood there wringing my hands. Every fiber of my body on fire.

"Mr. Jones, you don't want to do this." My voice didn't waver.

"Yes, I do!" He yelled. "I want to punish Doc Roy for being a cheater and a liar."

"Mr. Jones, I know you love your wife. There's a good chance you can win her back."

"How can I do that on a mailman's salary? I knew when I married her she was out of my league."

"Perhaps, but she saw something in you that made her want to marry you. If you kill my dad, you will throw away any chance of a reconciliation."

"How can I compete with a doctor?"

"What happened? Did you take her for granted? That's what my dad did to my mother. Even after years of marriage, you've got to romance your wife with flowers, date nights, and tell her that you love her, often. That goes a long way, Mr. Jones."

"Well, I…"

"And what about your children? If you kill Dad, you'll go to jail. Who will take care of them? They might be sent to foster care. Do you value your family above your need for revenge? Do you want to see them grow up, graduate, walk your baby girl down the aisle, and one day hold your first grandchild? That's what you'll be giving up, Mr. Jones, just to feel a moment's satisfaction from an act of revenge. Once you do so, there's no going back. It'll be a life behind bars … maybe without parole."

I heard a thud when Mr. Jones let the sword fall to the floor. He plopped into the chair he had occupied earlier. He hunched over and held his face in his hands, sobbing.

I looked at Dad, his face was wet with tears.

"Come on, Mr. Jones, go home to your wife," I said. "Forgive her and tell her that you love her. Hug your kids. No harm's done. We'll forget this ever happened."

Mr. Jones rose from the chair. His red teary eyes met mine.

"I'm so sorry … about all of this." He looked back at my father.

"I'm sorry, too." My dad said in a hoarse voice, regret filled his eyes.

Mr. Jones looked at me. "Thank you." He turned to my father. "You've got quite a young lady, here, Doc, I hope you appreciate her."

Dad let out a deep sigh. "I do, but now more than ever."

Mr. Jones stepped around the sword and hurried to the door. Sunshine lit up the hallway as he walked over the threshold.

As soon as the door closed behind him, Dad rose from the sofa, and reached for me. We hugged one another for a long while. Tears streaked down our faces.

"That was a close call." Dad looked at me and wiped a tear from his cheek. "If it hadn't been for you, there's no telling how this would have turned out."

"Infidelity hurts the whole family, Dad."

"I'm sorry, Pumpkin." He patted my shoulder before he picked up the sword and set it opposite its mate on the wall.

"Are you hungry?"

"I'm ravenous. Tell me something, what made you leave the kitchen to check on me?"

"I only had the spaghetti to cook. I checked to see if Mr. Jones had left. I stopped to listen and when the conversation took a bad turn, that's when I knew you were in trouble."

"Smart girl."

"I was afraid he'd brought a gun. It never occurred to me he'd threatened you with one of your prized swords."

He hugged me again and kissed the top of my head.

"Dinner will be ready in five minutes. I couldn't pop the noodles into the water until I knew Mr. Jones had gone home. I hate soggy spaghetti."

Let Freedom Ring!

When sister Anna rises in the morn, and the sun washes her face
with light,
she feels the shame of having had to lay down with her master
again last night.
Although, her pleas to dissuade him were bold.
To say no is denied by law, it's comply, be whipped or sold.

When brother Samuel stands on the auction block,
buyers pry open his mouth, strip him of his clothes and take
stock.
Disease could reduce the price of purchase or the loss of a foot
or toe.
The bright sunshine exposes his shame as he hangs his head
down low.

When Uncle Joe broke the law and forged a path to freedom.
At the bottom of the well, a posse of men and dogs found him.
As the rope tightened around his neck, his thoughts were
heaven-bound.
Oh, say can you see, death to those seeking liberty, ironic
democracy, confound.

When Aunt Sarah fled her cabin bed in the darkest night,
she sought the cherished freedom that her Joe held forever in his
sight.
Steal Away called her and others to follow in Harriet's
footsteps.
Sarah rang the Liberty Bell as the sky cried rain, and she wept.

Carol Thomas Horton
Conquering the Hill

We stood atop the white beast and looked down. It didn't look that intimidating. Hundreds had conquered their fear of Suicide Hill. Even now, an army of sledders was marching up the narrow snow-crusted pathway, re-mounting their sleds, and racing back down the slope with ease. No bloody noses. No broken bones. Piece of cake.

I'd heard stories of the Hill for much of my life and I wanted to conquer it. This almost vertical quarter-mile run was a legend. Every winter when the January snows roared into the small town of Fredericksburg, Virginia, thrill-seekers flocked to its summit. My husband, small son, and I were joining the excitement for the first time as we canvassed the snowy peak and planned our descent. Pumping up our pride, we waxed the blades of our six-foot-long runner sled while much smaller crafts glided past us.

"Who's going first?" I asked.

"This was your idea," my husband Jim reminded me.

"It's your sled," I replied.

"My feet hang off the back," he countered.

The minutes passed as we stood on the packed snow and stalled. We continued to watch as a convoy of confident individuals lined up their sleds, crouched low, launched into a sprint, and zoomed down the hillside—cutting to the left just before reaching the forest of trees at the bottom. Their screams and laughter trailed behind them and drifted back up to our ears.

"Sounds like fun," I hinted.

"Okay, how about I lie on the sled, stomach down," Jim suggested. "Then you lie down on top of my back, and Scott lies on your back. We'll all go down together."

Perfect plan. No one would take the plunge alone. We were a team. Rugged and ready. We could do this together. A dedicated family of brave hearts, although perhaps maybe temporarily weakened minds.

Settling the sled on a level patch of sleet, Jim climbed aboard and steadied the wooden luge with his outstretched arms. He pushed the sled back and forth a bit with his gloved fingers to test the strength and glide of the blades underneath.

"Climb slowly onto my back," he advised.

I lowered my body like a plank onto his spine, gauging my center of gravity for a successful sleigh ride and clamping down on his shoulders like a vice. Then clambering to the top, our son Scott lie prone against my backbone and put a chokehold around my neck. And there we were—linked together like a circus of trapeze artists who were ready to fly.

The launch was quick and painless. Free as a bird! We began soaring down the hill like an eagle diving for its prey with the wind stroking its sleek form. But our dismount was equally as swift and far from painless. Scott was the first to tumble, taking me with him in a side-roll. A few feet later and Jim joined us on the ground with his hands still gripping the sled. We had scarcely left the summit and our initial attempt had ended in bruised egos.

"Too much weight," Jim decided. "You and Scott try it without me."

Rising from our failure, we backtracked to the hilltop and strategized. This time, I anchored myself with a tighter hand-grip and curled the tips of my boots under the edges of the sled. Then I motioned for Scott to lie on my back and he climbed aboard. Standing at our rear, Jim gave us a gentle push. No flying this time. But no success either. About a third of the way down, the blades picked up speed, skirted sideways, and overturned us onto the snow. One hand on my son and the other on the sled, I slid to a stop. Suicide Hill had won again.

"We didn't make it," I announced, returning to the crest.

"Well, let's go home," Jim said. "Unless you want to try it alone."

I paused. It would be my third run down the slope and the perhaps the third time would be the charm. I was experienced now. Besides, if other sledders were making solitary zoomie runs, then so could I.

"Hold the sled," I told Jim.

Determined, I mounted my steed and grabbed the reins. I was on my stomach again, but now I widened my grasp for more control. In the back, I drew my heels close together, hoping to create a stabilizing rudder. Flattening my body and narrowing my eyes, I gave the word and Jim began to push. Three steps later and I was released onto the incline.

Downward I flowed, like water falling from a mountaintop. Smooth and flawless. Snow spitting into my face and air forcing its way into my nostrils. I was on roll. The speed was so intense that I reached the halfway mark before I could think. I was rapidly making a beeline for the bottom on a straight and perfect path. It felt like Dale Earnhardt on steroids. Victory at last! Until the forest at the foot of the hill came into view and I realized my acceleration would need to decelerate.

Ahead of me, other riders were veering to the left, which lengthened out their trip on level ground and allowed for an easy stop. My plan was to follow them and I prepared for the finish line as the distant trees grew closer. I clutched the steering bar in the front and turned slowly to the left. It seemed appropriate. But my speed was still rising and I was about to become intimate with a tall Virginia pine. Dropping my feet, I dug into the snow in an effort to slow my pace, but the force of my feet was too strong, and for the third time, I flipped and face-planted in the snow.

I groaned and rose to my feet, covered in dirty snow and wiping the slush from my reddened cheeks. I looked defeated. Glancing uphill, I wondered if my husband and son had noticed. They had. I had to think fast to avoid humiliation. My dignity was at stake. In a quick reaction, I threw back my shoulders, waved and then smiled. Afterall, I wasn't dead. I had actually made it. I had survived the gauntlet. Suicide Hill had been conquered.

When Sixty is Not the New Fifty

Society tells us that sixty is the new fifty. Health and wealth have been prolonged. Age is but a number and you are only as old as you feel. Rock the man bun and lace up the Stilettos. The voice of youth cries out within you.

For most of us, the engine still turns over pretty well at age 60. Our homes and careers demand our attention as always. Adult kids fly in and out of our abodes like birds paying a quick visit to the feeder, dropping off their fledglings, and then fleeing with their mouths full. New television series still spark our interest and our bones barely feel the pain of cutting a yard full of grass.

A couple of years slip by and 62 emerges from the fog. Our language evolves. "Where did I put my glasses? Now, why did I come into this room? Oh yea, I'm looking for the phone number of…What was her name again?"

But age 65 is the real clincher. Sure, it's only halfway to 70 and Medicare kicks in with free check-ups! That's when the doctor walks in and makes you draw the face of an outdated analog clock that hasn't existed outside the walls of an antique mall in two decades. The fear of failing your checkup makes your blood pressure rise just in time for the nurse to clamp on a cuff and squeeze your arm until a slight sweat oozes from your brow. The questions continue as the doctor runs down the checklist, writes up a referral to another physician for the undiagnosed imperfection on your cheek, orders a library of blood tests that normal humans cannot read, and hints that blood pressure medication might be the next step in your geriatric journey.

Arriving home in anguish, the high heels are expelled, never again to feel the warmth of your feet, and you search for a comfortable place to stretch out and rub your tootsies. But not down on the floor. No, the floor has gotten a lot harder of late and much further away. The floor is no longer your friend. You've even stopped squatting down on it to play with the grandkids without a master-plan on how to get back up.

You settle in and adjust to this new phase of life—at least you can retire now. No schedules! Stay up late and watch the game or a movie. Travel a bit. Join a club or two or three. Get asked to become an officer in each club. Volunteer one day a week for a non-profit and end up working three. Try out those new recipes you saw on TV. Gain ten pounds in two weeks.

Just don't blink, because now you've turned 67 overnight and you need to get one of those pill organizers marked with each day of the week. Hey, life's not over. You can still drive over and pick up the grandkids. Someone has to update the apps on your laptop and reset the digital clock on your Smart TV. And your daily walk-in-the-park is quite doable, as long as the path doesn't lead uphill. Plus, there's still date night at your favorite restaurant, but it must happen before sunset. No driving after dark.

But age 69 brings little comfort. Age 70 is breathing down your neck. Too many doctor visits and club meetings. Too much junk mail on taking European cruises and buying invisible hearing aids. Although at least one perk manages to appear on the horizon. You can cut back on dental visits. After all, most of your teeth are now either missing, capped, crowned, or completely false.

An Uninvited Guest

Nighttime noises were the norm in our first home together as a married couple. There were little creaks and soft groans, and even an occasional drone from the old upright church piano that we had bought for our children's music lessons. We were used to it. Not that the house was dated; we had purchased it brand new. But the land on which it sat was tired and aged—soiled by war and stained with bloodshed.

The surrounding forest encased the bodies of 19th-century soldiers and civilians—Americans who fought Americans, women who nursed the wounded, and children caught up in the heartache. All of them had faded away into a history that no one clearly remembered. Their memories now buried—marked by worn-down stones and cemetery weed. Their souls had been whisked away to another domain—another place beyond our time.

Our home stood steadfast near this woodland graveyard, where nighttime noises were frequent, but playful. "Must be Nanny Figg at the piano again," one of us would chuckle. We had grown up with the notion of Southern ghosts, who were polite and genteel. They were a reminder that family and friends watched out for each other, even after death, and the noises were often a comfort. None of these faint little sounds ever bothered my night-owl habits as I often stayed up and read by the lamplight. Then I'd end my day by tidying up the family room and checking the door locks. Tiptoeing down the hallway, I would check on the kids, and slip into the bed beside a snoring husband.

On this night, an autumn chill hugged the house. The wind raced through the dried leaves on tree branches and a quarter-moon barely shown from behind dark clouds. I lie awake in bed, my vision adjusting to the dull colors of the night as I deepened myself in the covers and stared down the long hallway outside the bedroom. I waited for sleep.

My eyes caught the first sign of movement in the kitchen beyond the hallway. It was silent, but unsetting. A tall figure was moving toward the bedroom and I knew someone had broken into our home.

"Jim, there's a person in the house," I nudged my husband, who slumbered beside me. The figure in the darkness was dim, but he was there, moving toward me in silence.

"Jim, wake up! "Someone is coming down the hallway," I whispered, shoving my husband toward the edge of the bed as he continued to sleep.

As the shadowy figure moved forward, I could barely see his outline, but he was a man. Slender and without expression—his eyes fixated on me and I froze when he entered the room. I had neither words nor weapon to defend myself.

The figure moved across the room, locking his cold gaze on me, and stopped at the foot of the bed. Lying motionless under the sheets, I slowed my breath and prayed for answers. I wasn't ready to die. The minutes passed like hours.

Then without warning, the strange apparition began glowing with light, like a sunbeam in the night, and I could see the callused face surrounding his sadden eyes. His hair was stringy and ungroomed. His clothes were tattered and worn. But his illumination did not brighten the room. His brilliance did not travel. Instead, it remained contained within him and radiated for only for a few seconds, then slowly faded away.

I lie awake in shock for a long time, not knowing what to think. I was not dreaming. Sleep had not touched my eyes. Fearful thoughts continued to flow in and out of my head in the quietness until I finally settled down to rest, and I began to drift off. Then in the last moments of my drowsiness, I stirred and mummered in a low voice, "Y'all please don't ever do that again." And they never did.

I Couldn't Help You Die

I spent time with you

Bathing your arms, tucking in your sheets, swabbing your lips.

But I couldn't answer every call for help.

Your new voice haunted me.

I needed the return of evenings spent in star-gazing,

Your patient tone filling up my curiosity.

I had followed your footsteps

While Mama cared for younger siblings.

I felt understood by you for we were the strong ones-You and I.

Now I was limited and broken.

No one taught me how to be your parent,

Cutting food into small pieces and grieving with hidden anger,

Wanting the return of my father.

As you lie dying, my brother bonded with you,

Maybe for the first time.

He held your hand as you slipped into a parallel universe.

But I stoically hid my heart as your body perished.

I really just wanted my Daddy again.

Valerie Horton

My Better Place

Minnesota in March is too snowy
Austin in August is too bright

There ought to be a place
cool in the summer
warm in the winter
sunny all year-round

I will wear a red bandana
and eat pickled beets
strutting under an umbrella
while rabbits crowd my feet

I shall escape to a tourist town
flat near the desert
high in the mountains
low by the beach

October looks enticing
December I could embrace
somewhere in these 12 pages
I will find my better place

Rereading

Over four long decades
I hoarded beloved books,
awaiting my earned leisure

I break open the stiff pages,
anticipating immersion back
into lost worlds with old friends

I start with *The Daughter of Time*,
recollecting an intricate mystery,
but found racism and a tedious plot

Two poems in, I'm wondering why
I carried *Gentle Wolves* across
2000 miles and three decades

Fantasies, thrillers, histories,
romance, mysteries, sci-fi –
not even the horror remained the same

With trembling wrinkled fingers,
I trace the creased cover of my most
cherished Ursula Le Guin

Longing to recapture bygone ardor,
I crack open the dried-out spine
and warily sank into brittle pages

VALERIE HORTON

unmoored

It's not quite cold,
but a bit damp,
lying on my back
looking up
at the night sky

Pushing against
each other,
a hundred billion
galaxies scream
ever faster apart

I should rise,
so much done,
with more to do,
and yet still more
left to undo

Why, God, this
one blue-green planet
out of trillions?
Do other worlds spin
waiting their turn?

I remain still
as the earth hurls me
thousands of miles
an hour through
the ever-expanding void

Fingers deep in dirt
Einstein said,
it is all relative
to a passive observer
in an indifferent cosmos

A Bowl of Stones

I've driven this lone and level road before,
but the sun had been high and my memories
were closer than they now appear.

Two states back, in my bedroom rests
a bowl of stones gathered from across the globe,
each holds a smooth hard piece of my story.

Some pretty, some painted, some plain
each rock once held a treasure now gone,
not the hand that mocks, only stones do.

Worse case is that this loss is an early sign
of that slow, wasting disease that robbed
my mother of knowing her own face.

Or perhaps there were too many nights
of shared azure moments in boundless places
for all of them to remain fast in my heart.

I crave a do-over so I can hold tight
to the tinsel-sweet and piercing hours,
and my memories never again creep away.

So many choices made, so many paths taken,
all my colossal wrecks coldly reflected
in that old, cracked rear-view mirror.
Stopping late, nothing remains for me
on this road, until by a faltering streetlight
I spot a rare, chipped piece of blue quartz.

***

In homage to Shelley's 'Ozymandias'

VALERIE HORTON

Elsewhere Trails

The dog and I've been down this path before
on a cool fall morning much like today.
The air reeks of dying leaves and moldy earth
preparing to settle into stillness.

My ex-marine father said he had itchy feet,
I wear his heel-worn traveling shoes
too tight and eternally ready to move on.

A slash of creeping red catches my eye,
through a buttonbush's dark green leaves snakes
poison ivy, that vine always turns early.

Ahead around that next curve, my knees
don't like the steep upthrust littered with quartz
and granite flecked with pinkish-gray feldspar.

My rambling back trail of homes cross ten states
and two equatorial islands, I stop for a second
to breathe while considering how much time
I have left to add to my I-used-to-live-there list.

On the downslope, I clamber over a deadfall,
a sharp dogwood branch tears at my pocket
as the dog circles, trying to herd me on.

The next long stretch is a gentle gradient,
no sun shone through thick-trunked river birches
crisscrossed above with aging sycamores.

A craggy grey basalt outcropping ahead tells me
it's not much further before the trail loops
around and returns to the beginning.

I miss a mud patch and slide forward,
arms flailing and heart racing,
as the dog heeled close in concern.

Steadying myself, I continue along the path,
considering which direction to go next
to meander down other elsewhere trails.

VALERIE HORTON

# of not forgotten lovers

it was during my youth
it was far from here
it was all so sharp and clear

we never danced
but we moved together
like hard rain at night

my sharpest memory
is the anise grief of letting go,
later I lost your ring

why now decades past
do I still wish to connect
not knowing what is left unsaid

do you also feel the words
hanging between us never said
long ago and far from here

What are dinosaurs for?

If a creator invented the dinosaurs,
I'd bet on the pantheon of Greek Gods
arguing about who made the biggest horns,
whose stony clutch had the bluest eggs,
whose oversized jaws would tear deeper,
as the feathered behemoths bow in homage
to the three-faced earthy Hecate.

Or across the vast ocean, maybe some
of the elemental and countless Kami
are half-remembered dinosaurs
honored and celebrated in Shinto shrines
beside Raijin, carved of cold grey stone,
raging thunder and throwing lightning
to ignite the energy of the universe.

Or maybe the Jesus-Jehovah-Holy Ghost
three-way made the dinosaurs to test,
Job-like, the faith of the pathetic young-Earthers
who believe the terrible, sharp claws
of towering, rampaging velociraptor
chased grandma down the Grand Canyon
looking for a quick, scrawny lunch.

Or maybe dinosaurs were made for children
as they jump over chipped dino tracks painted
on dusty museum floors, marveling
at the outrageous tyrannosaurus rex,
or cower beneath brachiosaurus bony legs,
tingling and almost reassured that their fears
would eventually turn from flesh to solid rock.

At night, do those aging children wake
to gaze at a comet-tossed, murderous sky
filled with impossibly distant galaxies
separated from this planet by immense
reaches of insurmountable time and space,
and ponder, cold in the dark, do the Gods
ever wonder what humans are for?

VALERIE HORTON

A Bear in the Burbs

 Unable to sleep-in before sunrise
on my first day retired after 40 years,
I ambled past neat and flowery homes
with my eager black lab, mulling over
my inertia toward my future work plans

I gasped as a young black bear shuffled
out of the birches, we three froze –
muzzle to nose to muzzle –
each aware of the wrongness,
meeting at this moment in this place

The bear, quicker of mind and reflex,
reared back, crashing into the grove.
The dog, undaunted and resilient,
crept forward to sniff at a scent
then squatted to cover the spoor

I remained frozen as my ambitions crashed
through those trees, shattering leaves
and bark like that bear fleeing the burbs,
knowing the path I had intended
was mine to walk no longer

My Life Without You

The yellowing frog with green splotches
didn't move in the afternoon heat

Removing the ice from my water
I slosh the drying amphibian

Wiping my brow, I see my life
withering in the heat without you

It creeps closer with each draw
on your cigarette, with each cough

As the sun blinks behind a cloud
I think the frog may have stirred

You step gingerly out onto the patio
pinching something deep within me

Action is required, I gently push
the motionless frog into the glass

I release it near the pond, close
by the briar-threaded, chainlink fence

Does it stir a bit in the grass?
No, the frog hasn't moved

You call my name, wondering
why am I standing still, staring down

Looking back at you, my love,
I wonder how far can I carry you

Allita Marie Irby

Missing You (3-poem set)

I Miss You

I miss you when I see your medic uniform hanging in the closet
and the photo album from Korea.

I miss you when I pick up the book, *Australia, Land of Many*
Dreams, by Lyall Rowe.
Australia that place where you lived for many years.

I miss you when I think of the 1985 trip to Hawaii to visit you.

I see you in every Hawaiian shirt I pick up and in the vacation
photos of our visit to Waikiki Beach. You were my tour guide – – –
my young brother, beautiful in your skin.

That is why I left my office in Washington D.C. one day in 1995 to
write a message to honor you, on the quilt on the National Mall with
all the other missing souls.

You

You confided your dreams to me and you trusted me
with your reality, your sexuality,
and I kept that truth to myself.

Why don't you leave that small town where the memories haunt
you of being bullied in high school.

Is it too late to try to be independent?
…too late to hold your head up?
…too late to find true love in a partner?

There are cities, towns, and states where you can hold your head up.
You can find a partner.
You can be independent once and for all.

If only you try…again.

NOW

Missing you today.
I'm sorry I was not there then.
Please forgive me now.

Love / 3-poem set

Fool Me Once

Fool me once, she said.
Your love was not really mine.
I wonder who will have the benefit of it.
Who will die from loving you.

Oh, Wine and Roses

Oh, wine and roses.
Oh, shower me like before.
The days of roses,
When you and I were coupled.
When you and I were in love.

Unrequited Love

Unrequited love
Unreciprocated love.
It's the damnedest thing.

You say you don't love me,

but I love you.

Books

Packed ten months ago, the boxes were stacked in the corners
and under the windows.

She cut the tape on the boxes gingerly
not to disturb the contents.

Then she ripped off the packing tape with energy and excitement
like a Christmas morning.

She lifted the flaps of cardboard
with reverence to see her collection of... books.

She saw **"A Little Yellow Dog"**,
with a collar of **"The Color Purple"**,
with eyes like **"The Bluest Eye"**
and she knew she was home.

JUNETEENTH (3-poem set)

Jubilation

Jubilation of the proclamation
across the nation!

Commemoration
not of tribulation, but of elation!

Remembrance of freedom day!

Galveston

Galveston!. Oh, Galveston, Texas!
The freedom from bondage!
My Independence Day!
Your Independence Day!
Galveston, Texas, June 19, 1865

The Juneteenth Flag

Blue above the horizon,
Red below,
White lone star within the nova,
A new beginning for African-Americans.
New freedom!
New people!
New world bursting on the horizon!

Easter

April 13, 2024

Decorating egg trees,
Bare branches,
Colored eggs.
Joy, smiles, Spring,
Rebirth flowering.

Warm, bare branches signaling the beginning of Spring.
Colored eggs in the breeze,
Like multicolored flowers, daring to be picked.
Bring smiles and joy to little eyes.

Grownups reflect on yesteryear,
When hats and gloves and patent leather shoes of white
brought squeals of delight.

A Thanksgiving Memory

Waking to the aromas of a roasting turkey with sage,
the house was filled with warmth, my memory from an early age.

Spices filled the air like cinnamon and nutmeg for pies,
visions of cakes and cookies for wide little eyes.

'Twas a lasting memory of Thanksgiving Day,
of family, of home, and hearth always.

Always a Fresh Cut Tree at Christmas

When we were at grandmama's knee
She lived in a two room cabin, in the country.

One great room, with one door in
(the same door out).
A kitchen room to the left, with one door in
(the same door out).

The great room had a fireplace; the kitchen had a wood stove.
The walls were wood and plaster and filled with Love.

There was no running water, just a pump.
No refrigerator, just an ice box you see.
At Christmas, always a fresh cut tree.

Many cows and chickens AND hens from Guinea.
At Christmas, always a fresh cut tree.

For lights, oil lamps, no electricity
But at Christmas, always a fresh cut tree.

The Circle of Life

Don't know quite know what to say or do
Want you to know we are thinking of you
We talk about the circle of life
Don't want to accept it, we acknowledge it
But find it difficult to swallow, difficult to digest
There is no sustenance in the meal we must all partake
That last breakfast
That last lunch
That last dinner
That last tea
That last Spring
That last Summer
That last Fall
That last Winter
That last "Hello"
That last "Good bye"
The last "I love you"

The Goat

Inspired by an interview, Tony Romo & Jim Nance,
February 9, 2024

The aura!
The mystic!
The magic!
Four out of five Super Bowls!
Is he chasing Brady?
Is he the GOAT? At 28 years old!
A Hall of Famer!
His name… Mahomes!

REM

His hands were all around her neck. She felt the pressure of the squeeze. In bed, in the dark, her eyes popped open as she began to fight him off. She slapped his face, kicked with all her might until he let go of her throat. He started snoring softly. It was then that she realized... he was still asleep.

Another thought came to her mind---was this REM Sleep Behavioral Disorder she had read about? Acting out dreams was something to discuss with your doctor. Was it time for a neurologist?

She had heard about Alan Alda's experience with this sleep disorder, and later his Parkinson's diagnosis.

Before she drifted off to sleep, she made a mental note that as a couple they would get through this together.

Dandelions

In concrete, and sand, in earth,
these flowers are grown
wherever the seeds are blown.

Dandelion, the official flower of the military child,
may bloom in the spring and most notably in fields of green,
wherever the seeds are blown.

This flower of sunny yellow so bright!
This flower can fold up and make seeds on a stem and change its
                    look completely.
These seeds can grow in concrete, in sand, in earth wherever the
                    seeds are blown.

March 2020

There's a plague upon the land. People are getting
sick and dying from something the world has not seen
before. It's something "novel", something new. I want to
call my folks to talk about it, but Mom is gone. She
passed in 2009. Dad is gone. He passed in 2010. Maybe
it's a blessing. They were in their late 80s and they were
not exposed to the virus that would ravage their
fragile bodies. I wonder…

So I call "G", my sister, my best friend. Eighteen months apart
in age, she has rescued me more times than I can
name. Afraid for me when I wasn't afraid for myself. I
was fearless, the first born, nothing could touch me, until
it did. Reckless with love and money. "G" was the one I
could call to dig me out of holes of my own making.
People say we look like twins. When I look upon her
face, I see a face that blinds me. A mirror image. She was
and is my touchstone.

Dave A. Kula

STOP SUICIDE

So many broken hearts and families,

Torn apart by life's painful cruelties.

Open wounds that will never heal while

Pretending everything is just fine.

So many thoughts of ending it all,

Under the guise of being joyful while using

Incredible skills of masquerading as okay.

Cannot change what dwells inside the mind as

Internally they desire to sleep forever more while

Doubting life will ever get lighter or better!

Everyone dies eventually, but why by their own hand?

Stopping suicide feels impossible when you've seen that end!

Stopping suicide is hard as people don't express their plans!

Stopping suicide can be simply checking on a friend!

Stopping suicide is aiding others to make new happy plans!

A Kula Cat's Tale: The Troubles of Mother's Day 2024

Told by: Persephone Kula
Written by: Dave A Kula

Hello to you, the reader of my story. My name is Persephone. No, I'm not the Goddess I was named after, but I am the Queen of the house I live in with my human mother and father. I have been told I am a tortoiseshell cat and was a kitten runt. I don't believe that, though, since I am the largest of my current siblings and I don't have a turtle shell. However, I know that I have the same wish my daddy has: to be a famous writer.

I know what you're thinking, I'm just a cat trying to tell a tale of how I rule the house. I assure you; I don't need to explain how I rule. I prefer to tell the stories of how my siblings and I contribute to our home. Our humans never had a human "child", so they treat us like babies and even talk to us as equals. When they leave us at home alone, they have us take turns being responsible for the house. We also have other responsibilities, such as catching mice, waking the humans up, reminding them to clean our toilets, and, most importantly, ensuring they feed us. We even try to comfort them when they are in pain, which is unfortunately often.

Our human parents are both witches, and they joke with friends about how they need cats as familiars. Although most people think that *only* black cats can fill this role, any type of cat, or animal for that matter, can be a witch's familiar. The best part about living with witchy humans is that we are typically treated better than the average "pet," and witches understand what we are saying much better than the average person. It isn't as easy as being in the Dr. Doolittle story, but we can have a conversation when we need to.

Throughout the year, we "children" have a tradition that all the cats work together to obtain gifts for holidays like Yule, birthdays, and our favorites, Mother's Day and Father's Day! My oldest brother, Alex, started this many years before I was born, along with another older brother, Hern, and a sister I never met named Solo. My older brothers passed on beyond the Rainbow Bridge since I joined the family. I have overheard Mom and Dad say several times that I was adopted because Mommy missed having a girl cat after Solo passed on.

I was part of a litter born in a barn about fifteen years ago. The human that found us brought us to this store to find us furrever homes. (Did she say furrever or forever homes?) She had put a hair tie around my neck like a collar and said she would keep me since I was the smallest. But then mommy came in, after all my siblings were matched up with other humans, and she picked me up to pet me. I remember curling up on her chest. It was so soft and warm. She held me for hours until all the humans started leaving. I really liked her, and she quickly fell in love with me. Fortunately, the human that found us allowed her to be my human.

Over the years with my humans, we had a grumpy runt of a sister named Lilly, who passed on a couple years ago. She was always upset with any cat larger than her, which was any teenage or adult cat, due to medical issues she had as a baby kitten. Then Willow joined our family around the same time that my two older brothers, whom I had grown up with since kittenhood, passed away. For a long time, I blamed Lilly and Willow for making Alex and Hern go away. Fortunately, I finally realized it wasn't their fault – just bad timing. That still doesn't make us best friends though.

I realized Willow was extremely nature-smart. She had several prior humans that didn't take good care of her before my humans rescued her. She was even thrown outside to fend for herself on many occasions before Willow became my sister. When she arrived, her fur was covered in fleas from her nose to the tip of her orange and white tabby-striped tail. She thought my humans were just going to abandon her like the prior ones did, especially after being locked in a bathroom by herself for her first week with us and subjected to the horrors of multiple baths and being taken to… the vet.

It's been over five years since she joined us. She still periodically tries to escape to chase squirrels, birds, and other cats that wander onto our land. She was confused by our humans' fear of letting us outside when they explained there are foxes, wolves, coyotes, and even birds that are big enough to eat a cat. She figured she could handle herself in the wild. Willow now takes this in stride and loves spending quality time with the humans. She even likes to help me plan nice surprises for our humans.

On Christmas day, Leonna was the next to join our family six seasons later. (Santa Claws should have known we did not request another sibling as a holiday gift.) He is an older Nebelung male that Mommy and Daddy thought was a girl cat for almost a year. We all thought it was hilarious that he was named after a strong female character from an animated show they watch, but he never seemed to care. He spent close to the full prior year surviving living outside by going between my grandma's house and her neighbor's. The neighbor fed him every morning, so he would hang out in their garage until they kicked him out to close their garage doors. He would then go to grandma's house, and she fed him at night. He spent those nights under a car or on her deck until the garage door opened across the street.

Lastly, my youngest sister, Freya, joined us a year and a month after Leonna did. She was just a baby when she got here after being found at Mommy's co-worker's apartment complex. Freya had been all alone, and cold outside, in the winter and needed a home. Lilly had unpredictably enjoyed having a smaller cat around. When Freya grew a bit, Lilly started being mean to her like Lilly was to the rest of us. Freya never understood why, but she was the only cat who truly got along with all four of us. She is the biggest troublemaker of us, but she also has the cutest face that nobody can stay mad at. (Mommy keeps saying she is a tuxedo cat, but she doesn't wear a tux, so that is confusing.)

Now that I have introduced you to myself and my siblings, I wish to regale you with how Mother's Day in 2024 almost got missed, and how it was all Daddy's fault.

*****

🐱 🐱 🐱 🐱 🐱

Normally, since Mommy and Daddy love these events called Renn or Renaissance Fairs, and Mommy only gets to go one or two times in the Spring, we take turns sneaking into the festival with Daddy when he goes by himself. While there, we take green paper we steal from Dad's wallet or other items of value to trade to get gifts for Mommy. When we don't have that, we have occasionally done odd jobs, like the year Lilly and Willow chased mice away from some vendors in exchange for a beautiful piece of pottery Mommy wanted.

However, this year, Daddy didn't go to the fair until Mother's Day. Normally, this isn't a problem; however, Daddy messed everything up. He didn't tell us he was going to the fair that day. He kept saying he would see Grandma for breakfast to celebrate Mother's Day. Then, Daddy stayed out all day and came home telling Mommy all about the things he saw and did at the Renn Fair with his nephew, who was also named Alex.

We were all very upset about the lie he told us. We had no gift for Mommy on Mother's Day, and we didn't know early enough to try ordering something using Daddy's phone or tablet. Willow and I spent that whole weekend trying to steal his phone without any luck. He took it with him when he left, and he had it in his hand almost all the time while he was home. We tried to use his tablet, but all it would do was show a big circle with "0%" in the middle of the screen before turning black again. (It must have been broken or something...)

The following Saturday, it was raining. We knew Daddy planned to go to the fair, and we were ready. The plan was for Willow, who knew the layout of the Virginia Renaissance Fair (VARF as Daddy sometimes refers to it), to sneak out to the car and get our gifts. We sent Freya with her since that little girl could charm just about any human who isn't a dog lover. (Why would any human prefer a dog over a cat anyway?)

We found several of the green papers with "20" on their corner in a box with Daddy's accessories he wore with his kilt to the fair. We snagged three of them and a small velvet pouch to carry stuff in.

Once we saw Daddy putting his green and yellow patterned kilt on, we knew this was the day to get Mommy's gifts. Freya snuck into Daddy's backpack while he packed water bottles in it. As soon as he opened the front door to go, Willow ran as fast as she could, jumped off the deck with a perfect four-paw landing, ran across the yard, and dove under the car to hide. When he opened the door to put his backpack and pouches inside, Willow climbed up and under the passenger side front seat. With that, Willow and Freya were on their way with green paper and instructions of what to look for.

Once at the festival, Willow snuck out of the car and ran toward the gates, passing under one vehicle to the next the whole way across the field used for parking. Freya was stuck in the backpack until Daddy opened it. He finally reached in to grab a water bottle while visiting his friend Alice, who worked at a booth selling crystals. Alice had helped find gifts for Mommy in the past, and she knew who Freya was, so Freya took the opportunity to hide under her table until Daddy left. The fact Alice was a witch, too, would simply make her job easier. With this in mind, Freya emerged from under the table to speak with Alice and explain the situation.

Freya immediately expressed how Daddy messed up Mother's Day and how she needed to get some gifts. However, she quickly realized Willow had the pouch with all their green paper. Luckily, Alice agreed to pay for a couple items for Freya if she ran some errands. Alice set some green paper on the table for Freya to use; however, Freya was distracted by a butterfly and didn't notice the papers float away in the breeze.

Freya first had to go to the baker's table to obtain some banana bread. Noticing she forgot to take the green paper Alice provided, she utilized her cuteness to steal some from a lady who just bought some. She rubbed against the woman's legs and meowed flashing her beautiful yellow-green eyes. As the enthralled lady reached down to pet her, Freya snagged the plastic bag with the small bread loaves and ran back to the crystal booth to deposit the sweet-smelling loot.

Next, Freya had to obtain a couple bottles of water. She found a vendor with water in a cooler in front of their food stand. One by one, she pulled a bottle out from between balls of ice, digging with her paws, while people took photos and video of her exploits with their phones. Little did she know, one of the people in line was kind enough to pay for the water she was trying to sneak away with. Once she had three bottles out, she started rolling them across the dirt path to the tent Alice worked in. (I'm just glad Alice didn't ask for soda…)

Freya spent the rest of the day hanging out with Alice and her friend, glad to be under a tent so she didn't get wet from the occasional light rain she already contended with to obtain the goods. This also gave her a chance to look through the smaller stones and necklaces to figure out what to pick for Mommy. Freya proudly selected a green stone cut to look like a cat attached to a cord creating a necklace. She also chose a beautiful, polished malachite, the same stone as Mommy's engagement ring carried in the form of a heart.

Freya was treated to some fried fish, and the outer coating removed by a girl that saw her drinking raindrops that dripped from the side of the pavilion. After, the girl laughed so hard at the small pink tongue catching water as it fell, she almost lost her fairy wings strapped to her back. Freya was also given a few small pieces of the bread she stole. (And to think Daddy keeps saying that stealing doesn't pay off…)

Freya was advised that Daddy always stops to say goodbye to Alice on his way out of the festival. Sure enough, as a few people wearing green shirts were announcing it was five o'clock, she saw Daddy walking up the hill toward where she had been enjoying her day out. As Daddy talked to his friend, Alice, her friend silently unzipped the big pouch of his backpack and placed Freya inside with her small bag of gifts. He just as quietly zipped it up enough that she was hidden among the empty water bottles, uneaten snacks, and trinkets Daddy had bought, with an opening to allow in some air.

*****

🐈 🐈 🐈 🐈 🐈

Willow spent the day at the festival excitedly roaming from tent to tent, searching for the perfect gift. She found a person selling bookmarks with small charms hanging from them. We *all* know Mommy loves to read books all the time, and she's always looking for a way to mark where she left off. The problem Willow ran into was the bookmark she liked the most was a metallic feather that did not have a cat charm attached, like the cats hanging from other bookmarks had. (Of course, she would choose a metal version of something you could find for free on almost any bird…)

Upset that none of the feathers had cat charms, she pulled a dragon shaped bookmark with a kitty charm dangling from it. Next, she selected the metallic feather, which had a peacock hanging from it. With both bookmarks, she approached the shop owner and explained that she wanted to swap the charms.

After several moments of confusion, the woman figured out what all the meowing was about. She pulled out some tools and swapped the charms. Willow handed her a green piece of paper from the pouch, and the kind lady placed two pieces of paper with a "5" and a "10" in the pouch, along with the feather bookmark – now with a cat charm – in a pretty box.

After realizing she had more money than she thought, Willow decided to buy more stuff until the velvet bag was full. (Of course, she never realized she didn't split the money with her sister as she was supposed to…) After roaming through several vendors' pavilions, she found a tent that smelled like lots of incense had been burned inside, the same way it smells in a room where Mommy and Daddy burn incense while staring at candles. Once she entered, the woman sitting near the entrance said, "Hail and Welcome, little kitty! Where did you come from?"

Willow explained her mission to the woman, including telling her how much Mommy loves incense and cats. She immediately helped Willow get a few boxes of scents that Mommy had burned in the past and a few that she never smelled in the house before but had aromas she knew Mommy would like. The woman also showed her a ceramic black cat she had made and painted herself. Willow knew this woman was a witch like Mommy and knew if another witch created a cat statue, her mom would love it.

Willow exchanged paper with the woman and realized the ceramic cat was bigger than her pouch. She looked at the woman about to ask for a bigger pouch just as the lady, seemingly reading her thoughts, presented a pretty flower decorated bag with a long handle. She helped Willow place everything in the bag and offered to keep it for her until the end of the day. She also pulled out a small piece of chicken, offering it to Willow. As she ate it up, the woman added a small dish of clean water to drink. Willow purred excitedly as she enjoyed the snack under the tent.

Once Willow finished her snack and took a short nap between the woman's feet, she took off toward the other tents. She saw Freya with Alice eating some tuna from a pouch she knew had to have been stolen from Daddy's backpack and lapping water up as it fell from the side of the tent. (If water is dripping from somewhere, you can be sure Freya will be under it within a minute to lick it out of mid-air before it hits the ground.)

Knowing her youngest sibling was in good hands, she didn't stop at her favorite vendor in search of something, figuring Freya would pick the best option available there. She hopped on top of a table with a higher view of the festival. She saw tents filled with clothing of all sorts, leather-made items, shields, swords, and other assorted weapons like Daddy collected, and lots of places with food or gemstones. Then she spotted the apothecary, the place with the herbs. Mommy loved working with herbs, too. As she strolled to that covered area, she realized she had no idea which herbs Mommy would want. She also noticed she couldn't reach most of them anyway. She tried to figure out what to do when a familiar scent filled her nose… catnip…

She looked around cautiously, making sure nobody was looking, before leaping to snag a small bag of the green heavenly herb. Running off with the plastic bag of herbs, she didn't realize she dropped the velvet bag with the remaining green paper. She hid under a picnic table with the smells of turkey, chicken, and bar-b-que above her. Ripping open the pouch with her front claws, she rubbed her face into the tiny dried green leaf pieces until her mind was overtaken by the effects of our favorite drug. Mommy and Daddy only give us some when they are gone for a very long time or as a reward if we kill a mouse that got into the house. Even then, never a whole pouch.

Willow devoured nearly the entire ounce of 'nip before remembering she was on a mission, and the evening was coming soon.

She stumbled out from under the table, bumping into multiple people's legs, other tables, and even tripped over a tent stake. She looked up from her 'nip-induced staggering to see something she knew Mommy would love more than anything…. a shelf full of books!

Upon investigating, she realized there were multiple copies of the same three books, and none looked like the ones Mommy already had at home. With some effort, she pushed one of each book together in front of the man, who explained how he wrote the books. He politely asked Willow if she wanted the books signed when she realized she had lost her money. She ran off looking for where she had left it without even giving a single meow to the man.

As she tried to retrace her steps, she heard the loud cheer of a crowd calling out, "To the gate!" This was immediately followed by the sounds of drums and bagpipes coming from the largest tent in the fair that Daddy called "The Tavern." She watched the men and women coming out of the tent, led by the music players. She remembered this was what happened right before Daddy would walk to the crystal-selling tent and say his goodbyes to Alice before going to his car.

Willow ran as fast as she could to where Freya and Alice stood under the green tent. Freya was excited to see her sister and asked her how everything went. Willow's tail went down between her hind legs as she explained she found cool looking books but lost the green papers on the way there. She conveniently left out how some 'nip might have had a role to play.

Freya chuckled and described how she had seen her at the herb tent with the velvet bag and how she watched her bolt across the field with a bag of green herbs and no velvet bag. She originally thought Willow traded the bag for the catnip until she went over to see if there was any more of the greatest herb on Earth. She rescued the remaining funds after finding the velvet bag on the ground below the makeshift wall of various herbs and resins. She even spotted the bags of catnip hanging at the top, but they were slightly too high to jump without running into the hooks that kept the herbs hanging. After looking around, the decision was easy to return to the comforts of spending time with Daddy's friend.

Relieved the money was not lost, Willow thanked Freya for the retrieval and explained how Daddy would be there any moment. She then ran to the other tent with the witch, who was holding the bag of gifts she had obtained. After receiving some petting and a little more water, she watched her father getting a hug from his friend while her fiancé placed Freya, the velvet pouch, and a small plastic bag inside Daddy's backpack.

On a sidenote, I think it is hilarious that this trick worked.

As Daddy headed toward the gate to leave, Willow followed behind at a safe distance to ensure she was not spotted dragging the bag of goodies. Once Daddy got to his car, as per his routine, he opened the driver-side door to start the car and turn on the A/C. Then he went to the passenger-side door and placed the bags and accessories he carried on his chain belt into the seat. Freya made a slight noise when dad's second bag, carrying his camcorder, tripod, and who knows what else, was placed on top of the backpack. By this time, Willow was already in position in the back seat under an empty box that was supposed to go to the recycling dump, whatever that was.

Soon after, Daddy drove home and carried his stuff into the house. Willow trailed behind him going up the stairs, then dove inside as soon as he opened the door to appear like she was waiting with me and Leonna for him. It was common for at least one of us to be in another room or sleeping away from the door when our humans came home, so three out of four cats by the door was not suspicious in any way.

As Daddy set his bags on the living room floor, Willow dragged her floral-decorated bag inside so the screen door could finally close. Knowing Daddy's habits on a festival day helped a lot. I knew he would next go to the kitchen to pour a cup of water from the fridge. After that, he would take the water to the bedroom or the bathroom to prepare for a shower to clean all the sweat and interesting smells of the day from his body. I sent Leonna to follow him to prevent him from wondering what we were up to. We waited a solid minute to ensure he didn't come back for something, as he sometimes does, before Willow and I opened the backpack zipper to release our youngest sister.

Instead of jumping out with her bag of gifts as expected, we found her eating some small dried-out meat snack she tore into from Daddy's munchies he kept stashed in there. After shaking our heads and rolling our eyes at her, Willow took the small plastic bag, and I took the empty package to place near the trash can. I hoped one of the humans would simply think it fell there and not overthink it.

While Daddy was in the shower, we placed the porcelain cat on Mommy's favorite chair and combined the other gifts in one bag. Before we could drag that to the bedroom to display our gifts on the bed like normal, Daddy had finished his shower and was heading into the living room. We quickly hid the bag inside a plastic bin with prayers to the Goddess Bastet that Daddy wouldn't find it. Our prayers were answered, but not the way we wanted. He moved several items around the room, including placing several other bags and small items into the bin, which buried our treasure trove.

*****

The following three weeks consisted of our humans doing their normal routines of leaving, coming home, watching TV with us, playing games, reading books, and Daddy going to his festival every weekend. The whole time, we could not move the heavy items placed on top of the gifts for Mommy. We decided we were not going back to the festival to get anything for Father's Day, as we have frequently done, because he was a very bad daddy. Since we couldn't rub his nose in his bad deeds like he does to us, we figured we would punish him by not getting him any gifts until he unearthed the Mother's Day gifts.

Finally, a couple weeks after Father's Day, he emptied the tote bin. Freya distracted him when the bag became visible by peeing on the floor across the room. As he got up to chase her, I grabbed the bag and handed it to Willow since she was faster than me... I mean, I handed it to Willow because I am the Queen of the house, and it is beneath a queen to carry a heavy bag around the house. That was the real reason.

Freya had successfully hidden under the bed so Daddy couldn't punish her. While he cleaned up her pool of yellow liquid, Willow and Leonna got the bag on top of the bed and started to spread the multiple gifts out to surprise Mommy. We all knew she would be confused by the timing, but we were proud that we finally delivered her the Mother's Day gifts she deserved!

That reminds me.... We bought Daddy a gift for Father's Day, but he was supposed to be getting punished until after he fixed the mess he created for us... Of course, that adventure is a different tale to be told later.

*****

There are more kitty adventures to come. Persephone has been collecting their antics for over a decade. Every birthday, Yule/Christmas, Father's Day, and Mother's Day, the cats would "write" a note to Mommy and Daddy explaining how they obtained the gifts they provided. Eventually, these tales will be recorded to share.

19 Years Happier

(Tanka)

Best times with my friend-
Now nineteen years of marriage!
Through good times and bad.
Years my love has ever grown-
She's made my life so happy!

Lake Anna View

(Tanka)

Low clouds in the sky
A duck bobbing along waves
Shadows of birds on the wakes
Birds flying over the waves to-
Tall green trees beyond the lake

Mountain Laurels Bright

(Tanka)

Trees never planted-
White flowers stained with brown lines.
Mountain laurels bright!
How did you come to my yard,
To deliver such beauty?

Sharon Lyon

The Pecking Order

A free winter banquet for one and all, the feeder drew many species of birds. Black-capped Chickadees, with their bobbing curiosity, vied for footholds with the dull brown Song Sparrows. Tiny House Wrens peeped from the bushes, awaiting their turns. On nearby trees, the White-breasted Nuthatches practiced their upside-down aerobatics. Shy Tufted Titmice scurried across the snow-flocked ground, searching for scatterings. Northern Cardinals flashed in magnificent scarlet, bringing messages from departed loved ones. And high on the dead pine, a last soldier from the Great War, a Pileated Woodpecker hammered for ants hidden within the phloem.

A Blue Jay flew in with his puffed-up chest. Brawny and antagonistic, he bullied his way to the feeder, rattling and fluttering. The smaller birds scattered in fright, hiding within evergreen branches, reduced to pecking at old cones.

A few European Starlings gingerly approached the feeder, dressed alike in their oily black feathers, speckled with spit. They trailed after the Blue Jay, mimicking his movements, hoping to be just as grand and impressive as he. The jay, recognizing the benefits of their obsequious manner, welcomed them as flatterers. More starlings arrived, gobbling the free food. The Blue Jay croaked loud, repetitious squawks, educating the flock on his methods. Soon, the Blue Jay, with his starling mob, commandeered the feeder, demanding respect from all the rest of the birds.

Winter came to an end. Robins returned from their snowbird locales, tanned and rested. Grasses began to sprout and seed. Insects emerged from cocoons and tunnels. The sparrows and wrens no longer bothered with the feeder as food became plentiful. The brilliant cardinals found their muted mates and busied themselves by gathering twigs for nests. Spring breezes called to the starlings, and they coasted away to open country, swooping and diving in murmuration.

The feeder was almost empty. The Blue Jay was all alone. And he was unhappy.

He strutted around the feeder. He screeched to passing birds. He gorged on the last of the stale seed, unwilling to go hunt for his own repast and leave his high-and-mighty perch. From a distance, he heard the starlings call to him. "We are still with you, but we're very busy now. Perhaps we'll see you in the winter when we need you again."

Now the Blue Jay was angry.

Abandoned, he fluttered his feathers and yawped an audacious cry. He leaped up and down, his crested head bobbing. He screeched and cackled and whistled, hoping to attract attention.

And attract attention he did.

For camouflaged against the bark of the Tulip Poplar, a Cooper's Hawk turned his great head and stared with predatory eyes. Big Blue was a meaty fellow and looked delicious. With one mighty whoosh of wings, knife-like talons extended, the hawk descended upon the jay, catching him by the throat.

The Blue Jay made a last strangling noise as the raptor's arcuate beak turned him into lunch.

Soon, blue feathers decorated the ground beneath the feeder.

A pair of noisy American Crows cawed the news across the meadows. The starlings took flight as one giant, black mass in the sky, finding comfort in their sameness.

Quiet descended. The sparrows and wrens flitted peacefully in the dogwoods. The nuthatches stuffed seeds into tree holes. The cardinals welcomed new hatchlings.

And the Cooper's Hawk rested, satiated, in a distant oak, waiting for the next plump bully at the feeder.

The Meadow

The meadow flourished in evolutionary splendor, each plant species sprouting at its predestined time. First, the dandelions emerged, their enticing golden blooms mimicking the sun. Next, buttercups offered opalescent contrast to the first emerald sprouts of grass. The delicate fragrance of sweet nectar floated in the air from lily-of-the-valley's bell-shaped chalices. Cornflowers and sunflowers raised open faces in solar worship. Queen Anne's Lace and milkweed bloomed late, with decadent, ivory flowerets. All timed exquisitely to blossom in turn, so the bees might feast throughout the summer.

For the bees ruled the meadow with their buzzing voices and flying arabesques. The bumblebees, with their philosophical nature, preferred the luscious lavender. The honeybees, with their hurrying intensity, preferred the coneflowers. The rest they shared in begrudging symbiosis.

Insects of all types lived in the meadow, of course - fleas, mosquitoes, horse flies, lacewings. Grasshoppers and crickets danced and thrummed. Dragonflies and ladybugs swooped and twiddled. They all yielded to the authority of the bees, however, cowed by the collective mightiness of their stinging weaponry.

All except the wolf spiders, who wove dangerous webs in rock crevasses, waiting in deceitful silence.

One Spring, a drought hit the meadow as cyclones headed north and heat islands expanded. Rain evaporated as virga. Dew became scarce. The daisies wilted and the blackberry bushes refused to set. Even the dandelions offered only one bloom of sun-heads, which seeded into puff balls and blew away like kites.

The bumblebees and the honeybees began to grumble at each other. "We were here first," said the bumblebees. "We're indigenous to this meadow. You arrived from distant shores."

"We're more useful," snapped the honeybees. "We make honey, and all you make is noise."

The bumblebees took offense. "We pollinate the flowers. And pontificate on important matters. We are not useless," they claimed.

"We pollinate the flowers too," said the honeybees. "From sunup to sundown. With much less fuss than you."

Temperatures increased as the summer progressed, the sun's arc higher, and the daylight hours lengthening. The colony of bumblebees rumbled, hungry, and miserable. The honeybees flew longer scavenging missions and their young grew thirsty inside their combs. No bee wanted to share the meager bounty left in the meadow. Tensions increased.

"We have bigger stingers," threatened the bumblebees.

"We have more soldiers," responded the honeybees.

A summit was called. The two Queen Bees met on the butterfly bush. Their fat, well-fed abdomens weighted down the listless branches on which they perched. Fawning drones served the sweetest nectar. Gifts of royal jelly were exchanged. The Queens conferred and made polite conversation. They touched forelegs together, emitting pleasant pheromones, as the legions of workers gave winged applause. The Queens flew back to their hives, pleased with themselves.

But the drought continued, the grasses turning brown and reedlike. Poison ivy spread and sticker vines climbed the sedges. And the bee factions continued to grumble.

"We have bigger stingers," threatened the bumblebees.

"We have more soldiers," responded the honeybees.

Autumn arrived and a few late-blooming black-eyed Susans and stalks of goldenrod offered sustenance. Brawls ensued over these flowers, resulting in a torn proboscis here, a wrenched stinger there. Skirmishes broke out. Both sides suffered casualties, with worker bees lost from each swarm. Spittlebugs carried the news across the meadow, and the stink bugs and ticks hid their glee under clouds of deference and feigned sorrow.

Polar air blew in from the north as winter approached, and the surviving bees, thin and weak, began their seasonal hibernation.

During their slumbering respite, they dreamt of former days of glory and abundance. Snow fell, percolating into the ground and soaking the husks of buried, dormant seeds.

The Earth completed its solar revolution, once again delivering the equinox of Spring. Vernal rain showered the meadow, and the wondrous scent of wet soil filled the air. The sun blazed and dandelions celebrated with early blooms. Johnny-jump-ups splashed the fields with indigo. Poppies blossomed like scarlet temptresses. The bees emerged, ravenous, buzzing and fussing, ready to greet Mother Nature's perennial banquet.

The bumblebees feasted on wild lilac. The honeybees siphoned nectar from the clover. But when they met on the sunflower heads, they bumped each other with bristly thoraxes and glared with untrusting, multi-lensed eyes.

"We found this sunflower first," said the bumblebees. "Finders, keepers."

"How eloquent," snickered the honeybees, mincing their mandibles. "Says who?"

"We have bigger stingers," threatened the bumblebees.

"We have more soldiers," responded the honeybees.

The ladybugs, hoping for resolution, sighed and frowned at the renewed rivalry. Swallowtail caterpillars turned their faces away, sheltered in self-spun, silken cocoons. While hidden inside manure piles, the dung beetles snuffled in gleeful debauchery.

And the wolf spiders wove dangerous webs in rock crevasses, waiting in deceitful silence to conquer the meadow.

Caitlin Niznik

A different view

I look upon a murky lakeside view
Bashful and shamed to learn something new
This day I shall fly, triumphantly I will soar

I place my legs unsteady upon this board
Casting off far from silt sodden shore
Buckling, I decide to sit, brooding upon my shaky fate

Swinging my paddle side to side struggling to liberate
My desire from my ability to glide and levitate
Above this lake, instead, I crawl like a tyke

Like a child, now, I cast off my injured ego, so contrite
Rise up and balance, content to teeter and totter
For every child knows what adults forget

That failing is a part of play, so continue rising,
                                    rising against regret
I sink into myself, both hands upon my paddle, ready and set
To stand tall and feel the strain that's settled around my limbs
                                          so pleasant

Balancing side to side basking in this sacred enjoyment
Of knowing that my body is strong and Oh so buoyant
I look upon a murky lakeside view

CAITLIN NIZNIK

An Autumn Beauty

Springtime, whose beauty shines with light by day
Finds Summer heat too heady to keep at bay
Autumn comes as a sweet relief
To serve as Winter's aperitif

The wind combs through the trees
letting loose golden and scarlet leaves
to drift upon our Mother,
And adorn her body with a downy cover

Here in Autumn, we find the artist
Appreciative of a season soon to supernova, stardust,
With Scorpio eye, they see the abundance of
Crops below and Life above

A hand picks up new material
From earth's creations, gone too soon, ephemeral
To be constructed and dipped into the River Lethe
To forget their past of sunlit wreath

Born anew as Pinecone Hedgehog
And needle crafted Pine Cones Treefrog
Autumn reminds us, that beauty may yellow and darken,
But Joy is to be found wherever we look and hearken

A Sweetened Love

I hear my mother calling me
From the kitchen table
I don't find her

She's not in the spaghetti
She learned from an Italian neighbor
As a newlywed

She's not in the Golimpki
She learned from her mother in law
As a wife

I find her in my cup of cocoa
She learned from her mother
As a child

For my mother's hot chocolate is
Not the same as yours
It's not powder mixed in milk or water

She begins with a hard bar
Of chocolate from Ibarra
Simmering in a soup pot

Adding condensed milk, sugar, and spices
Stirring and sipping, savoring and sweetening
Until it's just right

I see my mother's face reflection
And feel her hands' embrace
In every cup of cocoa

Miriam S. Pody

The Baba Yagas Create Life

In the frigid, wild lands of Rus', there were ancient things that lived where humans never dared tread.

Alkonost and Sirin had been there since the land was young. They had planted the forest that now grew dense and black and full of monsters. Like the creatures they watched over, they were ageless, hungry…and lonely.

"We have the forest," said Alkonost, the eldest. "We have the leshiye, the rusalki, and Ded Moroz visits every year without fail. We hardly lack for company, or for wards."

The younger sister tossed her long white braid over her shoulder contemptuously. Despite their great age, her hair still grew thick and healthy, and she was vain about it. "I'm not talking about stewardship, and you know it. I want to try something different."

Alkonost frowned, but she was intrigued. The truth was, she too was tired of the same conversations and dalliances they had been experiencing day in and day out for longer than they had cared to remember. The seasons had begun to blend into an endless tapestry of monotony, unless they went out to play with the humans, but there were so few of them who were really *worth* anything that even that had become boring.

"Different how?"

"I want a child." Sirin's pale eyes gleamed, alive with sudden passion.

"I'm sure there are plenty of willing creatures out there to help you make one," Alkonost said wryly. "Why bring this up to me?"

"Not like that!" Sirin snapped, flushing. "A child like *us*. Something *we* could raise, and teach. Someone who will help as we get older. Someone who could—" She gestured vaguely, her lips

142

pursing as she tried to find the words. "It's something I want to do with you. Something that's ours and doesn't belong to anyone else."

Alkonost looked at her sister. Opened her mouth. Closed it. Thought for a moment.

"...And how do you propose we accomplish that?" she said, eventually.

Sirin twisted her bony fingers in her lap. "We could use what the forest has. Create a child that could grow. Something that could...last for a very long time. As long as we do."

That would certainly be a thorny problem, but not an impossible one. It had been so long since either of them had really had a challenge, Alkonost thought.

"We would have to make the child more than flesh, then. Nothing mortal." She held up a hand to forestall her sister's delighted reply. "And this child is *ours*. We cannot fail to raise it properly. Are we agreed?"

"We are." Sirin was already rolling up her sleeves. "Shall we make a boy or a girl?"

"A girl. Boys are too much trouble."

"And what shall we make her out of?"

Alkonost levered herself out of her chair by the fire to cross to the front window. Beyond the confines of their oven-warmed hut, the long and relentless winter howled. "There is always the snow. A snow maiden would be pure and virtuous. A good child."

"And the moment she comes inside, or when summer comes, she'll melt. Pfuh! Just like that. Even the depths of the forest can only keep snow alive for so long. She would be useless with the chores then." Sirin joined her sister at the window. "We could use wood."

"The fire would eat her alive if she tended it, sister. And wood is even more mortal than snow. No, wood will not do."

All was silent for a long time as they thought. The house shifted and settled under them, trying to get comfortable.

At last, Sirin spoke. "We could use the earth. When the winter fades, the river clay is soft and moldable. It will hold our magic well, far better than wood or snow, and we can use the oven to fire it so it will hold its shape."

"Can you wait so long?"

Sirin shrugged. "What is a season more?" she murmured. "We can use that time to plan and prepare. Our daughter will not enter this world unloved, with no crib nor cover."

All that winter they worked, with loom and axe and needle and whittling knife and song. They worked spell and blessing into every stitch and whorl, so the eyes of the animals that danced across the cloth seemed to sparkle with inhuman intelligence, and the carved leaves in the new furniture looked as they might begin to grow at any moment.

As the snow began to retreat, the sisters went further into the forest to seek what they needed for the child. From the newly-released river waters they took their clay and black river stones, iron-strong arms easily bearing the burden back to their hut. To bind it they pulled shadows from the hidden places between the trees and under the hills, and from their mouths they pulled their own teeth, wet and glistening, immortal blood and bone to tie their creation to them. From these they fashioned a baby girl, with dark hair and eyes as black as chips of obsidian, and fired her form in the oven, and breathed life into her with their bellows.

The first lusty squall from the child's mouth seemed to them to be a cry of triumph.

A Tale of Two Brothers

Let me tell you a story, child, of our world. You see there, at the edge of our plains, cutting through even the highest of our mountains? There is the Great Rift, which no man can cross, for the gods have forbidden it. The Great Rift has split our land since time immemorial, when the Ages turned and the first world was lost in fire and steel.

The world was enlightened once, but in their greatness the old ones became flawed. They forgot the gods. They built large villages made of metal many times the size of our tribe. They were great healers, but the metal made the world grow poisoned around them.

There were some who remembered the world even as the gods were forgotten. Legend speaks of a man who had two sons of the same age. The boys were as devoted to each other as they were their father and their world. They were young still when the land darkened and monsters began to invade the minds of men.

The father created a world within the world with his old magic as the children made an offering to the earth. They planted two young oaks to remind the gods of the young children who loved peace and fed them with the lifeblood of the world.

But the gods would not be appeased. Enraged by the people, they sent madness, and the earth trembled with fear. Fire spat from the ground and lit the skies with blood. Death spread through the world in an instant. The father took the children into his sanctuary below to protect them, but one ran back. It is unknown why, for the secret has been lost to time. His brother followed, his voice echoing through the passageways for his brother to return to them.

As the child reached the tree he himself had planted, the earth split open behind him. The tree held fast to the ground, and the child to the oak. His brother had also been saved in much the same manner, but as the earth belched smoke and blood, it pulled them apart. Then the first child, the one who had fled the safety of paradise, was overcome by the earth's breath, and he knew no more.

It was a long time before the earth began to heal again. The large villages were scattered to the four winds. All but the young were left behind in the first world, never to be seen again. The child, touched by the gods, grew into a man. And the Great Rift yet remains as a reminder of what he, our grandfather's grandfather, had lost. The oak that saved him by the grace of the gods still grows, reaching across the Great Rift, still seeking his brother and father. Perhaps his tree may yet reach its twin on the other side, the only thing that still lives in that wasteland. Until then, their spirits wait, and reach, praying to the gods that one day the Rift will be crossed and they may be together again.

-from the legends of the Sanfron Plains, c. 1295 N.C.

Excerpt from "GenEns"

August trudged through the sewers with the rest of the group, all of them following the Master through a maze of tunnels that all looked exactly the same. Their way was lit by the gently pulsing glow of the electric cables that threaded through the entire city.

"When are we going to kill her?" he asked for the tenth time that hour. "You *know* the way to her lair, and given that you seem to have incredible knowledge of the Newmares, you more than likely know where she spends most of her time and where she would be least guarded."

"And right now, she and her army are on high alert," the Master snapped. "*Think*, boy. Even if you were up to full strength and able to destroy her, how would you get close? The humans look different from us. We cannot pass for human without special equipment and being much more careful than you seem to be capable of."

"...We can't?" August asked, baffled. "But humans can't see energy, and we have the same shape. We should look just like them."

The Master laughed without humor. "That is the key, my boy. *Looking* like them is far more difficult when you cannot *see*. Do you know what the biggest difference between GenEn and human is? Our eyes. To them, there is *nothing* in our eyes, only blank color. They have black holes that suck in what they can perceive."

Owen shuddered at the description. "Humans are *disgusting*."

"How do you know this?" August asked suspiciously.

"I'm very old, boy. I know things that no other GenEn could. For instance: how to effectively cover our tracks from cameras and how to break in past electronic locks without blowing them to smithereens."

August fell silent, considering. The Master did seem to know what he was doing, and all the other GenEns followed him without question. But the younger man was suspicious. GenEn and human were distinct and separate, and the Master *still* seemed to have intimate knowledge of them. If he didn't read as GenEn through and through, August would almost think he *was* human.

He shivered. The water around his calves was ice-cold, and it stank. It seemed to accurately reflect his situation, at least, but that only made him grumpier. He just wanted to get this whole mess over with and get the real war started.

After what felt like an eternity of trudging through the sewer tunnels, the air slowly became warmer, and August could see a gleam of energy growing ahead of them. GenEn energy, from what he could tell, and that heartened him and quickened his steps. The rest of the group broke into a trot, equally eager.

August and the other former prisoners stopped at the very end of the tunnel, overwhelmed by the sight that stretched glittering before them. It was practically a small *town*, built above the blackwater and connected by bridges made of active cables. The whole place was clearly built for GenEns, since the heat he could feel against his skin was a hundred times warmer than any lightbulb he'd ever encountered. No, the heat was from the mass amounts of power crammed into one large concrete shell, humming in the bodies of nearly two hundred GenEns.

It was the most beautiful thing August had ever seen.

The Master put a hand on August's shoulder as Owen and the others started climbing towards the city of light.

"Welcome home," he said, squeezing the younger GenEn's shoulder firmly. "From here, we can rest, we can plan, and we can take down the Newmare regime and take our rightful place in the world."

August nodded firmly. This was much, much more than he'd been expecting, and if it meant a better chance at reaching his goals, he would follow the Master to the ends of the earth and beyond.

But first, evidently, there was work to be done. They'd grabbed as much of the food stored in the power station as they could carry, and that had to be taken to a ramshackle distribution center. August spotted other groups lining up outside carrying bundles and plastic containers, presumably from other raids. Or maybe they were there for rations from the raid the Master's group was currently returning from…rations which would now have to be further divided to accommodate the new refugees, including August.

He really hoped they were returning from other raids. If not, that was another concern that he didn't want to get involved with but probably had to.

Was this what it was like to have a family? Responsibilities? Was this what living outside a cell *was*? August was quite frankly stunned and certainly more than a little overwhelmed. Not that the relative freedom from concern while being held prisoner and having your life forcibly drained from you day in and day out was really worth having in the first place.

Life was much, *much* harder than he'd initially thought, and he'd only been free and relatively independent for half a day at most.

August stumbled a little and leaned against a nice, solid slab of concrete to steady himself. It was too much for one person to absorb in such a short amount of time. He needed to get away, get time to think. He wasn't a philosopher—he didn't even know what those were—and realizing universal truths and the depths of how truly GenEns had been fucked over was an entirely new concept.

Had the refuge been anywhere but the underbelly of a sewer, August would no doubt have ended up in some sort of garden where he could have a nature-induced revelation. Alas, it was a sewer, and there were no gardens to be found for convenient recovery or meeting with one's destiny or whatnot. He only found the edge of the town, suspended hundreds of feet above raw sewage.

He sat down, feet dangling over the precipice, and took several deep breaths. He nearly ended up adding to the mess below, gagging from the stench. At least it was fainter up here than in the tunnels, he supposed, but he missed the brief moments he'd spent outside back at the university; the first and only free air he'd ever tasted.

He'd never really seen the sky. August only remembered a great darkness above him that night, and the air moving around him. It had felt like nothing he'd ever experienced before or since. They'd mostly been too busy running for him to take it in. The other GenEns hadn't really seemed to notice or care, but August had. And in order to stay *safe* long enough to kill Dania Newmare, he couldn't risk trying again.

"You should be with the others," the Master rasped suddenly from behind him.

August started, nearly falling from the platform in sheer shock. "Are you *following* me, old man?"

The older GenEn carefully lowered his frail limbs to sit next to the blond. He cleared his throat gently. "Would it make you even more suspicious of me if I said yes?"

"...Obviously," August sneered. "That isn't going to endear yourself to me, *Master*. I'm only following you because I want to destroy the Newmares, and I can't do that on my own. Not yet, anyway."

"You need my strategy, and you need my knowledge."

August gritted his teeth. He didn't need to see the old man to know he was smirking. "Yes."

The Master put a hand to his ear, leaning closer. "I'm sorry? Could you repeat that, young man? I'm afraid my hearing is going in my old age."

"*Yes*, damn you! I need you. You know more than I do about the enemy." August clenched his fists hard enough that his nails drew blood. "I *need* you...Master."

There was a soft huff of approving laughter. "Good. Never forget that, boy. Without me, you would be either dead or back in that cell of yours for the rest of your pathetic life. I am your best hope, and right now, you are mine as well."

August frowned, turning to face the Master. "I am?"

"Of course you are. Of all the GenEns I have seen, you are the freest mind I have ever seen, and you have *passion*. You can't create a revolution with free men alone, August. You need revolutionaries. And you, more than any GenEn I have seen, are a true revolutionary." He patted August's shoulder in a paternal manner. "Come with me.

We have some time to use before the Newmare woman lets down her guard, and I want you to be ready."

"I *am* ready."

"No," the Master said firmly. "You are angry, and you are determined, but that will not be enough. You must be strong, stronger than you are now, and focused. You must learn her weak points, and how to get close."

August gagged. "Get *close*? Are you insane?"

"You are to gain her trust. And once you *have* her trust, August, you can destroy her."

There was silence from the younger GenEn for the longest time. August wanted to accomplish this so *badly*, but in doing so he was indebting himself to the Master, and this GenEn disturbed him on a profound level.

"I will not be doing all of the teaching, if that is what you're expecting. Or fearing. There are other GenEns here educated enough to give you a basis. They can also serve as cover for later; your ideal group of rebels to throw her and her rabid bodyguard off the trail."

"…What bodyguard?"

The Master smiled to himself. "You see? You need to *learn* things before jumping right into action."

August was silent for a long moment before he levered himself to his feet. "…All right, old man. Show me what I need to learn."

Steven P. Pody

Earth Music

I hear the music in the hills
...hear music in the trees.
My heart, it resonates a score
that brings me to my knees.
The colored sky's a symphony
that helps my soul revive
with sparkling tears of gratitude
in awe to be so alive.
But mere living's not

           the stuff of enough

...'tis simply circumstance:
True merit I render the

           splendor

that so charms my nature to dance !
Defining joy

         is an echoed thing,

and words do bare suffice.
It takes harmonic

         note to play

'mongst the ensemble

         of paradise.

A Bard of Word-Song

I am a bard of word-song, given lyric hand to write.
As long as quandary tests the soul, I should be erudite.
Explore the world entire, every notion grand and fine,
and plumb all range of passion, scripting each perceptive line.

Not as eloquent as I might wish, I chronicle my times.
Some times I hit, but often miss; inadequate to my rhymes.
I balk, reciting horror, with a wordsy bark or bite:
Shame and blame, and evils,

quite unfit for human sight...

And yet I must articulate what the future might confuse,
and get it down in written form so truth is not abused.
We cannot hide the present, for someday someone might say
"What petty, ugly struggles brought us through each wretched

day."

Photographers and artists craft their light-play to dispel,
and the journalist or historian have their factoid yarns to tell,
the shadows of the narrative,

revealing some poignant core,

of a moment's hate or beauty, illumined forevermore.

Amid the brilliant doings, are love and sacrifice for good,
the simple, decent glories ...hardly noticed or understood;
these too earn right of telling, as admiring laudatory;
blooded virtue, never rare, within our very human story.

But dire news often dominates ...and simplifies the sorrow;
and tales, unfolding daily, translate obscurely on the morrow.
A thousand little things occur as versifier's fare,
and pass into the darkling void if no poet's light is there...

Thus, the poesy raconteur relates

                         the range of human theme;
the sad, the bad, the just, the saints, and all that's in between.
Amongst dream and acts of babble, darkness coming fast and

                                            thick,

I am the bard of word-song ...whose flame must spark the wick.

An Investment in WitCoin

Noble intent won't pay the rent,
nor dreams your pinch-purse fill.
Why, if dough you throw at every urge,
there'll be naught to line the till.

       'Tis prudent to be prudent !
       (Oh, how simple does that sound ?)
       But rainy days come fast and hard
       and clear-cut truths abound.
You'll feel the lout, if you're without,
and hunger haunts your frame.
Or if, in pursuit of beneficent credit,
you taint a once good name.

       Attention then, my impulsive friend,
       and yield not unto caprice !
       All things may come in their patient time
       if your future has not been fleeced.
...Not to preach 'gainst frivolous overreach,
but give the notion

                    some thought.
Tomorrow may deliver its every promise
if today was not whimsically bought.

The Sailor Man

"I yam what I yam"
        said the sailor man,
an' none could gainsay the quote.
A mouthful of spinach philosophy
an' little more need ever be wrote.

"To thine own self be true",
        offers but part of a clue,
in its subjective, obtuse little way.
But being yerself, because youse is you,
is a jolly good deal to say.

"I yam what I yam,
        an' that's all what I yam !"
No apologies need tabulate score.
Ya say what you mean, an' keep it all clean,
an' ya don't owe no swabbies no more.

If youse is what yam
        an' may declare, quite undamn'd,
in a confident voice, none too loud;
that ya stand for a self, integrity bound,
well, your momma, she'd be vasty proud.

By wharf or tall seas,
        ocean or land, as ya please,
adhere to horizon's line sight.
Faith a'minding your biz, hold fast to what is,
an' what's firm an' good in the right.

Yes, simple truths that stay true,
        both spoke an' tattoo,
are the hawseholes deploying your anchor.
Be you what youse is, but be it the best,
that none may unbend your spanker.

Notes: 'swabbies' = sailors. 'hawsehole' = hole/groove the anchor chain runs thru. 'unbend' = to take down. 'spanker' = a type of sail.

Footprints On The Roof Of The World

Tall in the airy heights and peaks,
  and mountain-vista stuff,
    I search in quest of Yeti,
      'tween summit, and
               deep-chasm bluff.
From roaring chute of river's rush,
  well surmounting Tibet's plateau*;
    above both tree and living line
      my Himalayan trek must go.
I seek the elusive footprint;
  document rumor of this or that;
    poke around for scraps of skin or fur,
      or rare, mythic, frozen scat.
I look with keenest sympathy, for
  what all high-country folk believe:
    This proof-less local beast of lore
      is no mere legend to deceive.
Supposed tracks, in lofty snow,
  where the transiting specter strolls,
    imprint, on imagination,
      more mystique than old Sanskrit scrolls.
Even hardiest part-thrive in green season,
  where the sinuous water flows.
    Perhaps Yeti inhabit some Shangri-La,
      in a coulee which no one knows.
So down and up, and in-between,
  I seek the buggers out:
    Massive, furry ghosts of human kin,

156

or inexplicable ape holdout.
At night I view a shock of stars,
   beyond flaps of warm-refuge tent,
     and I listen, most intently,
       for any echo of Yeti lament.
Frost-bitten and frozen danger;
   thin air, avalanche, and all,
     are worth mortal ecstasy
                 to purely once,
    hear that abominable, chilling call.

* Highest normal living space on Earth - at 14,400ft.

Should I Outlive Forever

A word like 'forever',
     in whatever font or ink or declaration,
has a mar and scar of untold desperate claw marks,
     unseen, but ragged and tainting and haunting.
No microscope will aid the revelation;
     but rather t'will be the questing, aching heart
     in a fit of infinite focus.
Always a concept, ever a hope ...and now,
     without living pledge; with no sound of comfort;
bereft of tender, simpatico touch,
     yawns cruel void for the single, lonely lover
     awash in an exile of memory.
Forever. ...And where are you now ?
Hanging onto forever was a shorter time
     than complete adoration had previously supposed;
than the mortal, clutching grasp,
     and my deepest love, could hold.

The Tremulous House

In the tremulous house of poetry
we hone our sharpened quills;
'pon responsive parchment
                                        falls the wit
our inspiration wills.
Or luck incites...
...or,
          muse mysteriously thrills;
or humor tickles, drop by drop
or acerbic intent kills.
Whatever incentive,
                                the lines are writ
through heat and rain and chills:
For a creator bears the mortal hour
paying all the Devil's bills.
Yet some Great Hearts hoard
                                        time enough
to jot glories, foibles and ills
'pon fragile rag, or skin, or screen,
passion
                writing alone fulfills.
Laud whatever steadies the hovered word
'fore ink-pot dries or spills,
or Death,
                it claims the mind-held hand,
and forever after stills.

Darwin's House Of Change

Were you killed by evolution ?
      Last year's model in quick-start speed ?
Need to trade your scales for feathers ?
      Uptake slow, to survive and breed ?
If you've proved to be so un-fit,
with your legacy prospects small,
why not roll your dice at Darwin's
for a chance to improve it all ?
We've got radioactive hot springs,
and smart predators, employed,
and for small consideration
could whip up an asteroid.
In the back rooms are some glaciers,
or, if tired of species slaughter,
please retreat to our expansive pool
and convert to breathe its water.
Perhaps you are embarrassed
by your smooth and tiny brain ?
So try out our diverse game room;
...see what skills you can obtain.
And if social life is dragging,
and you're picked off, one by one,
cooperation is your golden key,
or learn to hide or run !
To this end, at Darwin's,
nocturnal, or for the day,
we'll work on good communication,
or secrete you safe away.
Unless, of course, you've got bad luck
- your sea is drained, or land deluged,
in which case
      consult our morphologist

to engage some niche, unused.
We've got the answers to all your needs,
your genes will come out fine.
We'll accommodate any adaptation
...if given enough time.

Never Too Late

In a world of desperate people;
in the land of 'Screwed-It-Up';
splash remorseful thoughts, unbidden,
like sour wine in an unclean cup.

A life of bad decisions;
of ignoring some moral path;
of pooh-poohing a mom's sage counsel;
or inviting some god's
                    ugly wrath.

Bitter folk hold no answers:
Nor any of their wild-eyed kin.
Perhaps moving forward with bulk anger,
is not the wagon to be in.

Instead, focus on some forgiveness.
By all means go start -- on yourself.
Grow rightful from all experience.
Treat your scars as true personal wealth.

"Live and learn", the sages state.
Persevere, 'til you've understood.
Endure 'til the balance tips your way,
and you become
                  a force for good.

Tribute is paid in the following poem to two often overlooked women present and influential during deeply critical points in world history. Queen Anne Boleyn, wife of Henry VIII of England, already garners enough credit as a domestic troublemaker and, of course, as the mother of Queen Elizabeth the First. However, she was herself a distinct pebble in history who generated major ripples in the planetary scheme of things – first motivating change in the religion and allegiance of a nation; then the balance of power of a continent -- and eventually impacting the political, religious and social development of over a quarter of the world. She was, therefore, a mover and shaker in quite her own right. ...As for another inconvenient troublemaker, Wallace Simpson, she likewise deserves a reputation greater than as a historical footnote. Her personal, but timely, maneuvers of love happened to remove a very powerful negative player (King Edward VIII) from the pre-WW II chessboard that proved to be a decisive beginning step to the outcome of the largest war in human history. It was very likely that, still in power, a sympathetic king of England would have either surrendered or made a negotiated peace with Nazi Germany. It was a close-run thing. Sprechen Sie tausand-jahr Reich? Without her, we might have 909 years to go...

By Two Little Ladies, Shook

Two little girls, playing at love;
    flirty, skirty,
    smiles all perty.
All on a vibrant isle of fate;
    coy and clever,
    rule-breakers ever...
(Anne Boleyn and Wallace Simpson,
    face kingpin's whim in custom's sin.)

Henry and Edward, pivotal times;
    amused, enthralled,
    complacency stalled.
Marriages beyond the usual stake;
    move heaven and heart,
    shake landscape apart...

(Anne Boleyn and Wallace Simpson,
    accommodate the number VIII.)

Four centuries cast from one another;
    iconoclast dice
    craps paradise.
They rocked the earth and the turbulent seas,
    ashes falling,
    history calling...
(Anne Boleyn and Wallace Simpson,
    dubious self-success ...or happiness.)

Flamed one, a lovely Reformation;
    continent split,
    two truths legit.
Won one, a second world war;
    three years, it's sung,
    before begun...
(Anne Boleyn and Wallace Simpson,
    pitched their charms: A planet, alarmed !)

No ladies changed more, in a thousand years;
    popularity estranged,
    for love, exchanged.
Two winsome women, a globe upend;
    A present remiss,
    without their kiss...
(Anne Boleyn and Wallace Simpson;
    by course they took,
                twice, mighty world shook !)

Summer Light And Fireflies

In a charming ebb of twilight,
as I contemplate this day,
when the world was warm and sunny
and quite mellow in every way.
I muse on fate
                    and fortune
(oft inspiring balladeers...),
while twinkled lightning's kindled
'neath sky's dome of shining spheres.

Evenfall
            unleashes
                        beasties,
both in starry form and flesh.
Nocturnal roams such hunters;
cunning chase begins afresh !
With a majesty of planets,
and stellar heroes overhead,
sparkly fireflies grace the darkening space
which daytime bugs have fled.

Mind impressions yet endure from
the illume of golden hours,
but fading gloom, now bleached and leached
mutes the gaudy birds and flowers.
...One now discerns no butterfly,
seen bright in summer's morn.
Just celestial points,
                        and sporadic flash,
shadow-sculpted, moonlight-borne.
Late, past the vibrant glowing hue
and linger'd ways of solstice light,

stalks many a child, with jar in hand,
keen-hunting in ebony backyard night,
to savor a galaxy of personal stars,
with a youthful awe that never dies;
wide wonderment of myriad generations
beholding nature ablaze

>   with fireflies !

evenfall = the onset of evening, dusk / illume = to illuminate, educate,
enlighten, inspire / gloam = time of day immediately following sunset

Composed For You, To Last An Age

If you leave, angry and early, the world stage,
you'll miss the ending The Author intended : (.
Whupped into self-pity and silent rage
you might overlook eventual affection -- both glorious and splendid.
...And, in any case, years, foolish or sage,
> might yet be redeemed by your own generous love, expended.

Cadence Of The Sea

In detail,
>   it's all quite personal,
that each creature got its spark
from more than moon or

>   molecules

or Noah on his ark.
But since the planet cooled,
and filled   hole,
>   the   Pacific

>   great

the incubating Earth quite settled
in its maternal role.
And, as the creatures came and went,
and spread from sea to land,
the place had more than wind and rain,
and frequent sunshine planned.
And so it's been, since those first drops
composed the primal swells,
and long before crustaceans
scudded ocean rills in shells.
For, there's a heartbeat to the world;
to the surface -- dry, and wet,
that reflects our lunar neighbor,
to which we owe substantial debt.
For with widespread tidal heaving,
twice a day,
in race and reaches;
'round the globe, unlevel sea laps
'gainst the ports and sandy beaches.
...Lifting boats above the sandbars.
...Lowering waves
to harvest clams.
...Roaring rips to fatten estuaries.
...Flats exposed to rich exams.

A vast recycle is underway
within each seaboard's grip;
and commerce,
international,
flows and ebbs with every ship.
Seafarers, birds and fish adapt
to dynamic sea
and coast.
...And to such rhythms of life itself
as our kind blue home may boast.

Goddesses Of The Morn

Well-served, the early morn,
that breathes
      autumn's bouquet;
when cool and clear, the light evolves
into a sparkling day.
    For harken, you of mortal sense,
    though be thee beast, or flora;
    as daybreak hour
        bears stirring kiss
...of Ersa ...and Aurora.
'Pon peak or noble forest;
moist verdant dale or lawn;
there comes caress, magnificent,
from deities
      of Dew and Dawn.
    Same-wise-strong
      unto a warming Spring,
    and summer's early dim, and coolest;
    and amid the diverse solar year
    with winter at its cruelest.
...Even seasoned with
      a hoarfrost tinge,
Ersa daubs the Earth's fair skin.
And Aurora upholds her rosy vigil
through Mother Gaia's
      cyclic spin.
    Dividing night from vibrant day,
    with multi-hued
      and varied graces;
    'tis daily blessing (a waker's gift !)
    ...to behold
      their beautiful faces.

For Those In Vernal Glory

Well, it's coming again, my friend.
A hint, and then a wide burst of bud, bud.
It's that fling of Spring thing,
coming fast, hitting hard and smelling good.
A mass of a flash of green, seen
…plus the famed and fabled flower scene,
kicking poets and lovers in that sacred heart part.
Rejoice !
Fresh start. New hope.
Warmth; a luminous inspiration to every artist's eye !
Rebirth, and the dearth of death.
A time of aspired plenty !
The Earth reverberates in new song
and every natural creature knows the tune.
Come join the chorale, pal,
for I sing with the best:
Verdant trees a'twitter with a clamor of birds,
elk and bear and ferret know all the words,
the salmon in the lifeblood of the land;
the froggies courting loudly in their swamps;
cicadas wondering if their year to shine,
and emerge in obnoxious splendor of their kind…
Squirrels, roses, white-tails, dogs,
pigeons, yaks, apple and plum,
cats and cattle, roses and hogs;
the renaissance of the world, chum !
Awaited hope …and, promise to come,
and what else could any blessing bring ?
All senses pitched to high delight:
Brace yourself for a thrill of Spring !

STEVEN P. PODY

East Virginia

In the loving arms of rivers, East Virginia's lands unfold.
From the Blue Ridge to the ocean,
a most magnificent tale is told.
We may catalogue her virtues, nature blessed each verdant mile;
you may rush along her trail ways,
or kick back and pause awhile...
North, along a pretty valley, and to the south runs too,
the lifeblood of Virginia,
found in story, song (and view !)
The James and Shenandoah,
tumble-flow to bay and sea.
Appomattox and Rappahannock,
likewise course through history.

Respect to Chief Powhatan, the first Virginian named;
though he knew of no such boundaries,
still, he's fated to be thus famed.
At future Jamestown, new dreams landed
...ships presaging bold migration,
melding local and fresh-quest destiny,
as blended-culture; mighty nation !

But beyond old native spirit,
and colonial overlay.
Beyond uncivil battles; blood and tears that soaked the clay.
Surpassing shackle, and imperfect triumph,
with men and women, heads unbowed,
panoramic Ol' Virginny
lies lovely, bountiful and proud.
As cascading waters turn eastward,
and calm to sluggish flow;
and likewise, high Appalachia
levels east, as fields to sow;
and the easterly-sea ...gifts vistas,
on the abundant Virginian shore,

they round out vast variety that each person should explore.
The glories of a remarkable State,
                    endow grandeur for hand and heart;
                            bestows delight to every eye,
                                    and sets Virginia
                                        quite apart.

Word Dancer

Shall I tell you of life's secrets ?
Of patterned rhythm near at hand ?
Define
            what your eyes should tell you,
            so, with grace, you'd understand ?
I am
            but a modest poet,
who has thought-played quite a span,
but would gladly dump my squirreled facts
            to tell you what I can.
Yes, it's true,
                        I dwell atop no mountain,
and I network, nary a stroke;
...my ashram's clogged with tumbleweeds,
            and its cred's been long revoked.
So there's no particular reason,
            why any folks should seek a key
from a life of recurring pandemonium
            and random serendipity.
(None ventured to ask me
            anyway;
                    ...thank you all, so very much.
So when reality goes sideways,

well, my agent won't be in touch.)
Yet, humbly, I offer a line or two
      as you encounter humanity's writ.
...As seeking minds, they skip and leap,
'pon grammatical gems and wit.
So, by all means carry out your quest
      to find out all you may;
from pundit
      to online philosopher,
            many paths will come your way.
For you, sages
         will try to calm your fears
(with more queried angst than answer)
...but when their music becomes a bore,
      return to me, your imperfect
                 Word Dancer.

Andrea Williams Reed

Beauty is Found

Beauty is found-
In a long scenic drive to
distant relatives,
after a fast-paced work week -
a time to relax.

Beauty is found-
In a surprise phone call from a friend,
when home alone pondering
a difficult day.

Beauty is found -
Among old clothes when a favourite dress
still fits and sparks memories
of slimmer days.

Beauty is found -
In holiday letters with updates
of the year's events -
reminders that someone has
thought of you.

Beauty is found –
In a luncheon with old friends to chat and
catch up with each other reminds you that
you are not alone.

Beauty is found in-
a compliment to keep you going,

after a series of disappointments and
blunders can lift your spirit.

Beauty is found in-
Reflecting with contentment after a family
get-together, where forgotten stories and
dishes were shared and savoured.

Beauty is found in-
Waking up a few minutes before the alarm goes off,
after a refreshing night's rest
Can give you a head start on your day.

Beauty is found in-
finishing a captivating book and
being the wiser for the knowledge absorbed.

Beauty is found in-
a satisfying movie on a cold winter's night with
loved ones gathered around.

Beauty is found in the gratitude for the moment.

I Write

I write…
to get it out,
to get it right
to understand
to know myself
to let others know me
to share joys and triumphs
to process losses and disappointments.
I write…

Waiting

The anticipation mounts for the arrival of company,
  the long afternoon of planning, preparing, and cooking.

The longing for the significant other to enter a life;
  filled by sifting through the possible candidates.

The child that has not appeared, science-has no answer;
  meanwhile teach other people's children.

The swollen spot that will not go away;
  doctors, tests, two hours in one waiting area –
  diagnosis- cancer.

The craving of dream employment which passes –
  occupied with duty, responsibility, and family.

As we listen for the final sleep; a last breath,
  a final hand squeeze;
  among nurses, machines and tears.

Fall of Autumn

Temperatures dip
Hues darken,
sun's glare abates

Trees shake off their summer
attire for fall ensembles
To decorate trails
for hikers, and bikers.

Breezes lift leaves and spirits
And fill the soul with anticipation.

173

ANDREA WILLIAMS REED

She Kept Her Thoughts To Herself

Smiled, and waved,
to the public, danced
with world leaders.

Being a wife,
mum, and granny, she was
a mother to an empire.

Always there
for us in times
of need or celebration.

We never heard her share,
thoughts, opinions,
or feelings.

As time moved on
and the
world changed.

Her presence a constant
source of strength
and stability for a nation.

Summer Road Trip

Atlas opened and destination highlighted.
Old suitcase out- new clothes packed!
The family car gassed and loaded up.

Food and drinks carefully
stored.
Home secured.

The gratification of the destination-
A success or disappointment
Yet, guaranteed new sites, faces, and food.

Experienced and enjoyed with
shared memories to savour
and reflect upon for a lifetime.

Shopping at the Mall

Made a few rounds in parking lots for spot to land vehicle.
Walked in familiar entrance,
Started quest for special item.
Walking among the stores, lights and displays,
Fresh crisp offerings in the latest styles,
Shapes that dazzle and lines that draw one in.

Food court teases our senses with smells and tastes.
Snacks and drinks to keep our energy going for our quest.
Lest we forget our cast of characters we interact with,
The bored salesclerk
Bothered by any questions,
Regarding products or services,
The over worked food service person,

Busy wiping trays and tables.

The consumers tall and short,
Young and old, some walking with speed
Some walk with the assistance of others
Or supported with scooters, walkers and canes.

George P. Coleman

The year was 1952.
I stood up with my feet
firmly in the sands of Yorktown
and stretched out my long steel frame,

across the historic York River.
Where I claw my fingers
into the wild sea grasses
of Gloucester point.

The naval weapon station
to my left
and a coast guard station
on my right.

Along my 3,750-foot length spine
I carry commuters back and forth,
between neighborhoods.

I twist my midsection.
to allow ships to pass through
causing motor traffic jams and
prompting commuters
to shout bad words about me

Dazed and confused individuals
have abused and used my shoulders
as a jumping off point to their demise.

I used to be thinner,
until surgery in 1998,
doubling my width, adding a
toll for my procedure.

I have been slapped, knocked
a time or two, by the ships passing through
and got stuck in my twist.

After treatments and adjustments
I was able to untwist
resume my job
connecting communities.

Freedom Marchers

They came in droves:
Some walked, others rode.
Makeshift boxes
of cardboard for shelter.
A place to eat, sleep, and
wash before each freedom march.

Most participants, friendly,
others with a glance dismissed,
me with their gaze, their distrust,
indicating their belief,
I was part of the oppressive system
which brought them to this
point.

Dr. King in his eloquence
spoke sensible words…
to every race and made us
reflect on freedom.

She said Yes

The call went out;
she answered it
with an enthusiastic yes.

Sleeves rolled up.
Running shoes in place,
she went to work.

Organized,
Directed,
and facilitated.

An example of a leader
who mentored the next
generation of leaders.

Goals achieved,
accolades received,
appreciation shared.

The world made better,
because she said
yes.

Grocery Shopping

Armed with list.
We enter the labyrinth
Of consumer goods,
Stacked high and wide
Light precisely striking them

Smell of fresh baked breads,
Apples and zucchini with smooth shiny skins
Pebbly rinds of oranges and cantaloupe
Whiffs of raw fish, pork and meats
Employ all our senses!

We roll through a maze of aisles
Checking off our list,
While mostly showing restraint
Sometimes with considerable strain
Against impulse buying
We scurry towards the
Perimeter of store to
Secure household staples

Before leaving,
We are tempted in check-out lane.
Our minds speculating about
Contents of periodicals as
We scan the headlines
Hands organize coupons
As we inch along
To settle purchases
And exit with bags in hand.

Advisors and Mentors

As offspring mature and
enter the world on their own,
Family players transition
from protectors into
advisors, examples and mentors

The person we run to in a storm,
 shields us from the rain.
The one who is calm in the gale.
 And soothes our anxieties.
The guide we seek when lost,
 points us in the right direction.

Earliest coaches and instructors,
offering their strength,
when we could not find our own.
who taught us how to hunt,
gather and trade in a harsh world.

Our favourite advisors are the ones,
who can clear up the uncertainty,
and give peace of mind.
They are the ones who know what to say,
when we are at a loss for words.
By example show us how to walk, talk,
and dress to be a part of the larger community.

Our mentors prepare us.
to carry on in times of hardships
and not give up.

Indiana Boy

I am from the corn fields and
limestone of the mid-west,
where, fathers favor daughters
and never sons.

Where peonies burst forth and
color the landscape after
winter's deep snows and
harsh winds.

I rode long roads, without bathroom breaks,
to feasts of grandma's beef and noodles,
aunt's potato salad, uncle's stories
and competitive games of pinocle.

I endure never ending chores,
assigned by harsh father,
with stern words, exacting
hands, who was never pleased.

I spend the lonely summer spackling
and painting, to sounds of drills, saws
and swearing; mowing bought
the smell of grass and nosebleeds.

I hauled the golden harvest,
admired the full pantry,
waited for winter and
next visit with grandparents.

ANDREA WILLIAMS REED

Final Tour of Duty

New and last assignment,
Briefed and accepted.
Expected to last 3 years.
could be shortened,
or extended.

Depending on progress
and effectiveness,
will be reviewed
periodically.

Grueling tasks of tests,
treatments, falls,
hospitalizations, ambulance
rides, tubes and shots.

Mission thud by occasional
Setbacks due to doctors
and providers with little experience or
knowledge regarding condition.

Fatigued by hospital stays,
complications from dialysis
maneuvers – too little,
too much and misdiagnosis

Focus of mission-
living
assignment was extended,
to six years.

Jorge R. Robert-Saavedra

A Vision

I saw a vision, bright as a star!
Mounted on a white horse,
Galloping, not touching the earth!
Brandishing a sword,
High above his head….
Dripping with blood and love.

And the knight,
Through the field rode,
Unchallenged!
Under the drumming of the steed's hoofs,
The uprooted dandelions flew!
While the irises pointed the true path,
Along the trail of sand.

And the sword flew,
And cut both right and left!
Vanquishing the dragons.
It Shielded humanity!

And the vision rode,
Until it was no more,
But the wind still stirred,
From its passing.
The trail bore the stallion's marks,
And the irises and daffodils,
Spoke of the warrior's might!

Dearest Love

Dearest Love.
You are,
The wind in my sails,
The rudder in my life,
The light in the window,
Guiding me home at night....
Without you, life would be an endless desert,
Wine, would have no taste!
And music,
Would be noise,
Keeping me awake at night!

I am the Soap

I am the soap,
I hold your hand,
I caress your face,
I kiss your body.
I am the soap,
Lather with me!

I am the soap,
I cover your body,
I fight the water,
     And leave a film!
I leave my scent…,
     We are one!
I am the soap,
Lather with me!

Of Flowers and Love

As the sun melts,
    The layers of frosted dew.
And the crocuses and daffodils,
    Inch their way.
Through the matted brown grass,
    And rotting leaves….

As the early flowers of spring,
    Gather strength!
From the sun's,
    Softly kissing rays of gold!
I look at you,
    And see you in full bloom!

Maisie, Ken & Peggy's Havanese

Maisie had a fur coat,
Made of gold and silver.
Her reddish aura,
Was a glow with her love for us.

Sitting between us in the couch,
She was our baby girl.
On the leash, during our walks,
She was my buddy.

A car ride to her,
Was an out of this world adventure.
So simple to please!
So much love she gave us.

185

She

And my heart drums,
As our finger touch,
And I feel your warmth,
And my body quivers!

And I hold you close,
As embracing a newborn;
And I love you so!
And time is not…

But life is!
And it takes us apart!
And the moment is gone!
As life moved to the right…

And our bodies caress as they part,
Making the moment last,
Dizzy with your scent!
Trembling with your impression…

And I long after you,
As I stare into the night.
As I know not where you are!
Even though I have you within…

As my hand crumples the petals,
Of a rose that was,
And find the essence is still in the essence!
Your love is still in my heart…

Thomas "Jerry" Lee

The careless storm,
Tossed his ship,
From left to right,
And back again!

The roiling seas,
Bucked his vessel,
Up and under,
And then again!

And all those about,
Lost sight of the course!
But he did not!

And if there was,
A call for help,
He tossed a line!

While his ship,
Was swamped to the Gunwales,
He still gave aid, to fellow man!

The Turtle

I have always liked the desert at sunset.
As the sun slips away,
The stars, one by one, can be seen,
To start twinkling in the sky,
Until, as if with a crescendo,
They cover the entire firmament!

187

Before dusk,
With my feet propped on the fire pit,
A cognac on my hand,
I see a distant stone moving.
A Very discordant vision,
In this flat, sandy soil.

As the wind shifts,
It roils sand and dust,
Lifting racing whirlpools,
On this hot and arid landscape.
The stone stops, and like a periscope,
It lifts a head.

Realizing now the rock is local fauna,
And sensing its need for survival,
In these inhospitable, dry surroundings,
Which lacks water and vegetation for miles,
I race inside the cabin,
And retrieve water and fruits.

The weathered, leather being,
Made older and worn,
By dust and sand,
Stops.
Drinks and eats its fill,
And in the blink of an eye continues.

I don't know where it came from.
I don't know where it goes.
I don't understand its haste!
We met once in a desolate land.
We shared a moment of ourselves.
We made a difference in our lives.

Vietnam Veteran
(Viet Vet)

Late at night,
Trying to sleep.
I toss and turn,
I sweat and tremble cold.
As wind and rain and thunder,
Tremble wet and cold,
Against my roof,
…And windowpanes.

I hear the muffled,
Grating, shuffle made,
By leather boots!
The slap, slap, slapping,
Of rifle slings!
Snare drums!
Keeping cadence,
Marking time.

Late at night,
I wake from sleep,
I pull the covers,
I warm my feet.
I hear the choppers,
I smell the jungle steam.
The faces I see,
The names I have lost!
I toss and turn,
I sweat and tremble cold.

Crunch, crunch,
Crunching on!
Singing in unison,
Chanting on!
Marching, marching,
Running on!
Youth and hope,
And dreams!

Innocence, and strength,
And courage!
Dropping off, mile-by-mile,
Day-by-day!

Late at night...!
Trying to sleep.
Snare drums!
And marching music.
Memories of a bonding past!
A hand extended,
An encouragement voiced!
A memory,
Of life, and death!
Alive in me!
Unshared!

Yesterday, I Thought I Saw You...

Yesterday...,
In the mall,
I thought I saw you!
I turned my head...,
...and in the crowd,
I saw your hair!

Yesterday...,
Among the crowd,
I saw your shoulders turn!
It was your gait...,
That caught my eyes,
...and turned my head!

It could not be true...
I KNEW!
But I hurried-up...,
To see your face!
To make sure!
To see your eyes...

I hurried!
I strained to look...,
I still knew!
But just in case,
I tried to see...,
Your smile and deep blue eyes!

I strained,
Through the crowd.
I caught-up with you!
I craned my neck...
Such hard eyes!
Such chiseled smile!

Today,
At the restaurant…
I looked-up.
I thought I saw you…
At the bar…
I did not look back.

As Time Escapes

At 94 years of age,
He stood before a headstone.
"Born: 1947, Died: 1972."
"How fast time flies!"

The double Headstone
Announced: "Husband and Wife,"
66 and 60 years, respectively…
"Not enough time!"

It was not bigger than a brick.
A young Soldier's name,
    And dates engraved in it,
The grass hugged it.
"Where did time go?"

A beautiful guardian angel,
Embraced the headstone.
My name was missing the dates….
"I will join you soon…"

Fathomless Blue Eyes

A fathomless pond,
Mirrors,
The light blue sky.
And at its border,
I stand!
Looking....

Looking!
Held transfixed,
By the fathomless depth!
As I look into,
The light blue,
Of your eyes!

Fathomless!
Fathomless, light blue eyes.
That beckon me,
Holding me transfixed.
Drawing me,
To their depth!

Conscience...,
I am deaf!
Intellect...,
I answer to instinct!
In utter disregard for convention,
I drown!
In fathomless,
Delightful blue!

David Anthony Sam

A Matter of Gravity

The weight is borne in the bone,
suspending us above the hard
center which draws us down.

We walk by stepping forward
into our falling, catching
ourselves in time, stepping on

the roundness of a space
which curves us into itself,
desiring reunion in dust.

The equation may be calculated
in a mathematics of distance,
mass, and the absolute unseen.

We are worn like the wind
grinding time against stone,
sculpted towards dissolution.

It is a heavy matter to rise daily
against the pull, and in that
resistance, define ourselves.

Originally published in *Blue Heron Review*

Fatherhood

There was the valley,
the Youghiogheny cutting
through rounded mountains,
the red clay my father dug
with pickax and shovel
to force a home from
the grudging hillside.

The time was new, the clay
dark red with iron,
the wind warm enough
for summer, but not so
hot you'd think of death.
My father grunted with
each heft and swing.

He sculpted that clay
with the same careful
touch he used when he
etched our busts in
redwood. He showed me
the meaning of the red clay,
the river in the valley

cleft, the rounded mountains.
He showed me the tracks
of the deer, the shy brown
flash of doe between
green undergrowth. He
showed me how to find
wild onions by their

leaves, and how to
recognize wild cherry
trees by their black
bark and sweet sap.
And with the sunburnt sweat
of his rippling back,
and with each heft and swing,

he showed me how to cut
a home from a red hillside.
So with a shaping word
I have tried to hew
a human place from high sun
and the hunger within
the world's rich clay.

Originally published in *The Wayne Review*

Above Emile Creek

The old valley
      the sandstone rocks
            in the black loam

like valuable ore
      on the steep hillside
            the clambering boy

getting the black loam
      under his fingernails
            scrabbling up the hill

to grab the cut wild
      grapevine as thick
            as his wrist to swing

full of wild free across
      the creek above skitterings
            of salamanders and

crawfish and echoes
      of joyful hillside
            landing on the other

bank full of wisdom

Originally Published in *FLARE: The Flagler Review*

DAVID ANTHONY SAM

Treehouse Summer

In a warm treehouse summer when one world
of hills and muddy creeks gave way to another
world flat and filled with meandering old water,
he rode the black Ford station wagon between
states in the company only of his father.

They stayed in Flat Rock, named for the flat stone
where canoes and river barges once beached
from the Huron River just upstream from its mouth
into the larger Detroit. They stayed with his father's
sister and her husband and his cousin for one summer.

There he made two brief friends, and found they
too were builders of treehouses. He was the one
to use the blue-lined notebook paper to draw
with his messy hand a plan to take the abandoned
wood from a construction site and raise it towards heaven.
They three assembled the scraps of boards with bent
and rusting nails scavenged from a derelict shed
found in the copse of trees, owner unknown.

In that same school notebook, he cobbled pieces of his
boyhood imaginings and dark dreams gleaned from
the black and white Sci-fi movies he'd seen while still
in Pennsylvania. He nailed the pieces of his stories
together with pens and fingers full of a boy's hopes.

Both the treehouse and the notebooks are long lost.
The trees have been felled for some larger subdivision,
the treehouse dashed by progress, rotted by gravity

to the ground below. His aunt and uncle, his father
and mother now all dead. And still he scribbles dreams
on trees, assembles houses to reach skyward,
and calls it all from silence just before he sleeps.

Originally Published in *From the Depths*

In a Winter of Ice and Stars

I weigh the seasons of my madness,
my circles around the wrong lake,
my deepest footprints just shadows in snow,
in a winter of ice and stars.

Just one place to fold time
for a few moments in the universe,
I am one winter walk beside a frozen lake
in this season of ice and stars.

I pull against my own atoms,
my weak force, my strong force, my gravity--
masks I wear when laughter falters
             in a falling of ice and stars.

I try myself and weigh all evidence in
brittle choices that crunch the snow
under my feet. Resolved: my singularity
under the wisdom of ice and stars.

Originally published in *Hurricane Review*

DAVID ANTHONY SAM

He Reconciles the Scientist and Poet

Bent on quarks and omega mini,
eyed by the cosmic bits
that you eye on a photoplate
[spy into infinity),
you might deceive yourself.

Breaking worlds into worlds,
banging clocks together
in infernal time till
the gears spill
like guts in streaks of white,
you might spy yourself
peering back; or
spin a beam
around the rim of universe
and see the back of your own head
bent over a retreating horizon.

Backed inside the whirling particles,
you watch your watching in a gas darkly.
Each time you break
something, it only makes something,
and the journey spills your guts
like gears,
and tells you stories
in different words.
You might receive yourself
coming back another way.

Originally published in *Great River Review*

Ex-voto

"I saw that words grouped a certain way
made it possible to live without
the things they described."
  •   *Adélia Prado*

What do I have worthy
offering the all that is
the interweaving emergent one
the multiplicity of its examples?

I have no boat to draw drydock
and leave before the waves
as surrender.

No painting because I have
no hand that can brush
color from unimagined
daydreams.

No cane or crutch to prop
against the altar of death
in thanks for being lame.

No charm or bit of gold,
no amulet or cameo pin,
no bone cross or stone ankh.

I have no chalice to exile
from my lips so wine there
transubstantiates to air
and dregs the color of dried blood.

No fisher's lure, ballcap,

communion dress or artifact
from the dear dead
to leave behind with my memory.

The most blessed thing I can
abandon here
is this offering of words
that no one values much
but are my flesh made syllable
from old clay and water
mixed briefly to be me
in the time of sentence end.

And, forgive this lessening of couplet
maimed by absence of due rhyme.

Originally Published in *The Crucible*

In Any Season

Trout--- rainbow; bass--- small or large
mouth; pike, walleye, and bluegill;
he fishes them all from their water
in or out of season. He stands above
them on the dock, at the shore,
careful that the sun not shadow him
across early water. He baits hooks,
selects lures. He wades into running
streams with hand-woven flies and casts
loops of line into the very spot
where the trout mouths bubbles, waiting.
He walks on ice, cuts two holes,

202

drops a tripline into each and waits
in winter winds for a bell to ring,
signaling. And when the fish is beached,
panting on the sand, pulled into the boat,
netted from the stream, lying on the ice,
he slips the steel loop through its gills,
out its lipless mouth, and snaps it shut.

In every season, under any sky,
he passionlessly pulls fish from
their water, locks them by the gills,
and lets them down in the clear air
he himself must breathe. He may admire
the silvered flesh, the arc into the air,
the splash of red-stained water at sunset,
the tug of line, the whiz of reel,
the fight of fish into the straining net.
But--- pike or trout, bass or salmon,
muskie, perch or bluegill--- he pans
them all like gold from the rushing
of water. He pans them all in butter
above the snapping fire. He builds
his flesh from the meat of fish
dragged stupid but magnificent from
the cool dark shallows. He touches
the hook to his thumb, brings out a bead
of red, and tastes fish blood in his.

Originally Published in *Great River Review*

DAVID ANTHONY SAM

The Work of the Body

Breathe into the pain, she said.
Our muscles tend to gain our losses
and remember. That must explain
those places where death has entered
and remains. How the touch into
a certain tenderness brings forth
the hidden sorrow. How sorrows
gather in knots and ache themselves
to our dull awareness when we
seek to fall asleep after long days.

Breathe in the pain, locate yourself
there where a father passed and left
his memory in your sinew, a mother
held her last word into the story
she inscribed in fasciae, where long
ago a dog died into the joint he
jammed while dragging you down
stairs to his daily run along alleys.
Our muscles contain our lives, make
power from our memories, walk us.

The work the body does is more than
what the physicist makes formula,
more than what the anatomist
describes. The body etches biography
into our bones, leaves indentations
and striations in the hard remnants
that abandon us at our own dying.
Breathe with the pain, she said; know
it and become it and it remains, no
longer minding our exhaling here.

(Originally published in *Touch: The Journal of Healing*)

Suzanne Shelton

Chair Time

They call it "chair time".
Rows and rows of recliners,
IV poles, dressing carts and
some bedside tables.
The mood is somber.
Pale faces, head scarfs, wigs,
supportive family members and friends.
Nurses carrying IV bags of "the hopeful cure".
Occasional laughing and " what's your name
and date of birth?" Doctors walking briskly
in and out the treatment area. Alarms sounding,
IV rates and tubing adjusted. Idle hushed chatter,
blankets offered, some people reading or sleeping.

They call it "chair time". Will it be over soon?
Will this "chair time" work? The Oncology team
educates and works with a positive approach.
However only the "higher power" knows the outcome.

They call it "chair time".
Prayer, strength and trust
can help lead to cure.

I know. I have done "chair time".
I am so thankful for the Oncology team
that helped me believe.
I am so thankful for the professional support.
God Bless all of you.
What you do matters.

Elizabeth Spencer Spragins

Dawn Chorus   (after Emily Dickinson)

a soft grace note falls
deep within this well of dark
where music echoes
arias and dirges blend
as hope unfolds her feathers

First published in *Page & Spine: A Weekly Literary Magazine*, 11 March 2022. Web.

Vespers

the slant of twilight
burnishes a chapel bell—
daylilies trumpet
names on broken headstones
to an empty gravel road

First published untitled in *Skylark: A Tanka Journal*, vol. 5, no. 1 (Summer 2017): 59. Edited by Claire Everett. Northallerton, England: Skylark Publishing. Print.

Slave Cemetery

anguish overflows
levees lined with unbleached bones—
a channeled fury
gathers silt of centuries
and the river roars their names

First published in *Writers Resist*, Issue 136 (23 June 2022). Web. https://www.writersresist.com/2022/06/23/slave-cemetery/.

Heirloom Roses

an untended rose
clambers over rustic rails
where cedar splinters
daughters of forgotten blooms
find a foothold in the sky

First published in *Freedom-Rapture: Black Bough Poetry*. Ed. by Matthew M. C. Smith. Swansea, Wales: Black Bough Poetry, July 2021, p. 41. Print.

Latticework Pie

granny smith apples
nestle deep within their crust
a perfect circle
as I hold the knotted hands
that held my heart in childhood

First published in *Founder's Favourites*, no. 2 (Jan. 2018): 5. Edited by Monique Berry. Ontario, Canada. Web.

Heirlooms

Richard Collins whipped out a business card and flashed his perfect teeth. "Our offer for your land still stands. We would have demolished the house, anyway."

Ava MacGregor's scarred boot stirred the ashes of her front porch. Her eyes followed the child scampering among the skeletons of heirloom fruit trees.

"Gramma, I found apples in the orchard! The rotten ones had yellow jackets on them, so I had to be careful." Six-year-old Isla beamed as she hefted a tote bag from the scorched grass. "I'll help you plant the seeds."

Ava gestured with her chin. "There's your answer, Mr. Collins."

First published in *Terrain.org*, 26 May 2022. Web. https://www.terrain.org/2022/fiction/heirlooms/.

Opening Night

behind black curtains
robins tune the orchestra—
a song without shape
gathers notes that flood the night
and breach the dam of darkness

Songs of the Southern Rim

Quiet calls
From the corners of these walls
As a frosted sun descends
And lends flame to painted halls.

Raven wings
Whisper when the canyon sings
Lullabies of lavender
On her harp of piñon strings—

Grace note soars!
Condors row on silent oars,
Ferry cargo of my dreams
Over streams to heaven's shores

As dusk falls.
One last breath—the warm wind stalls
Just before the daylight dies.
Red rock sighs and quiet calls.

~Grand Canyon Village, Arizona

Notes: During daylight hours, differences in temperature generate air currents within the Grand Canyon. Local lore holds that at nightfall, when warm air rises and cooler air sinks for the final time, the canyon breathes its "last breath of the day."

First published in *Time of Singing*, Vol. 47, No. 2 (Summer 2020)

At the Rio Grande

No one stands by the empty grave
Reserved for bones I could not save
From the maw of a hungry wave.

My brother chose to stand and fight.
He uncovered the graft and blight
And took up his pen, dared to write
A truth that they never forgave.

Our father was the first to die.
They claimed that those who vilify
The state must pay for every lie
With lives of loved ones prone to rave.

That night my mother disappeared.
A neighbor said that blood was smeared
Across the steps, and when she peered
Inside she saw a broken stave.

We fled on foot and left no trace.
By day we slept in sacred space;
At dusk we left our hiding place
In search of rectory or nave.

We crossed the river at high tide.
My brother carried me astride
But could not reach the other side.
I mourn the man and what he gave.

First published in the *MacGuffin*, vol. 36, no. 3 (Fall 2020): 132.
Print.

Shades of Loch Ness

Beneath the waters dark and deep
The bones of clansmen stir from sleep,
Rise from spell-bound bed.
Magic calls the dead—
Runes are read:
Castle keep

Will crumble into hatred's hand
If fear can forge the sword you banned.
Long-forgotten lore
Holds the oath you swore
When peace tore:
To command

That children study music, art,
And deeper matters of the heart;
That dirk and crossbow
Never cripple foe;
That none throw
Spiteful dart.

Since tapestries of peace will fray
If glory rests in tombs of clay,
The dead haunt the heir
Of a dragon's lair—
Dreams sail where
Dark meets day.

~Loch Ness, Scotland

Notes: The legend of Nessie, the Loch Ness Monster, has persisted for more than 1500 years. Ancient lore proclaimed her a water horse, a mythical creature that lured its victims into the depths and then devoured them. Modern sightings are suggestive of a large reptile. Despite numerous attempts to document Nessie's existence through photographs, film, and even sonar, definitive evidence has not emerged. First published in the *Lyric*, vol. 99, no. 1 (Winter 2019): 5. Print.

Curse of the Canyon

The old ones listen for the sound
Of life within this painted ground.
Spellbound creatures in tableau

Were once a race seduced by greed.
They hoarded every nut and seed
With no thought to feed the crow

Or leave a single prickly pear
For Sister Deer or Brother Bear.
With no care for earth below

Their feet, the Legend People preened
And strutted while the hungry keened
Or gleaned in vain where rocks grow.

Coyote, in the guise of friend,
Prepared a feast, bid foes attend,
Penned them there, and struck his blow.

The Trickster turned them into stone
That desert winds harass and hone.
Day fire sets their bones aglow.

Their eyes are blind; their tongues are mute;
But when the night wind plays her flute,
Paiute hear a moan pitched low.

~Bryce Canyon, Utah

Notes: According to Paiute tradition, the greedy Legend People once inhabited Bryce Canyon. Coyote, who oversaw the land, decided to punish them. He lured them to a great feast and then cursed them, turning them to stone. First published in *Parabnormal Magazine*, Vol. 2, Issue 2 (June 2020): 80. Print.

Eilean Munde

The Highland mist conceals a sacred isle
Where green of moss embraces gray of stone
That marks the grave of one who fell to guile
Of clansmen who betrayed him to the throne.

In life he donned the mantle of a laird
And rested hand on hilt of sword or dirk
But slept unarmed by winter hearth he shared
With those who broke his bread and shamed the kirk.

The daughters of the dead succumbed to snow
And prayed with frozen lips for shelter's grace.
At death's approach they glimpsed a jeweled bow
That bridged the clouds from loch to holy place.

But duty tethered falcons to the wrist,
And souls foreswore the sunrise for the mist.

~Loch Leven, Scotland

Notes: Graveyard Island, a burial ground for several Scottish clans (including the MacDonalds), is located on Loch Leven.

In 1690 William of Orange defeated James VII of Scotland at the Battle of the Boyne. To erode any remaining support for the Stuart (Jacobite) cause, King William offered to pardon rebels who swore allegiance to him by New Year's Day of 1692. Delayed by a snowstorm, the Laird of the MacDonalds of Glencoe did not swear fealty promptly. When the king's men (under Robert Campbell) subsequently requested shelter from the laird, he welcomed them as guests. The soldiers enjoyed his hospitality for several days and then rose up against their host before dawn on February 13, 1692. Thirty-eight MacDonalds, including their chief, died in what came to be known as the Massacre of Glencoe. Dozens of women and children died of exposure when they fled their burning homes.

First published in *Glass: Facets of Poetry*, no. 4 (Apr. 2017): 13. Print.

A Two-Minute Tale

"Time's up." Rosemary McCay tapped the bathroom door.

"Don't come in," Dillon shrieked.

Shaking her head, his new foster mother trotted down the hall to answer the call of the tea kettle.

A tuneless whistle on the porch announced her husband's arrival. After wiping his boots on the mat, Miles strode in and washed his hands at the kitchen sink. "I was listening to the radio in the barn, and the forecast isn't good. The Patawasket Dam is at capacity, and the river's expected to crest this afternoon."

Rosemary shoveled scrambled eggs onto a chipped stoneware platter. "Will we have to evacuate?" When the toaster popped, she snatched two pieces of whole wheat and added them to a growing stack.

"Maybe. Maybe not. Breakfast first." He grinned, circled an arm around her waist, and dipped her back for a long kiss. Rosemary tapped his shoulder when Dillon appeared in the doorway. Her partner released her with a blush that matched the boy's. Miles slid into the nearest ladder-back chair and Dillon followed suit.

"The tractor will never make it through the mire, so I thought I'd spend the day cleaning tools. Dillon, I'd welcome your help."

The child stopped nibbling the crust from his toast and tucked his chin. "Sure," he mumbled. When Rosemary parked the bacon on the table, his nose wrinkled. "Excuse me. Forgot my watch. Be right back."

Miles snared two strips and attacked his plate with the determination of a starving man.

"I'm worried about Dillon," Rosemary whispered. "We've fostered lots of kids who had issues, but he takes anxiety to a whole new level. Maybe he's afraid we can't afford to keep him. He won't shower unless I set a timer for two minutes. And what nine-year-old kid turns down an offer of cookies and milk at bedtime?"

"We've only had him a week. He's just skittish. Give him time." Miles squeezed her hand and nibbled her ear. "Nobody can resist the charms of Rosemary McCay for long."

A door slammed in the back of the house. "Shh. He's coming."

As the child trudged into the kitchen, he glanced out the window and turned as pale as the ivory sheers. "The river's flooded," he whimpered. "It's covered the boxwoods."

Miles leaped to his feet and yanked the curtains back. "Looks like we're surrounded." The two adults exchanged glances.

When the air conditioner clunked into silence, Rosemary's calm voice filled the void. "Dillon, please stuff this towel under the door to the porch. Miles, could you kill the electricity from the circuit-breaker panel box?"

By the time Dillon wedged the towel under the door, water was flowing over the threshold. The sodden cloth slipped through his fingers and lodged against a table leg. He jumped onto a chair and stared at the incoming tide.

Grim-faced, Miles sloshed out of the utility room. "Rosemary, hold the step ladder for me, would you?" Hooking a hammer into his belt, he scrambled up. "I'm going to knock out the skylight so we can climb onto the roof. Everybody look down and close your eyes." Six hard blows brought the morning mist within reach. Rosemary tossed him her apron, and he draped it over the frame as protection from shards.

"Rosemary, you first so you can pull Dillon up."

His wife's ballet flats danced up the rungs and disappeared. "Ready."

"Dillon, it'll be easier if you take off your flip-flops."

Wide-eyed, the boy shook his head. "I can't get my feet wet."

Miles took a deep breath and gritted his teeth. "Right. Up you go." Rosemary reached down and tugged the child's thin body through the opening.

"Coming aboard." The ladder wobbled, and Miles fought for balance as he heaved himself over the edge. Plopping down with a grunt, he wiped a bloody hand on his shirt. "Good thing this old house has eight-foot ceilings. Any higher and we wouldn't have made it." He surveyed the lake that covered the farm. "I think we can take the apple harvest off the calendar." The arms of submerged trees waved in agreement.

Dillon stood up and shuffled toward the chimney. "Careful, son. It's slick," his foster father warned. When the boy hesitated, his flip-flops lost purchase on the tiles. Miles' wounded hand shot out and clutched nothing but air. The child tumbled over the edge and disappeared in the murky water.

The McCays locked eyes across the hole in their home. Rosemary spoke with the cool demeanor of a general. "I've got this."

"I know you do. Wish I could swim." He forced a smile.

Rosemary kicked off her shoes and executed a back roll into the flood.

Riding the current downstream, she scanned for Dillon's crimson T-shirt. A minute passed, then two. Rosemary's sense of smell sharpened as she reclaimed her place in the water. She homed in on the scents of fear, despair, and . . . seaweed. *Ah, child, why didn't you tell me?* Whipping past the hedgerow that bordered the orchard, she spotted the boy beneath her. The shrubbery had slowed the waters here.

Rosemary swam into a tree's embrace and perched on one of its branches. Cupping her hands around her mouth, she called down. "Dillon, can you hear me?"

He didn't raise his head. "You have some sort of underwater megaphone?"

"Nope. Don't need one."

"Well, now that you know what I am, you can go away and leave me alone."

Rosemary's eyes caressed his hair, drifted down his torso, and settled on his tail. "You're a member of our family. That's who you are. Look up, Dillon."

When he did so, his jaw dropped. "You're a mermaid!"

She waggled her tail. "We merpeople have to stick together. Let's go back. Miles will be worried."

"But he'll see this!" Dillon thrashed the aqua appendage below his waist.

Rosemary grinned. "Nothing fazes Miles. He changed our daughters' diapers. Their tails were turquoise striped. Time to go home, little merman."

First published in *Ligonier Valley Writers 2022 Flash Fiction Contest Winners*. Ligonier Valley, PA: 27 Oct. 2022. Web. https://www.lvwonline.org/past-winners.

The Dissident

Sleepless eyes
Stare, unblinking, at black skies,
Sweep the corners of the night,
And alight where rebels rise.

Words inflame
Dissidents they vowed to tame.
Armed with rage, the censors took
All the books that bore my name

And burned them.
Torching leaves without the stem
Was futile. I slipped away,
Praying courts would not condemn

My loved ones.
Those fears never fed on guns.
Weapons targeted my wife;
My life bought hers— and our son's.

In this cell
I endure a hidden hell.
Broken bones and bruises heal:
Time steals truth my wounds would tell.

I am cold.
Blankets reek of mice and mold,
But sagging spirits rise when
Unpenned hopes my fingers hold

Meet the page.
Papers that you smuggle wage
War from bases underground:
Unbound books escape this cage.

We must part.
Thank you for your faithful heart.
These walls weaken every year,
But I fear the poisoned dart.

Please erase
Every footprint, leave no trace—
Watchers lie in wait. They seek
All who speak to power's face.

Darkness dies—
Dawn's caresses tantalize
My shackled limbs. Friend, take care
Not to stare at sleepless eyes.

Stephen Spratt

Hurricane Ian

Hurricane Ian was the deadliest hurricane to strike the state of Florida since 1935. It became a high-end Cat. 4 hurricane on Sept. 28, just before hitting FL slightly north of Fort Myers Beach. It has tied with several other storms, becoming the 5th strongest hurricane on record to hit the US mainland.

There were 146 casualties in FL. and damage estimates exceed $50 billion. The 10' to 15' storm surge flooded at least the first floor of every building on Fort Myers Beach where my brother Rob lived. Sixty-one deaths occurred in Lee County where FMB is located. In Lee County alone, there was minor damage to 16,314 structures, plus major damage to 14,245, and 5,369 were total losses.

So, just how strong is the wind in a Cat 4 hurricane? We had a high wind event of around 50+ miles per hour in Fredericksburg in

June, 2022 that blew out many branches and toppled several large trees. Add 100 MPH and you get a wind that is strong enough to blow over an elephant...

...and blow the blades off a ceiling fan.

My brother Rob's house is located on the sound side of Fort Myers Beach, which is a barrier island about ½ mile wide at that point. In this picture taken by a neighbor across the street in a 2-story house,

Rob's house is the one behind the telephone pole. The debris from the beach front houses destroyed by the 20' waves, flows by in the strong current. The water is about 4' to 5'deep on the houses and only got another 1' to 2' higher. Rob's cinder block house was built in 1965 and had never flooded before. His trailer, used for storage, floated over and ended up on top of his Camry. The cab of his black Ford Explorer in the driveway is barely visible close to the front of the house. The force of the current and debris burst in the front door and the upper sash of one window behind the tree. Very few items, once soaked with seawater, were salvageable. Rob dejectedly observed, "Now I know what it feels like to be homeless."

It was a week or two before anyone was allowed on the island. Rob, his wife and two teenage granddaughters moved in with Gail's 93-year-old father Calvin, whose trailer was located inland not far away, but not badly damaged. A tremendous amount of debris ended up in Rob's front yard.

Rob received an insurance payment from GEICO for the underwater vehicles and they were towed away. FEMA set up an impressive debris removal program that cleared his front yard and continued picking up piles of trash every day. By Oct 28, there were

125 debris removal trucks with a grapple plus a trailer doubling the load capacity to a maximum of 80 cubic yards, that worked 7 days a

week. As of 11-14-22, 3 million cubic yards of debris had been collected from Lee County, and there's a lot more to go. That's equal to 78 football fields filled 18' deep.

Much of the debris has been dumped temporarily in an open area just south of Fort Myers Beach on Lovers Key. At this enormous dump site, scaffold platforms were set up for FEMA employees to look down into the back of the double debris-removing trucks and visually estimate how many cubic yards are in each truck. The owners are paid $50 per cubic yard by FEMA. Multiplied by 60 to 80 cubic yards, that's $3000 to $4000 per trip to empty the debris in the temporary pile. These trucks don't have a dump mechanism; both truck and trailer are unloaded with the same grapple that loaded them- -one bucket at a time.

These giant piles of debris are later loaded into open 100 cubic yard dump trailers and hauled to a nearby landfill. The closest landfill is 3 miles away, but may not be able to handle 10 million cubic yards of debris. The next landfill is 50 miles away. The Lee County board of Commissioners voted just before Thanksgiving to increase the amount paid per mile for these huge dump trailer trucks from $5 per mile to $40 per mile. That's an 8 times increase! While $5 per mile is low, $40 per mile is high. The rate increase will end up costing taxpayers millions of dollars in added fees if the debris has to be hauled to the next nearest dump 50 miles away. FEMA will likely pick up the bill (i.e., future taxpayers including us). The commissioners and the hauling company (Crowder Gulf) declined to talk to interviewers.

Because Fort Myers Beach was on the right-hand side of Ian's counter clockwise spin, the Cat. 4 (140+) winds pushed 10' to 15' of sea water onto that section of the coast. Luckily, Rob's home was on the back side of the island with no waves like the giant ones that destroyed many beachfront homes on the Gulf side of the island. However, the 6' of seawater that flowed inside the house ruined almost all of their possessions.

Rob's wife Gail was particularly distressed that her recently deceased mother Sylvia's ashes were on a table in the bedroom.

Incredibly, the table floated up to the ceiling and down again

without spilling Sylvia's ashes. Sylvia never did like to get her face wet in the ocean and even outlasted Hurricane Ian.

Rob did a great job removing all the rest of their   possessions with some hired help. There was a very slippery thick layer of mud covering everything.

The interior debris was placed next to the road with all the debris that washed into their front yard. FEMA contractors hauled everything away with their grapple trucks. Next, Rob had to get the sheetrock removed from the walls and kitchen ceiling and let things dry out. It had started to get moldy, so they sprayed for mold.

When my sister Sarah and I got there on Nov. 3, the house was clean, wide open inside and dry. The concrete floors were topped with Terrazzo and Rob power washed them. He had a structural engineer certify that the house was structurally sound and an electrical expert said everything that was underwater had to be replaced, even the wire. That was Sarah's and my job. Sarah is 8 years younger and enthusiastic with lots of energy. She worked cleaning the yard that first day while I figured out the best way to attach a plastic box to the cinder block walls that had ¾" furring strips. Rob didn't want to knock holes in the cinder block for every box or pad out all the exterior walls. So, we used thin electrical boxes attached with plastic

anchors and screws. Once the procedure was established, Sarah removed the existing metal boxes and wires. She then attached the new boxes and pulled new wire which I had brought from Fredericksburg in Sarah's trailer. I spent the next several days identifying each circuit in the old panel box.

Sarah and I slept one night in the trailer park and then one night on cots at the beach house with no lights or plumbing. We alternated between the beach house and the trailer after that. We used Sarah's Porta-Potty under Rob's gazebo which survived the hurricane. Sarah used the portable shower she brought under the gazebo and a full moon one warm night. I guess the neighbors might have seen two full moons that night.

Rob got his electrician JB, who was very busy, to install a new meter base with a 200-amp disconnect on Friday, Nov.4th. JB inspected what we had done so far and OK'd it enough to call Florida Gas and Electric to hook the house up to electric power, which they did on Tues Nov 8th. That gave us one outside outlet we could use without activating the new 200-amp 40 space panel box. I also installed a new front door and frame to replace the one that burst in.

We brought the new door from Fredericksburg, tied on top of my Chevy Equinox. I started installing the new 200-amp main panel box on Monday, Nov. 7 and after stripping a screw, got the feed wires hooked up on Tuesday. Sarah flew back to Fredericksburg on Thursday, Nov. 10th as she still had a business to run.

While Sarah and I were working on the electric, Rob tackled his pool, which was full of nasty water and mud. He told us about the 16" Grouper and dead bird he had pulled out of the black water earlier. Rob bought two 1" electric sump pumps which ran on the generator that his daughter Kim had brought to the house shortly after the hurricane. It took a couple of days to pump out the pool and Rob worked on scooping out the mud as the water went

down. He finally got the last bit out, but the mud had left a dark stain on the pool, even after pressure washing. A spray of half chlorine and half water made it a lot cleaner and he started refilling the pool.

Rob kept the chlorine strong and the filled pool looked great. A "contractor" had offered to clean a neighbor's similar pool for $11,000.

Unfortunately, the Spratt's cat Sophie, was left at the house on the night of the evacuation. Rob rode a bicycle to the house two days later and saw no sign of the cat. They were not allowed on the island again until 12 days after the storm. Not much chance of anything surviving that long with no food, especially a house cat that was skinny to start with. On that visit 12 days after the storm, Rob saw

some tracks in the mud that could be a cat. Was Sophie still alive? Claire looked around back under the shed where the cat sometimes went and Sophie popped out. How did she survive the tidal surge and then no food for almost 2 weeks? Must have used up most of her 9 lives, but she sure didn't gain any weight.

On Nov. 17, we had the inside lights working in all the rooms except the Lanai. Rob took a picture and it was encouraging to the family, 7 weeks after the hurricane.

Elizabeth (Liz) Talbot

COVID-free Paradise

It was two years since COVID-19 had shut down the world. My husband and I had longed to travel overseas, but there was one requirement that we feared the most.

We would have to test negative for COVID before being allowed to return to the United States.

Several months earlier, we had gotten the three am in the morning call from our daughter who had been visiting Ireland. "Mommy, I tested positive for COVID and I can't go home!"

We couldn't do much for her. She was forced to isolate herself for a week in an airport hotel until she produced a negative test.

"It says here we wouldn't need a test to go back to the states," my husband said as he pointed to his laptop.

"What country is that?" I ask.

"The Virgin Islands, a U.S. territory," my husband replied.

"There's gotta be a catch somewhere.:

"You just have to test negative three days before your departure date," he explained. It couldn't be any old test off the drugstore shelf. We got ours from one of those Minute Clinics after complaining about the "sniffles." My husband then entered the results on a website provided by the Virgin Islands territorial government and we were good to go.

We had everything planned out. We'd fly to St. Croix and stay at a resort on the north coast for several days and then transfer to a hotel in Christiansted, the main city, for the rest of the stay. And then we would squeeze in an overnight visit to St. Thomas where my husband's fraternity brother now lived.

After landing at the airport, a National Guardsman inspected my COVID-19 vaccination card before waving me on. They are stationed everywhere in the airport.

230

"Why are they here?" I ask, "Is something going on we don't know about?"

My husband shrugs, "Maybe it has something to do with the hurricane last fall."

"This is February," I reminded him. Another Guardsman directs us over to the car rental desk across the parking lot. After signing the necessary paperwork, the attendant hands over the keys. "Now remember, drive on the left side of the road."

I can't fathom why car rental companies still rent cars to mainland tourists. My husband and I had agreed beforehand that I would be the driver since I am left handed (at least in some things) and better able to adjust. Without knowing anything about where we're going, we head for the east-west road linking the two major cities of St. Croix, Fredericksted and Christiansted.

We were supposed to get phone service on the island, but for some reason, my phone's GPS then decided to go on vacation. We know the resort is on the north coast, but we cannot find the road north. After an hour of indecisive driving, we finally waved down a highway patrolman who showed us the road to the resort. It was a narrow two lane road that twisted and turned through fields and jungle until we arrived at the most astonishing vista, unspoiled by hotels or condos.

I am not mentioning the name of the resort which has received decidedly mixed online reviews. My husband assured me that the worst reviews could be attributed to the damage caused by last fall's hurricane and the damage had been repaired by now. But between the hurricane and COVID-19, he thought he had found a bargain.

I was glad to have arrived when there was still light, not wanting to have been caught on some curvy road in the dark. We were assigned a villa, with its own kitchenette and screened patio, except the screen was torn at the bottom corner.

"Honey, there's a hole down here. Aren't you a little concerned?"

He shrugged me off. "It's no big deal. What can possibly get through that little tear? Don't you hear the waves? There's not many hotel rooms where you can do that."

There's also the cacophony of sounds from the jungle, which can be unnerving, although one can simply turn up the TV. When we had pulled our luggage up the stairs and entered the room, a cat had been waiting for us. He was a domestic shorthair mix of stripes and white fur. The cat walked into the kitchenette, as though this was his home. I fed it some leftovers which I had found in the refrigerator before shooing him out. We hadn't been informed that each room came with a cat.

We would first lounge at the resort for a couple of days. Before leaving for our vacation, I had ordered snorkeling equipment, imagining that I would be able to snorkel at will off the coasts of St. Croix. During our honeymoon years before, we had gone snorkeling off St.Thomas for the first time and I had fallen in love with the shimmering fish and colorful corals and feeling at one with Nature. I tried out my equipment in the waters off the resort the next day, but the water appeared to be disturbed by some unseen force and I couldn't see much.

The day afterwards, we set out for Fredericksted, on the southwestern corner of the island, which promised good snorkeling near a gigantic pier where the cruise ships docked. On the way, we would visit a bar in the rainforest that featured beer drinking pigs. The road at first appeared to be well paved, but then began to deteriorate.

"You're not driving on the left side," my husband reminded me.

"I'm trying to avoid the potholes!"

It no longer mattered whether I was driving on the right or left hand on the road. Worse, the rainforest was pressing in on all sides.

"Did you turn on the correct road?" my husband asked.

"I thought so," I replied, "We should be going in the right direction."

Soon I am driving less than 20 miles per hour, trying to stay on any available pavement. The steering wheel jerks every time I inadvertently pass over a pothole.

"I hope we don't break the axle on this thing," my husband remarked..

"I'm sure triple A will make a visit to the rainforest," I deadpanned. If we could make a call on our cell phones in the first place. The thought must have crossed my mind that we could wind up as an item on the evening news back home. Couple from Virginia disappears in rainforest! Their empty rental car abandoned on the side of the road! Details at 11:00.

Thankfully, the forest thinned out and then a ship glided by, giving a surreal impression that it was traveling on land. Fredericksted had to be nearby. After parking, I rented a larger pair of fins, crossed the street, and lowered myself into the water near the pier. The water is comfortable, no wetsuit is required here. My husband headed for the bar.

Fortunately, no cruise ships were docking that day, although I had heard they had begun sailing again, though under more restrictions than before COVID. The water was calm and clear, with few fish. I could spot some sea turtles fifty feet away from me. I returned the fins and located my husband at the bar. After dressing, I visited the old fort, built by the Danish in the mid-1700s.

Before the U.S. had purchased the territory in 1917, which consisted of St. Croix, St. Thomas, and St. John, the islands had been ruled by Denmark. I can't wrap my mind around how one of the smallest countries in Europe aspired to a colonial empire in the Caribbean. Maybe they wanted in on the lucrative sugar trade. Abandoned sugar mills, aptly described as "upside down thimbles," still dot the countryside.

The governor general, Peter von Scholten, had declared immediate emancipation at the fort in 1848 to stem off a full blown slave revolt. The slave owners were infuriated at the sudden loss of their property, and he left the island after suffering a nervous breakdown.

We drove by some nice Victorian homes on the way back to the resort, but nothing historical, as most of the town was burned down in the "Great Burn" of 1875. Following the main road across the island, we stopped at a supermarket to pick up beer and chips, which has an excellent Latin food section to serve the large Hispanic population on St. Croix.

A supermarket display advertises the "Paqui Chip Challenge." "Please read this warning," reads the sign. The Paqui chip is a tortilla chip made with the Carolina reaper pepper, not intended for anyone sensitive to spicy foods or who is pregnant or has any medical condition. Keep out of the hands of children and wash hands after eating. Side effects include general discomfort, sweating, nausea, or vomiting.

Such a product would never be sold stateside. I'm thinking it would have been neat to bring a package back and place it in the break room of my former office. We had a tradition before the pandemic that every time one of us returned from vacation, a box of candy or salt water taffy from our destination would be left for our coworkers, as some kind of gratitude offering. I'm sure everyone would have been howling in laughter at such a product being marketed in a supermarket.

Because of the pandemic, my coworkers and I were forced from our offices and there is no word on our return. It may never happen. What will happen to the traditions and the customs we originated to make our work days more enjoyable?

I fall asleep immediately after a full day. My husband was sitting on the screened patio, enjoying the sound of the waves.

I feel a tickling. "Honey, I'm too sleepy," I murmur. My eyelids flutter open. He is not beside me. I know I felt something, and I can't just go back to sleep. I turn on the light and after leaving the bed, I find out he has fallen asleep on one of the rattan chairs on the patio.

I shake him awake. "Honey, something's in here. It woke me up."

"Whaaaa?"

I return to the bedroom and flip over the comforter. A small lizard darts out.

"Oh my God, it came in through the screen!"

I shoo it off the bed and into the kitchen. As soon as I open the door to leave it out, the cat rushes in. Now I figured out why every villa was assigned a cat. It immediately corners the lizard near the refrigerator before it decides to make its getaway into the stairwell. The cat follows in a hot pursuit. Now I wish I had picked up some kitty kibble at the supermarket as some kind of gratitude offering.

My husband is still rubbing his eyes when I shut the door. "That thing came in through the screen." I grab a pillow from the sofa and place it over the hole. There are not going to be any more nighttime visitors.

The time for our car rental is coming up soon, so the next day we plan to visit the most easternmost point of the territorial U.S. The GPS on my phone briefly revives and points us in the right direction. The rainforest recedes, replaced with chaparral and towering cacti. We reached the end of the road, where a Stonehenge type of monument was erected at the turn of the millennium.

The hill then makes a dramatic slope down into the waves, which we can hear up here. This is where the sun's rays first arrive every morning, as New York or Washington continue to slumber in the darkness.

There's an abandoned seaside hotel in the area which was the subject of a photo exhibit I saw somewhere. It opened to much promise and hope but had been plagued by litigation until its destruction by Hurricane Hugo in 1989. I've been haunted by the images of abandonment captured by the photographer and I would have gladly made the hike to see the ruins.

"Are you sure it's near here?" my husband asks.

"I think so," I reply.

"It's just a ruined hotel. We have to get the rental back to the airport."

We finally returned the rental, but not before I revert back to my right hand driving habits. Fortunately, there were no accidents, and we took a cab to Christiansted. Our hotel is not in Christiansted proper, but on

Protestant Cay, a four acre triangular island right 200 yards across the boardwalk from the King Christian hotel.

The island is so named because when St. Croix was under the rule of Catholic French kings of the late 1600s, burials of non-Catholics took place there as only Catholics could be buried on St. Croix. Unmindful of the Cay's history as a possible mass cemetery, we take the ferry across, consisting of a small boat ride of a few minutes.

The hotel has seen better days, because of the pandemic. A grand hall, once used for conventions, is vacant, with sheets draped over the furniture. Iguanas, the size of small dogs, scamper in and out of the drained pool. They peer into our rooms, as if trying to decide if they are worth a visit.

"Under no circumstances are we leaving the sliding door open," I warn my husband.

The next day we booked a charter to Buck Island Reef National Monument, which lies just off the coast. Most of the park lies submerged, the Holy Grail of snorkeling. While the sun is shining, there's a breeze from the north. The captain sets anchor and the snorkelers enter the ocean via a ladder set out by the crew.

I feel as though I am snorkeling in twilight. The light from above appears to be diffused even though the sun is shining. The coral is there and the fish swim by, but the colors appear to be muted. When we re-board, the crew passes around paper cups of rum punch.

"It was a little murky today," the captain admits, "You probably heard about that weather system up north. Sometimes it affects us down here as well."

After the snorkeling adventure, I set out on a stroll. The streets retain their names from the colonial era. Fisker Gade runs parallel to Bjerge Gade. A few buildings still display the Danish royal signia. Across from the old Danish Customs House stands the vacant Lutheran *Kirke,* awaiting the return of its Danish congregation. A monument to Peter Carl Limpricht in Danish stands in a nearby park. To the Crucians, he's probably as relevant today as an Egyptian pharoah.

A sign warns all visitors to wear a face mask at all times and sanitize their hands upon entering and exiting the park. This strikes me as a curious regulation since I cannot recall anyone who contracted COVID-19 in an open air park.

The city and harbor is guarded by Fort Christiansvaern, where Alexander Hamilton's mother, Rachel was incarcerated by her first husband, John Michael Lavien, for several months. The same Alexander Hamilton that inspired the Broadway blockbuster.

The site is normally staffed by the National Park Service, but no one is available due to COVID-19, at least according to a handwritten sign at the entrance. They did leave behind some displays to tell the story.

When she was released, she fled for St. Kitts. She returned to St. Croix with her son Alexander. They both contract yellow fever in February 1768. Alexander survived but Rachel died. Lavien made sure Alexander did not receive anything from his mother's estate.

While the Fort and the Danish custom house are well preserved, I notice that many buildings have been boarded up and left to the elements until a few arches remain standing against the sky.

I don't want to give the mistaken impression that Christiansted is crumbling into the harbor. There are many fine restaurants available in the old warehouses. In the morning, after being awakened by the sound of crowing, I take the boat over to have my coffee along the harbor. There I crumble part of my croissant on the sidewalk to attract nearby baby chicks as the mother hen pushes them on. I'm charmed, although I am not glad to be awakened at 5:00 am every morning by roosters.

One evening, we are dividing a sushi roll when the owner strolls over to start a conversation with us. A couple of decades ago, he was a resident of New Orleans. Now he regards himself as a permanent resident of St. Croix We bring up our plans to take the ferry to St. Thomas to visit my husband's fraternity brother. A look of horror strikes his face. "Not the ferry! Take the seaplane!" He's taken it many times to go to medical appointments on St. Thomas for only $99.

We've never seen one before, except in Tarzan movies. Now every morning and afternoon we see it take off and land across from our hotel. The next day, my husband goes to the office to inquire about fares.

"How much is it?" I ask.

"Two hundred each, if we leave today." He's clearly disappointed.

"I guess the closer you are to the departure date, the more they hike up the fare."

"What could be wrong with the ferry," my husband asks. "We're in the Caribbean. The water should be calm, the skies are sunny. It should only take an hour."

We walk over to the ferry and take our place in the open air section on top. A woman takes her seat a few rows behind us and eats her lunch out of a takeout container. The boat proceeds smoothly as the mountains of St. Croix recede.

The first warning is the sound of crashing waves. They rise higher and higher, causing small rivulets under my feet. They finally breach the rails, soaking us at intervals. The passenger who had been enjoying lunch behind us has long disappeared.

We retreat to the center of the deck, which is no guarantee of remaining dry. The water and wind work in tandem to chill us. How I regret leaving my parka back home. We'd like to go downstairs to escape, but fear slipping on the deck, which is wet by now. This journey has to be over soon.

Finally, the peaks of St. Thomas appear and the seas resume their placid appearance. I wonder if the extra clothing in my backpack has been soaked as well.

My husband's fraternity brother drives up in his SUV. "Welcome to St. Thomas." he greets us. We notice a plastic cup with fresh ice cubes in the cup holder near the driver seat. "Had to leave a reception early." There is no open container law in St. Thomas.

He drives us past the piers where the cruise ships had docked earlier, and the bars and souvenir stands that are now shuttered for the day. "There are parts of this island where I wouldn't be caught at night." Apparently there has been a change from the idyllic paradise where we honeymooned years ago. After a few minutes, he stops at a gated community and presents an ID to the security guard, who then waves us through..

Our hosts present us with dry shirts and towels. A hot shower had never felt so good. We go past the kitchen to the balcony, which opens over the bay. We're sipping our drinks and enjoying the view, when I suddenly realize what we're looking at.

"That island out there, isn't that Little St. James?"

"Oh, the island that Jeffrey Epstein owned," our host replies nonchalantly. "It's for sale now."

I recognize one of the buildings. Epstein, a notorious sex trafficker and pedophile, would fly his victims to the island where they would be unable to escape. No one living in the condo community where we're now staying knew what was taking place. Now they are reminded of Epstein and his crimes every time they look out the window.

We leave to have a substantial meal at the restaurant serving the community before we return to our host's balcony for more drinks. This time the island is shrouded by darkness and haze.

My husband's fraternity brother has lived on St. Thomas for almost two decades; even raised his youngest daughter there. Everyone has fantasized about living in the Caribbean but few realize the challenges. "Where did your daughter go to school?"

"Private school. You wouldn't want to send your kids to the public schools."

"What about travel teams?" I ask. "Did your daughter join one?"

"We'd just fly to St. Croix." St. Kitts, Puerto Rico, or Florida must have been too far away. The airfare must have been immense.

"What happened when the pandemic struck?"

He shrugs. "We stayed home for a few weeks and baked bread like everyone else."

He is calm, considering the fact that the hospitality industry he is employed in crashed during that time. He becomes more agitated when my husband mentions the hurricane.

"We had no electricity until December!"

"Wasn't the hurricane in September? How could you live for almost four months without electricity?" my husband asks.

His wife chimes in. "I returned to the mainland while my husband stayed to protect our property."

"Couldn't the government have done more?" I ask.

Our host makes a sardonic smile. "We're just a territory. They're not worried about us back in Washington." I couldn't imagine the condo's up to date appliances sitting silently for months on end. My husband and his friend stay up until 4:30 am catching up on old times while I sleep on a comfortable four poster bed.

The next morning we go down to the private beach while our host attends to some business. I can't think of many gated communities with such a wonderful beach. But I still can't take my eyes off LIttle St. James, lying beyond the cove. Would I have been willing to brave the currents and sharks to escape?

Our host returns to take us to the afternoon ferry. Before dropping us off, he tells us he's been thinking a lot about retirement lately. He's already living in a situation most retirees work and save for a lifetime. "Maybe I'll return to the states." We're shocked at this admission, but then he quickly adds, "I don't know if I can ever go back to driving on the right hand side of the road."

We're left at the dock where the return ferry waits. It's one deck and completely enclosed. "We won't get wet this time!" I exclaim. After downing a few rum punches at the bar, we're allowed to take our seats. I notice barf bags tucked in the pouch in front of each seat, just like the kind the airlines provide. "What are those for?" I ask, dismayed.

"Just in case," my husband reassures me.

The ferry sets out a normal pace and then suddenly goes full throttle into the open seas. It doesn't go over the waves, just through them. They react by thumping furiously against the sides of the ferryboat. A glance outside the porthole reminds me of what the view inside a washing machine must look like.

I bend down between my knees. "What's wrong?" my husband asks.

"I want to say motion sickness, but I'm not nauseated."

I wish I could just throw up, but it's not that simple. I'm simply in pain everywhere in my body. I mentally go over a checklist of the most painful situations I've found myself during my past life: toothache, falling off my sister's pony, my first hangover, childbirth, broken ankle. This ride doesn't compare with anything on the list.

"When will this be . . .over . . .with?" I croak. 1 try to shift positions in my seat, which doesn't give me any relief. No signs of land. Glancing across the aisle, a young man is curled up, asleep. What's his secret? I'm envious.

Someone cuts the engine and the boat glides into the harbor. "Am I going to need a stretcher?" I ask. My husband looks at me worried. He had bought travel insurance before the trip but hadn't anticipated using it.

The boat docks, and to my amazement, I am able to stand up and walk off the boat. My pain recedes and I feel normal.

We are enjoying our last night out on the harbor before returning home tomorrow. We've just polished off a platter of fish tacos at a dockside cafe when we notice a small crowd gathered near the dock. They're looking down, pointing in amazement.

"Look at the fish,"

I go over and there are fish over a yard long, floating just beneath the surface, unconcerned about the crowd hovering over them. They know they are in the safest place of the entire ecosystem. I didn't need to have invested in that snorkeling gear after all.

William T. Tang (Long Tang)

Winning

An arrow sailed through the air and struck the ground ten paces in front of them; a plume of bright red horse mane fluttered from the tail of its shaft. A cloud of dust billowed from a saddle between two hills, and a column of riders cantered into a line blocking the road. Two riders trotted out from the group in the lead.

Master Tim raised his hand and fired a whistling signal arrow into the air to alert the rest of the mercenaries, then said to James: "Get ready to fight. They don't seem to be satisfied with a small road tax, too many of them. We'll stall for the rest of the band to back us up."

James felt the rush of blood through his veins. He remembered the horror and shame of the disastrous loss at Chang-Ping, but that was then, and this is now. This time, he is determined to win. James loosened his grip on the crossbow, wiped his palm dry on his tunic then gripped the weapon tighter. He did not like the crossbow; he preferred the longsword, but the bow could shoot at a distance, and James was reluctant to let it go without firing a bolt.

A tall ivory-skinned woman with flaming red hair led the approaching bandits who all sported bright red beards. A tall male bandit rode close behind the female leader. As the riders drew closer, James saw the reddish-pink freckles that dotted her face, neck, and arm; he then understood Master Tim's earlier comment of sparrow pips on the bandit leader, and she was the only bandit that did not wear a red beard.

The trailing bandit spurred his horse forward ahead of the woman and sang out, "we planted these trees, we built this road; those that wish to pass must pay the toll."

Master Tim laughed at the ritual singsong demand of the highwaymen. He advanced in slow steady steps, "I would be willing to pay a reasonable sum, but I need the permission of my big brother."

"And where is he?"

Master Tim looked back toward the caravan and saw the rest of his mercenary band had formed their battle line; he turned toward the bandit and shook his six-foot-tall walking staff, "he's right here." A bronze grimacing tiger's head glowered from the top of the tough ironwood.

"We'll see if you are as brave as your words," the bandit roared and charged.

Instead of dodging or retreating, the mercenary leader leaped forward then crouched low. The bandit lost sight of his target; his view blocked by his own steed's head. He yanked the rein and pulled the horse to the left, only to be surprised as his enemy jumped high into the air. The bandit shifted the point of his lance, but too late. The tiger's head rammed into the rider's face. His head snapped back in a shower of blood, followed by a scream that ended with abruptness as the man choked on a mouthful of teeth and blood, then fell off his saddle.

The female bandit chief shouted and launched her mount at Master Tim, and the massed riders followed.

The mercenary leader grabbed the empty saddle pommel of the dismounted bandit and allowed the horse to drag him out of harm's way.

The sudden attack surprised James. He found himself facing a charging stallion. He lifted his crossbow but gave up when he realized its uselessness at close range. He dropped the crossbow and reached for his sword. But the horse was already on top of him. He felt a strike against the side of his head and the world went spinning.

\#

James awakened to a splitting headache. He blinked his eyes and took time to survey his surroundings. The aching head told him he was injured but alive, or else it would not have hurt so much. His one functioning eye worked its way around the room, and the dancing light glinted on a spearhead leaning by the doorway. The tuff of red horsehair at the base of the blade reminded him of the Red Beards. He could not remember getting there, then the binding of his limbs brought to mind his captive status, *not good, not a good way to survive a battle. That's one more score on the losing column,* as he drowsed off again.

Footsteps awakened James, this time he was glad to be able to see with both eyes; someone had cleaned his face. His vision cleared enough to reveal the ivory-skinned bandit leader towering over him. Close up; she did not look as tall as when she was astride a horse. She looked to be thirty-something, twice his own age, with large emerald-green eyes, thin but wide sensuous lips, broad high cheekbones, and reddish-pink freckles that covered every visible part of her body. He could not help but stare at her red hair. He had never seen a person with flaming red hair. She was close enough for him to smell her musty scent. Suddenly, she seized his hair knot and swung his head to one side, sending new spikes of pain into the side of his head.

"Aaagh," he moaned weakly.

"I suppose you'll live, can't say the same for poor Torbrich." His tormentor released her fingers, and his head plopped back onto the hard-packed ground with a thud accompanied by another jolt of stabbing pain. He saw stars fluttering, and it was a while before his eyes regained focus on his tormentor. She saw his questioning eyes, "yes, you are my prisoner. No, we did not kill your friends, and no, I don't know where they are at. Although I must thank your friend for killing Torbrich for me, he was getting to be unwieldy. It was his idea to attack your caravan head-on to demonstrate his leadership expertise, I suppose.

"I grabbed you when I saw your people advancing to attack us; most unusual for men on foot to charge at cavalry. I ordered my men to pull back. Your friends were very smart and disciplined, and they did not try to chase us and rescue you. If they had, we would have ridden around and then ambushed them before returning to attack the caravan proper. You have a smart leader in that caravan." James sighed; *I suppose the other side wanted to win too.*

The woman continued, "as it is, we are even. Your people killed Torbrich, and we've got you." She pursed her lips, "give me your word not to escape if I release your bonds?" James nodded his head, setting off another pain spasm. She smiled at his ready compliance, pulled out a curved dagger, and cut his bonds.

James rolled and then crawled onto his feet, ignoring the aching head and numbed hands, stumbling a few steps before gaining his footing against the dirt wall, then rushed out the door. "Hey…" the surprised bandit chieftain followed her prisoner out of the door only to see him watering the bushes with gusto.

James dressed then turned back toward the female bandit, "thank you, thank you, aah…" He said with a somewhat slurred speech accompanied by a sheepish but satisfied grin. For some reason, he was not afraid of her; in fact, he liked being near her to smell her musty scent. She looked capable, confident, and very exotic.

She laughed and waved the metal blade in her hand, "if you can run like that, I suppose you have more or less recovered. Besides, it was only a glancing blow, and you had a metal helmet. Come, let's go eat and introduce you to the gang." James lifted a hand to touch the injured and still swollen side of his head and mentally thanked Master Tim for his helmet.

James followed her into another cave dwelling. A group of men were eating and playing loud drinking games near the fire pit that doubled as the cooking and eating area.

In the center of the room, two dozen men sat on piles of thick rugs gambling with dice. A slim young woman lay naked on her back in the midst of the gamblers, trembling lips spoke of her fears. An upturned helmet on her crotch served as the dice bowl, a dent on its side told James that he was its previous owner.

The bandit chief led the way toward the fire pit and ladled up a bowl of the contents from the cooking pot, then sat on a pile of cushions and started eating. She gestured for James to help himself. He picked up a wooden bowl and a spoon and then filled the bowl with the aromatic mixture. The cuisine was a pleasant surprise; it was tenderer and a bit spicier than the caravan fare.

"I am Nydia, and you?" the bandit leader asked.

"I am James." She gestured with the bowl for him to continue. "I was the scout for the caravan you attacked."

"You are young for a warrior; but you would not have been so far ahead of the rest of the caravan otherwise. Now you must decide, join our band, or die. I cannot allow Torbrich to die without reparation. I grabbed you for a reason. If you join the band and take Torbrich's place, then the score is settled. Otherwise, it is a life for a life, your choice."

James thought, then shrugged his shoulders and was rewarded with another pain spasm. "Since you put it that way, I'll join, but I will not fight my caravan. The man that killed your Torbrich was my master. If you fight him, I will join his side."

"I don't think I want to tangle with that pack of wolves. I might win, but the price would be too high. There are other herds of sheep that are easier to fleece." She paused with an imperceptible smile, "but you agree to take Torbrich's place, is that right?" She waited for James's nod, then added, "finish your food and come."

James gulped down his last bite, tossed the bowl and spoon into a bucket then followed her to the center of the room. The spicy stew revived his body. He was able to walk with minimal discomfort. Nydia stepped through the ring of gamblers, then reached down and picked up the helmet from the woman's crotch. The bandit chieftain banged the face of the small shield with her knife handle, and the room fell silent. "Boys, this is James. He will take Torbrich's place, so make him welcome," she chuckled, then tossed the helmet to one of the men before walking out of the room, leaving James standing in the midst of his new comrades.

One young bandit of about James's age and height stepped forward while the rest of the men formed a circle. James recognized it was a warrior challenge that he could not refuse. However, he was still weak from his earlier injury and in no shape for a prolonged engagement.

James circled his opponent, watching for the man's movement. When his opponent charged, James feigned right, stepped left then crouched down. It forced his opponent to slow and change direction. When the foe pivoted, James dove down, palmed the ground, and swept his feet forward. The bandit was surprised and tried to stop, but his momentum carried him onward. He attempted to hop over the sweeping feet, too late. The bandit broke the fall with his hands and shoulder, then tried to spring back up. However, he fell back with a loud thud when James's left heel connected with the back of the man's head.

James rolled back onto his shoulder and then got onto his hands and feet while he shook off a slight dizziness. He was ready to reengage, but there was no need. His opponent was down for good.

Even some of the people in the front row did not see all the action that took place. The men stamped their feet and cheered at the lighting victory while many asked for details of the bout.

James's body shook from the adrenalin-filled excitement. He'd been in battles before, but this was his first personal one-on-one combat. He couldn't tell if his dizziness and shaky hands were the effects of his head injury or the excitement of the battle, or a combination of both. He walked over and knelt to check on the fallen foe.

The bandit glanced up cross-eyed, shook his head, then rolled to his feet. He teetered a bit and shook his head again, then laughed sardonically, "that was a good trick; I won't be so rash next time." He shook his head a third time and gave a throaty grunt, "welcome into the brotherhood. I am Nicolas, call me Nico."

"I was lucky," James chuckled. *Yes! He finally won one.*

"Where's our ransom prize?" One grizzled bandit shouted over the din; as the excitement of the fight subsided, he glanced about and found the woman cowering in one corner of the darkened kiln bed area. "Don't be in such a hurry for bed, sweet thing; you'll get there soon enough. First, we must pick your mate for the night. Now, come back here and lay down."

James watched the men resume their gambling and asked Nicolas, "who is she?"

"She was to be the new concubine of a local village chief's son. We came upon her wedding procession while returning from the fight with your caravan. It was bad luck to return empty-handed from a raid, so she was a fortuitous encounter. We held her for ransom, which had yet to be delivered. The deadline was set for dawn today, and it's almost dusk, so I don't think she'll be redeemed.

"We were gambling to see who got to own her. The boss had set the ransom at ten pieces of silver, and the boys were trying to win enough to pay her ransom fee. All would then share the ransom. This way, everybody got something out of the venture."

"So, this is not your base camp?"

"Nah, it's a day's ride from here, in the mountains to the south."

"Oh, and what happened to your red beards?"

The young bandit grinned, "it's a stringed contraption we wear during raids. The chief came up with the idea, and it had great psychological value. Some caravans just gave up without a fight on seeing our red beards, and some people joined our band because they liked the sound of our name."

"I'm tired. Where do I sleep?"

Nico gave him a weird grin, "since you are taking over Torbrich's place, you get to sleep in his hovel. Come, I'll show you." Outside, he pointed toward a cave with a horsehair standard, "it's that dugout by that standard."

***

James walked through the flap at the entrance. Nydia was leaning on a pile of cushions, her bare feet protruding from a white fur blanket.

"My apologies, I...I must have entered the wrong door," James stuttered to the woman, but he couldn't tear his eyes from Nydia's body, which was partially covered by the blanket while exposing a chasm of cleavage.

She gave a throaty laugh, "come in and sit down. We need to discuss your duties. I don't like to look up at people."

James crossed his legs, sat down on a cushion, his eyes focused on the stallion in the tapestry behind her. She waited then said in a slow even tone, "relax, I don't bite. You agreed to take Torbrich's place within the band, right?" He nodded. "Well, among other things, he was my lover." James's jaw dropped, his eyes snapped down to Nydia, and he felt his face burning. He was rewarded with another throaty laughter, "ha, I do believe I have gotten myself a spring cock. At least, you don't have any bad habits to unlearn. Shall we get started on your duties?" she pushed an elbow against a pillow and lifted herself off the carpet.

The blanket slid off, and James saw a fine coat of freckles covering her body from head to toe. *Master Tim was mistaken about the bandit chieftain; she, too, wore a full red beard.*

James nodded to himself; *alright, let's win this one.*

END

The Sheared Sleeve Habit

"The Sheared Sleeve Habit,"—断袖之癖 （Duàn xiù zhī pǐ） is the Chinese poetic euphemism for the homosexual tendency.

***

By tradition, Chinese emperors maintained at a minimum of three thousand concubines. Occasionally, a few stags got in to run with the doe(s). Imperial historians recorded the existence of hundreds of male concubines, "Nan Chong (男宠)," that served the pleasures of the emperors. Forty percent of the Han dynasty emperors maintained male concubines. The term Nan Chong literally meant "Male Pet(s)."

***

The most famous of all male pets was Dong Xian (22 BC – 1 BC), a favorite companion of Emperor Ai (27 BC – 1 BC), who ascended to the throne after the passing of Emperor Cheng. Dong Xian was handsome to the point of being beautiful. He had soft, unblemished, smooth skin, accompanied by an alluring face and a lithe, swaying body. He was the son of Dong Gong, a courtier of the Han Imperial Court.

By tradition, senior government officials often sponsored their children into the government service. In 7 BC, the elder Dong used his influence and secured a post for his son on the household staff of the Eastern Palace – the traditional name for the palace of the crown prince. The phrase "Eastern Palace" was also a standard term used when referring to the crown prince. At the age of 15, Dong Xian became a new aide in the Crown Prince Liu Xin's retinue. However, before the youth got a chance to meet the crown prince, Emperor Cheng (51-7 BC) died; therefore, within months after the young Dong Xian reported for duty, he rolled up his bedding then moved with the rest of the crown prince's retinue into their new home, the Imperial Palace.

Crown Prince Liu Xin ascended to the throne and took the title of Emperor Ai. Despite his youthful age, Dong Xian's pedigree earned him an assignment as an officer of the imperial guard; however, his lack of military training and experience, plus his obviously feminine physique created problems in performing the duties of an imperial guard officer. Eventually, he ended up as one of the official time barkers. Each day, he stood at his post at the entrance to the imperial court and announced the hours of the day in his melodious voice for the emperor and the members of the court.

Young Dong Xian was proud of his new job as a guardian protector of the emperor, and he was able show off his shiny armor to the elder Dong. But the job of a time barker was tedious and boring to say the least. Then fortune smiled on the young guard officer in the person of the emperor. In 6 BC, within a year of ascending to the throne, the new emperor took notice of the handsome warrior that stood guard daily at the gateway of the court. Emperor Ai saw the strikingly beautiful youth that stood out from the rest of the roughhewn guardsmen, and the man had a clear crisp voice that matched his graceful mien. The emperor summoned the guard officer for a closer inspection and was besotted by the elegance and beauty of the youthful time barker. Emperor Ai immediately promoted Dong Xian to be an Imperial Attendant of the Emperor; thus, within a year of entering the imperial civil service, Dong Xian got a second boost in his position, he became a personal companion of the emperor, an imperial concubine – the emperor's favorite Male Pet.

The emperor doted on his new boy toy, and the two were inseparable. Dong Xian rode in the same carriage with the emperor, ate the same meals and of course shared the same bed. The imperial ministers fumed and raged in futility; except for Dong Gong who was pleasantly surprised by his son's unique position as the emperor's favorite companion. The imperial courtiers had only recently survived through the sexual excesses of Emperor Cheng (the previous emperor) and his male pet, Zhang Fang; they now had to deal with another imperial brat of an emperor who appeared to have acquired the same habit as his predecessor.

A few months later, the emperor promoted the sixteen years old Dong Xian again. This time, he became the Imperial Guard Commander of the emperor's personal entourage. A few years later,

Emperor Ai created a lordship for his young guard commander as befitting his august position. However, the emperor's newest edict met with opposition from his senior courtiers. Prime Minister Wang Jia counseled the emperor against the idea of creating a lordship for Dong Xian. Although the young man was of noble birth, he lacked the stature and experience to serve as an equal among the imperial ministers and generals. Wang Jia's opposition infuriated the emperor. He threw the prime minister into the gaol for the audacity to dispute the emperor's wishes. Despite Wang's protest, the emperor named Dong Xian as Lord Gao-An. While in prison, Prime Minister Wang refused food for twenty days in protest against the emperor's abuse of power, then expired in his cell.

After Wang died, Lord Gao-An got another promotion. He became the 大司马 (Da Shi Ma), the senior minister of the imperial court. At the youthful age of 21, the young male pet was the highest ranked official of the empire. He ranked below one person – the emperor, and above all others; even his father, Dong Gong, had to bow down to the youthful senior minister of the empire.

Emperor Ai showered his young lover with treasures, gifts, and estates. Dong Xian had his own palace. The emperor shared everything with his young lover, even directed Dong Xian to use the best utensils while he (the emperor) ate from the next best set of the porcelain ware.

Dong Xian informed the emperor that he had a younger sister who was just as beautiful as her brother. At his (Dong Xian) recommendation, the emperor summoned her, and she joined her brother in the ranks of the imperial concubines. She was not the only member of the Dong family that benefited from the emperor's largesse. Every member of Dong Xian's immediate family was given positions in the imperial court; and even servants of the Dong household received gifts from the emperor.

Dong Xian had a wife, and the emperor granted the male pet leave for conjugal home visits, but Dong Xian refused and insisted on remaining at his emperor's side. Emperor Ai found the perfect solution, Dong Xian's wife too moved into the imperial palace, albeit there was no record of her sharing the emperor's bed in the presence of her husband.

One morning, the emperor awakened from his sleep but could not get out of bed because his bedmate was lying atop the sleeve of the imperial robe. Instead of awakening the young man, the emperor drew a knife and slit off the sleeve to leave the bedchamber without disturbing Dong Xian in his sleep. That episode became the source of the phrase "The Sheared Sleeve Habit,"—断袖之癖 （Duàn xiù zhī pǐ）which referred to a man of homosexual proclivity.

The emperor saw to being together with his lover in the afterlife. Next to the imperial tomb that he constructed for himself, Emperor Ai had a mausoleum built for Dong Xian. Early in the year 1 BC, at an imperial banquet, once again the emperor managed to shock his courtiers. He announced his desire to abdicate in favor of his male pet. The declaration horrified the assembled courtiers but in view of ex-Prime Minister Wang Jia's experience no one dared to contradict the emperor's wishes. All save Wang Hong, a senior aide of the emperor. The intrepid courtier rose and spoke against the proposal, "The realm was created by Emperor Gao-Ju (Liu Bang—the founder of the Han Dynasty), and it is not the personal property of Your Majesty. The throne should be passed on to legitimate imperial heirs. The Liu clan's imperial bloodline and the realm were sacrosanct. An emperor should not jest about such matters, Your Majesty should reconsider." His statement infuriated the emperor, but it did prevent further discussions regarding his abdication in favor of Dong Xian. Wang Hong succeeded in the intervention and prevented the emperor from passing the throne to Dong Xian. Wang was lucky to be spared from the same fate as the ex-prime minister, but the courtier was shunned by his master, and was never again invited to another imperial banquet.

A few months after the failed abdication banquet, Emperor Ai died of an undetermined illness. Emperor Ai had neither an heir nor designated a successor; Dong Xian, as the senior minister, became the official ruler of the realm. As predicted by Wang Jia, the youthful male pet lacked the expertise, experience, capability and more importantly the prestige necessary to govern an empire. Of immediate concern was the imperial funeral arrangement for Emperor Ai, about which the senior minister had no clue. He spent his days moping and crying over the death of his lover, Emperor Ai.

The Dowager Empress Wang Zheng-Jun stepped into the power vacuum. She summoned her very capable nephew Wang Mang to administer the funeral arrangements for the deceased Emperor and manage the affairs of the state. Wang Mang was an ambitious and self-righteous adherent of Confucian ethics. He had been despaired by the corrupt excesses of the imperial court. He seized the opportunity to set things right. Before Dong Xian realized what had happened, he was stripped of his rank and evicted from the palace for dereliction of duty in the proper attendance of Emperor Ai during his illness. Dong Xian was shocked out of his lethargy and realized the perilousness of his fate and refused to endure further abuses. He decided to join his master and lover in the afterworld. That evening Dong Xian and his wife committed suicide to preserve his dignity. However, he lost even that when Wang Mang believed the reported suicide to have been faked. He exhumed Dong's body from the mausoleum built by Emperor Ai, stripped the corpse of clothing to verify its identity then dumped it in a hastily dug hole on the grounds of the imperial prison. Following the eviction and death of Dong Xian, his family members also lost their august positions and estates; the entire clan, including Dong Gong, was banished to the western frontier settlements – a traditional form of punishment for criminals and undesirables of the realm.

END

The Orchestrated War Over the Taiwan Strait

At 6:30 pm on August 23rd, 1958, the Communist Chinese People's Liberation Army (PLA) launched a violent artillery barrage against Kinmen and Matzu island groups. Kinmen was less than two kilometers from the mainland Chinese city of Xiamen, off the Chinese coast but controlled by the Republic of China (ROC), also known as Taiwan. Within three days, more than 30,000 shells hit the tiny island. The initial barrage caused thousands of casualties, including the killing of three deputy commanders of the Kinmen Defense Command – Generals Jí Xīngwén, Zhào Jiāxiāng, and Zhāng Jiézhèng. General Yu Dawei, the ROC Minister of Defense, was also wounded in the initial artillery attack. When President Chiang Kai-shek of the ROC received the report on the artillery attack on Kinmen, he exclaimed, "good hit, good hit."

***

In 1949, after suffering a string of defeats on the Mainland of China, Chiang Kai-shek fled to Taiwan, off the southeastern coast of China, with 600,000 Nationalist (KMT) troops which once numbered four million only a year ago. Chairman Mao Zedong, the leader of Communist China, planned to invade Taiwan in the Fall of 1950 to complete the unification of China. In 1948, President Truman of the United States had written off the Chiang Kai-shek led Nationalists in Taiwan as a corrupt lost cause and refused to risk any more U.S. resources on Chiang.

Fate intervened in the form of the Korean War. On June 25th, 1950, North Korea attacked South Korea, then, three days later, the U.S. Seventh Fleet sailed into the Taiwan Strait, thus saving Taiwan from the Communist onslaught. The PLA units poised to cross the Taiwan Strait were shipped north and then marched into battle in Korea. (See "The Chinese Slant – Rising to Dominate", History

Publishing Company, LLC, July 2021, for details regarding U.S.-China-Taiwan relationships.)

On December 2nd, 1954, following the end of the Korean War, the United States signed the Mutual Defense Treaty with the ROC guaranteeing the security of Taiwan, backed by the U.S. Seventh Fleet. However, the treaty only applied to the defense of the island of Taiwan and the Pescadores. Kinmen and Matzu islands were not protected under said treaty.

The increased tension during the Cold War engendered U.S. concerns over an accidental incident across the Taiwan Strait that could draw the U.S. into a war with the People's Republic of China (PRC), and eventually with the Soviet Union. Frequent cross-strait military raids against the PRC from Taiwan-controlled offshore islands along the Mainland coast only aggravated U.S. security concerns over the region.

On January 18th, 1955, PLA attacked and captured the Yijiangshan islands off the coast of Zhejiang province, China. The next day, PLA followed up with preparatory attacks against the nearby Dacheng archipelago, just south of Yijiangshan, forcing Taiwan to withdraw its forces from the archipelago on February 11th. By the end of the month, PLA captured all islands off the coast of Zhejiang province. The loss of the island groups was a personal blow to Chiang because they were his ancestral homeland in China.

American military leaders, who initially supported the U.S. defense of Kinmen and Matzu islands, began to have doubts over their position. U.S. Joint Chiefs of Staff and the Department of Defense advised President Eisenhower to have the ROC withdraw its troops from Kinmen and Matzu islands to reduce the potential for a major conflict in the Far East. A retreat from the two island groups would create 150 kilometers of geographic separation between Taiwan and the Mainland, a more defensible position than two kilometers of water at Kinmen. In April 1955, President Eisenhower sent an emissary to

Taiwan to urge Chiang Kai-shek to withdraw his troops from the coastal islands.

Chiang Kai-shek was furious at the U.S. suggestion. Giving up those islands would be an insult to his ancestry. Besides, the political value of Kinmen and Matzu far exceeded their military worth. He felt control of the two island groups symbolized Nationalist Taiwan authorities still ruling over parts of the Fujian Province, and by extension retained dominion over the Mainland. Thus, Chiang Kai-shek loathed acceding to the American suggestion. Additionally, it would be a blow to his troop's morale and threaten his political survivability in Taiwan. Finally, it could lead to the division of China into two countries, an unacceptable prospect for any Chinese who had just endured The Century of Humiliation (See "The Chinese Slant – Rising to Dominate").

On September 29th, in the face of continued pressure from the United States and Western allies, Chiang Kai-shek declared at a press conference that Taiwan was determined to hold on to the Gold (Golden Gate/Kinmen) and the Horse (Horse Ancestor/Matzu), and that Taiwan would 'not consider the attitude of its allies. Taiwan would fight on independently.' The next day, U.S. Secretary of State John Foster Dulles said bluntly that although the United States and Taiwan held frequent and close contact on defense issues, the two sides had not been able to reach a consensus on the defense of the outer islands. He further pointed out that if a reliable ceasefire could be achieved across the Taiwan Strait, it would be foolish, unwise, and ill-advised to maintain a large military force in Kinmen and Matzu. On October 1st, Chiang Kai-shek rebutted Secretary Dulles' suggestion as a unilateral statement, and that the Taiwan government was under no obligation to abide by it. Chiang insisted Taiwan would never withdraw its troops from the two island groups. But the refusal of President Eisenhower's wishes risked continued U.S. support for the ROC.

Bellicose rhetoric aside, Chiang realized his survival in Taiwan depended on continued U.S. support. It should be noted that throughout the ongoing cross-strait military conflicts, there were frequent communications between the two belligerents across the Taiwan Strait, mainly through intermediaries via Hong Kong. In the spring of 1956, Zhang Shizhao, a prominent academic, delivered a letter from Mao Zedong in the name of the Central Committee of the Communist Party of China to Chiang Kai-shek. The letter advised Chiang Kai-shek that his ancestral home was well maintained and ancestral graves undisturbed. It also promised Chiang continued military and political power in the event of unification. In 1957, in the wake of the U.S. pressure to withdraw from Kinmen and Matzu islands, Chiang sent a letter via Cao Juren, a renowned WWII war correspondent and Hong Kong journalist, to Zhou Enlai. The letter requested that the PLA **'Give a good attack against Kinmen'** to distract, diffuse, and alleviate U.S. pressure on Chiang to withdraw from the offshore islands.

Despite their political differences, neither Mao nor Chiang wished to see a China divided. Both men had experienced The Century of Humiliation that China suffered under foreign domination during the past century. They saw Kinmen and Matzu islands as linchpins that tied the two Chinas into one; the alternative would have meant a divided and weakened China. On August 23rd, 1958, PRC complied with Chiang's special request to 'give a good attack against Kinmen.'

***

The Good Attack

Kinmen is only 120 square kilometers in size and 1.8 kilometers from Xiamen at its closest point. The KMT maintained 92,000 men and four hundred artillery pieces on the Kinmen Island group, with Taiwan-based air and naval support. The PLA deployed 569 artillery pieces and 215,000 troops against Kinmen with another eighteen divisions available in ready reserve.

According to official ROC statistics of the battle, KMT suffered 618 dead and 2,610 wounded (combined military and civilian casualties), plus two Landing Ship Transports were sunk, one Landing Ship Tank was damaged, one cruiser was damaged, and three pilots were captured. Two U.S. advisors were also killed at Kinmen, along with one wounded.

PRC officially admitted 460 military and 218 civilian casualties; two torpedo boats and one ship (not further identified (NFI)) sank, and one ship was damaged (NFI), plus eleven airplanes were lost.

Three days following the August 23rd shelling, President Eisenhower ordered the U.S. Navy to prepare for escorting supply ships to Kinmen and Matzu islands. On September 4, President Eisenhower and Secretary of State Dulles jointly issued the "Newport Statement", announcing that the United States would escort Taiwan's warships to the besieged islands. Concurrently, the U.S. transferred two aircraft carriers from the Middle East to the Pacific theater. By mid-September, the United States claimed to have assembled the largest US atomic strike force overseas since the war in the Taiwan Strait. The United Press further reported that the U.S. was ready for a nuclear strike.

Escalating military tensions and the nuclear threat in the Taiwan Strait alarmed the Soviet Union. Nikita Khrushchev, Premier of the Soviet Union, sent two letters to Eisenhower on September 7 and 19, warning that if the United States launched a nuclear attack on China, "then the aggressor will immediately be counterattacked by the same kind of weapons." On September 13, Khrushchev summoned the PRC ambassador to the Soviet Union and offered military assistance. An offer that Communist Chinese leaders declined.

Eisenhower believed loss of Kinmen and Matzu would demoralize KMT troops, which would lead to the fall of Taiwan, setting off a domino effect on Japan, Philippines, Thailand, Vietnam, and South Korea, thus threatening the interests of the United States. On the other hand, he had no wish to be dragged into another protracted war *a la* Korea. Many people in the U.S. government raised the possibility of using atomic weapons against the PRC. Secretary of State Dulles said, "we have so many atomic bombs in our arsenal, what's the sense of keeping them?"

General Twining and the rest of the Joint Chiefs of Staff recommended to President Eisenhower to use tactical atomic weapons against Xiamen to protect the Island of Taiwan from the PLA.

Senior General Ye Fei was summoned by Chairman Mao at three o'clock in the afternoon on August 21st, 1958, for a report on preparations for the bombardment of Kinmen and Matzu. Mao asked, "will you kill Americans with so many artillery shells?" At that time, the American advisers had been assigned down to the battalion level of the KMT military. General Ye answered in the affirmative. The Chairman did not speak for more than ten minutes and then asked, "can we avoid hitting the Americans?" and Ye responded in the negative.

Mao suspended the meeting, then on the next day, he declared, "we will fight as planned. I want you (General Ye) to command from Beidaihe. (Nicknamed the "summer capital," Beidaihe is the Chinese counterpart to Camp David of the U.S. It has been the site of many key decisions in the history of the PRC leadership.) The purpose of the artillery attack is not to capture Kinmen, it is a political battle."

General Ye was concerned with hitting the American ships. Chairman Mao ordered, "only attack Chiang's ships, not the U.S. ships." General Ye was to avoid hitting U.S. escort vessels, and not fire until the KMT ships arrived in port at Kinmen, and the PLA will provide situation updates to Beijing every half hour.

General Ye asked, "what if the escorting U.S. ships fired on us?"

Chairman Mao immediately replied, "if the American ships fire, PLA is not allowed to return fire." General Ye repeated the question three times and was told 'no counterattack'. As it turned out, when PLA guns sounded, American ships turned around and left.

On October 5th, Mao Zedong ordered the PLA to cease fire for seven days, then on October 13th, Mao gave orders to stop the shelling for two more weeks.

The United States Navy stopped escorting supply ships to Kinmen, and the Taiwan Strait situation eased. However, the United States misread the Chinese initiative for the two-weeks cease-fire. Washington thought Beijing had acquiesced to the United States' "Draft Proposal" in the previous Sino-U.S. ambassadorial meeting for China to "abandon the threat of the use of force against the Kinmen and the Matzu islands." Assuming there was a ceasefire, the U.S. government resumed its pressure on Taiwan to retreat from the coastal islands of the PRC. On October 14th, U.S. Secretary of State Dulles met with ROC Ambassador Yè Gōngchāo in the U.S., and again pressured him to persuade Chiang Kai-shek to withdraw troops from Kinmen and Matzu. Dulles scheduled a visit to Taiwan on October 19th, to discuss the issue.

Upon learning of the pending trip by Secretary Dulles to Taiwan, at 5:30 pm on October 20th, when Secretary Dulles was about to depart for Taiwan from Alaska, the PLA resumed bombardment of the coastal islands, firing more than 11,000 rounds within two hours. On October 21st, Secretary Dulles arrived in Taipei to seek an end to the conflict with Chiang Kai-shek. Dulles reminded Chiang that the current situation could easily lead to a world war with possible nuclear ramifications. And if the Soviet Union joined the war, Taiwan could also be attacked with nuclear weapons. However, Chiang Kai-shek would not budge, and Dulles had to agree to deploy Matador nuclear missiles to protect Taiwan. On October 23rd, the two allies issued a joint communiqué. Dulles recognized that Kinmen, Matzu, Taiwan, and Penghu were linked in defense postures; and Chiang Kai-shek promised to give up the use of force to restore the mainland.

On October 25th, Mao announced, "I have ordered the Fujian front line not to hit the airport in Kinmen, the wharf, beach, and boats in Laoluo Bay on even days, so that the military and civilian compatriots on the islands of Dajinmen, Xiaojinmen, Dadan and Erdan can be fully supplied with grain, vegetables, cooking oil, fuel, and military equipment, so that you can subsist. If there is a shortage, just ask and we will supply your needs. It is time to turn enemies into friends. On odd days, keep your ships and planes away. We won't necessarily shoot every odd day, but you shouldn't come, to avoid possible losses. This way, you can resupply during half of the month. Some of you may suspect that we are attempting to sow dissension between officers and men between your army and the people. No, comrades, we want you to strengthen your solidarity so that you can unite abroad. It's not a trick, but a normal product of the current situation. No airports, docks, beaches, or boats will be attacked under the condition that no American escort vessel be introduced. ...there is only one China in the world, not two. We agree on this. The American design for the creation of two Chinas is absolutely not acceptable to all Chinese people, including you and the overseas Chinese." And the PLA guns went silent.

In the following twenty years, the PLA bombarded Kinmen and Matzu on odd days only; they hit only deserted beaches, and the KMT responded in kind. Propaganda leaflets were often substituted for explosives in artillery shells. Kinmen and Matzu became "links" connecting the Mainland and Taiwan. During the Lunar New Year and other festival days, both sides celebrated together. In time the artillery fire became ritualized, only after mealtime, and was preceded by loudspeaker broadcasts for people to get into protective shelters.

In 1972, President Nixon visited China and signed the Shanghai Communiqué with China acknowledging the one-China policy. However, the Odd-days artillery dueling policy lasted until the establishment of diplomatic relations between the PRC and the United States on December 16th, 1978 (the last shelling took place on December 15th, 1978). The artillery battle officially ended on January 1st, 1979, when General Xu Xiangqian, the PRC Minister of Defense issued the "Statement of the Ministry of Defense on stopping the shelling of Kinmen and other islands."

Chiang Kai-shek orchestrated the artillery duel with the PRC to convince the U.S. government of the importance of Kinmen which should not be given up handily. Concurrently, the PRC used the artillery duel as a special signal to maintain "contact" with the Chiang government and prevent the creation of a divided China.

***

As of 2022, despite their political differences, China remains Taiwan's largest trading partner. The United States is Taiwan's second largest trading partner, accounting for 13.3 percent of total trade and 10.6 percent of Taiwan imports. China accounts for 22.6 percent of total trade and 19.6 percent of Taiwan's imports. Other major Taiwan trading partners include Japan (9.7 percent), Hong Kong (7.3 percent), and the Republic of Korea (6.2 percent). For all intents and purposes, Hong Kong can be considered a part of China. The statistics say a lot about Taiwan's economic dependence on China.

China has become the ranking regional power in east Asia, and the second most influential nation around the globe. Through its Belt and Road Initiative, China is developing an asymmetric counter to U.S. power. It can be said '**China has no enemies, while the U.S. has few friends.**'

Taiwan maintains a dwindling number of diplomatic relations (12), all of which are members of third-world countries, including the Holy See. China's growing political, economic, and military powers will only diminish Taiwan's survivability as an independent political entity.

Under the leadership of past and current leaders of the Democratic Progressive Party, the Taiwan government struggled, without success, to wean itself away from China's influence and achieve independence, which is China's line in the sand. In the event of a cross-strait conflict, members of the Association of Southeast Asian Nations (ASEAN) will not come to the aid of Taiwan, because ASEAN forms the largest trading partner of China. Japan, Korea, and the Philippines might even withhold authorization for U.S. forces to use facilities in those countries in a Taiwan conflict due to potential targeting by China and North Korea.

Taiwan survives on U.S. dependence on microchips produced by the Taiwan Semiconductor Manufacturing Company (TSMC). It makes 24% of all the world's chips, and 92% of the most advanced microchips found in today's iPhones, fighter jets, and supercomputers. Taiwan counts on the U.S. dependence for TSMC chips for its (Taiwan) security; and the U.S. is maneuvering to move TSMC's chip production expertise to Arizona. What will happen to Taiwan when the U.S. no longer needs microchips from Taiwan (TSMC)? Worse yet, what happens if China achieves monopoly of the chip production and market?

China can take Taiwan militarily; the crux is its willingness to suffer the economic and political consequences. Conversely, is the U.S. ready and willing to risk a hot war with China over Taiwan, with Russia and North Korea waiting in the wings?

The unification of Taiwan with China is not a question of if, but when and how. The hundred thousand men strong Kinmen defense force has been slashed down to a mere three thousand. U.S.

Representative Nancy Pelosi visited Taiwan in August 2022, causing China to unilaterally erase the center line in the Taiwan Strait and commence routine air and maritime close surveillance of Taiwan. A PLA invasion of Taiwan could be accomplished within three days.

With growing Chinese strength and influence around the globe, it may well be on its way to achieving victory without battle; then the orchestra can play taps. The alternative could mean WWIII.

END

Dan Walker

THE HEMLOCK PASSES, two-poem set

The Hemlock Goes Extinct: A Call for Sanctions

They say a *moth* did this? Like bloody Hell.
I say it's human. Somebody let this slip,
someone whose job it was, may he lie where he fell
on a slice of sun-baked rock where adelgids strip
the tender nail-roots from his epidermis
and larvae lay their eggs inside his Thermos.

I hope those worms bore through *his* hairy bark
to the skull where dull Forgetfulness and black
Neglect left toothsome pleasures, dark
and vulnerable to an alien's attack.
I hope *his* guardians spew an equal stench
of decadence. May I suggest the French?

And may that woolly moth, or its larval spawn,
eat through his plush and secret vestibules
of organs, eyes, and out onto the lawn
of his death-slab—and on to what foreign fools
conspired to aid that foul invasive clutch
at this fair forest. (I suspect the Dutch.)

Elegy for the Hemlocks

(Verse form based on the Welsh *awdyl gywidd* stanzaic pattern and used in J.R.R.Tolkein's "Eärendil was a mariner" in *The Two Towers*.)

On the eighth of Creation He set a
tree in Heaven's lea, forever green.
As Eden's guard the hemlock stood,
in shadowed wood all glimmering.

With fragrant frond of coolest green
in gorge half-seen and valley dim
there stood the hemlock tall and fair,
an angel's heir, to point at Him.

And round about from richest earth
there grew a girth of orchids bright
and rhododendron—whites and reds
and mossy beds of dappled light.

And guarding all, on ancient peak,
too blank and bleak for sheltering,
there stood the spruce and balsam fir
but straight they were, unfaltering.

And thus they stood for eons there,
thru summers bare and winters grim.
Nor fire nor flood nor feral trail
nor ice nor hail could topple them.

Till something came across the sea—
an enemy of tiny size,
but Hell's own appetite for leaves.
And tree by tree it felled its prize:

Through dell and valley, gorge and glen,
through field and fen it ate its way
till every stand of hemlock stood
a ravis hed wood of ashen-grey.

℘

Let not this crime go un-avenged.
The gates are hinged to open Hell
for them who let this crime occur,
unless they stir to break the spell:

Let them look up from creek to crag,
to summits jagged from abuse,
and lift their hands to save their souls
and make their goal to save the spruce.

Where these still live on wind-flagged crest
with eagle nest and berries wild,
the virgin forest long is gone,
but these live on through summers mild.

Let those whose hands are stained with
blood of ancient wood now moldering
put forth their might to save those heights
from blast and blight, and save them green.

THREE CHRISTMAS STORIES

Life Lessons

The after-Christmas chores are left to grownups, a group my wife's still not sure I belong in. "The man's nearly sixty," she says to her sister on the phone when she doesn't think I'm listening—or maybe doesn't care— "and he can't fix a faucet. Can't even slice up a box without cutting himself."

She's talking about what we're supposed to do for recycling cardboard at the dump, which is very busy during the holidays— flatten it so it slides through the slots into the big green bin. Sometimes just stomping on it works, but with tough boxes made to hold something heavy, like a tricycle, say, or cat-litter for the new kitten, or that Christmassy green-and-red-colored salt block, you have to tear them or cut them up. Which takes time, and if you use a knife you can—as has been observed—cut yourself.

"OK," I say, "you're so smart. You do it."

And she does, carefully, neatly, taking five minutes.

"There," she beams.

"One box." I wave my hand at the garage. "There are six more of these things. That'll take half an hour."

"Then don't do it. Just throw them in the garbage. Be wasteful."

I don't respond to that. You can't respond to that.

So I go to the dump.

At the dump there are generally two types of men. Type 1 is a local guy with a half-size pickup which is shedding paint and has a load of stuff his ex-girlfriend left behind in the trailer after the holidays, and he's done going through it for anything he can use or sell and is going to dump the rest. Type 2 is from one of the gated developments on the Lake with a name like Olde Creek, spelled with that archaic final "e", even though it's less than ten years old, and it's not even on a creek, but an inlet. He probably has a Range-Rover loaded with empties from the wine-and-craft-beer festival at the marina—all sorted and crushed for recycling.

I teach creative writing, so I can be either type if necessary. Today it's Type 1.

I'm getting my paring knife into the first box, and the guy with the truck says "Hey, I can show you a way to do that a lot easier—you don't mind, do you? OK, watch this."

He puts a box in front of his right front tire, another in front of the left, and pushes an open flap of each box firmly under the tire. Then he rolls the truck over both boxes, which drag a foot or two and then flatten. But that's not all. They also pop, with sides split out, filleted like trout.

"There," he beams. "Now you do the others."

I mess up the first two. You have to get the flap under there just right. But the last two pop out quick and flat. I'm impressed.

"You *could* stomp them flat," he grins, "but this is way more fun." Then, as if reading my mind: "Four at a time doesn't work because the back wheels lose too much traction."

"Did you figure this out?"

"No. I got it from somebody at the Wal-Mart warehouse where I used to work. You got any glass? OK, watch *this*."

You have to put the bottles inside something like a heavy box or a blanket that you're also going to dump. Then you run over *that*. He demonstrates with a rug remnant and some beer bottles, and it works for him, sort of—we have to collect some escaped glass—but I decide not to chance it. The dump doesn't require it, for one thing, and there is some risk. He points out that you could say the same thing about deer hunting.

I don't hunt, so yet again I have no answer.

Still, I now realize that these are some of those things—tips, life lessons—that get passed along man to man, father to son or whatever, and I feel like I've passed some threshold—a bit late maybe, but a step up. God knows how many steps I missed by going straight through college into teaching instead of off to Nam—probably a bunch of them there. Hunting, for sure. But a man has to make choices, and every choice is a step, right?

This dump has a trash-masher for whatever can't be recycled. There's a booth where an attendant, a middle-aged woman wearing a hard hat and a red vest with a holly pin, works the masher. I'm thinking I might let her in on the cardboard tip. I'm a step up on the manhood ladder now. I can be generous. But when it's my turn to dump, she's talking on her cell to somebody, maybe her daughter-in-law.

"Don't worry about it, Hon. If Johnnie told you he'd pick it up today, he will. But if you want him to speed things up with those boxes, remember what that lady at the Wal-Mart showed us... yeah with the wheels. ... Well, sure, it does take practice, but that'll make it more interesting, and men need that sometimes. ... I have to go, Sweetie. I'll call you back."

She smiles at me. I smile back. I'm already shrinking.

"Can I help you with something, Sir?"

"No thanks, I'm good." I tip my ball cap with the little antlers.

"Happy New Year," she says. "Those are cute."

Since then, they've gone to a hi-tech mashing system where it's almost better if you don't try to do them yourself, but I don't feel more advanced. And I don't have anything to pass on. Next thing they'll have is a self-changing tire.

At least she didn't call me Sweetie.

The Good-Enough Christmas Story

My friend Alan, a writer, had promised a Christmas story to a local monthly. My favorite thing about the magazine, *Virginia History Tales and Trails*, is that its first issue had misspelled *Tales* as "*Tails*" on the cover. That issue sold out. But circulation declined later.

"I'm at a loss," he told me over coffee at Panera. "I totally forgot about the Christmas feature."

"Just make something up," I told him. "I've seen ghost stories in there that have to be fiction. What did you want to show me?"

What he had was a letter from an ancestor, a sergeant in a Virginia regiment of Confederate cavalry, posted along the Rappahannock and Rapidan rivers in the winter of 1862-63.

"You had ancestors in the war, right?" he asked me. "Mostly from the North?"

"The ones I know about, yeah."

We were from all over. McCulloughs from Maryland. A bunch of Italian Pirellis and others from Pennsylvania and New York.

"Well," he said, "this isn't much of a story," he said, "but it's all I've got."

I looked at the letter briefly and then more closely. The hair on the back of my neck—yes, really—it stood straight up.

"But—" I said, looking down at it, then up at hims. "It may be. It may *be* enough."

Here's what it said (spelling uncorrected):

In Camp near Rappidan, Dec 23rd 1862
Dearest Lizzie—
Like most soldiers when they get low I write to folks at home to tell them I am as alright as that may be with as little as we have here. I have coffee most days now because I don't smoke and I can trade my plentyful tobacco for those deliteful grounds.

271

It has been COLD here, as I expect it has been where you are. The Company has been on picket duty along the rivers ever since Fredericksburg.

I have arrangements with a yankee sargeant from a Penn. regiment on the other side to meet every few days down at the point where the 2 rivers come together.

His name is Sal. I'm not sure what Sal is short for, but he has two boys like me, plus also a girl. He showed me a tintype of her. She is very pretty, and since I can draw a bit, I got a sheet of newsprint with nothing on the back and used a char stick from the fire to do a sketch for him. Last week I give it to him when we met. It really pleased him. He asked if he could do anything for me "beside surrender"—and we had a laugh. I said well if he could make it warmer that would be nice. I had to take my horse's saddle-blanket for a cloak it was so cold now.

But I wanted to tell you this – yesterday there was a sharp skirmish at the ford with a few wounded and dead on both sides, and by the time I rode down to the point with a sack of tobacco Sal wasn't there, just a few things that looked left from the fight, mostly small arms and a couple of haversacks. Also I found on a tree limb a pretty good blue top coat. I didn't see any blood, so I figured it may have been used to cover somebody killed till he was buried.

I waited to see if Sal would come down, while we picked up what was worth saving. He never came, so I left the tobacco bag with a red bow made out of braid from an artillery sargeant's cap. I wrote Merry Christmas on the sack. I hope Sal will be first to get down there. When I got back to camp and looked at the coat, ready to cut off the US buttons which we usually do, I saw that the ones on the front had already been cut off and re-sewed with brass blanks. I knew they'd been changed because the turn-up collar still said US. So it may have been from one of us. Who knows?

My horse is going to have a merry Christmas, though, because he will get his saddle blanket back now because I am KEEPING the coat! I won't get a chance to thank whose-ever it was because we're pulling away now.

Let me know how you are. I hope the war stays away from the south side.

All my love to you and Tom and little Elisha,
and may God bring you a blessed Christmas.
Samuel.

What made my hair stand up was this:

The War is an interest of mine, and I had been studying the role of cavalry in that winter of 1862-63. One Union regiment with duty there was the 8th Pennsylvania, a well known outfit with a good unit history published, plus a number of soldier journals and letters. D Troop lists a first sergeant named Salvatore Pirelli. There were other Pirellis in the regiment, but only one Salvatore.

Here is the end of one of his letters:

. . . . . .

At the ford, I and a rebel sergeant on the other bank have an arrangement for our men not to shoot at each other without two pistol shots in the air first to warn us. My boys sometimes bring coffee to trade for things like tobaco and testaments. They have a lot of tobaco and testaments. It seems we both worship the same God and pray for his vengeance on each other.

Every few days we try to meet at the little spit where the two rivers join, and we can talk over things. A few days before Christmas we were to meet, but there was a fight back at the ford and I couldn't wait around to see him, but I left a coat for him. He had said he had to take his horse's saddle blanket for a coat. This one was blue, but that does not seem to matter to them. I took off the US buttons, which they often do. I wrote MERRY CHRISTMAS on a piece of paper, but couldn't see how to attach it. I guess he'll know.

I do not doubt that we'll soon be shooting at each other again. Why that is, I'm not wise enough to know. But I have to hope it's part of God's Plan. And I hope the Plan means I'll see you all again soon, in Peace and Love—

With all my heart,
Sal

When I met Alan for coffee two days later, I had something for him. As he already knew, his ancestor had survived the war. Sergeant Pirelli, alas, did not. He was killed in action the next spring. According to a letter from the company Captain to Pirelli's wife, when Perelli was killed, Confederates had taken his shoes and blanket, but for some reason had left his uniform jacket—maybe because of the sergeant's stripes—and the contents of a pocket. I managed to retrieve these and a transcript of the above letter from my cousin in Harrisburg—a direct descendent of Sergeant Sal.

I showed the letter to Alan and then took out a Ziploc bag containing the pocket contents.

"Alan, I believe that the Sal in that letter was my great-great-great uncle—maybe once removed—and these," I said, pushing the envelope forward, "are the rest of the US buttons from that coat. You now have all of them. And you can see the drawing on the paper. Be careful with it. It's just newsprint." It was a very much smeared charcoal sketch of a little girl. "Merry Christmas," I said.

We looked at each other.

"Are you sure?" he asked.

"Well, sure enough for me and my cousin…and Ancestry.com. Now go write your story."

"Well, thank you. I don't know what else to say."

"Well, let's just say this: All those political things we disagree about—let's agree never to shoot at each other about them."

"It's a deal. Or we shoot in the air first, right?"

We both laughed.

How sure am I? Have I really checked the age and provenance of those letters and buttons and that newsprint? Let's just leave it at this: If you *think* you know something that makes somebody else really, really happy, why on earth would you check?

Will Payer's Holiday Story

William couldn't wait to clean the barn lot that morning, in spite of the early snow. Actually because of it. First off, if he got to it right away, the piles of horse poop would still have that nice pyramid shape and come right up out of the snow, which was dry and cold for this early in the season, and wouldn't weigh much even if it stuck to the poop he pitchforked up into the wheelbarrow. But second, and more important, he could get out to his mom's riding ring while it was still an unspoiled blanket. He had to cross it with the cart in order to dump the manure on piles at the end of the ring—why she wanted it put out there, he never understood—but that was the fun part.

See, William had built the piles into an impressive-looking mountain range, which he liked to think of as the location for a big resort, with streams and hiking trails and a nice condo development on top near the ski runs—like the one where his Dad had had property till the crash and they had to sell some of it. Today, he went through the gate—not easy to open with eight inches of snow, even dry snow—and about half way across the hundred-meter diameter of the ring, he stopped, his breath taken away, not by the effort, but by the fresh plain of snow and the mountain of snow-covered manure on the other end. Beyond that end of the ring was pasture—all of it snow-covered. He got out his phone and took a picture of the wheelbarrow pointed out toward the pasture with his empty gloves on the handles, as if waiting for him, or maybe worn by some ghostly presence. Then he pushed the cart out closer and took a couple of shots where no fence was visible and his piles would look like real mountains shot from a plane, maybe the Brooks Range.

He wondered what they would look like with lights. In fact, he was wondering if he could arrange a string of the tiny battery-operated lights—which his parents usually put around the spruce in the front yard—so they'd look like the holiday lights his imaginary development would have, and he was wondering this as he looked through his viewfinder and his phone suddenly sang out with its Darth Vader ring tone, causing him to drop it into the snow. He dug it out and brushed it off.

"Hello?" he said. He didn't recognize the number on the other end.

"Hello yourself… Hey, shut that damn thing off back there…"

"What? What thing?"

"Sorry," said the voice, "I was talking to somebody else. Bill?"

The voice spoke English but sounded Nordic or Scottish or something. And it sounded hoarse and gravelly—not so much from age and infirmity, but maybe just from…hoarseness.

"Are you there, Bill?" the voice continued.

"You mean William? Yes."

This was a sore point. Why, oh why, would his parents, Ed and Melinda Payer, give him a name that could be used for jokes that never got old: "Don't worry, guys, old Bill Payer here will pick up the check." And eventually there would be: "Well, it's good to know if I go out with you, at least you'll be the Payer. Ha ha ha." At least that's how it would go if he ever did ask a girl out, but so far his only actual Date had been to the Junior Prom and was arranged by the girls in the lunchroom who had all those things figured out (You should ask Nancy…Oh she wouldn't go with me…Oh yes she would…Oh no, she… Yes. She. Would. Get over there. Or we'll call you Bill…hee hee.) It just never got old.

"Well, all right," the gravelly voice said. "I guess I can see why." Then after a pause: "I guess 'Willie' wouldn't work any better, would it? Willie Payer! Ho ho ho!"

Ho ho ho. He'd heard that one, too. He didn't answer.

"Well, listen, Will—I'm going to call you Will because I'm too old to waste syllables. You're 18, right?"

"Yes, why."

"You have to be an adult to make a Wish."

"A wish? About what?"

"Look, Will. You're supposed to be gifted…."

"That was in middle school."

This was yet another sore point: his father, the Gulf War hero, was fond of pointing out that William was not actually smart, just good at taking tests, which is not the same thing, and by now he was old enough to know his father was right.

"Will, you are in the Mete-head Club, right? The Meteorology Club? Something you've shown an aptitude for."

"So?"

"So, I need a forecast made. And what's in it for you is the Wish."

"The Wish. Are you some kind of Genie?" This was a very weird dream.

"No. And you don't get any wish, either. In fact, I've already made it for you. You see, the real Genie at Mount Olympus—Oh, never mind. I live very far to the north—extremely far north—and I won a bet and got the three wishes. I used one to settle a labor dispute here with the Elves and wound up with a bunch of bad Hobbits. I used the second to get my wife a nice car, which she's been wanting, but I was misunderstood and now she has an ICE car. Get it? So I can't waste this one and be misunderstood again, so—I need you to go look at your models and forecast Christmas Eve for me."

"That's two weeks away. Christmas Eve for where?"

The voice cleared its throat.

"Ninety degrees north latitude."

"The North Pole! What—are you—?"

"Yeah. Not so loud."

"So why not a real forecaster. I'm just a kid. And it's cold out here."

"Well, who says I haven't asked? But here's the deal: You make the forecast—all I really want to know is wind speeds and directions at the 500 millibar level—the jet stream, you know—and where the polar vortex will be that night. And you get that story."

"Story?"

"You know what I'm talking about: You promised the creative writing teacher you'd write a holiday story for the last day, which is the 23d."

"But what if my forecast turns out to be wrong—on the 24th?"

"Then the story disappears and all memory of it."

"You can do that?"

"If I can do this, why can't I do that?"

There was a beep and William saw a tiny red light begin to flash on the flat area between two of his mountains—which he had been thinking of as a parking lot for the visitor center. The red point became a line, then widened to the shape of a door. This was beginning to freak him out. He looked back toward the barn. But then he heard, in a sort of miniature version of the other voice:

"Come in, Sir."

He snapped back around to see a small and—yes—Elvish-looking figure standing in the doorway. Behind him looked like steps going down to....

"Come where?" he said. "Where does that go? And who are you?"

"So many questions! It goes down. And my name is Virgil, and"

"Virgil? Hey, I've read the Inferno. This isn't—?"

"No, no, no, no—I was named after my maternal grandfather. Come on!"

So he turned and headed down the stairs, which were lit by those red lights, and William followed—because this was clearly a dream, and he was probably delirious, lying in the hospital after nearly dying in a snowdrift or—

"All right, Sir, to your right... Now that's the door to the Geospatial Northern Oceanic and Meteorological Exploratorium. The GNOME."

"The what?"

"It's basically a computer and a rack of monitors. You'll figure it out. You're supposed to be good at that." And he flung the door open.

William was half expecting something that looked like the deck of the Enterprise, but instead it was just about the size of his school IT lab with three rows of computers—nice ones with big flat screens. He turned to ask about it, but the elf—if that's what it was—was gone, and when he turned back he saw in front of him three goats—yes, goats—sitting on stools, one at the end of each row. They wore blue tee-shirts with "GNOME I.T." across the chest.

"I'm Gruff!" one said and elaborately licked his chops, if that's what goats have.

Right away the second one said (or croaked—"gravelly" wouldn't do it justice): "Don't let him get your goat! Heh heh."

"Who in the world are you?" William asked.

The third one sounded like what might be female for a goat:

"We are the goats of Christmas Future."

Hilarious. But it turned out the three did have some talents. Their hooves split neatly into fingerlike prongs that could interact with the smart-screens, and their tails converted into cables: "USB 6.0," the third one said, "which is faster than 6-G wireless." And their network had a nice fast Web-connection with access to the weather sites where William had log-ins.

"How long do I have?" he asked. Not very long, as it happened.

After what might have been a couple of hours, he heard that first gravelly voice from the room speaker.

"Well, how's it going? Nothing got your goat, I hope?"

The big monitor in the front of the room showed what he'd been expecting, the red suit, the white beard and all—except without the outdoor hat. And a big smile.

"No, they were very helpful. Where did they go to?"

"They were holograms—good for jokes. What have you got?"

"Well—" (he punched up a map) "Can you see what's on my screen? OK, the European deterministic doesn't go out that far, but its control model and the US model both..." and so on for a while till Santa, if that's who he was, waved his hand.

"OK, but do you have the jets plotted?"

"Well," he said, "I like the Japanese for that, and here it is."

"So—what do you think? Can I fly through that, laddie?"

"You're flying a—a sleigh?"

"Well, of course: a Supersonic Light-Entropic Inter-temporal Geospheric Helio-copter—SLEIGH— 2022 model XLE. The speed is classified."

"Then I don't know, but you'd have quite a tailwind going south. Here's the map."

The man in red put his glasses on and punched something on a keypad, then held up a printout, waved it at the camera, and smiled.

"Good work, young man."

When Virgil the elf showed William up the stairs and out into the still snow-covered ring, he had to ask: "How am I going to find out if it—you know—?"

"If it worked?" he laughed. "Well, I guess if nobody gets anything on Christmas, that's one way. But you'll know." He smiled and waved toward the wheelbarrow. "You'll know." William retrieved his phone, dumped his manure, pushed his cart back to the barn, and instead of waking up he got a call from his dad: "Where in Hell have you been? Your mom's been worried sick. She thought you'd fallen into a snow-cave or something."

* * *

279

In Christmas week there was indeed a deep vortex over the Northeast—so at least he'd got that much right—and it snowed enough on the 22nd that school was out that day and the next—which meant he was off the hook for the holiday story, which he still hadn't written.

Still, on Christmas morning with a few inches of new snow on the ground, he awoke, embarrassed to feel the excitement of a kindergartener: either his forecast would verify or it wouldn't, and he would know, somehow. Hadn't that been "Virgil"'s forecast? He would know. At least in dreamland he would.

At first light, he ran to the manure pile as usual, but there was no sign of any doorway in his mountain of poop. So if knowledge was going to dawn, it would take its time. Sure it would.

Back at the house, his little sister grabbed him by the hand, pulling him toward the tree:

"Come on, Will! Santa's been here!" and she yanked him through the room.

Will, she had said. Not Billy? Not Willy-the-poo? OMG. Interesting.

It got even more interesting on the first day back at school when Ms. Herrera called his name in homeroom: Will Payer.

At the name he felt goose-bumps— real, not-dreamlike—on his scalp. She had not pronounced it Pay-er, but Pie-er. As he walked to first period—Creative Writing—his heart was pounding.

"What's my name?" he asked Nancy, who was still in the doorway.

"What do you mean? Is this a joke?"

"No. Just say it, please. Read it on the board up there."

She looked at the white board, the day's agenda, and sighed.

"You're such an egotist. 'Will Payer's Holiday Story.' There." It had rhymed with Pie-er. PIE-er! She turned with hands on her hips. "What? You look like you've seen a ghost. You forgot all about it, didn't you?" She smirked. "I can't wait till it's your turn."

But when it was his turn, he was ready. Yes, there were risks: How his name had been pronounced might give his friends ideas for mockery. But if he left that out, he'd have to make up something else about the wish and whether it was granted.

280

It was complicated.

So in the end he decided to leave that hanging—to be continued next year!—and let Nancy wonder if she was going to be part of it. Maybe she had made a wish.

The possibilities were magical.

Lea Walker

The Marriage

I was 20 the first time I saw him. I was on a date with Joseph, who was from one of my classes at the liberal arts college we all attended. He – I would later find out that his name was Thomas – was charming his way across the stage that night. Vibrant and funny, tall and lanky, he was riveting, and I was riveted.

After the show Joseph introduced me to Thomas, and he and I held each other's eyes too long as he stood in the receiving line with his castmates. When he extended his hand to shake mine, I knew that he too was feeling the thrum of electricity.

Joseph perceived the sparks going off, and he tried to drum up some lukewarm jealousy. But he was gay and struggling to come out. Neither of us had much invested in our relationship, so I felt no betrayal of Joseph in my reaction to Thomas.

My heart simmered down as Joseph drove me home, but I told my roommate/best friend what had happened. "Do you think you'll see him again?" she asked.

"I don't know anything about him," I answered, "Except that he works with Joseph and goes to NSU."

She looked pensive. "If it's meant to be, you'll see him," she offered with the wisdom of her 21 years.

———

I did see him again. Three months later we both went to a Halloween party. I was half-heartedly passing as a cat; he and his best friend were all in as the Blues Brothers. I still have the pictures from that night. We spent the whole evening doing our best flirting, and by midnight, I was smitten.

What I didn't know at the time was that he was dating two other girls concurrently, which I guess explained why he didn't ask me out right away. We did exchange useful information: I learned that he was a finance major and in a fraternity. I told him I was the middle of three girls, a marketing major with a secret wish to be a writer, and that I generally looked unfavorably upon the Greek system. We ended our evening with a vague agreement to meet again.

We saw each other from afar on campus, but didn't come face to face again until late January. By then our mutual attraction was so undeniable that our friends had noticed and were giggly. A group of us met at the college basketball game on Saturday night. By the time we all settled into a dark corner booth of a restaurant, Thomas and I could see only each other. I remember nothing else about that evening except kissing him.

We saw each other the next day, and the next. On Monday night, he told me he loved me. I didn't hesitate when I said it back.

On February 25 he asked me to marry him. I was 21 and he was 24. We were both still in college. We had been dating for three weeks. I had not met his family and he had not met mine. Except for casual meetings, we had known each other for less than a month. I said yes immediately.

We got married outside in August in the garden of a historic mansion whose cost I could not afford. In Texas. The high that day was 104 degrees. We waited until 8 pm for it to "cool off." Everyone looks melted in the wedding photos.

When we got married, I worried that I should have told Thomas about the $1,200 I had in student loan debt, but his family was more well-off than mine, and I was embarrassed to talk to him about money. That was my secret. But I soon discovered that he had secrets that dwarfed mine:

He had been suspended from the university for the spring semester for failing grades – for the third time.

He had crippling depression and, in the future, often would go days without speaking to me.

He had a raging temper.

We had been married for a month the first time he went into a cycle, and the cycles always followed the same pattern: rage and violence, depression, days of silence.

I don't remember what set him off – when he got close to a cycle, he used anything for an excuse; I just remember that I had never seen anything like it before. He got a look of absolute hate on his face – hate for me, hate for the video game he was playing, hate for the world.

Then he started throwing and kicking things and screaming at me. He called me names, cursed, made guttural noises. I stood in stunned silence. He grabbed his keys and stormed out, slamming the door so hard it bounced open again. He was gone for eight hours.

From a distance of years, I want to shake my 21-year-old self and tell her to get the hell out of there. To admit to her mistake and get away from him. But she didn't tell anyone. She thought she could fix it.

When he returned, I initiated the pattern that lasted the next 15 years: I apologized and asked what I had done wrong, what I could do better, how I could make him happier. He didn't answer or even acknowledge me. He went into the bedroom and closed the door and locked it. Two days passed before he spoke to me again, and when he did, he gave me a warning look not to mention what had transpired.

Thus, my life on eggshells began. In retrospect – and post-therapy - I realize now that he was abusive from the beginning, but at the time, I truly believed that he was suffering and desperately needed my help. Occasionally, he would apologize for his silence or raging and beg me not to leave him, and I would promise that I would never leave him, could not live without him.

In March of our second year, Thomas locked me in the bedroom for three days. My sin was going with my best friend to help her shop for her wedding dress and failing to be home to do the laundry properly. When I got home, he called me sweetly from where he was sitting on the bed. When I went to him, he went to the door, turned and looked at me and said, "I'll tell you when you can leave this room."

The door was not actually locked. Theoretically, I could have walked out of that room at any time. But I was deeply afraid of him. I had watched him beat the shit out of inanimate objects on a daily basis. He had shoved me into walls, pulled my hair, twisted my arm behind my back. I knew that he had a cruel streak that was deep and wide, and I wasn't willing to test him.

And still I remained silent. I didn't tell a soul the truth of our lives: the pattern of rage, depression, silence, passion, brief normalcy, repetition. Many people won't understand this; they won't understand why I didn't stand up for myself, fight back, tell someone, leave.

If you knew me, you especially wouldn't understand this. I've always been assertive and confident. I don't take people's shit. If I had confessed to my family and friends the truth of my marriage, they would have been stunned that I of all people had put up with it.

But I'm also an empath, and fatally loyal. I had the lethal combination of shame for marrying a man I did not know, love for him despite myself, and a determination to fix him.

Another significant element to this story is that between the torturous cycles, Thomas was funny and kind, charming and thoughtful. He put a lot of effort into wooing me. Appearances mattered more than anything to him - as they did to his mother - so he liked for others to see him being romantic or for the two of us looking shiny together. I always knew that his efforts were partly for me, but mostly for his perceived audience.

Thomas's father died when Thomas was 20. His mother was alive, and they were close, but she had not always been there for him. His two sisters were several years older than he, so he grew up a bit like an only child and with little discipline. In other words, his family didn't offer stability. I suspected that they knew about his rages and silences, but discussion about such things, or anything uncomfortable, was never an option.

Thomas was readmitted to university and applied himself to doing well. He was brilliant – exceptionally so to the point that he could hear or read something once and remember it. Once he actually started going to class and doing the work, he made the honor roll. He graduated two years after we got married and got a job working in finance. Our lives improved when a father figure entered his life.

Doug hired Thomas to work as a loan officer at the bank the summer after Thomas graduated from NSU, but Doug became much more than Thomas's boss. Doug had been a Marine in Vietnam and still had the self-discipline and team spirit instilled by the military. Thomas's deep concern for Doug's good opinion of him kept him on an even keel more days than not, and his downward cycles became less frequent.

I graduated the next year and started teaching high school English and journalism. Thomas was probably the most stable of our entire lives during the first three years he worked for Doug and I began teaching. He had only three or four yearly "episodes" as I called them then, during that time, and I was lured into thinking we could have a normal life.

Was I arrogant or stupid enough to think that I had "helped" Thomas? That my staying with him, my loyalty and devotion to him, had driven his demons away? Who knows what I was thinking? I know that because of embarrassment, shame, love, devotion, pity, and about 20 other reasons, I didn't want my marriage to end. I also know that I didn't have a clue about mental illness. I did try to talk to Thomas more than a few times about getting treatment for depression, but he shut me down before the words were out of my mouth.

Into this clusterfuck that sometimes simmered rather than boiled, I decided it was time for a baby. My mother once told me that most people can talk themselves into just about anything, and how right she was. I talked myself into believing that Thomas was stable enough to be a father, and in January of 1989, I conceived.

During my pregnancy, Thomas's cruelty and rages returned, and fear coursed through me. He locked me outside one night. He hammered holes in the sheetrock in the baby's room because he couldn't get the curtains hung right. Always especially sensitive to noise, he repeatedly screamed at the neighbors and even called the police to report them because he thought they were too loud. These things are all quite minor compared to later years, but if my young self had only been wiser, I would have recognized them for the flaming flags they were.

Every time he raged or was cruel to me or one of our cocker spaniels, I would think to myself, "I'm having a baby with this man?"

It was about this time that I began to ask myself a question about every woman I met: "I wonder if she's afraid of her husband?" And because the process down a dark road was far gone, my answer to myself was always, "Probably."

On a Tuesday morning in late October, I woke up in early labor with our son. Later that same day, Thomas's mother, a school guidance counselor, stood up from her desk and fell to the floor, dead from a ruptured aneurysm.

I attended the funeral and associated events while in labor. When she died on Thursday, my contractions were 20 minutes apart. On Sunday night, I finally told Thomas I couldn't wait any longer. We reached the hospital at midnight.

Gage Thomas Walker was born in October of 1989, and from the moment the nurse put him in my arms I was afraid to put him down. Death lingered in the air, but something else was there too: I was afraid his father would hurt him.

Although Thomas did find moments of joy in Gage, he was despondent over the death of his mother. He retreated to bed and slept as much as possible, like he did during his depression cycles. When he had to return to work, he put on his "appearances are all that matter" hat and took it off the minute he stepped through the door again.

Gage was colicky for the first five months, crying every night for up to five hours. I was terrified that Thomas would hurt him, but my parents didn't live nearby, and my best friend had moved out of the country. I had nowhere I could immediately go. My solution was never to leave Thomas alone with the baby.

Thomas picked up on this and forced me to leave Gage alone with him once. The baby was three weeks old and Thomas insisted on having Italian food from a local restaurant and that I pick it up. I resisted. He questioned my reason, knowing the answer and knowing that if I said it aloud, he would explode. I went to pick up the food. When I returned, Gage was wailing. Thomas shoved him into my arms and said, "You're lucky I didn't throw him against the wall."

Never again.

Yet he hadn't.

Leave and go where? A hotel? With a baby? He would come after me and it would be so much worse.

And there was this: his family was well thought of in this community; I was an outsider. As I well knew, he could be infinitely charming and manipulate sympathy to suit his purpose. I had no doubt that a judge would likely give him unsupervised visitation with Gage.

Of all the bad decisions I made, I know with every atom of my being that refusing to risk allowing Thomas to have unsupervised time with the kids was the right decision. After that first time, I didn't leave Gage alone with Thomas again.

Despite my fears for myself and my child, I still believed that Thomas needed understanding and healing. I knew that he had a mental illness, even if he refused to discuss that reality, but I believed I could help him overcome it. As I write these words, it strikes me how ridiculous and inane the situation was we were living in:

1. My husband was mentally unstable, emotionally abusive, and constantly threatened violence.

2. He refused to consider help or even discuss his condition.

3. I, although I had no training or even any experience with mental illness, believed I could help him overcome his serious mental illness while caring for a newborn and working full time teaching 200 high school students.

Not surprisingly, my efforts failed. Thomas grew increasingly depressed, with his cycles of rages and silences lasting longer, and he added an element to these cycles: talk of suicide.

After going for three days or more of not speaking to us (although apparently functioning normally at work), Thomas's first words to me would usually be something like, "I've been thinking a lot about killing myself," or "I don't want to live anymore."

I can't overemphasize the dichotomy of my emotions during these years. I loved him desperately. When I looked at him, I saw the man I loved – the man who made me laugh, who loved to read as much as I did, who could finish my sentences, who shared my taste in TV and movies, whose eyes crinkled when he looked at me.

And I believed with my soul that I could help him fight his demons, that I could change things for him and for us, that he needed me.

But the other part of me was terrified of him for both myself and Gage.

He truly beat me for the first time when Gage was four and our second son was a year old. I got paint on the carpet when I was painting the playroom. He kicked me repeatedly, pulling my hair to keep me in place. Gage saw him doing it, and when I was putting him to bed that night, he told me that he had a dream he was a big bird who flew down from heaven to save Mommy from Daddy.

My heart broke into a million pieces.

When I had accepted that Thomas was the type of father he truly was -- that I had to stay with him to keep him from being alone with Gage, I decided that if this was going to be my life I was going to at least have another child, because I thought that I was a good enough parent for us both.

The paradox of this is not lost on me. I believed myself to be an excellent mother, but was I really, when I knowingly had children with a man who was sometimes a monstrous father, a threat to their very existence? I still ask myself that today.

After Fletcher was born, Thomas's career began to bloom and we moved twice within four years. Feeling good about himself and his performance at work helped keep his cycles down, and I constantly secretly coached the boys to tell me if their father ever was mean to them or hurt them.

I still had my policy of never letting Thomas be alone with the boys. I rarely had to go out of town with the school district, but when I did, I would ask my mother to come and "help" Thomas with the kids. On this, I was absolutely unbending, and surprisingly, he gave in to my demands without much fuss. Mom ended up taking care of the boys while Thomas stayed in his room the whole time, which was what I wanted, anyway.

Both of our children were – are – brilliant, which has always garnered them attention, and Thomas soaked in the accolades by virtue of their being his progeny. They were sweet and happy boys, and I shielded them from Thomas for the most part. They understood that Daddy stopped speaking to us sometimes. "I knew we had to walk on eggshells," Gage says, "But I thought we were pretty happy." Fletcher has some different memories.

"Dad took me into the bathroom one time when we were on a family trip and punched me in the stomach. I was six," Fletcher says. "He told me that if I told you (Mom), he would do it again."

That was just the beginning of Thomas's abuse of Fletcher. Thomas would make up offenses that Fletcher had committed and punish him for them, both physically and otherwise, all without my knowledge, all while I thought I was shielding both of them from him. So much for my protection policy.

When we had been married for 15 years and the boys were 10 and 7, I began formulating a plan: when Fletcher was old enough to tell a judge he didn't want to go to his dad's, that he was afraid of his father, we would leave. ...But the best laid plans and all that.

For the next few years, we were the ideal family on the outside: I won Teacher of the Year; the boys won awards in academics, sports, and music, and Thomas climbed the corporate ladder.

On the inside, we were a happy family sometimes, but mostly, Thomas continued to emotionally abuse us, and sometimes his abuse turned physical as well. Often, the boys and I were nervous about Thomas coming home, and we constantly took the metaphorical temperature of the house. The three of us could communicate volumes with glances and shorthand.

And then, in 2004, the demise began in earnest. Thomas was fired from his job for viewing porn on his computer at work.

We had to sell our house, pay off all our debt so that we could live on my teacher's salary, and move across town into a smaller, older home.

Thomas became truly suicidal then, but still refused to get help. I expected to find him dead every day when I returned from work. He had little to do with the boys during that time, and they thankfully were busy with their friends and activities.

He did something during this time I had never seen him do before: he took accountability. "How could I have been so arrogant?" he asked me. "I thought I was too important to the company, that even if they caught me, they wouldn't fire me."

I thought about it: I considered how easy it would be to take my kids – Gage was 15, and Fletcher was 12 by now, almost old enough for a judge to consider his opinion – and wash my hands of Thomas once and for all. To tell him I had given more than enough of myself to his lost cause.

But I couldn't do it. I couldn't walk away when he kept talking about killing himself. I realized later that he had been using that tactic for years, whether sincere or not, to control me. So I dug in, found us a new house, fixed it up, got everyone settled in. And Thomas found a new job making about half of his previous salary.

But losing his job had pricked Thomas's already troubled heart, and the barely-tethered civility he had was sometimes used up by the time we all returned home in the evenings.

Thomas's new job required him to office at home, so he sometimes left the house and saw people during the day, but he was sometimes isolated for eight hours or more. When I was home from school and he was working, I would hear him screaming during conference calls (having muted himself), throwing things, cursing, slamming doors. Our gentle and sweet golden retriever became even more afraid of him.

When he had worked in an office, Thomas had to behave himself. Now that he worked from home, he was free to rage, and so he did. He spent his days screaming and cursing on mute.

Thomas's new bosses were all about numbers and quotas. They liked for their people to reflect a certain pace, healthy or not. Thomas's stress level soared, which meant that the trembling in our house soared with it.

You can undergo physical stress only so long before your body begins to rebel, and my body did just that. In one year, I had three surgeries, including a double mastectomy and reconstruction.

I have a wonderful extended family. I always say that when God gives you parents as wonderful as my sisters and I had, he expects a lot from you. I've always been close to my family, but Thomas didn't come from a close family, and from the beginning he made it difficult for me to remain close to mine.

When Thomas and I met, I usually visited my family at least once a month. I thought he would go with me to see them after we got together. Not only did he refuse to go, he complained so much about my going that I cut down my visits. Abusers isolate their victims from friends and family, and that's just what he did to me. I went from seeing my family every month to seeing them three or four times a year.

In addition to the all-day rages of his job, Thomas became increasingly paranoid. At the time, I didn't know about location services on the iPhone. In an accusing tone would call me and ask, "Why are you at the corner or 66th and Main? Who are you with?"

"I'm at Old Navy," I would answer. What I didn't say was that if I ever got free of him, I would never look at another man.

By now, the boys were as big as he was, so I no longer had to worry about the physical abuse. But the emotional abuse was worse than ever. Fletcher and I were still his favorite targets. He was convinced that we were talking about him, whispering about him.

Then Thomas lost his job again. Maybe those calls hadn't all been muted, after all.

It was summer, so school was out, and he followed me everywhere I went and did everything I did. His jealousy of mine and Fletcher's relationship worsened. He criticized or undermined everything Fletcher did. Fletcher, who had always been a magnet for friends, was losing his self-confidence. I told him I thought we should leave.

"No, Mom," he said. "Dad's sad. We can't leave him."

"We can," I said.

We had moved into a bigger house again when Thomas landed the job working from home. His office was on the second floor, and he fell coming down the stairs and badly hurt his back. He had had surgery, but remained in pain much of the time.

Now with no job, his paranoia, rages, long-term depression, and near-constant pain, Thomas was worse than ever, and he became actively suicidal. I came home one day to find a knife stuck in the wall in our bedroom. Thomas was in bed. When I asked him about the knife, he told me he was too big of a coward "to do it."

I walked to the closet to find my clothes pulled off the hangers. Many of them had been slashed by the knife in the wall, it seemed. "What happened here?"

I was more afraid of him than ever because he was more unstable than ever.

I had finally accepted that I couldn't help him. My kids were grown; Gage lived on his own, and I could take Fletcher and leave. But I was afraid that Thomas would snap and kill us all. He had told me recently that he had a gun. He had also told me that he was afraid he was the kind of person who could shoot up a school.

"You care more about your clothes than you care about me," he said as his explanation for shredding them.

I didn't bite. I started putting things back on the hangers, tossing aside the ones that he had ruined. Then I pulled his knife out of the wall and took it with me.

Thomas got another job, this one making about half the salary of the last one.

I had developed excruciating migraines when he lost his job for the second time, and the preventative medicine I took caused weight loss. I was already thin, probably because I trembled a fair amount of time. Before long, my 5'7" frame was down to 106 pounds, and my head hurt most days.

I was actively trying to save Thomas's life every day. He bought utility knives in batches and used them to cut his arms, trying to "get up the nerve" to cut his wrists deeply enough to bleed to death.

He became an alcoholic, hiding a flask of Crown Royal in his desk at work. At home he drank all evening.

He became addicted to prescription painkillers and sleep medicine – the kind that are so strong they must be special-ordered. He especially liked to take a pill and have a drink together.

He started sleeping in the closet because he said that was the only place he felt safe.

And then the end really began.

Thomas and I went on a short trip in my effort to alleviate his paranoia and depression. When we returned, Gage – who had recently graduated from college – was at our house with his girlfriend. Fletcher was on the sofa, and I could tell that he had been crying. It was August; classes would be starting again soon.

"Fletcher needs to tell you something," Gage said, looking at me and pointedly not at Thomas.

"Sit up!" Thomas barked at Fletcher "What is it?"

I sat down beside Fletcher and held his hand.

Painfully, slowly, and through tears, the news emerged that Fletcher had become addicted to synthetic marijuana. He had flunked out of school and was suspended for the fall semester.

Thomas jumped up. "Get your shit and get out!" he boomed.

I turned on him. "Or better idea: you get your shit and get out."

The boys and Edie froze.

The fury on Thomas's face that I had seen a thousand times bore down on me. "What did you say?"

"You heard me."

He stood over me, glaring down. I held his gaze, daring him.

He turned and stormed out, shaking the house when he went.

I made Fletcher go home with Gage because I was afraid Thomas would return with a gun.

When he did come home, I was upstairs in my sewing room bedded down in the daybed but far from asleep. I heard the garage door go up and then him come up the stairs, and I quickly got up and stood behind the door. The lamp was on, giving me enough light to see when he pushed open the door that he had nothing in his hands. I could also see that he was drunk, high, and still mad.

"Them or me," he said.

"What?" I asked, knowing what he meant, but incredulous.

"Choose. Them or me."

My laugh had no humor. "Them. A thousand times them. No woman worth anything would choose a man over her children."

He pulled his fist back to punch me.

I straightened. "Go ahead," I said, "Punch me and you'll never see any of us again."

Again, he turned and left.

I left him the next day. I took the dog with me and went to a hotel and registered under a fake name. By then I had learned how to turn off location services. I called a good friend and told her what I was doing, and I made sure the boys stayed away.

He called my phone over and over and over again. I finally answered. "I'm not coming back."

"I'll do anything. Whatever you want."

"You'll go to a psychiatrist? You'll take medicine?"

"Yes."

"No more fits? No more rages?"

"Whatever you want."

"I'm not keeping your secret any longer."

He hesitated. "Do whatever you want. Just come home."

I had hope that medicine could help him. I had little hope that he could stop raging. But I was so tired, and I wanted to tell my family about the last 30 years. I wanted to tell them I was sorry for all the time I had missed with them.

I went with Thomas to the psychiatrist because I knew he would downplay his problems. I was right. He tried to tell the doctor that I got angry because he went to the movies by himself.

The psychiatrist prescribed a medicine for bipolar depression. I made a note of the number of pills so I would know if Thomas wasn't taking them.

After three weeks, he was like a different person. He quit noticing every little noise; he quit exploding; he hugged Fletcher and told him he loved him. Here was the man I had been searching for – for 30 years.

I went to visit my family and stayed for a long weekend. I didn't worry that the world was going to blow up without my holding it together with spit and glue.

But after six weeks I noticed that Thomas was remarking on noises again and acting a bit moody. A few days later things were worse, and by the next week I could tell he wanted to go into a rage, a rage he had promised me not to have again. I counted his pills and my heart sank. There were too many pills.

I asked him about it. "Have you stopped taking your pills?"

He looked at me with challenge in his eyes. "You know I'm too smart to need those pills."

I let a beat pass. "You know that was the deal."

He didn't answer. That was Sunday night.

I told him on Tuesday. Fletcher was at work when Thomas got home, and the house was quiet. We sat on the fireplace hearth. "I want a divorce," I said.

"I know," he said.

I was still worried about Thomas's stability, especially with the alcohol and drugs thrown in, so I had Fletcher stay with Gage to be safe, and I stayed with a friend. I also told my principal what Thomas had said about shooting up a school. He posted police at the entrances with Thomas's picture on their phones.

Thomas told us that he was going to see his sister, that he would need family support.

Instead, he drove to a beautiful rest stop, put a gun in his mouth that he had bought that morning, and pulled the trigger.

He sold his wedding ring that morning to pay for the gun.

That was ten years ago.

We were paralyzed with grief, shock, and guilt for the first year.

My own guilt went on and on and on.

I knew how badly he wanted to die, yet I kept thinking that if I hadn't left, he would still be alive, that I killed him.

But slowly, my life returned. With skilled and compassionate therapists. By seeing my beautiful children thrive. When the nightmares subsided. When I moved 2,000 miles away.

Now, I come and go as I please.

Now, I never think to wonder if a woman is afraid of her husband.

Now, I don't worry incessantly about my children.

Now, I don't have to guard anyone's life.

Now, life is beautiful. Now, I have peace.

Frank M. White

The Deceitful Monkey Tale

The Monkey and the Elephant were playing Jacks,
The Monkey was winning and making wisecracks.
The monkey bounced the ball, grabbed eight with one scoop,
Then he opened his mouth and let out a whoop.

Came the elephant's turn and he bounced the ball,
He picked up eight, but he let one fall.
The monkey looked up with a grin on his face, he said
"You are clumsy Mr. Elephant, you ain't got no grace."

The monkey bounced the ball and he picked up nine,
He was way out front, feeling real fine.
The monkey looked up with a glint in his eye, he said:
"You know Mr. Elephant, you couldn't beat a fly."

The monkey bounced the ball and he picked up ten,
Then he looked at the elephant and scratched his chin.
He bounced the ball and tried once more,
This time he left one lying on the floor.

He looked at the elephant and said with a smile,
"I could've won old boy, I will beat you afterwhile,"
"You do pretty good when you stay in your class,"
"But when you play with me, you know you can't last."

The elephant bounced the ball, picked up eight, nine, ten,
Then he put them all down and tried it again.
He grabbed them all up and was reaching for the ball,
He was just about to win the game after all.
The monkey leaned over and bumped into his arm,

He said: "Excuse me Mr. Elephant, I didn't mean no harm",
The ball went one way, the jacks went the other,
"I'm so sorry said the monkey, but accidents do happen
brother".

The elephant looked down with tears in his eyes, he said:
"You did that on purpose, don't tell me no lies."
"I was winning this time, and I just had you beat,"
"You couldn't stand to lose, so you just had to cheat."

The monkey looked up shaking his head, he said:
"Before I cheat you brother, I'd rather be dead."
"For all I know it was just one of those things,
That happens to the best of us when bad luck rings."

"It's a hard blow to take and I know how you feel,
But I beat you fair and square, and that's for real"
You played a good game, a very fine one,"
But in the end brother, the best man won.

I would play you another, but I just have to go,
I don't have the time to beat you anymore.
So with a wave of his hand, he got up and left,
As he strolled down the road, he was singing to himself.

He passed the word through the whole neighborhood,
He had beat Mr. Elephant and beat him good.
Then he started on home to his treetop to rest,
But he met Brother Elephant in a ring type contest.

The elephant threw a left and a very hard right,
The monkey was getting the worse of the fight.
The elephant hit the monkey and he bounced off a tree,
"Please, please cried the monkey, please stop slugging me."

The elephant threw a right and he knocked the monkey down,
He said "This time brother, I am not fooling around,"
The elephant bent over, brought the monkey to his feet,
He said, "Now Mr. Monkey, we will have a repeat."

So he gave Mr. Monkey a few more licks,
Some for old times and some just for kicks.
One to bend him over and one to stand him up,
A right to the belly and a left uppercut.

The elephant warned the monkey as he let him go,
Act like that again, you will get twice as much more.
As he lay there on the ground with his eyes to the sky,
He made a vow to never, ever again, deceive that guy.

Suddenly the monkey woke up from his sleep,
Sweating profusely, and feeling very cheap,
He was having a nightmare, much to his relief,
So he wiped his face with his dirty handkerchief.

Now the elephant had many close friends around,
They caught Mr. Monkey laying down on the ground.
They walked up to him and told him to please rise. They said:
"Now look Mr. Monkey, you have to apologize."

Now you and Mr. Elephant were playing Jacks'
"And you claimed you won, but we have all the facts"
"You wanted so badly to win so you just had to cheat"
"You thought you were so good that you couldn't be beat."

But old Homer Eagle flying way up in the sky,
Patrolling the Jungle with his great eagle eye,
Saw the whole entire thing from way up above,
He saw you give Mr. Elephant's arm a shove.

He flew down to the Jungle, passed the word around,
"You better come clean, if you want to stay earth bound."
The two got together in a large jungle grove,
Mr. Monkey apologized in the cool cove.

Uncle Sam's Armed Services

The Army, Navy, Air Force and Marines,
All have fine men and women in their scenes.
You can even throw in the Coast Guard too,
Also a part of the Red, White and Blue.

They all wear a different uniform,
But Officers and Enlisted are the norm.
Though certain ranks and pay grades are the same,
Some are addressed by a different name.

One summer day in 1962,
When the wind was calm and the sky was Blue,
I listened to a retired NCO,
Tell me something he wanted me to know.

He said "Young man, you are Air Force, that's fine,
But other service branches are on line,
You know what they are as well as I do,
Let me tell you something about them too.

They are all part of your great Uncle Sam,
One for all like water over a dam,
They all reside in the same old stable,
In different stalls, this is not a fable."

Each Branch has its own Head Secretary,
Each Branch has its own vocabulary,
Sitting alone at the top of the fence,
Is the lone Secretary of Defense.

Seated in the White House is the one man,
Who has the title they all understand.
The President and Commander-in-Chief,
That is the whole story, the truth and brief.

MILITARY LIMERICKS

U.S. AIR FORCE

Enlist in the Air Force High School Lad,
Become an officer, college Grad,
You will be wearing Air Force Blue,
It will be becoming to you.
Either way you will be Glad.

U.S. NAVY

If you want jingle in your jeans,
Join the Navy by all means,
The whole world you will see,
Traveling over land and sea,
Eating all those Navy Beans.

U.S. MARINE CORPS

The Marines wanted a few good men,
At least that was their slogan back then,
Since times now have changed a bit,
That slogan is no longer a hit,
They now seek a few good women.

U.S. ARMY

Be all you can be,
The Army said to me.
So I took a stand,
And raised my hand,
To see what I could be.

U.S. COAST GUARD

'Always Ready' like a Saint Bernard,
The motto of the U.S. Coast Guard,
No matter whether on land or sea,
The Coast Guard will come and rescue thee,
And fly you to a safe Harbor Yard.

The U. S. Military Parking Lots

The Army, Navy, Air Force and Marines,
Are all different from each other so it seems,
Yet at all their military bases,
You will find in many of the cases,
Parking lots for their war fighting machines.

U.S. Military Families

In every military branch that you know,
There are families with many kids in tow,
Whether Army, Navy Air Force or Marines,
Families are a major part of various scenes,
Kids were military brats, not GI Joe.

Teamwork

A basketball team consist of five,
A baseball team of nine,
Eleven make a football team,
Together they really shine.

They run out on the field,
Or on the basketball floor,
And as they play the game,
They really go, go, go.

Some are tall and slim,
Others are short and fat,
But all of them are good,
When handling ball or bat.

They pool their skills together,
They work in harmony,
This fine display of teamwork,
Often results in victory.

Smile

Smile when you are feeling blue,
It will bring out the best in you.
Smile when you are down and out,
Don't stand around and fret or pout.

Don't frown when you are feeling sad,
Things just can't be all that bad.
Cheer up, be gay and throw a smile,
A smile is always worthwhile.

Everything goes wrong when you frown,
The whole world seems upside down.
Nothing seems to work out right,
And people seem so impolite.

Your day is wasted from the start,
You walk around with hate in your heart.
You don't care much about anything,
It's only unhappiness you bring.

Wear a smile all day long,
Smile even when things go wrong,
A smile will thaw the coldest heart,
A smile is like a work of art.

Letter to a Friend

Just a few lines to say hello,
Are you well and still on the go?
Or are you sick and lying in bed,
With the covers pulled over your head?

What have you done since I last wrote?
Have you travelled by plane or boat?
How have you spent your leisure time?
Are your family up and feeling fine?

Everything is nice and swell down here,
I'm feeling fine and full of cheer.
It's very hot and there is little shade,
So I stay inside and drink lemonade.

Tell everyone that I said 'Hi"
When I'm home again I'll stop by.
I don't know when that will be,
But one day soon you'll be seeing me.

Answer this letter one day soon,
Don't wait until the next blue moon.
I'll be waiting to hear from you,
I wish your friends would write me too.

The Highly Famous MA-TA-PO-NI Historic Rivers in One

Out in the county, by fields and woods,
Four small rivers flow thru neighborhoods,
Each is so tiny they look like a creek,
But they are rivers and very discrete.

They all form in the very same county,
But that is only part of their bounty,
One aspect that is unique to me,
Spotsylvania is the County you see.

But that is only part of the fame,
There is more coming in this game.
You soon will understand this story more,
As these rivers you come to adore.

Now the MA, the TA, the PO and the NI,
Are the names these rivers are known by,
But these names only begin the story,
Other aspects bring them fame and glory.

Now first the MA and the TA join together,
And they become the MA-TA River,
Then the PO and NI do the same,
Guess what the PO-NI becomes their new name.

Don't think that is the end of the tale,
As these rivers flow past valley and dale.
The MA-TA become one with the PO-NI,
As they pass each other by.

As they flow through the County of Caroline,
It's the MA-TA-PO-NI you will find.
But that is not the story's ending,
It is just another beginning.

Down by West Point in King William County,
The MA-TA-PO-NI has an encounter,
It meets the Pamunkey River,
And then there is another name giver.

The MA-TA-PO-NI loses its name,
And it will never again be the same.
It's now called the York River today,
The York continues along the way.

Then it flows past a town with its name,
Known for Revolutionary War fame,
Headed toward the Chesapeake Bay,
The Atlantic Ocean Waterway.

There's a young lady, sharp as a tack,
Who knows the river's history front and back
There is nothing about this river's fact
That this young lady lack,

She can quote stories, and give out facts,
Like shoes on shoe store racks.
Who is that lady that's sharp as a tack?
That lady is none other than Ms. Mack.

The Green Side of the Grass

One warm, sunny, spring afternoon.
In the mother's month of May,
I walked upon some hallowed ground,
Just before Memorial Day.

Song birds were cheerfully singing,
A lovely, sweet melody,
Soft breezes were gently blowing,
Nature was in harmony.

I visited former comrades,
Loved ones of families past,
All who now stately lie reposed,
"Neath the green side of the grass.

Mothers, fathers, sisters, brothers,
Officers, enlisted, all types,
Soldiers, seamen, airmen, marines,
They wore stars, bars, leaves, or stripes.

Grandparents, cousins, in-laws too,
Husbands, wives, daughters and sons,
Aunts, uncles, nieces and nephews,
All held dear by their loved ones.

Some suffered the anguish of war,
Others waited from afar,
But even though they were apart,
They were esteemed in someone's heart.

Some sailed oceans and foreign seas,
Some served abroad in strange lands,

To uphold, protect and defend,
That for which old glory stands.

Some made the supreme sacrifice,
On battlefields far away,
Some lost limbs, became lame or blind.
Yet lived to see another day.

As time moved on from year to year,
Others also passed away,
To that great land beyond the sky,
Where we hope to meet someday.

Now those of us who still reside,
Atop the green side of the grass,
Pay honor, tribute and respect,
To you our dear friends of the past.

Female Black History Month Down Through the Years

When I was a kid playing 'Hide and Seek'
We celebrated Negro History Week.
It was during the second month of the year,
The month my sister Gladys was born here.

I attended old Stafford Training School,
To learn reading, writing and the golden rule.
It was for Colored kids back in the day,
I passed Stafford High School along the way.

With the exception of teachers I knew,
Professional Black females were few.

I knew house maids, babysitters and cooks,
But none of them made the history books.

Now a few Black midwives lived down my way,
They delivered babies, back in the day.
They received a call from both Black and White,
A baby was about to come in sight.

Now Ain' Sally Culley and Ain' Dee White
Two mid-wives who lived close to my home site,
In Stafford, down near Wildcat Corner way,
Delivered many kids still living today.

Booker T. Washington and Dr. Charles Drew,
George Washington Carver, were just a few,
Of the men we studied during that whole week,
In our little school house near Accokeek Creek.

But things began to change down through the years,
After many heartaches, prayers and tears.
Peaceful demonstrators, both young and old,
Males and Females became very bold.

Now when you pass my old school by the creek,
You will see a new name, just take a peek.
It is the Rowser Building now, you see,
A teacher and principal, there was she.

A historical marker sits near the road,
That building is now in another mode.
It's a State historical landmark sight,
Shining brightly in the National Spotlight.
And for Black females in this day and time,
On the Local, State and National Line,

Many more are in the History Book,
Just open one up and take a look.

You'll see Generals, Lawyers and Physicians,
School Superintendents and Politicians.
And many more have some type of fame,
Many of whom I don't even know their name.

Now deep down in that media Hall of Fame,
Is my sister, Gladys White Jordan's name.
Connected with a college application,
With Mary Washington as its destination.

She was denied admission in fifty-six,
Due to a skin condition, she could not fix.
And Mary Washington turned her down,
Because her skin color was not white but brown.

Then sixty years later in twenty-sixteen,
Mary Washington had changed its routine.
They presented Gladys the Monroe award,
The President and Staff were in one accord.

Here in August of twenty, twenty-four,
There are many black females we adore
A special one is now topping the list
U.S. Vice President, Kamala Harris.

Mendie Williams

Heart's Door

Some lovers use cruel and disparaging words
Their treatment of you is a sin
Sadistically cruel lovers will happily induce pain
They'll torment you over and over again
Devilish lovers will knock on your heart's door
Pleading to be let in
Lovers beware
Do not dare open your doors to them
Lock your doors, lovers of love
Recognize your foe is not your friend
Heed my warning, little Lilies of the Valley
Don't let the devil in
Cruel lovers are not your Morning Star
This savior - God did not send
Recognize your abuser for whom they are
Attackers of hearts who want to make your head bow
and your knee bend
For those who don't take this advice
Your fairytale will not have a happy end
Just remember, when the devil knocks on your heart's door
Little lambs,
don't let the devil in!

Jessica Wolski

Lights of Memory

Gazing through memories,
Through whatever changes,
Through time golden as sunset,
I still fancy you.

I started by running
Through blended views,
Bulwarks all around me,
Blooming flowers turning to dust.

I was never fast enough,
Though I was still lost.
Light all around me
Turning to dust at my touch.

Your light never went out,
Hung in stillness of time,
Brighter than the North Star
Though I willed myself cold.

Memories fade like old shirts
Very few return to mind
But your memory stayed
And you returned to my life.

You came looking for me,
Finally with barriers down.
One look in your radiant eyes
And you have me spellbound.

Happier Times Ahead

"This is wrong," Nick stepped away from Anna with his face red and his heart beating so fast that he could feel it in his throat.

Anna had opened her eyes and looked at him. He could see the mix of disappointment and confusion in her expression. They stood there, in front of the office building, out in the freezing December evening after a very lively office holiday party and the exchange of gifts for Secret Santa.

He had almost kissed her. He almost kissed his friend and it made him feel . . . weird. She was a holy object to him. Something sacred that should be admired from afar and never touched. But he almost did. He almost kissed her, his friend, whom he had forbidden himself from thinking about as more than a friend.

"Nick, what's--" He didn't let her finish.

"Anna, we've known each other for a long time. You're my friend. We can't go and start kissing each other!"

Well, now he sounded like a childish madman. Anna was standing right there, everything directed at her, and even she thought he was being irrational. *Has anyone ever explained to this man what a relationship is*, she thought.

She did her best not to laugh at what Nick was saying. Granted, when most people hear something like this, they might be mad or even upset, but Anna knew that Nick acted this way over pretty much everything. His behavior wasn't out of the ordinary for her, even if he was skipping a few steps ahead in his mind. "I know where you're coming from, Nick, but there's nothing wrong with this." She took his hands into her own, trying her best to calm him down. "Many friendships turn into relationships. It strengthens the bond between two pe--"

"You don't understand," he exclaimed, pulling his hands away. "I can't kiss *you*! If I kiss you, I'm not going to want to stop. I'll like it too much!"

"And that's bad?"

"*Yes!*" Nick said loudly, maybe too loud as people passing by began to give him weird looks. His hand touched the silver watch; the watch Anna had given to him at the party. He twisted it back and forth on his wrist in nervousness.

And it was that watch, a simple silver watch that led them to this moment. If he had just stayed home that evening, they wouldn't have been there right then. They wouldn't be standing out in the cold, where he made the comment of how beautiful she looked when they stepped outside, the dim light of the streetlamps making her eyes sparkle in the night and the smile on her face radiating with a positive energy that made him want to smile too.

He couldn't help but feel how wrong this all was—how everything should be at the status quo. They were *friends*. Nothing was supposed to change that.

As much as Nick loved the damned watch and would treasure it forever, he wished she hadn't given it to him. It only brought all these old feelings back from when they were teenagers with acne and raging hormones. Of course, for Nick, his personality and outlook on things hadn't changed. He was still trying to hold his feelings back in fear of losing his closest friend.

Anna had felt feelings for him since college, when she felt a spark really form between the two of them. She had dropped subtle hints over the past few years, but Nick refused to acknowledge the existence of those feelings for the same reason why he was freaking out over their almost-kiss.

That's not to say she wasn't nervous and having a mental freak out about the fact that they almost kissed. Of course she was, but she wasn't freaking out about it out loud and sounding absolutely ridiculous. She knew that wouldn't get them anywhere.

It was to the point with Nick where he'd suggest guys for her to go out with or try to set her up with someone. In one light, it's a sweet concept to have a supportive friend like him who wanted to see her happy. However, if you were in love with him like Anna, it would feel heart breaking for him to do that. Anna thought that Nick saw enough chick flicks with her to realize that. Now she wondered if he ever paid attention or learned anything from them.

Nick's thoughts might've seemed childish, but it was a fear that ran through his body like his own blood. Fear that he would date her and they'd hate each other, he wouldn't be good enough for her, or they'd break up and he'd just die of a broken heart. He had thought of all of this, not on the spot, but over the many years they've known each other. Since high school, through college, and even during that moment on the sidewalk in the bustling city, these thoughts and more ran through his head. These *"what ifs,"* that just seemed to multiply and grow like a virus in his head.

He had tried to make it stop, but it was as if life wanted to torture him by having her in every aspect of his life. Her second choice college just happened to have been his fifth choice and they both ended up there together for four years. After spending a year and a half apart, they both just happened to get jobs at the same office building at around the same time. One would find this purely coincidental and so did Anna, but Nick kept wondering what he did to deserve such a life. A life where the woman he loved, the one whose happy life he wanted to witness on the sidelines, was always shoved into his space.

He felt like they were in a genderbent version of the story of Narcissus and Echo. Anna's always doing her thing and hanging around the same places as Nick where he's just admiring her from afar and not wanting to get too close and cramp her style with his presence. Nick knew that this wasn't how that story went, but this was his version.

"Nick," Anna placed her hands on his shoulders firmly. "We can both agree that we have feelings for each other. We came very close to kissing a few moments ago. All of that is fine. It's human to have those thoughts and feelings, even between the closest of friends. Just because we want to kiss each other, though, doesn't mean we should jump into a relationship. No one gets into a serious relationship on a dime."

"But the thought that we *could*," he insisted, genuine fear reflecting in his eyes. "It's a domino cffcct! One thing leads to another and then another! If we kiss now, that could lead to a date, which then leads to a second date, and then a third, and then a relationship, marriage, and then it could take drastic turns from there! We could hate each other and end up divorced! One of us could die and the other ends up widowed! Or--"

He wasn't able to finish his thought as Anna let out a laugh.

"Don't laugh! I'm serious! I don't want to risk losing you just because we kissed!"

Why isn't this getting through to her, he thought. In his mind, he was trying to salvage their friendship before it got destroyed by this meteor called the power of romance. In his experience and seeing it in real time, it was destructive and could destroy a relationship like theirs if they weren't careful. However, his thoughts were jumping ahead of the present day and making him crazy with his own irrational fear.

As far as he was concerned, Anna wasn't taking any of this seriously at all. She wasn't thinking of the consequences and fearing this as much as she should. It wasn't something to laugh about but to worry and try to ignore like he'd been doing for so long.

If Anna heard any of those thoughts, though, she would drag him to get his head examined. She knew that there are risks and fears with putting your feelings out there, even if it's just a kiss and nothing more than that.

"Nick, you aren't going to lose me. Nothing bad's going to happen if we were to kiss right now."

Nick blushed deeply at the thought and immediately started shaking his head, as if the idea was a spider on his head that he desperately wanted off. "You don't know that!"

"You're right. I don't. I also don't know why you're acting like a stress-induced maniac! There's no rule stating that if you kiss someone you have to commit yourself to them. You understand that, right?"

Nick stopped shaking his head and kind of stood there for a moment, not looking at her in the eyes as he tried to think of a logical argument. As no surprise to Anna, he couldn't find any.

"Hey, look at me,"

He didn't. He kept looking down at her shoes, cream colored wedges that met toe to toe with his black dress shoes. For the first time in those moments they had been standing outside together, he realized how close they were to each other. So close that when he finally looked back at her, he realized that it wouldn't take a lot for one of them to kiss the other. Not too close, but close enough to make chills go up and down his spine.

He looked her in the eyes, his mind captivated once again by how they sparkled in the dim lamplight of the city, snow sticking to her long black hair and melting on her dark blue winter coat. Nick's mind drew a complete blank, just staring at her and, despite her lips moving, not hearing a single word—having been drowned in the screaming voices in his head.

What the heck am I doing, he thought. *She's so pretty and nice, but I can't kiss her! That would go against our entire friendship and I don't want to lose that! Would it even be worth it? She seems to think so, but maybe . . . she had too much to drink? Yeah! She drank too much and the alcohol isn't making her think straight! But wait. We didn't drink enough to get that drunk—*

"Hey, get out of the way!"

Immediately coming out of his own thoughts, Nick saw a cyclist on the sidewalk, heading straight towards them.

Without a second thought, Nick grabbed Anna and pulled her up against the side of the office building as the cyclist rode past them.

"Jerk, you aren't supposed to be on the sidewalk!" Nick called after the guy.

"N-Nick," Anna whispered, her face turning a pale pink.

He looked back at her and turned red, realizing why she was so frazzled.

Any space they had had between them had disappeared and he was now holding her in his arms, holding her close to his body in a protective way. There was nothing provocative or scandalous about it. They just kind of stood there, his arms wrapped around her torso while she held herself against him, her hands on his chest. They stared at each other as they tried to gather their thoughts.

Anna's face became a darker shade of red the longer they stood there, burning with embarrassment. Her eyes glanced around at her surroundings. Nick's pale green eyes reflected all worries and concerns that he had voiced and kept silent all evening. She glanced from there to his blonde hair, which was littered with small clumps of snowflakes, to his lips that had intrigued her all evening.

They continued to stare at each other as Nick held her, mentally screaming in his head yet not really saying or doing anything. It was like his mind was shouting out various commands of what he should be saying and doing but his body just stopped working. Nothing came out of his mouth, he didn't move to let Anna go, nothing. He just stood there with his arms around her and stared at this girl who was staring back at him.

Finally, as if his body finally wired back up to his brain, Nick collected all his thoughts and found the will to speak again.

"Anna, I--"

He didn't finish. He probably would've continued their argument, using this moment as an excuse to not kiss. In his mind, he thought that if they felt this awkward being this close together, how would a kiss feel? Well, he didn't even have to ask.

The moment those words left his mouth, Anna grabbed him by the lapels of his jacket and brought his face down for his mouth to reach hers. For a moment, he was in shock as a tingling sensation resonated through his body while her lips still rested on his. The kiss took him so off guard that he almost forgot to breathe, feeling as if his heart were trying to shove its way up his throat.

Although panic rose through his mind, his lips were on autopilot and he managed to kiss her back. Her lips were soft on his, feeling like a puzzle piece that had been missing from his life that had been put back into place.

The kiss itself was very slow and soft, the two of them feeling much closer to each other and as if they weren't even in front of their office building in the middle of the city. It felt like it was just the two of them, eyes closed and melting into each other.

When they finally pulled away, they slowly opened their eyes and could see the other's burning face. In that moment, they managed to back away from each other to collect their thoughts, both the good and bad, while not really looking at each other.

From the moment their lips touched and even in that moment after, Anna couldn't stop smiling and could feel her entire body squealing with delight from the kiss. She felt as if she was on Cloud Nine, like she was made of air and everything would go right.

However, a wave of doubt washed over her for a moment. She enjoyed it, yes, but what about Nick? Granted, she probably shouldn't have kissed him after he kept saying how he was against it, but he did say that he liked her. He couldn't have hated the kiss, right?

She gave him a few glances, her heart beating out of her chest and her cheeks burning. *How does he feel*, she thought over and over again, as if on a loop. Would he even tell her? What was supposed to happen now? Neither of them had ever really gone this far with anyone to really know for sure.

In all honesty, Nick still had many concerns. He hadn't even had the chance to touch on the fact that they worked together or how hardly anyone ever ends up spending the rest of their lives with someone they went to high school with. And although those thoughts still plagued his mind, he gave himself a moment to stop. For now, maybe it was time for him to push those thoughts aside. Maybe, for however long it lasted, he could enjoy having feelings for someone he really cared about.

"H-Hey, could I walk you home?"

Anna looked back at him and gave him a small smile. "Really? It's a long walk."

He chuckled. "I'm sure I'll manage."

Would they talk about the kiss? Not tonight, but perhaps maybe tomorrow or the day after that. For one night, though, they just wanted to enjoy each other's company and not worry about what tomorrow may bring.

The two of them walked away from the office building and into the dark, cold December night. Neither of them had any clue what would happen tomorrow, after the New Year or even every year after that. For once though, Nick seemed okay with that. They both did.

That night, they could just walk together and enjoy the sight of the snow falling from the sky. In that moment, they just enjoyed each other's silent company as they walked to Anna's apartment building, hands intertwined and the joy from the kiss on their minds.

The Bear of the Woods

"Run,"

That's all he told me. The bravest, strongest man I knew, my father, was white as a ghost and sweating bullets before we even broke into a run. I guess even the greatest of men have their moments of weakness. For my father, it was the moment IT appeared.

It was the biggest, most human-like bear I had ever seen in my life. Not like the cartoon ones with the hats and bow ties but like a werewolf or the minotaur. A bear-human hybrid with paranormal strength that chased us, egged on by a masked man covered in blood, who called after the creature, "Make sure not to mutilate them. We need to eat tonight."

The memory of those words, the words of that sick, twisted man still make me feel sick to this day. The only other thing I could think was, *This can't be happening.* This was supposed to be our last hunting trip of the summer, our chance to finally catch the beast that had been rumored to have plagued the forest for years. The one my uncle said no one ever saw and lived and if they did manage to survive, they were never sane again.

I know what you're thinking. If it was so dangerous, then why were we out there in the first place? My father and I were two self righteous peas in a pod. We were what my mother would call, "Intelligent idiots." We were both very intelligent people but when we put our minds to something, even something as life threatening as this, something we believed to be as real as BigFoot, there was no stopping us. Unfortunately, I was cursing our collective, danger seeking mindset because I knew for absolute certain that we were going to die in those woods that night.

We just continued running, running faster than I ever had in my life. Even if we were going to die, to be killed and later eaten by this monster and the psychopath with him, we were going to try our hardest to save our butts before the creature even got the chance.

The creature bellowed out a roaring battle cry as we heard it charge faster.

"Go right!" my father shouted at me, using his right arm to push me in that direction as I could hear him running to the left, splitting us up.

In hindsight, I understood why he did it but, really, I wonder now if he had ever seen any horror movie ever. Splitting up was always one of the most idiotic things someone could do in one of those movies yet, at the same time, I understood that he was hoping that the beast would follow only one of us while the other tried to find a way out.

For a little while, I thought I was in the clear. There were no sounds or signs of the beast and I seemed to be all by myself. That is, until I started hearing footsteps behind me. Loud, running footsteps as if something or someone was trying to catch up to me. This only made me run faster, trying so hard to run out of the forest, away from this horror show I had stumbled into.

I could hear a low growling from the thing chasing me, something inhuman in nature though the footsteps and movements itself sounded very human-like to me. I was too freaked out and focused on my own life to really turn around and catch the sight of what or who was chasing me.

Unfortunately, I was also too focused on leaving to really focus on my surroundings because I couldn't see the tree root that I ultimately tripped on. I also must've hit my head because I blacked out after my head hit the forest floor.

I'm not entirely sure what happened after I fell. I woke up here and the beast hasn't bothered me at all. I also haven't found my father, so I could only suspect the worst could've happened to him. That was over fifty years ago and the beast is still in there with his master, feeding on whatever and whoever stumbles into their domain.

So you've heard my tale. What will you do now? Will you be smarter than me and my father and leave with your lives? Or will you continue into the woods to search for the beast and his master? If you choose the latter, I won't stop you. Step forth, enter into the forest beyond and be mindful of your souls. Maybe you'll find my father or you'll stay here and keep me company a little longer. Until then, I bid you farewell and hope we meet again someday in the worlds beyond.

Lynn H. Wyvill

Caught You

The moon grinned a guilty smile.
"What have you done?"
Mother Nature asked.

"Nothing," the moon said
With his mouth full
And crumbs on his lips.

Mother Nature said,
"You've gobbled up all the stars!
Why did you do that?
I was saving them for
Everyone who looks up in the sky!"

"I didn't eat all of them,"
The moon said.
"I'm sorry I did it
But you make the best stars.
They're so sweet and buttery."

"Now I need to make more,"
Mother Nature said.
But she didn't mind.
She just laughed when she
Saw her moon's crooked smile
And heard him say,
"I love you, Mama."

Hold Hands

We clutch cell phones in our hands, captivated by all they offer us. We never want to take our eyes from them, never want to be without them. We are consumed by our love for them.

This obsession isn't healthy. Our bodies and minds are worn out. Our senses are numb. We are missing so much that no cell phone can give us.

If we never look away from our phones, we won't see the tree frog hiding in a carpet of fallen leaves.

If we don't take off our headphones, we'll never hear the rain falling.

If we never seek refuge in nature, we'll never find the peace that the Canadian geese enjoy when they fold their ecru wings against their bodies and rest quietly in the shade.

Without nature, our spirits become like a decayed hole in the base of an old tree that still lives but is missing a piece of its heart.

Nature wants to hold our hand for a short walk in a city park or a day along a wooded trail or a weekend by the water. "Spend time with me," nature beckons. She says, "I will wipe away stress that rests as heavy as boulders and turn them into skipping stones you can cast into a lake's deep water."

"Spend time with me," nature says, "so your mind can freely wander like clouds drifting in a delicate blue sky."

Only then will we gather our own thoughts, as plentiful as wildflowers, which no amount of staring at a screen could ever conjure.

LYNN H. WYVILL

Grandma's Girl

The low, sturdy stone wall where I sit still holds the warmth of the sun, now hiding behind the gray clouds. Far away, thunder grumbles under its breath. The sky bulges, ready to burst with rain.

When it does come, it's so light I can't see it, but I can feel every single drop lightly tap my back.

A breeze carries the faint scent of a boxwood hedge, just like the ones that surrounded my grandma's house. It brings with it tender memories of how she stopped everything to listen to every silly thing I had to say and didn't mind if I woke her up early just to be with her.

Her house was very different from our house. Everything was softer – the colors on the wall, the overstuffed sofa, and the chime of the doorbell. The place I loved the most was the kitchen with its old-fashioned appliances and huge porcelain farm sink. I remember the first time I was alone in that room and discovered a hidden treasure behind a worn wooden cupboard door. I could barely reach the black snap latch, but when I did, I found a butter dish containing the softest, creamiest yellow butter I had ever seen.

I knew I didn't have to ask, so I slathered some on a slice of velvety white bread and took a bite. The flavors melded together and bathed my tongue in salty, sweet, yeasty perfection. And then I made another, the butter thicker and heavier.

As I ate, I stared out the window at the huge oak trees that shaded the backyard and listened to the murmuring conversation of the grown-ups. When I was done, I found Grandma and climbed into her arms for a nap.

My memories of Grandma come like small white butterflies that play as the breeze runs its gentle fingertips over the creek's green grass.

Twinkles in the Night

The sun's high beams kick up smoking heat and send blinding white light everywhere you look. Summer's bounty of ripe fruit and vegetables bursts out of gardens. Thunderstorms boom and jagged bolts of lightning slash ominous skies.

Big, old flashy summer is here, and she will not be ignored.

So, who could blame us if we overlook the lightning bugs flying in slow motion as the sun sinks in the sky? Silently, their bodies blink on and off, on and off, in the sticky humid air, pinholes of light in twilight's curtain.

As a child, I would beg my mother for a glass jar, one that, despite being washed, always retained the distinctive scent of pickles. I poked holes in the top so the captured lightning bugs could breathe. I lined it with grass so they would be comfortable.

Even though I was a curious child, it never occurred to me to ask why these bugs blinked. Their luminescence enthralled me.

I would tiptoe up to the lightning bugs, capturing one at a time. Trapping a new bug without releasing any of the ones already in captivity was an art form. And I was good at it. My goal was to fill the entire jar, but I rarely caught more than three at a time.

Before I went to sleep, I would place the jar by my bed, hoping my little friends would flick on and off, illuminating my room all night. But I was always disappointed.

Maybe they were upset that they couldn't roam free or they missed their friends. Perhaps they didn't like the pickle-scented jar.

Maybe they were frustrated that I had interrupted their search for a sweetheart. Turns out those blinks are winks meant to attract a mate.

Maybe my punishment for their capture was to turn off their lights. But I don't think that's what happened.

My companions still blinked on and off, but one pulse of light on its own in a closed pickle jar can be missed. It takes a blink - one here, one there, another and another, all together twinkling in the night sky – that creates magic.

Dance in My Moonbeams

Tonight, a panda bear plays in the balloon of my moon. I've seen hills, valleys, a bunny, and occasionally a man in the moon before, but never, ever a panda bear.

Tonight, though, is special.

Do you know they've named you Super Moon because you are bigger and brighter than you've been in a long time? That's funny because I think you're always a super moon.

You are nearer to me tonight than usual, but couldn't you come a little closer? My fingertips can't quite reach your smiling face and the panda bear within you.

I don't know, and I'd like you to tell me, please, Moon: Are you soft and squishy like a marshmallow, or dusty like talcum powder, or cool and smooth like granite?
Silly me. I know what you're made of.

You're a downy, warm pillow in the snug cradle of the sky where you catch all my sweet dreams and tuck them in so they are safe and won't get lost in the dark. Maybe that's why somehow I'm less lonely when I see you looking down on me from the night sky.

Now you are full to bursting with all of my dreams. They bubble up around the panda, tickle his nose, and make him giggle.

"Dance in my moonbeams. They are full of your dreams," the moon says to me. "They are ready now, and so are you."

I open my arms as I twirl round and round to receive my bright and shining hopes bundled with your loving wishes that all my dreams come true.

I know, Moon, it's time for you to go. But before you do, please sprinkle some dream dust across the sky in the form of stars to remind me to dream a thousand more dreams and fill you up once again.

LYNN H. WYVILL

Turtle Dreams

I was out for a walk Saturday morning
Everything was quiet until
I heard voice and
Felt the ground vibrate.

I look. It's children.
Lots of them.
Running toward me.
The first one to reach me
Squeals, "It's a turtle!"

They form a circle around me and
Bring their faces close to get a better look.
I don't mind, but I am a little shy, so
I pull my head and legs into my shell.

Then I hear them say the most thrilling thing
I've ever heard. They want to
Take me home with them.

My heart is beating so fast.
I'm going on a trip.
I'll have kids to play with.

This will be the most exciting
Thing that's ever happened to me.
Just as they reach for me
I remember that I'll have to
Leave my mom and dad
My brothers and sisters!

Wait, I'm not ready to leave home!

Their teacher saves me. She says
I'm happier here and they shouldn't
Take me home.

The children are disappointed
And I'm a little sad too
To lose my new friends
But I really like it here by the creek.

Before the Rest of the World Rises

The dark presses against the windows

The house settles and creaks

The moon shines on the grass

The stars are still

The birds murmur in their dreams

The leaves rest in deep sleep.

I am awake in this sacred silence

With nothing to disturb my peace.

LYNN H. WYVILL

A Long Life

I was born and grew
Into a sturdy tree
Sprouting branches
Searching for life's purpose.

Some limbs barely grew at all
If it was in the wrong direction.
Some dropped to the ground
When they had served their purpose.

Most stretched and grew long
Reaching for sunlight
Touching others
When things felt right.

You may think I'm old
I'm not, just older
Wiser, happier
Contented and at peace
Still reaching for the sun.

They Don't Know

The robin sings
But doesn't know
He soothes my aching heart.

The creek washes over my feet
But doesn't understand
It cools my fevered spirit.

The oak pushes its roots deep
Not realizing
It inspires me to stand strong.

The primrose bursts from the icy ground
But doesn't see
It gives me courage to face the day.

The moon glows
But doesn't know
It encourages me to shine in the darkness.

The sun beams bright
Unaware
That it fills me with hope.

Rachel Young

A Mother's Love

It was so easy, almost too easy, she thought, as she quickly got back in the car with the little dog in her lap. She had never thought of herself as a thief before, much less a dognapper, but this was for her little boy, her *dying* little boy. There was nothing she wouldn't do for him. She shook the rain from her hair, put the car in drive and made her way down the street, just as the dog owner, a little girl not much older than her own boy, came back out of the house looking for the dog.

She pulled into a parking space in her apartment complex and sat for a moment, not looking at the little brown, fuzzy dog eyeing her expectantly. She had prepared for this, at least somewhat. She had a leash, two dog bowls – one for food and one for water - and a bag of dog food. She didn't get any dog toys, not sure of the type or size of dog she was going to dognap. She started to feel guilty but pushed the feeling aside as she looked into the deep brown eyes of the little dog next to her.

It wasn't her fault that the local animal shelter wouldn't adopt to her because of where she lived. It wasn't her fault that local animal rescue groups were too expensive for her to adopt from. None of that was her fault. It wasn't her fault that her son was dying.

He wanted a dog, a friend, a comforter, and she was damned well going to get it for him. Once he was, well, once he didn't need the comfort or friendship anymore, she would return the dog as quietly as she got him. It was only a matter of weeks the doctors said, before he was back in the hospital, for good.

She took the leash out of the shopping bag and fastened it onto the collar of the dog, "Let's see what we should call you, huh?" She said to him, as she looked at the tag dangling from his collar. "Oh, I see. Your name is Ewok. A Star Wars fan, I see. You do have a little

Ewok face, that's for sure. You are a cutie." She ruffled his head and he licked her hand.

"Let's take you inside so you can meet my Kenny. He's going to love you." She opened the car door and wrestled Ewok, her purse, and the bag of dog supplies out of the car. She managed to close and lock the door to her car without dumping anything or losing Ewok. Finally, she made it up the three flights of stairs and wrangled her keys into the lock of the door.

"Oh, wow! What a sweet little guy!" Emily, the teenage neighbor who sat with Kenny when she had to go out, gushed. "What's his name?"

"Ewok, from the Star Wars movies."

"I can see the resemblance, definitely." Emily laughed.

"How has he been tonight?"

"He finally fell asleep about an hour ago. He said he didn't hurt too much tonight, but I think he was just saying that for my benefit. He didn't turn down the pain med like he usually does." Emily's eyes were sad. She couldn't stand the pitying look in them.

"Well, thanks for looking after him for me. It means a lot to me. He really likes you."

"It's no problem. It's a nice break from my sisters, believe me. I also got most of my homework done and I get to watch what I want to watch on tv, so it's a win-win for me."

She reached into her purse for her wallet, to give some money to Emily, but Emily was quick to stop her. "No, it's not necessary, really. I enjoy Kenny, I really do. I meant everything I said, it's such a relief to be away from my life for a couple of hours, I should pay you for letting me come over here. Really, I appreciate the offer, but I insist you keep it."

"Well, that's very sweet of you, Emily. Thank you. You are a big help to Kenny and me. We don't know what we would do without you."

Emily walked to the door and opened it to let herself out. She turned back one last time and said, "He doesn't have much time left, does he?"

"I'm afraid not, no."

Emily just nodded her head and left her with Ewok, standing in the living room. He was looking around at his new surroundings and pulled the leash from her hand when he wandered into the small galley kitchen off to the left.

"Well, you might be thirsty, huh little guy?" She took one of the bowls out of the bag she had set on the rickety coffee table and went into the kitchen. She turned on the tap at the sink and filled the bowl, setting it on the floor. Ewok had just started to lap up water when she heard Kenny call from down the hall. Ewok's head popped up and his floppy ears perked forward.

"Mommy, are you home now?"

"Yes, Kennybug, and I've brought you a present." She scooped up Ewok and made her way down the hall.

"A present?" Kenny asked groggily, "what kind of present?"

"The best kind of all." She stepped into his bedroom through the doorway holding Ewok, who was squirming to get down. She unhooked the leash and walked forward to put the little dog on the bed next to Kenny.

"A dog! You got me a dog?!" Kenny was instantly alert, and her heart broke at the joy on his precious little face. "What's his name? What do I call him?" Kenny pulled Ewok closer to his face and patted his head and ruffled his ears. Ewok loved the attention.

"His name is Ewok," she said, "from a science fiction movie called Star Wars. An Ewok was a cute, fuzzy little bear-like creature, just like this little guy."

"Ewok, huh? Well hello, Ewok. My name is Kenny and we are going to be best friends, the best of friends, and you can sleep with m-"Kenny started to cough and couldn't stop, not even able to catch a breath it seemed.

After a coughing fit of what seemed like minutes but was only seconds really, Kenny threw himself back on his pillow, ready to cry. At that moment, Ewok nestled into the crook of his left arm and laid his head on Kenny's chest. Kenny began stroking Ewok, and the crying fit, the rage of "why me, why am I so sick, why do I hurt", never materialized.

She tiptoed backwards out of Kenny's room. She had never thought of herself as a criminal before, but she would gladly steal this little dog all over again to give her son this peace.

******

It's been three days since she dognapped Ewok from the front yard of that house on Tripaldi Street in Broadland, VA. Three glorious days for her son. He's still sick. He's still dying. She knows that. But he's happy. He has a friend to tell his secrets to. He's only 6 years old, it's not like he can journal his feelings. This is great therapy for him. He's even playful at times, but he tires quickly, and he and Ewok take naps. It's like Ewok knows Kenny's not long for this place and he wants to comfort Kenny while he can. She thinks about that and has cried herself to sleep these last two nights.

It's eleven o'clock and she flops down on the lumpy couch. She's too keyed up to go to bed tonight. She doesn't want to cry tonight, at least not over Kenny and Ewok. So she grabs the remote, ready to watch something, anything to take her mind off of her own life. Instead, she lands on the news and sees the face of an 8-year-old girl, pleading for the safe return of her beloved dog, Ewok.

"His name is Ewok," this little girl says, standing bravely between her parents, looking directly into the camera. "He's a Brussels Griffon dog. He's very sweet. He loves to be petted and to cuddle. His favorite treats are blueberries and carrots. Please, if you have him, bring him home. I miss him so much." The little girl is crying and hugging her mom. Her dad steps up to the microphone.

"We are offering a reward for the safe return of Ewok. A five-hundred-dollar reward and we will not prosecute if he is returned in good health unharmed. Please, we just want him back. Thank you."

He steps away from the microphone. The phone number to call flashes on the bottom of the screen. She stares at it like it will come out of the tv and eat her alive.

She turns off the tv and runs to bathroom and throws up in the toilet. *What have I done?* She thinks. *In bringing joy to my son, I've brought heartache and fear to a little girl.*

"Mom?" She turns to see Kenny, in his SpongeBob pajamas, leaning against the wall opposite the bathroom doorway, Ewok by his side. "Who is that girl on the tv? Why is she talking about Ewok?" Kenny is near moaning now and is having trouble standing.

"It's nothing, Kenny. It's time to get you and Ewok to bed. It's late." She holds his fragile little hand in hers and walks him to his room. She tucks him into his bed and pulls his rocket ship comforter up to his chin. He's been complaining of being cold lately. She knows it's only a matter of time, short time, before they are off to the ER and he is admitted, this time for good. His coughing fits have been getting worse and the inhalers and nebulizer treatments aren't working.

"I know it's something, Mommy. Promise you'll tell me someday?" His eyes are closing, and Ewok is on the bed between him and the wall, head on his chest.

"Yes, I will tell you all about it someday." Hating herself for lying to him. She kisses his forehead, pats Ewok on the head and slips out of the room.

*****

"I'm sorry, but there isn't much more we can do except make him comfortable." The doctor explains to her, as she fights back the tears.

"How much time does he have left?" She is whispering, barely able to say the words.

"I would say he has a week, at the most."

She collapses onto the floor crying and sobbing as a nurse asks if she has anyone she can call for her.

*****

Thankful for Emily, who is at the hospital sitting with Kenny, she rushes home to do the one thing she promised herself she would do. She opens the door and finds Ewok sitting on Kenny's bed. She bursts into tears. She wipes her nose with the back of her hand and dabs at her eyes. Ewok is looking at her expectantly, waiting for Kenny? She isn't sure. She looks around Kenny's room, trying to find the leash and happens upon a folded piece of paper on his nightstand. Written on one side it says: "*Mommy, tape to Ewok's collar.*" She unfolds the paper and reads his childish letter:

Thank you for lending Ewok to me and my mom. By now I am probly dead and my mom is sad. Ewok made me happy and that made my mom happy. But it was not rite that my mom took him, so she is giving him back. Please don't be mad at her. She did it for me.

Ewok's friend, Kenny

At the end of the letter, Kenny drew a picture of himself and Ewok. She sobs as she folds the letter and tucks it into his collar. She gives up on the leash, instead carries him out to her car.

Under the cover of darkness, she drives down Tripaldi Street and parks down the block. She tucks Ewok under her right arm and walks up the street to the fenced in yard where just last week she took him. Just before she sets him down, she makes sure that the letter from Kenny is securely tucked under his collar. She turns him around to face her.

"Thank you, Ewok. Thank you for everything you have done for me and especially for my son." He licks the end of her nose. She lets out a laugh through her tears and sets him down just inside the fence. She then retreats down the block before calling the phone number that imprinted itself on her brain the night she threw up.

"Hello, Hollarman Residence."

"I am so sorry. Ewok is back in your front yard. He has a note in his collar for you." She hangs up quickly, before the sob can escape her.

She watches from the shadows as the front door bursts open to shouts of "Ewok?" turn to shouts of "Ewok, you're home!" She sees them look around for a moment and then hears the father remark about finding the note. Satisfied that her son's wishes have been met, she turns and goes back to her car and back to the hospital, where she sits and waits for her son to die.

*****

It's been two days since she returned Ewok. Kenny doesn't wake much, but he did ask her about Ewok. She told him Ewok was fine.

"Did you return him?" Kenny asks breathlessly.

"Yes, I did. What I did was wrong, Kenny, but I would do it again, for you. I won't apologize for that." She gently squeezes his hand.

He turns his head and looks at her, "Did you find the note? The one I wrote to Ewok's family?"

"Yes, I did. And I did just like you said. I put it on his collar so they would see it when I gave him back. He's a special dog and they know he was special to you, too."

"Good. I'm tired, Mommy. I miss him."

"I know you are and I know you do, sweet boy. I brought you something to remind you of him." She pulls out a stuffed fuzzy dog from a bag sitting at her feet.

"I know it doesn't exactly look like Ewok, but you can pretend, right?" She asks.

"I love it, Mommy. Thank you." Kenny takes the stuffed dog and hugs it tight. He drifts off to sleep and she sits by his side.

A knock comes at the door to his room and a nurse pokes her head in.

"Can I speak with you for a moment?" The nurse asks her.

She gets out of the chair, grateful for a reason to stretch her legs, but not wanting to leave him for fear he may wake up.

"Nurse Sharon can sit with him for a minute while we talk." Nurse Chrissie says. Sharon nods and heads in to sit down where she was sitting as she walks out to talk with Chrissie.

"Is everything okay?" She asks.

Chrissie leads her to the waiting area where there is a family sitting. There is also a young man in khakis holding a camera.

"This is the Hollarman family. They own Ewok, the dog that went missing a couple weeks ago. They have a letter from Kenny that moved them and asked for special permission to bring Ewok to see Kenny." The man with the camera gets up from his seat and begins snapping pictures.

She is surprised and looks from one face to the other. She doesn't see hostility or anger. She is confused. Where are the police? Why aren't they arresting her for dognapping? Surely, he didn't mean it when he said they wouldn't prosecute. She stole their dog, after all.

"Hi." The man steps forward with his hand outstretched. Click, click, click goes the camera. The cameraman moves around the waiting area getting different angles.

"I'm David Hollarman. Thank you so much for taking such good care of Ewok. He is none the worse for wear, as they say." He looks around at the others, his wife, she guesses and the little girl who was crying on TV.

"This is my wife, Janice and my daughter Heather." They both say hello, as does she. She is still confused and unsure what is going on, but then hears that familiar little bark from one of the chairs behind them. Ewok is here! Click, click goes the camera.

She looks back at Chrissie.

"Yes, as I was saying, they asked and got permission for a one-time pass for Ewok to visit Kenny. They also hope to get pictures of Ewok and Kenny together." Click, click. "This is a photographer from The Daily Broadland Gazette, he's here to capture the moments, and Janice is a freelance writer, who will write a story for the paper." Chrissie is smiling warmly.

The photographer, who introduces himself as Greg while he brushes long hair out of his face, says he understands time is of the essence, so he has brought along an old-fashioned polaroid camera. He wants to take pictures of Kenny with Ewok that Kenny can keep with him while he's in the hospital. He smiles softly at her as her eyes well up with tears. She looks around at these people, at a loss for words.

She had done such a horrible thing, stealing their dog. Taking a family pet, a member of their family, really. How lonely Heather must have been, how sad she must have felt to not know where her little Ewok was, if he was safe, warm, fed, loved. She felt like such a terrible person for doing such a mean thing, but on the other hand, there was her son. What was she to do? No one would give her a dog, allow her to adopt a dog or sell her a dog she could afford. She was a single mother on unemployment taking care of her terminally ill child. She desperately wanted to provide this one bit of comfort and happiness to him. Was that really so bad? She didn't have any answers. But the Hollarman's did. They had forgiveness and kindness. They wanted to share their beloved Ewok one more time with her beloved Kenny. Who was she to question them?

"I am happy to meet you all." She says, wiping her eyes, sniffling, "Kenny will be so happy to see Ewok again and to meet his wonderful family." She looks at Greg. "Thank you for taking pictures for him, he will treasure them, I know."

Color Blind

Closer than sisters, we completed each other's sentences. We laughed at our own jokes that no one else understood. We lived in a world of our own making, acting on every whim and curiosity.

After trying to dig to China in my backyard, creating a four-foot-deep hole, we felt quite a sense of accomplishment for two five-year-olds; however, my dad was not amused. We were banished from the backyard into the house.

Left to our own devices in my house, we decided to play mad scientist in my bedroom and create bubble gum. We used lotion, water, flour, and shampoo, mixing the foul concoction on the desktop in my room. The gooey mess soon ran over onto the carpet and had us squealing and running from the room. My mom was not amused. We were banished from the house back to the outdoors.

On school days, we would ride the bus home together and be apart for only as long as it took us to run to our respective homes to put our book bags down and change into play clothes. We would yell "bye!" to our moms and head back outside to meet each other at the top of the cul-de-sac and plan our afternoon activities; digging holes, cooking up bubble gum, or whatever other idea came to us, until we were called in for dinner. We'd say our goodbyes and goodnights and do it all over the next day. Madonna was truly my best friend, my confidant, my sister in every sense of the word.

One Saturday, Madonna's mom let her spend the night with me. My parents took us to my grandparent's house for the evening. After dinner we played dress-up with my grandmother's sparkly costume jewelry. I was enamored with her gold peacock brooch with large blue-green shimmery feathers. Madonna took a shine to her many sparkly tear-drop earrings. The jewelry accentuated the beautiful evening dresses and high heels we donned. All dolled up, we'd sing and dance to old jazz records played on an old-timey record player, putting on a show for the adults. What fun we had wearing those gowns, trading them back and forth, deciding which one looked best on each other.

Then we had this delicious thought - wouldn't it be fun to trade our regular clothes with each other and see if my parents and grandparents could tell us apart? We were convinced that if I dressed and did my hair as Madonna, then my parents and grandparents would think that I *was* Madonna. If Madonna dressed and did her hair like me, they would think she was me. It was the perfect plan! We laughed and giggled at how we would fool them. Oh, what fun it would be! We clunked back into my grandparent's bedroom in her high heels and evening dresses to change clothes.

What if I went home tomorrow to Madonna's house and fooled her mom?! Wouldn't that be hysterical? What if she stayed at my house as me? We laughed until we cried as we hurriedly changed. Madonna dressed in my tee shirt and shorts and I slipped into her romper dress. Lickety-split, she brushed out her many braids, while I put my long hair into ponytails and braided each as best I could. We looked into the mirror and were astounded at our transformations. I was Madonna and she was me! Certainly, the grownups in the living room would be fooled!

We skipped into the living room holding hands and announced ourselves to my parents and grandparents. They kept looking from one to the other, mouths open, brows slightly raised. Speechless, they stared at us. We did it! We fooled them! We giggled as we told them of our trickery. We laughed at them, full belly laughs. I took my hair out of the ponytails and braids to prove it was really me, on the off chance they didn't believe us and were still fooled by our mischievousness.

Years later I realized the truth of their astonishment. They weren't fooled by our deception. No one thought I was Madonna. But their shock wasn't a fake attempt to join in our prank. No, they were amazed that Madonna and I truly believed we'd fooled them. They realized at that moment that neither Madonna nor I saw color.

You see, that little five-year girl with ponytails and braids was white and her best friend in the whole world, Madonna, was black.

The Gravitron

The Gravitron! She is so excited as she runs through the fairgrounds because this year is the year she can finally ride the Gravitron! She just knows she'll be tall enough this year. After all, she only missed it by an inch last year.

She runs through the midway, leaving her brother behind. She dodges families, kids, and teenagers. She's laser-locked on her goal, the Gravitron. She sees it up ahead and it is beautiful. It is lit up like a neon alien spaceship in the night sky. The brightest colors she has ever seen, neon blue pulsates around the middle of the ship, while red outlines the opening where people enter and exit. Yellow and orange are at the top and bottom, and the entire rainbow of colors blinks along the body from top to bottom and bottom to top, meeting in the middle; in synchronized harmony to the beat of the rocking music coming from deep within somewhere. She makes it to the end of the line and stands mesmerized.

This is it. She thinks. *The ride I'd been waiting for all year. This will be better than riding with my brother in his Mustang on that back road.* She is giddy with anticipation.

She imagines what it will be like to climb the rickety metal stairs and enter the belly of the spaceship known as the Gravitron. She wonders if she will be nervous or excited to walk up to a space along the wall and pull down the waist bar and slide behind it and then click it into place at her mid-section, locking her into an upright position. She imagines grabbing the handlebars on either side of her to help hold her in place. Will she wait impatiently or with anxiousness for the ride to start? Then the door will close.

It will start slowly spinning at first, she knows. She has watched it from the outside enough times to know that it will quickly speed up. She has heard the screams of excitement and fear from the people inside. She has heard horror stories from her brother, of course.

"This one time, a kid threw up and his puke just hung in the middle while it was spinning. Only after it stopped did his puke splat

347

on some poor sucker! Man, I'm glad I wasn't on the Gravitron that time."

"Yeah, right. As if." She told her brother. "Like I believe you or your lame friends."

"Fine, don't believe me. But I tell you, I was on the ride when this one kid was so freakin' scared he peed himself. Hope that doesn't happen to you." He laughed.

"Shut up, Todd. You're such a loser."

Now that she is in line, the conversation comes back to her. She sure hopes she won't be like that kid and pee herself. Todd would never let her live it down. He would probably tell all his friends, too.

"Hey guys, guess what? My little sister was so scared on the Gravitron that she peed herself. Hell, no I didn't take her home. I wouldn't let her sit in MY car in piss clothes. I called mom to come to get her." Yeah, that would be just like Todd. He could be so mean.

The line to get on the Gravitron is moving closer to the front. She can see now that she is tall enough to ride. Whew! That's one thing she doesn't have to worry about at least. That would've been totally embarrassing if she would've been turned away again for being too short. Being short sucks. She's mostly used to it, but sometimes she wishes she was taller, like at the grocery store or the library, so that she could reach stuff on the top shelf. It would be cool to be able to just reach up and grab what you wanted.

The line moves closer still. One more ride and then she will be on with the next group. The Gravitron holds about forty people she figures. She tried counting all the people that come off, but always loses count around thirty. More people come off after that so her best guess is forty.

O-M-G! She shrieks silently in her head. It's her turn. She sees all the people coming off and most have someone waiting for them. She wishes stupidly that her brother was there waiting for her. She'd like him to see how brave she is. Oh well, maybe he'll let her tell him all about it later on the ride home. She's supposed to meet him at 8 o'clock.

She files up the rickety steps with the other riders, big and small, old and young. Some look anxious, others confident. Most are with friends or family. She is alone. She doesn't care, she isn't going to let being alone stop her from the sheer joy of riding the Gravitron! She's waited all year!

She walks into the spaceship and picks her spot on the wall. She slides behind the waist bar, clicks it into place, and grabs on tight to the handlebars. She says a little prayer, *Lord please don't let me pee myself. Let this be the best ride of all time. Amen.* As soon as she finishes, she feels the room begin to spin. No turning back now.

It spins faster and faster and then something she didn't expect, that no one told her about happens. The floor drops away and she's just stuck to the wall! She really does scream then. A scream of excitement and fear all rolled into one. The room is not only spinning around and around, but it begins to move up and tilt slightly as well. She is prepared for this, having watched from the outside. She still screams as the G-force pushes her further back against the wall, feet dangling into nothingness.

She turns her head to the side to look at her neighbor. He is screaming and crying, eyes shut tight. She feels a little better, she is still screaming, but at least she can look, well a little bit, anyway. She closes her eyes as they begin to water. *I am NOT crying!* She scolds herself.

She feels the floor come back and touch her feet. A wave of relief hits her. A sense of normalcy comes back. She feels the room tilt back right the way it should be and begin to slow. She is breathing heavily but is no longer screaming. She risks letting go of the handlebars with one hand to wipe her eyes. She doesn't want anyone to see her watery eyes when she gets off the ride. Not that anyone is waiting for her, but still.

The ride comes to a halt and her waist bar clicks. She pushes it forward and takes a wobbly step around it. She takes another wobbly step forward and another, until she finds herself under the bright lights of the Midway, looking around.

"Hey, there she is! You really did it! How awesome is that?!"

She hears his voice before she sees him. She looks to her right as she comes down the rickety stairs to the exit. There, waiting for her, after all, is her brother.

Riverside Writers Photo Gallery

Howell Library, Nat'l Poetry Month Open Read, April 6th, 2024. Allita Irby, Andrea Reed, Liz Talbot, Dan Walker, Steven Pody, Beth Spragins, Malanna Henderson. Photo by Allita's husband.

The Poe Museum Tour, Richmond, VA, on 28 Apr 2024
RW members: Steve, Bronwen, Malanna, Dave, Miri, Liz & Andrea.

351

In Edgar Allen Poe's Footsteps (and garden). 28 Apr 2024

RW members Andrea, Bronwen, Dave & Malanna. Poe-sies!

The usual suspects…

Jim, Jorge & Larry
…Larry, you are missed.

Riverside Writers 2024 Anthology / Author Biographies

Barbara Beaumont / pen name: Shashana. In my twenties a local park had a snap a-poem contest. I took a photo, penned a poem and won 2nd place. I was shocked. I still have the trophy they gave me. …And somewhere around here the poem. When 43, I secured a job at a local magazine. I did photo shoots and wrote for them PT for three to four years. I continued to enter poetry contests and often would place or get honorable mention. One day, I was asked to write an article for the Grand Opening of the new Hospice Building. There was a beautiful life size painted portrait of a donor in the lobby. I was inspired by the majesty of the painting and penned a poem about it, as well as authoring the article for the newspaper. After my article was published, I was invited to the grand opening where I met the governor of the state, read my poem to the crowd, and received accolades for my work. What an honor for me. I hold the position of webmaster in Riverside Writers. At my current age, much of my inspiration feels lost. However, memories of past accomplishments and putting pen to paper to create a story still brings me so much joy!

Madalin E. Jackson Bickel is originally from Huntington, West Virginia where she taught in a public-school setting for thirty years and served as an adjunct professor at Marshall University. She holds a master's degree in gifted education and completed over 45 additional post graduate hours in math and science. She completed nine more years of teaching in Stafford County, Virginia. Following retirement, she pursued her love of writing. She is an award-winning poet and storyteller. Her poems have been published in a variety of anthologies including *Scratching Against the Fabric*, published following the first Bridgewater International Poetry Festival, and Virginia Writers Centennial Anthology. She is currently a member of the Poetry Society of Virginia, Riverside Writers (Fredericksburg), the Virginia Writers Club, and the West Virginia Writers Organization. She has published three poetry chapbooks and four cozy mystery novels. Her most recent poetry chapbook is *If You Never Lived in the Mountains*. Her most recent novel is *Wined to Death*. Her works are available at Amazon.com under the pen name Madalin E. Jackson. She recently relocated to Tallahassee, Florida and is currently working on the fifth novel in the *Writers Block* series.

Don Bishop/T.S. Pedramon grew up in music, playing the clarinet from middle school through college, and has worked as a music teacher, a US Marine Musician, and Cyberspace Warfare Officer. He began writing two novels in his childhood and he read fantasy and science fiction along the way. Gaining fluency in Spanish as an adult (he speaks English, Spanish, and Dad jokes), he still values continued learning and expanding his horizons. Pedramon participated in National Novel Writing Month in 2009 and 2010. He finished neither, but his 2010 attempt has held his imagination since then, growing into a need to finish the story, the *Grendhill Chronicles*, as a full-fledged epic fantasy series. As of 2024 it's still not complete, but he is currently publishing his *Nightshade Unicorn* saga under the imprint Grendhill Media, named after the *Grendhill Chronicles*! Pedramon resides on the US East Coast with his wife, children, a parakeet named William Cutie, and a one-eyed black cat named Skippy.

James F. Gaines and his son **John M. Gaines** write fiction and poetry together under the pen name **J. M. R. Gaines** for their sci fi universe called *The Forlani Saga*. Besides the story appearing here, their short works have been published in various print and online journals, while their first two novels in the series, *Life Sentence* and *Spy Station* are available from Amazon and in Barnes and Noble stores. *Life Sentence* is also available in audiobook format from Audible. James, a retired professor, has also written a collection of non science fiction pieces, *Beyond the Covenant and Other Stories*, and a volume of poetry entitled *Downriver Waltz*. John, a librarian, writes continually for Librarypoint.com.

Malanna Henderson is a Detroit native who is a novelist, playwright, singer, songwriter, and Zumba enthusiast. She won two first-place awards in one-act playwriting festivals. Sponsored by the Tulsa Library, and Fredericksburg's Stage Door Productions, for the plays *A Question of Color* and *The Eclipse,* respectively. She earned a Liberal Arts degree from the University of Detroit, and later an MFA from the City University of New York. *'Tis All a Game of Chance*, a one-act play was later developed into a musical comedy. A 2025 production is planned. Her short story, *Me and Mrs. Jones*, was her Golden NIB entry of 2023. She is the current Vice President of Riverside Writers.

Carol Thomas Horton grew up in an extended family of front-porch story-tellers near Fredericksburg, Virginia. She is a former national award-winning journalist for Media General, where she wrote for multiple periodicals, including the *Richmond Times-Dispatch* and *The Free Lance-Star*. Carol also holds a doctorate focusing on education and writing, and has authored several education documents and curriculums while serving as a school teacher and later, as a principal. Her additional hobbies include genealogy, traveling and photography. She currently lives and gardens with her family on a portion of her late great grandparents' farm, where she continues to write about people and places, including co-authoring two books.

Valerie Horton has professionally published three books through the American Library Association Publishers; *Library Consortium: Models for Collaboration* was a bestseller in the profession. I have also edited a self-published book of my brother's poetry titled *The Inner Journey North*. I was an academic librarian for 40 years, working as an academic library director and library consortium director. I served as one of the two founding editors of a professional journal, *Collaborative Librarianship*. Currently an officer in Riverside Writers (Secretary), I am fulfilling my creative impulses by writing poetry, non-fiction works, and family memorials.

Allita Marie Irby has a Masters in Business Administration and a Certificate in Organization Development. She's been seriously writing since 1995 and is the co-author of the novel, *Fourth Sunday, the Journey of a Book Club* by B. W. Read. Allita's writing has appeared in numerous anthologies and online journals. Her memberships include: The Lake Authors of the Wilderness, Riverside Writers and the Pen-to-Paper writing groups in Virginia. She is a past board member of the Zora Neale Hurston/Richard Wright Foundation in Washington, DC. Allita writes fiction, flash fiction, micro fiction and poetry inspired by nature, cosmopolitan issues and current events. You can find her on Twitter @airby9.

Dave A. Kula is an aspiring Virginia author working to publish his first book in a series he started writing in 1991. Dave has many works "in the works," including several short stories, three novels of his series, poems, and even a zombie novel. Dave enjoys both writing and running Dungeons and Dragons games. He obtained enjoyment from writing news articles in high school where he spent three years on the school newspaper writing articles and becoming an editor. His favorite activities include spending time with his wonderful wife, Renata, and their four cats – his children. Dave hopes to complete his many works in progress and publish them... if he can keep his attention from Renata and RPG games long enough.

Sharon Lyon is a geologist, science educator, and author. She recently retired as a Professor of Physical Sciences from Howard Community College (MD) after a thirty-year career in education. Ms. Lyon earned a Bachelor of Science degree from The College of William and Mary, and a Master of Science degree from The

University of North Carolina – Chapel Hill. Both of the novels in her *Fossil Woman series* are #1 Amazon Bestsellers. Her *Fossil Woman* audiobook won a 2023 Benjamin Franklin Silver Award from the Independent Publishers Book Association. Follow her at www.sharonlyon.net and on Instagram @fossilwomanauthor.

Caitlin Niznik is a writer from a small town often confused with much larger towns in Virginia. When Caitlin is hard at work not working on her current manuscript, she writes poetry and oil paints in her cabin in the woods.

Miriam S. Pody has been writing, sketching and illustrating since she was very young. She found new outlets on the internet, and has been a long-time participant on many fan fiction and creative writing sites. This anthology will be the first widely-distributed print publication of her work, but several pieces have been on her DeviantArt account under the username DarkestElemental616 for years, including a previous iteration of *The Tale of Two Brothers* and the first draft chapter of *GenEns*, along with concept art and illustrations. She finds particular inspiration in fantasy and science fiction, and is the proud bookwyrm of a large library, rich in folklore and fairy tales. She currently serves as the social media liaison and A/V technician for the Riverside Writers, finding speakers for our meetings and running technical support.

Steven P. Pody, since his first poem in 1969, has published a 137-page volume of verse, entitled *The Panoptikon* (64 poems). A new 138 poem, 200+ page volume, entitled *The Flutter-By Two-Step* is coming out soon. His work is additionally represented in printed anthologies from Arizona, California, Maryland and Virginia, as well as e-represented on the internet. Current president of Riverside Writers, Steven is a military vet (U.S. Air Force, 4 years), and was a citizen of Alaska for ten years. He also lived 1 1/2 years in the Middle East, and 4 1/2 years in Africa. His current tally stands at 53 countries and 48 U.S. states visited, including crossing the Arctic Circle four times. Africa time was mostly covered by two tours in the U.S. Peace Corps. Steven met his German wife at an archaeological dig in the Golan Heights of Israel, and they have three wunderbar now-adult children. They supported a girl in Ecuador, under "Plan International USA", for 17 years. A Delaware native (Jill Biden was a U of D classmate -- both graduating AS75), Steve and Beate have called Fredericksburg, VA, home for 20+ years. Comment or contact: s_pody@msn.com

Andrea Williams Reed has served as Secretary and President for Riverside Writers. Her writing experience began with developing curricula for Work Ready and Family and Consumer Science School curriculum. Her poems have won numerous awards and appeared in four Riverside Writers anthologies, as well as several Poetry Journals. She enjoys walking, reading, travelling, and storytelling. A native of Gloucester County, Virginia, she now makes her home in Fredericksburg, Virginia, with her husband John.

Jorge Rafael Robert-Saavedra writes under the pen name of **J. R. Robert-Saavedra.** A life member of Riverside Writers he now resides in Denton, Texas. Jorge was born in San Juan, Puerto Rico. He is an alumnus from the University of Notre Dame where he graduated with an BBA in Financial Management. Later he obtained a MBA from the California State University in Turlock, California. During his active military service Mr. Robert lived three years in Germany, one in South Korea and in various installations in the continental United States. He retired from the Army Reserves. Jorge also retired as a civilian from the Department of Defense, Defense Logistics Agency. One of his last assignments was as an International Audit Manager where he traveled extensively representing the overseas contracting interests of the United States. From 1998 to 2007 Mr. Robert worked as an efficiency consultant to industry and the Federal government. He is presently licensed as a Realtor in the Commonwealth of Virginia. Mr. Robert published his poetry book *Poems by El Capitan* in 2012. Jorge volunteers in various local civic and professional associations; he enjoys analyzing the stock market, writing and photography. Much time is now spent with family and friends at sidewalk cafes.

David Anthony Sam lives in Virginia with his wife, Linda. His poetry has appeared in over 100 journals. His collection, *Writing the Significant Soil,* was awarded the 2021 Poetry Prize by Homebound Publications, the 2022 Poetry Prize by the Virginia Professional Communicators, and the poetry prize by the National Federation of Press Women. Seven other collections are in print including *Stone Bird* (2023) and *Dark Fathers (*2019). *Geographies of the Dead* will be published in 2025. Sam teaches creative writing at Germanna Community College and serves as Regional VP of the Poetry Society of Virginia.

Suzanne Shelton, born and raised in Maryland, grew up traveling and visiting extended family in Tidewater region of Virginia. As an adult she made her home in Virginia and retired from a nursing career. She is a member of Riverside Writers, she does not remember a time when she did not write.

Elizabeth Spencer Spragins is a fiber artist, writer, and poet who taught in North Carolina community colleges for more than a decade before returning to her home state of Virginia. Her work has appeared in more than 100 journals and anthologies in 11 countries. She is the author of three original poetry collections: *Waltzing with Water* and *With No Bridle for the Breeze* (Shanti Arts Publishing) and *The Language of Bones* (Kelsay Books). elizabethspencerspragins.wordpress.com.

Steve Spratt. I was born and raised in Fredericksburg, went to Jack and Jill Kindergarten on Franklin St., Montfort Academy and James Monroe High School. I graduated from Johns Hopkins

University and married my wife Linda in 1972. I worked for my dad at WC Spratt Inc., until I started Steve Spratt Improvements in 1978. Forty-three years later, I retired in 2021. While cleaning out a closet that contained a bunch of old pictures, they reminded me of stories about those pictures. With my memory becoming weaker, I realized the only place those stories were saved was in my memory. It occurred to me that I should write them down to share these exciting, interesting, funny, unlikely stories with others before they were gone. My story about Hurricane Ian is one of the more recent memories.

Elizabeth (Liz) Talbot did not start writing in earnest until she moved to the Fredericksburg area in 2001 and joined Riverside Writers. Somehow, she found time to write and serve as a club officer between raising two daughters and a legal career. The group encouraged her to submit one of her first poems, *I am Rappahannock* to a contest sponsored by the West Virginia Poetry Society, which then won second prize. Lately her writing has been focusing on the profound changes which the pandemic of 2020 wrought in American life, and her contribution to the anthology (*COVID-free Paradise*) reflects the desire of a married couple to return to the Caribbean vacation of the pre pandemic era. She has also recently completed a novel (unpublished) with the working title, *My Post Pandemic Wedding*. She wants to thank Greg, Sheila, and Dave for their suggestions as well as the staff of the Howell Branch of the Rappahannock Regional Library.

William T. Tang. Long Tang is the author of five books and numerous articles on the history and culture of China. He graduated with honors from the General Political Warfare College, Taiwan, and taught Chinese history and culture at the Eckerd College in Saint Petersburg, FL. Before retirement he was a research analyst with 40+ years of experience working on China issues. He is fluent in three dialects of Chinese and Spanish. Long Tang is a Board of Directors at large of the Virginia Writers Club (VWC), and Treasurer of Riverside Writers. His most recent article, *Need A Date For My Mom*, appeared in the June 2024 edition of Chicken Soup for the Soul. He lives in Fredericksburg, VA, with his wife, a dog, two cats, four parakeets, and a forest full of denizens.

Dan Walker is the author of three published novels-- *Huckleberry Finn in Love and War: The Lost Journals; The Iron John Trilogy, Parts 1 (The Boy and the Princess), 2 (What Could Go Wrong),* and *Part 3 (The Stunning Conclusion);* in addition to numerous articles and prize-winning poems. About writing, Dan says, "I once thought I was a Serious Writer. Once I got over that, I was fine." He has taught in Spotsylvania County Schools, the University of Mary Washington, and the Virginia Community College's Career-Switcher program. Dan has also worked as a seasonal Park Ranger. He is official liaison between Riverside Writers and its parent group, the Virginia Writers Club (VWC). Dan and Mary, his wife of fifty-two years, live on a small farm, with four cats, three dogs, two horses, and a small flock of semi-feral poems— which will consent to be fed but *not* picked up and taken to the vet.

Lea Walker is a retired high school and university English teacher and current Department of Defense writer-editor. She has two adult children and lives in Fredericksburg, Virginia. She is a member of St. George's Episcopal Church, and volunteers for Community Dinner, and other organizations. She is a cookier and a crafter, and lives with her two cats, Hamlet and Horatio.

Frank M. White. A member of Riverside Writers, he was born in Stafford County, Virginia. Frank immediately joined the U.S. Air Force upon High School graduation, serving for 26 years. He began writing poetry in elementary school, when he became fascinated with nursery rhymes. In May of 2022, he published his first book of poetry: *Frank's Homespun Poems from the Heart*.

Mendie Williams is a new author who was a former school librarian. She has a degree in Economics, a Master's of Arts in Pre-Elementary Education, and a School Library Media Science certification. Writing became an interest after her lesson plan, a graduate school assignment, was submitted by her professor and published in *School Library Media* magazine. She decided to join a local writer's group after she published an article in *Naval History Magazine* online. She is a wife, and mother of two adult children. She works as a realtor when she is not writing. She also recently started a butterfly business with her husband. Her hobbies are swimming, gardening, and flea market shopping.

Jessica Wolski. I have been a member of the Riverside Writers since joining the Young Writers Club in 2019, and have lived in the Fredericksburg area for over 20 years. I've been writing since I was 13, and am working hard to be both a book editor and a published novelist. I am a student at Germanna Community College, and active in their creative arts journal (*The Roar*) -- both in publishing my own work, and by being the head editor for three consecutive years. All of my pieces published in this current anthology were originally in different editions of *The Roar*. *Happier Times Ahead* was a story which won second place, regionally, in the Virginia Writers Club-sponsored 'Golden Nib' contest in the summer of 2020, and subsequently published in *The Roar* (Fall 2021 edition). The story was written with my hope for my own future, and was originally named *Is This Wrong? The Bear of the Woods* was written during my own horror writing workshop, putting myself out of my comfort zone. It was published in the Spring 2023 edition of *The Roar*. Finally, *Lights of Memory* is also from the Spring 2023 edition, and was written for someone very special in my life.

Lynn H. Wyvill is the author of three books of poetry, *Nature's Quiet Wisdom*; *Morning Light, Quiet Nights*; and *Abundant Strength: A Caregiver's Prayers*. Lynn finds inspiration in spending quiet time in nature. She is mesmerized by ocean waves, soothed by walking forest trails, and captivated by birds and butterflies playing in flower gardens. Her joy is sharing her love of nature in her poetry. Before writing books, Lynn worked as a radio/television broadcaster and video producer for the Federal government. Her second career was as an owner of a communications consulting and training business. She is a lifelong learner, avid reader, and small-town explorer who lives in Virginia with her artist husband.

Rachel Young. I'm an aspiring novelist with a penchant for weaving tales of suspense. Nestled in the serene countryside, I draw inspiration from the rustling leaves and distant howls of my two loyal dogs. My cozy home is a sanctuary where creativity thrives. While my heart flutters at reading the pages of romance novels, the novel I'm writing takes a darker turn. Characters with secrets and shadows tend to die. However, my personal essays and short stories are not so sinister. It's this juxtaposition – the light and the macabre – that fuels my creativity. My sister is an accomplished author herself. I often dream of literary success such as hers; her legacy is inspiring my own!

Riverside Writers Past and Current Officers

Riverside Writers Roster of Presidents:

1. 1997-2000 Betty Marcum
2/3. 2001-2002 Greg Mitchell, Stan Trice
4/5. 2003-2004 Sharon Hite, Jim Gaines
6. 2005-2006 Chris Valenti
7. 2007-2008 Diane Parkinson
8. 2009-2012 Larry Turner
9. 2013-2014 Madalin Bickel
10. 2015-2018 Jim Gaines
11. 2019-2020 Andrea Reed
12. 2021-2022 Nate Hoffelder
13. 2023- ...the current editor, still earning some undefined measure of his accolades as lucky 13.

Current Officers, Riverside Writers, Autumn 2024:

Steven P. Pody, President
Malanna Carey Henderson, Vice President
William Tang, Treasurer
Valerie Horton, Secretary
Barbara Beaumont, Webmaster
Miriam S. Pody, A/V Master & Recruiter (guest speakers)
Bronwen (Chisholm) Robinson, Book Festival Liaison &
Planner

Made in the USA
Middletown, DE
09 November 2024

63721174R00210